LEE BROOK

The Shadows of the Past

First published by BrookHarvey Press 2024

Second edition

This book was professionally typeset on Reedsy.
Find out more at reedsy.com

For you, kind reader—
For constantly supporting me.
Merry Christmas, and thank you.

Contents

Chapter One

Detective Inspector George Beaumont sank into the sofa, his arms full with the warm bundle of his baby daughter, a sigh of contentment escaping his lips as he glanced around the living room of his modest semi-detached house in Morley. Little Olivia gurgled happily against his chest, her tiny fingers curling around one of his shirt buttons. He smiled down at her, drinking in that pure baby scent.

Beside him, Isabella, his fiancée, nestled close, her hand finding his under the woollen throw.

George soaked in the moment—the twinkling lights of the Christmas tree, the cinnamon and cloves lingering from Isabella's holiday baking, the sound of his children's breathing... it was everything he had been chasing.

"There we are," Isabella said as she flipped off the lights. "All ready for our Christmas film."

A quiet family Christmas, though a simpler dream than most, had always felt just out of his reach. But now, here, with Isabella's head resting gently on his shoulder and his baby girl lying cosily in his arms, he had found it.

Peace.

"I love this," George murmured, his voice a low rumble of satisfaction. It had been a great day with family visiting and staying for Christmas dinner, but this was the part he'd been looking forward to.

Isabella smiled, her eyes reflecting the flicker of the fireplace. "Yep, it's perfect," she agreed, her gaze flitting between the two children. Jack, nearly two, was building a haphazard tower of blocks, his concentration fierce and brows knitted in a mimicry of his father's usual expression.

"Want me to press play?" George asked, reaching for the remote. The Christmas tree in the corner of the room stood guard, its ornaments a testament to the family's love—a mixture of Isabella's elegant taste and the more whimsical, child-friendly decorations Jack had insisted on.

"Please," Isabella replied, shifting slightly to accommodate Olivia, who gurgled happily in her lap.

The screen flickered to life, the opening credits of a classic Christmas film rolling. George's eyes, however, were not on the screen. They were watching Jack, observing the way his son's small hands deftly manoeuvred the blocks, a frown of concentration etched on his cherubic face.

"Look at him," George whispered, a note of wonder in his voice.

"He's got your determination, George."

George chuckled softly. "And Mia's stubbornness."

"He's also bloody cute, just like his dad."

The compliment brought a smile to George's lips. This was what he had longed for—these simple, unadorned moments of family life. The world outside, with its chaos and crime, seemed a distant reality.

"Remember our first Christmas together?" Isabella asked, her voice tinged with nostalgia.

George nodded, the memory vivid in his mind. "I was so

nervous to meet your grandparents. Thought I'd mess it right up."

"But you didn't," Isabella reassured him, her hand giving his a gentle squeeze. "You charmed them just like you charmed me."

The film played on, a backdrop to their reminiscing. George's thoughts drifted to his work, to the cases that had kept him away from moments like these. The weight of responsibility and the pursuit of justice—they were his calling, but they had come at a cost.

Isabella seemed to sense the shift in his mood. "You're thinking about work, aren't you?"

George hesitated, then nodded. "It's hard not to. Even on Christmas Day, I can't help but think about the cases still open, the families waiting for answers."

"That's what makes you a good detective," Isabella said, her voice soft but firm. "But tonight, let it go, just for a little while. Be here with us."

George's eyes met hers, and he saw the truth in her words. "You're right," he said, a decisive edge to his tone. "Tonight, it's just us."

As the film's laughter and music filled the room, George allowed himself to be fully present, soaking in the peace of the moment. Olivia's cooing, Jack's giggles, Isabella's warm presence beside him—these were the treasures of his life, a relief to the harshness of his profession.

The Christmas film's festive jingles faded into insignificance as George's phone came to life, vibrating against the hardwood of the coffee table. His hand, previously relaxed and intertwined with Isabella's, tensed as he recognised the caller ID—Detective Sergeant Yolanda Williams.

He ignored it, not wanting anything to pierce this long-awaited Christmas Day perfection.

Bella tilted her head up, raising an eyebrow at him. "Aren't you going to get that?"

George shook his head. "Not today. Today is just for us."

Isabella considered him a moment, then nodded, settling back against his shoulder.

The phone rang again. And again. On the fourth ring, Bella gently extracted Olivia from George's arms.

"Just see what they want, gorgeous," she said softly. "Then come back and be with us."

George reluctantly grabbed the phone from the end table.

"Sorry, love," George muttered, his brows knitting together in an all too familiar expression of concern.

Isabella's eyes followed him with a mix of understanding and disappointment as he stepped away, the glow of the Christmas lights casting elongated shadows across his face.

George stepped outside, the chill of the winter night biting through his jacket as he closed the door behind him. The street was silent, save for the distant hum of traffic and the muted sound of Christmas celebrations from neighbouring houses. He stood there for a moment, letting the cold seep into his bones, a stark contrast to the warmth he had just left behind.

He gazed up at the night sky, the stars obscured by the city's glow, and took a deep breath, trying to steady the turmoil that churned within him. The air was crisp, tinged with the scent of frost and distant woodsmoke, a sensory reminder of the season that was supposed to be filled with joy and peace.

George answered the call, his voice a low, cautious hum. "DI Beaumont."

"Sir, it's Yolanda. I'm sorry to call on Christmas Day, but

something's come up." Yolanda's voice, usually steady and composed, carried an undercurrent of urgency.

George's gaze drifted to the window, where frost etched intricate patterns on the glass, a stark contrast to the warmth of his home. "What's happened?"

"We've got another one, George. Another murder. And it's eerily similar to the Santa Claus killings."

A chill that had nothing to do with the December frost crept up George's spine. The desire to return to the comfort of his home, to Isabella and the children, was a physical ache in his chest.

"Are you sure it's related?" George's voice was a whisper, his eyes narrowing as he processed the information.

"The MO is almost identical. The victim was found dressed in a Santa suit, just like the others. And there's a note, George. Taunting you specifically."

George's mind raced, piecing together the fragments of the case that had been consuming him for weeks. The Santa Claus murders had sent shock waves through Leeds, a series of brutal killings masked by the festive attire of the victims.

"Where?" George's voice was barely audible, his detective instincts fully awakened. He could still picture them in the living room: Isabella's gentle smile, Jack's wide-eyed innocence, Olivia's peaceful slumber. The image was a balm to his soul, yet it clashed violently with the professional obligation that called him away.

"Harehills. The body was discovered an hour ago. We need you there, sir."

George nodded, even though Yolanda couldn't see him. "I'm on my way."

As George ended the call, his thumb lingered on the disconnect button, the weight of the conversation heavy in his hand. The joyous background noise of his family's Christmas celebration became a distant hum, overshadowed by the echoes of Yolanda's words.

The Santa Claus murders, a series of chilling cases that had plagued Leeds in both December 2013 and December 2023, clearly hadn't been solved at all. The faces of the victims flickered through his mind like a macabre slide-show—each one dressed in a Santa suit, their festive garb a grotesque contrast to the horror of their final moments.

"George?" Isabella's voice floated through the slightly ajar door, laced with concern. "Are you alright?"

He turned, catching a glimpse of her silhouette framed in the warm light of the door. "Just needed a moment," he replied, his voice barely above a whisper.

"Come back inside. It's freezing out there," she urged, her tone soft yet insistent.

He stood motionless for a moment, the weight of responsibility settling on his shoulders. He returned to the living room, where the film played on, its cheerful scenes a stark contrast to the darkness that awaited him.

Isabella looked him in the eye as he approached, her expression shifting from warmth to concern. "What is it, George?"

"It's nothing, just work," George replied, attempting a reassuring smile that didn't quite reach his eyes.

Isabella studied his face; the familiar lines etched deeper by the burdens he carried. She knew him too well, knew that his 'just work' often meant sleepless nights and a mind consumed by cases.

"George, talk to me. I can see it's serious," she pressed, her thumb stroking his arm in a comforting gesture.

He hesitated, his gaze flitting towards Jack and Olivia, blissfully unaware of the world's harsh realities. "There's been another incident. It's related to the Santa Claus case. I have to go."

"I know you have to go," she said after a pause, her voice tinged with resignation. "But it doesn't make it any easier, does it?"

George shook his head, the internal conflict evident in his stance. "No, it doesn't. Every time I leave, I feel like I'm abandoning you all."

"But you're not," Isabella replied, her voice stronger now. "You're doing your job, George. A job that helps keep us safe. We understand that even if it's hard sometimes."

Her words were a comfort, but they did little to ease the guilt that gnawed at him. "I just wish... I wish it didn't have to be like this."

Isabella stepped closer, her hand reaching out to touch his arm through the open door. "We'll be here when you get back. We always are."

George looked into her eyes, seeing the love and strength that had been his anchor through so many difficult times. He nodded, a silent acknowledgement of her support.

Isabella reached out, her hand gently brushing his. "You're thinking about them, aren't you? The victims?"

George nodded.

Isabella's face fell, but her voice was steady and supportive. "We understand. Be careful."

He leaned down, kissing her forehead softly. "Always am." His voice was a murmur, a blend of promise and reassurance.

George knelt down, pulling Jack into a brief, tight embrace. "Daddy has to work, buddy. Keep an eye on Olivia for me, OK?"

Jack nodded, his young face serious beyond his years. "OK, Daddy."

George stood, his gaze lingering on his family. The contrast between the peace of his home and the violence of his work had never been more stark.

"Back soon, Daddy?"

"I will, son. I promise." George ruffled his son's hair, his heart aching at the innocence in Jack's eyes.

He then turned to Olivia, asleep in her mother's arms, and planted a gentle kiss on her forehead. Her peaceful slumber, undisturbed by the shadows of the world, was a stark contrast to the turmoil within him.

With a final glance at his family, George grabbed his coat and warrant card, the symbol of his duty. The warmth of the room seemed to recede with each step he took towards the door. The festive cheer, the laughter, the comfort of family—all faded into the background as the detective in him took over.

Outside, the crisp winter air bit at his skin, a stark reminder of the shift from domestic bliss to professional duty. The quiet streets of Leeds, adorned with Christmas lights, felt eerily desolate, and with a final glance at the house, the embodiment of the life he cherished, George turned away, his footsteps echoing on the frost-hardened pavement. As he walked towards his car, the internal struggle continued to rage within him.

As he drove, the serene image of his family lingered in his mind, a bittersweet juxtaposition against the grim reality awaiting him. The festive tunes on the radio were a jarring contrast to the gravity of the situation, and he quickly turned it off, the silence more fitting for his thoughts.

His grip tightened on the steering wheel, the weight of the

case settling upon him like a heavy cloak. Each turn of the wheel took him further away from the haven of his home, deeper into the shadows of his profession. In the rear-view mirror, the festive lights of his neighbourhood faded into the night, a symbol of the life he momentarily left behind to face the darkness that awaited him.

The car's engine hummed quietly as George navigated the snow-dusted streets of Leeds, the festive lights twinkling in the periphery of his vision. Each street was adorned with the colours of Christmas, reds and greens flickering in the windows of houses, their cheer a stark contrast to the sombre mood that enveloped him.

George's hands were firm on the steering wheel, the leather cold beneath his touch. The windscreen wipers rhythmically swept away the gentle snowflakes that seemed to fall in sync with his deepening thoughts. The soft patter of snow against the car was a stark contrast to the silence within, a silence filled with the weight of the task ahead.

He drove past families gathering in warm homes and children playing in the snow, all oblivious to the darkness that lurked just beneath the surface of the city. George's gaze was fixed ahead, but his mind was elsewhere, replaying the conversation with Isabella, the details of the new murder case, and the faces of the victims.

The festive atmosphere around him felt almost surreal, a world apart from the one he was heading into. The bright, joyful decorations seemed to mock the grim reality of his profession. The city, usually a place of comfort and familiarity, now felt alien, its streets leading him back into the depths of criminal investigation.

The journey was a transition, a bridge between the warmth

of his family life and the cold, analytical world of his work. With each mile, George could feel the shift within him, the detective taking over, pushing the family man into the background.

Chapter Two

The crisp evening air of Harehills in Leeds was pierced by the sharp sound of police sirens as Detective Inspector George Beaumont arrived at the crime scene. A narrow, snow-covered ginnel, usually inconspicuous amongst the urban sprawl, was now cordoned off with police tape, flashing blue lights casting an eerie glow on the pristine white.

The persistent hum of the media was already palpable. Camera lenses and microphones jostled for position, eager to capture every move of the police. George's jaw tightened as he stepped out of his car, his breath forming clouds in the frigid air. The presence of the media only added to the pressure, the weight of public scrutiny palpable in the air. Paige McGuiness, a known figure among the local press, made a beeline towards him, her recorder at the ready.

He pulled his coat tighter around him, his eyes immediately scanning the scene with a practised gaze that missed nothing. The lamplight cast long shadows across the snow, shadows that seemed to accentuate the solemnity of the situation.

Detective Constable Jay Scott, already at the scene, approached George, his face etched with concern. "Morning, boss. It's a bad one."

George nodded, his expression set in grim determination.

"Show me."

"Detective Beaumont, any comments on the similarities with the previous murders?" she asked, her voice betraying a mix of professional curiosity and sensationalism.

"Not now, Paige," George replied tersely, his focus elsewhere. "This isn't the time."

"But the public has a right to know if there's a serial killer on the loose," she persisted.

George shot her a sharp look. "My team's working on it. Now, if you'll excuse me."

Turning away from her insistent questioning, he approached the crime scene, his expression set in a grim line. Donning a Tyvek suit, mask, gloves, and shoe covers, he prepared to step under the police tape. The ritual was familiar, yet the sense of foreboding never lessened.

The body lay in the narrow ginnel, a stark contrast against the snow. George's practised eye took in the scene, noting the disturbing similarities with the previous murders.

As he surveyed the scene, George's thoughts turned to the case that had haunted Leeds for months. Christian Ross, now dead, had left a legacy of terror that seemed to be resurfacing. The methodical display of the victim hinted at a sinister possibility—either a copycat was at large, or Ross had had an accomplice.

Detective Inspector Beaumont stood up and scanned the area, his heart heavy with the knowledge that he had pulled his team away from their families on Christmas evening. The flashing blue lights of the police cars cast a surreal glow on the snow-covered ground.

Detective Constable Jay Scott, Detective Constable Tashan Blackburn, and Detective Constable Candy Nichols were huddled together, their breaths forming small clouds in the cold air as they discussed the scene before them.

"I'm sorry for dragging you all away from your Christmas evening," George apologised, his voice tinged with genuine regret.

"It's part of the job, boss," Jay responded, his tone professional yet understanding.

Candy nodded in agreement. "We're here to do what's necessary, sir."

Tashan, always focused, interjected, "Let's focus on what we have here."

Jay stepped forward, his expression solemn. "The victim is Ethan Turner, boss. He was the St John's Centre Santa Claus from the previous case."

George's brow furrowed at the mention of the name. "Ethan Turner?" George thought about the tall, lanky fellow with short-cropped black hair and piercing blue eyes he'd interviewed only a couple of weeks ago.

"That's him," Jay confirmed. "He's dressed in his Santa Claus outfit and very much dead."

George approached the body, observing the stark contrast between the festive red suit and the lifeless form of Ethan Turner. "He was a popular figure. This is going to send shock waves through the community."

Candy, who had been examining the area, added, "There are no obvious signs of a struggle, sir. It looks like he was placed here post-mortem."

Tashan, flipping through his notes, remarked, "No identification on him, but we matched his prints using a Lantern device. The outfit... it's almost theatrical."

George looked around the secluded ginnel, his mind piecing

together the scene. "The killer wanted him found like this; it's a statement. Any witnesses?"

Jay shook his head. "It's been quiet, Christmas evening and all. But we're canvassing the area."

George stood up, his gaze lingering on Ethan Turner's body. "This changes the dynamics of the case. Turner was well-liked; his portrayal of Santa Claus brought a lot of joy. Why target him?"

Candy looked thoughtful. "Could be personal, or perhaps his role as Santa Claus played into the killer's narrative."

Jay said, "Could be because he was mates with Oliver Hughes, the victim from a decade ago, and Liam O'Sullivan, Alex Green, and Ryan Baxter."

George nodded whilst Tashan added, "We'll need to look into his background and see if there were any conflicts or connections that could point us towards a motive."

George nodded again, his mind racing with possibilities. "Right. Let's get back to the station and start digging into Turner's life. We need to understand who he was beyond the Santa suit."

As George crouched beside the body, Dr Lindsey Yardley, the newly promoted pathologist since Dr Ross' death, joined him. She was a young woman with a serious expression, her professionalism evident.

"Lindsey, what can you tell me?" George asked, his eyes scanning the scene.

"If it's all the same to you, DI Beaumont, I'd prefer Dr Yardley now," she said, her voice devoid of emotion.

George narrowed his eyes and said, "I apologise, Dr Yardley."

"Thank you," Dr Yardley said as she adjusted her glasses,

her voice steady. "Preliminary observation suggests the time of death was in the early hours of Christmas morning. It narrows down our timeline for the killer's movements."

George nodded, processing the information. "That's helpful. Any signs of struggle?"

She shook her head. "None that I can see here. I'll know more after the autopsy."

Crime Scene Manager Stuart Kent, a meticulous man in his early fifties with a neatly trimmed beard, approached them. His limp, a remnant of an old injury, did not slow him down.

"DI Beaumont, we found some of Turner's personal effects," Kent reported, holding up evidence bags containing a wallet and a mobile phone. "These could be crucial in understanding the events leading to his death."

George stood up. He smiled at Stuart, glad the man was finally back at work and fully recovered from the awful attempt on his life by the Bone Saw Ripper. "It's great to see you, Stuart."

"And you too, DI Beaumont." he paused. "What's it been, like two years?"

"Nearly, aye," said George. "Feeling fit?"

"As fit as I can be, yeah," the Crime Scene Manager said.

"Good, good," said George, taking the evidence bags from him. "And this is good work, Kent. It might give us an insight into Turner's last hours."

Detective Constable Jay Scott, who had been conversing with the forensics team, joined them.

George's gaze lingered on the personal effects. "Did you go through the phone, Jay?"

"Not yet, boss. We thought it best to wait for your instruction," Jay replied.

"Let's get it to the tech team immediately. See if they can pull up recent calls or messages," George instructed, handing the phone back to Jay.

"Will do, boss," Jay said, heading off to coordinate with the tech team.

George turned back to Kent. "Stuart, I want the area canvassed thoroughly. If the killer left anything else behind, I want to know about it."

"Understood, DI Beaumont. We'll comb through every inch," Kent assured him, his tone reflecting his dedication.

George looked back at the crime scene, his mind already formulating theories. The killer's choice of a Christmas-themed display was a statement, but what exactly it signified remained to be seen.

"Thank you, Dr Yardley, Stuart. Keep me posted on any new findings," George said, his tone indicating that he was ready to move to the next phase of the investigation.

The chill of the evening in Harehills was palpable, not just in the air, but in the mood that hung over the crowd gathered behind the police tape. Detective Inspector George Beaumont, his gaze methodical and sharp, couldn't help but notice the concerned and scared faces of the onlookers. Their whispers, though hushed, carried an undercurrent of growing public fear. Each glance towards the crime scene was tinged with unease, reflecting the community's distress.

A SOCO approached him, holding an evidence bag. "Sir, we found this near the body," he said, his voice betraying a hint of unease.

George took the bag, his eyes narrowing as he saw the note inside addressed to him. Carefully, he opened the bag and unfolded the paper, his expression stoic yet alert. The note was written in a bold, mocking script:

"Dear Detective Beaumont,

Welcome to the game. I thought it was time we got acquainted. You chase shadows while I walk in the light. Let's see if you can catch up before the next gift is unwrapped.

Tick-tock, George.

Your admirer."

George's jaw tightened as he read the note, a mix of anger and determination setting in his eyes. The audacity of the killer, taunting him directly, was both alarming and provocative.

Detective Constable Jay Scott, who had been overseeing the collection of evidence, joined him. "What does it say, boss?"

He handed Jay the note, watching as his expression mirrored his own upon reading it.

"This is personal, Jay. The killer is not just playing with the victims; he's playing with us," George said, his voice low and controlled.

Jay looked up, his eyes unwavering. "He's trying to get into your head, boss. But we won't let him throw us off. We're going to catch this bastard."

George nodded, his gaze returning to the note. He handed the note back to the Scene of Crime Officer. "Get this to forensics. Check for fingerprints, DNA, anything that might lead us to him."

As the officer walked away, George took a moment to survey the scene once more, his mind racing. The killer was intelligent, calculating, and now blatantly challenging the police.

George stepped away from the ginnel, and the flash of cameras and the murmur of reporters waiting for a statement pulled his attention. He walked towards them, his expression composed, the epitome of professionalism in the midst of chaos.

"Detective Inspector Beaumont, can you give us any details about the investigation?" one reporter asked, her voice urgent with the need for information.

George stopped, facing the sea of cameras and microphones. "We're in the early stages of the investigation," he began, his voice steady and controlled. "Our team is working diligently to gather evidence and piece together what happened."

"Is there a connection to the previous Santa Claus murders?" another reporter probed, eager to draw him out.

George maintained his composure. "It's too early to draw any conclusions. We're exploring all possibilities and following every lead."

He glanced back at the crime scene, where Crime Scene Manager Stuart Kent's team was meticulously collecting and bagging evidence, including unique Christmas-themed items left by the killer—a grim signature that added a disturbing layer to the crime.

"We ask for the public's cooperation," George continued, addressing the reporters and the onlookers beyond. "If anyone has any information, no matter how insignificant it may seem, please come forward."

The reporters nodded, scribbling notes and murmuring amongst themselves. George, aware of the importance of public perception, knew his words were carefully measured to reassure yet not disclose too much.

As he turned to head back to the crime scene, he noticed Stuart Kent signalling him. Walking over, he saw Kent holding up a sealed evidence bag containing a small, intricately decorated

Christmas bauble stained with what looked like blood.

"This was found near the body," Kent said, his voice low. "Looks like the killer left it deliberately."

George took the bag, examining the bauble closely. "A message, or a taunt perhaps," he mused, his mind already racing with the implications.

Kent nodded. "We'll get this to the lab for analysis. There might be fingerprints or DNA."

"Good work, Stuart," George said, handing back the evidence. "Keep me updated on any new findings."

As George prepared to leave the crime scene in Harehills, a new commotion caught his attention. A group of people, led by a determined-looking woman, arrived carrying placards. They gathered near the police tape, their banners calling for increased safety and community vigilance.

The woman, her voice clear and resonant, began to address the growing crowd. "We cannot let fear take over our community," she declared. "It's time for us to come together and take a stand against this violence."

George observed her closely. She was in her mid-thirties, with a commanding presence that belied her slight frame. He recognised her. Her name was Emma Clarke, an activist known in the community for her leadership and commitment to social causes. Her words seemed to strike a chord with the onlookers, many nodding in agreement.

As Emma coordinated with volunteers, distributing flyers and speaking with concerned citizens, George's curiosity was piqued. Her dedication was evident, but he couldn't help but question her motivations. He approached her, his approach calm and measured.

"Miss Clarke," George began, introducing himself. "I

couldn't help but overhear. You seem deeply invested in this."

Emma turned to face him, her expression one of resolve. "Detective Inspector Beaumont, yes, I've seen you on the news. This is our community. We can't just stand by while this... madness continues." Her passion was palpable, her gaze unflinching. "We need to be proactive, work together to ensure our streets are safe."

George nodded, understanding her perspective. "I agree, community involvement is crucial. But these are dangerous waters. We don't want to incite panic."

Emma's lips pressed into a thin line. "It's not about panic; it's about empowerment. People need to feel they can contribute, make a difference."

George regarded her thoughtfully. "And what about you, Miss Clarke? What drives you to take such a proactive stance?"

Emma's eyes flickered, a shadow of something deeper behind her determined façade. "I believe in justice, Inspector. In making sure that no one else has to suffer."

Her sincerity was evident, yet George sensed there was more to her story. "Your efforts are commendable. But be careful. The killer is still out there, and we don't yet know what we're dealing with."

Emma met his gaze squarely. "I understand the risks. But I can't just stand by and do nothing."

George gave a slight nod of acknowledgement. "Just ensure you keep us informed of your activities. Cooperation is key."

As he walked away, George glanced back at Emma and her group. Her leadership had a rallying effect on the people, her voice a beacon in the midst of fear and uncertainty.

Chapter Three

The icy wind whipped around George Beaumont as he exited his car, the snow crunching under his feet. Elland Road police station loomed before him, its façade more imposing under the grey, overcast sky.

He reached for his phone, dialling Isabella, his partner, feeling a pang of guilt for leaving her and the kids at home on Christmas day.

"Izzy, it's me," George said as soon as she answered, his voice tinged with apology.

"George, are you OK, gorgeous?" Isabella's voice was laced with concern but also an understanding that came from being a fellow detective.

"I'm sorry for all of this. How are the kids?" George asked his mind still partially on the case.

"It's fine, George, we understand. But Mia was extremely frosty with me when she came to pick Jack up," Isabella replied, a hint of unease in her voice. "She was pissed off that you'd left Jack to go to work."

George sighed, rubbing his forehead. "I'll talk to her. I know this isn't easy on any of you."

There was a brief pause before Isabella spoke again. "We're OK, George. Just be careful, alright?"

"I will. I love you, Isabella," George said, his words carrying the weight of his affection and the unspoken fears that came with his job. "Don't wait up."

"I love you too. Stay safe," Isabella replied before ending the call.

Stepping inside, George was immediately engulfed by the frenetic energy of the station. Officers and detectives bustled about, their movements quick and purposeful. The murmur of hushed conversations filled the air, punctuated by the occasional ring of a phone or the sharp rap of footsteps.

Detective Sergeant Yolanda Williams caught his eye from across the room. Her face was etched with concern, mirroring the gravity of the situation. She beckoned him over with a nod.

"I've set up an Incident Room for us, sir," Yolanda said tersely as he approached. "We're gathering in five."

He nodded, his mind already racing with the details of the case. The Santa Claus murders had cast a long, dark shadow over Leeds, and this new development threatened to deepen the gloom.

As George made his way to the Incident Room, he passed clusters of officers engaged in hushed, intense discussions. The snippets of conversation he caught were laced with anxiety and speculation, a stark contrast to the usual composed professionalism.

The Incident Room quickly filled up as George entered. The faces around him were a mix of determination and apprehension, each person bracing themselves for what was to come.

Detective Chief Inspector Alistair Atkinson stood at the front, his expression grim. The room fell silent as he began to speak.

"Thank you for gathering promptly," Atkinson began, his

voice steady but his eyes betraying the gravity of the situation. "As many of you are aware, we've had a development in the Santa Claus murder case. A new victim has been found in Harehills, bearing the same signature traits as the previous murders."

A collective murmur rippled through the room, a mix of frustration and resolve.

"We're awaiting the full report from forensics, but preliminary observations suggest we're dealing with either the same perpetrator or a copycat who knows intricate details," Atkinson continued. "I want patrols doubled in key areas, and I need all hands on deck for this investigation."

After Atkinson told the team George was SIO and left, George convened his core team. The atmosphere was sombre, the air thick with anticipation. Detective Constables Jay Scott, Tashan Blackburn, and Candy Nichols gathered around the table, their expressions taut with concern.

George cleared his throat, breaking the tense silence. "Right, let's get to it. We've all seen the preliminary reports. This latest murder at Harehills—it's chillingly similar to our Santa Claus cases." He laid out the photographs and reports on the table, the grim reality displayed in stark detail.

Jay leaned forward, his youthful face etched with seriousness. "The same MO, sir. The victim was in a Santa suit, positioned just like the others. It's like the killer is following a script."

Tashan, usually stoic, frowned deeply. "But why? What's the pattern here? There has to be a connection we're missing."

Candy, her red hair a stark contrast against the room's drabness, interjected softly, "The note, sir. It's directed at you personally."

George rubbed his temples, feeling the weight of every unsolved question. "Yes, it's a clear message. As is the link between the victims. But what are we missing?" He paused as the obvious question no doubt lingered in the minds of the detectives, and the team fell into contemplative silence, each lost in thought.

Jay broke the silence, his voice hesitant. "We obviously couldn't interview Christian Ross, so we don't know whether he had a partner or not."

Tashan nodded in agreement. "We need to dig deeper into Dr Ross' past relationships, employment history, anything that might connect with the victims."

Candy leaned back, her brow furrowed in thought. "I feel like this is worse than before Christmas. No forensic leads, no witnesses—nothing. How does someone commit these crimes without leaving a trace?"

George listened, his mind racing through the possibilities. "We need to think outside the box. This killer is careful and meticulous. But everyone makes mistakes. We just need to find it."

The conversation ebbed and flowed, theories and ideas bouncing around the room like a tense game of tennis. Each team member brought their unique perspective, their collective experience weaving a tapestry of investigation.

Yolanda, who had been quiet, stood. "How are we handling this, sir?"

George stood up, his presence commanding attention. "We'll need to act as if Dr Ross wasn't the only killer," he explained. "Revisit every piece of evidence, re-interview witnesses, re-examine the crime scene photos. Anything that can give us a lead. Jay, I want you to focus on the forensic reports again. Tashan, dive into the victims' histories. Candy, coordinate with the other departments and see if they've picked up anything we might have missed."

The team nodded, their determination renewed. They were a unit, each playing their part in the intricate dance of investigation.

As the meeting concluded, the team dispersed, heading back into the fray. George remained behind, his gaze lingering on the reports and photos spread across the table. The faces of the victims stared back at him, a silent plea for justice.

* * *

In his office, George sat hunched over a sprawl of evidence photos and murder reports. The fluorescent light above flickered intermittently, casting an eerie glow over the grim details of the latest Santa Claus murder. His mind, usually a fortress of logic and reason, now waded through a swamp of personal conflict and professional duty.

Each photograph, each line of the report, whispered to him, hinting at a truth he was reluctant to acknowledge. The killer's method, so meticulously executed, bore an unsettling resemblance to the work of Christian Ross, the mastermind behind the original Santa Claus murders. But it was the nagging suspicion about his father, Edward Beaumont, that clouded his thoughts. Why had Christian visited him on the night of his death? And why did he threaten to kill Edward with a revolver?

George's fingers traced the edge of a photo, his mind replaying the conversation he had with his father weeks ago. Edward's words, once dismissed, now echoed with ominous significance. "You never know the secrets people hide, George. Not until you peel back their masks."

The room felt smaller, the walls closing in as George wrestled with the implications. Could his father have been an accomplice to Ross? The mere thought sent a shiver down his spine, a mix of dread and disbelief.

A soft knock on the door pulled him from his reverie. Detective Constable Jay Scott peeked in, his expression cautious. "Everything alright, boss?"

George looked up, schooling his features into a semblance of composure. "Yes, Jay, come in."

Jay stepped inside, closing the door behind him. "I've been over the forensic reports again," he began, unaware of the turmoil churning inside his superior. "There's nothing new, boss."

George nodded absently, his gaze returning to the photographs. "Thank you, Jay. Keep at it. Something's got to give."

Jay hesitated. "Boss, if you don't mind me saying, you seem... troubled. Is there anything I can help with?"

George weighed his response, the burden of his suspicion heavy on his shoulders. "It's just the case, Jay. These murders... they're getting under my skin."

Jay nodded understandingly, though George knew he couldn't possibly comprehend the full depth of his dilemma. "We'll crack it, boss. We always do."

After Jay left, George turned back to the evidence, his father's image looming in his mind. The parallels were too striking to ignore. And the addition of the note suggested a new culprit. But who was it?

And if it was his father, why would Edward be involved?

What connection could there possibly be? George's thoughts spiralled, a maelstrom of professional duty clashing with filial loyalty. The idea that his father could be linked to such heinous crimes was almost too much to bear, even if he did hate the bastard.

He pulled out his phone, hesitating over Edward's contact. A part of him yearned for reassurance, for a simple explanation that would dispel his fears. Yet, another part dreaded what he might uncover.

The clock on the wall ticked steadily, marking the passage of time and the urgency of the case. With a deep breath, George made a decision. He dialled Edward's number, his heart racing.

Outside, the snow continued to fall over Leeds, a blanket of purity over a city grappling with its demons.

* * *

The rain pattered steadily against the window of Luke Mason's office, the rhythmic sound a stark contrast to the storm brewing within George. Seated across from Detective Inspector Luke Mason, George felt the weight of his suspicions like a physical burden.

Luke, a figure of experience and wisdom in the force, regarded George with a steady, knowing gaze. "You seem troubled, son. More than usual. What's on your mind?"

George hesitated, the words stuck in his throat. Admitting his fears felt like a betrayal, yet the need for guidance was overwhelming. "It's about the Santa Claus murders, Luke. I... I have a suspicion, and it's tearing me apart."

Luke leaned forward, his interest piqued. "Go on."

"It's my father, Edward," George said, the words tasting bitter. "I think he might be Ross' accomplice. I can't shake the feeling that he knows more than he's letting on."

Luke's expression shifted, a mix of surprise and concern. "Edward? That's a serious accusation, George. What makes you think he's involved?"

George ran a hand through his hair, his mind a tumult of emotion. "It's just little things. Comments he's made, his knowledge of the case details, the fact he seems to know everyone involved." He paused. "And I feel like I need to know why Christian visited my father with a revolver; why Christian would want to kill Edward."

Luke nodded, absorbing the information. "I understand your concerns, George, but we need to tread carefully. Suspicions alone aren't enough. We need solid evidence."

"I know, I know," George replied, frustration edging his voice. "But how do I investigate my own father without bias?" He left out the fact that he loathed his father.

Luke's voice was soft but firm. "By remembering why you're a detective in the first place. Our duty is to the truth, no matter how difficult it may be to face. If there's evidence implicating your father, it will come to light. But until then, you must be cautious."

George sighed, the weight of the situation bearing down on him. "It's just so hard, Luke. The thought of him being involved in something like this..."

Luke reached across the desk, placing a reassuring hand on George's shoulder. "I know it's hard. But you're one of the best detectives I've worked with. You have the strength to see this through, no matter where it leads, son."

The rain continued to fall outside, a steady reminder of the world moving on, oblivious to the turmoil within the station walls. George sat back, the comfort of Luke's words a small beacon in the fog of his doubts.

"You're right, Luke. I'll follow the evidence wherever it leads. It's just going to be one of the hardest things I've ever had to do."

Luke nodded, a gesture of solidarity. "I'll be here for you, George. Whatever you need."

As George stood to leave, he felt a renewed sense of purpose tempered with caution. The road ahead was fraught with personal and professional challenges, but he was not alone. The guidance and support of Luke Mason were invaluable, a guiding light in the murky waters of the investigation.

Stepping out into the hallway, George took a deep breath. The station was quiet, the usual hustle of the day subdued by the evening. He knew the path ahead would be difficult, but he was resolved to uncover the truth, no matter the personal cost.

Outside, the rain continued to fall on Leeds, washing away the grime of the day, a natural cleanse in a city struggling with its own darkness. Inside, George Beaumont prepared to delve deeper into the case, armed with caution and the unwavering pursuit of justice.

Chapter Four

George Beaumont sat motionless in his office, the only sound the faint ticking of the clock on the wall. The room, usually a haven of order and control, now felt like a cage, trapping him with his spiralling thoughts. The dim light cast long shadows, mirroring the dark doubts that clouded his mind.

The possibility of his father's involvement in the Santa Claus murders was a corrosive thought, eating away at the foundations of his life. Christian Ross, the orchestrator of the original crimes, was dead, leaving behind a trail of unanswered questions. And now, with another murder mirroring those past horrors, George's world was tilting on its axis.

The silence of the room was oppressive, each tick of the clock a reminder of the urgency of the situation. George's mind raced, replaying every interaction with his father, searching for missed signs for any hint of the truth.

His father's voice echoed in his memory, snippets of conversations they had shared. Had there been any indication, any subtle clue he had overlooked? But each memory only deepened the confusion, painting the picture of a man devoted to his family, not a criminal mastermind.

He stood up, pacing the room, the confines of the office suddenly too small. The detective in him demanded evidence, facts, something tangible to pursue.

The weight of his profession, the oath he had taken, felt heavier than ever.

George stopped in front of the window, looking out at the city lights of Leeds. Somewhere out there, a killer was walking free, and it was his job to find them. But the path to the truth now seemed fraught with personal landmines, each step a potential betrayal of his family.

The room felt colder, the walls bearing down on him. This case was pushing him out of his comfort zone, forcing him to confront fears and doubts he had long buried. But there was no turning back. Christian Ross was dead, and the Santa Claus murders were continuing. He had to find the connection, even if it led to his own doorstep. So he made his mind up.

The weight of his decision hung heavy on George Beaumont as he gathered his team in the cramped Incident Room. The walls, adorned with maps and photos of the case, felt like silent witnesses to his internal struggle. He cleared his throat, drawing the attention of Detectives Jay Scott, Tashan Blackburn, and Candy Nichols.

"We need to look at every angle of this case, no matter how personal it might be," George began, his voice steady despite the turmoil within. "I want you to delve into any possible connections between the new murder and... my father, Edward Beaumont."

A ripple of surprise passed through the team. Jay's eyebrows shot up, Tashan's stoic expression faltered slightly, and Candy's eyes widened in shock.

"Boss, are you sure about this?" Jay asked, his tone laced with concern.

George met his gaze squarely. "Yes. It's necessary. We

can't leave any stone unturned, not with what's at stake." He added, "Edward may be innocent, and that's fine, but we need to know for sure."

Tashan nodded slowly, his professional resolve taking over. "We'll handle it discreetly, sir. You can count on us."

Candy chimed in, her voice firm. "We'll get to the bottom of this, sir. Whatever it takes."

"Good, but bear in mind I may not be leading this case," George explained.

"Because of Edward, boss?" asked Jay.

George nodded.

Determined, George made his way to DCI Atkinson's office. The corridors of the station seemed longer, each step echoing with the gravity of his request.

Atkinson looked up as George entered, his expression one of expectation. "DI Beaumont, what can I do for you?"

George took a deep breath, choosing his words carefully. "Sir, given my... personal connection to a potential suspect in the Santa Claus murders, I need to ask if I should hand over the case."

Atkinson leaned back in his chair, regarding George thoughtfully. "I've considered this, George. Your integrity isn't in question, but the situation is delicate."

George braced himself, ready to accept whatever decision was made.

Atkinson continued, "I want you to stay on the case. Your knowledge and insight are invaluable. However, I'm bringing DI Luke Mason in as well. He'll act as SIO alongside you."

Relief and apprehension mingled within George. "I understand, sir. I'll work with Luke closely on this." He paused, then looked Atkinson in the eye. "Thank you, sir, I really appreciate this."

"It's the best course of action," Atkinson said firmly. "Keep me updated, and remember, George, we're after the truth, no matter where it leads."

"Understood, sir," George replied, a renewed sense of purpose steadying his resolve.

Leaving Atkinson's office, George felt a weight lift, replaced by a focused determination. He headed straight to Luke Mason's office, ready to face this new chapter of the investigation.

George sat in the quiet of his office, the steady hum of the police station outside a distant backdrop to the conversation he was about to have. He picked up the phone, dialling Luke Mason's number, each beep resonating with the gravity of the call.

Luke answered promptly, his voice steady and calm. "Luke Mason speaking."

"Luke, it's George. I wanted to discuss the new arrangement Atkinson's put in place for the Santa Claus murder case," George began, his voice betraying a hint of the turmoil he felt inside.

"Ah, yes, George. I've been briefed. I understand this must be difficult for you, given the potential personal connections," Luke replied, his tone reflecting a deep understanding of the situation.

George leaned back in his chair, the leather creaking softly. "It is. I'm not sure how to navigate this. The thought that my father might be involved..." He trailed off, the words heavy with unspoken emotion.

There was a brief pause on the line as Luke considered his response. "I know this is tough, but you're not alone in this,

George. I'll be here to support you, not to step on your toes. Think of me as your deputy in this."

The offer was a lifeline in the storm of George's thoughts. "I appreciate that, Luke. Your experience will be invaluable, especially now. I just don't want my personal involvement to cloud the investigation."

"You've always been a straight shooter, George. If there's a conflict, we'll handle it together. We're after the truth, whatever it may be," Luke reassured him, his voice unwavering.

George felt a sense of gratitude mixed with relief. "Thank you, Luke. That means a lot to me."

"No problem, so what's first?" asked Luke.

George leaned forward, his hands clasped together. "First, we need to establish a solid timeline for Ethan Turner's last hours. We know he was a popular figure, so someone must have seen something."

Luke nodded in agreement. "Right. I'll have the team start canvassing the area around St John's Centre. We'll also need to review any CCTV footage available."

"Good. And let's not overlook his personal life," George added. "We need to understand who Ethan Turner was beyond the Santa suit. Friends, family, any known disputes."

"I'll have the team dig into his background, check his financials, phone records, the works," Luke said, making notes.

George's gaze was intense, focused. "We also need to consider the possibility of a connection to the previous Santa Claus murders. Could be a copycat, or maybe Turner knew something he shouldn't have."

Luke considered this. "I'll review the files from the previous cases and see if there are any links we might have missed."

"And the Christmas-themed items left at the scene... they're a signature of sorts," George mused. "We need to analyse them thoroughly, see if they yield any clues."

"I'll coordinate with forensics on that," Luke assured him.

George stood up, his mind already racing with the tasks ahead. "I'll also notify Mike Clarkson and Danny Roberts. If there's a pattern targeting individuals related to the previous case, they need to be aware."

"Sounds like a solid plan," Luke said, standing as well. "We'll catch this killer, George."

As they continued to discuss the logistics of their new working relationship, George found comfort in Luke's measured approach and sage advice. The conversation was a blend of professional strategising and personal reassurance, a balance that helped steady George's resolve.

As the call drew to a close, George felt compelled to express his appreciation. "Luke, I just want to say thank you again. This... it's more personal than any case I've worked on."

Luke's response was warm, tinged with affection. "No bother, George. You're like a son to me. We'll get through this together."

The words resonated with George, a testament to the bond they had formed over the years. It was more than just a professional relationship; it was a mentorship and camaraderie that had stood the test of time and challenge.

George hung up the phone, feeling a renewed sense of purpose. The path ahead was daunting, filled with personal and professional obstacles. But with Luke Mason by his side and the support of his team, he was ready to face whatever the investigation unearthed.

The office felt less confining now, the walls no longer

closing in on him. George stood up, his movements more assured. He had a case to solve, a truth to uncover, no matter how close to home it hit.

Stepping out of his office, George Beaumont was a man on a mission, driven by duty and bolstered by the support of a trusted colleague. The journey ahead was uncertain, but he was not walking it alone.

* * *

The clock on the wall of George Beaumont's office ticked steadily, marking the passage of time in a rhythm that seemed to echo the steady beat of his heart. Seated behind his desk, he was the picture of resolute determination; his eyes fixed on the file open before him. The dim light from the desk lamp cast shadows across the room, mirroring the complexity of the case that lay sprawled out in front of him.

Every so often, George would reach out, his fingers tracing the lines of text as if trying to physically connect with the clues they held. The Santa Claus murders, a case that had once seemed straightforward, had now woven itself intricately into the fabric of his personal life. The potential involvement of his father, Edward Beaumont, was a twist in the narrative he could never have anticipated.

George leaned back in his chair, the leather creaking under his weight. He let out a slow, measured breath.

The phone on his desk rang, piercing the silence of the room. George answered it, his voice steady despite the storm raging within.

"DI Beaumont," he said, his tone all business.

It was Detective Constable Candy Nichols on the other end.

"Sir, we've found something in the Ethan Turner's financial records that might be worth looking into."

"Good work, Nichols. I'll be right there," George replied, his detective instincts kicking in. The professional in him took over, pushing aside personal doubts and fears.

He hung up the phone and stood, feeling the weight of his profession more acutely than ever. He looked at his warrant card, which was a symbol of his commitment to justice, a commitment that was now being tested in ways he had never imagined.

As George left his office, he felt the shift within him. The detective, the seeker of truth, was at the forefront, ready to face whatever lay ahead. The personal conflicts, fears and doubts were still there, simmering beneath the surface, but his resolve to uncover the truth was unwavering.

The corridors of the station were quiet, the usual bustle of activity subdued by the late hour. George's footsteps echoed as he made his way to the Incident Room, each step a reaffirmation of his purpose.

Arriving in the Incident Room, George found DC Nichols waiting with a series of documents spread out before her. She pointed to a series of transactions that stood out. "These are recent large deposits into Turner's account, originating from an offshore account. But here's the interesting part," she said, her finger tracing the paper to a name that made George's heart skip a beat. "The account is linked to a charity known for its influential members, including Edward Beaumont."

George's professional demeanour faltered for a moment, a frown creasing his forehead. The mention of his father in connection with the case brought a personal dimension that he couldn't ignore. Yet, the detective in him pushed personal feelings aside, focusing on the evidence at hand.

"Do we know the nature of these transactions? Why would my father's charity be sending money to Turner?" George asked, his mind racing through potential scenarios.

Nichols shook her head. "Not yet. But the amount and the timing are suspicious. It's just before Turner's murder."

George nodded, his instincts telling him this was more than a coincidence. "We need to dig deeper into this. See if there's a pattern or a connection with the other victims. And discreetly, DC Nichols. We can't afford to tip our hand."

Nichols acknowledged with a firm nod, her expression resolute. "Understood, sir. I'll get on it right away."

Chapter Five

The morning Boxing Day sun filtered through the kitchen window, reflecting off the snow, and casting a warm glow. George Beaumont stood there, a mug of coffee in hand, staring out at the quiet Morley scene that had been his sanctuary from the chaos of his work. But this morning, the tranquillity of the scene was lost on him.

In his mind, a storm raged, thoughts swirling around the possibility of his father, Edward Beaumont's involvement in the harrowing crimes he was investigating. The bitter taste of the coffee did little to dispel the bitterness of his thoughts.

His fiancée, Isabella, entered the kitchen, her presence a soothing balm in the unsettling silence. "Morning, gorgeous," she said softly, noting the distant look in George's eyes. "You're up early."

George turned, offering a faint smile that didn't quite reach his eyes. "Couldn't sleep," he replied, his voice a low rumble.

Isabella made herself a cup of tea, her gaze fixed on George. "You're thinking about the case again, aren't you?" she asked, her voice laced with concern.

George turned from the window, offering a faint smile, an attempt to mask his inner turmoil. "Yeah, it's the case. It's... complex."

Isabella moved closer, her eyes searching his. "You've handled complex cases before. But this one seems different. It's affecting you more."

He hesitated, then nodded slowly. "It's a challenging one. We think it might be a copycat of the Santa Claus murders."

Isabella's brow furrowed. "A copycat?"

George's heart skipped a beat. He turned back to the window, looking out but not seeing the peaceful street. "Yeah, I think this is just someone trying to emulate those crimes." He paused. "And my father might be involved."

There was a momentary pause as Isabella digested his words. "It must be difficult dealing with something so close to past family experiences."

George nodded, keeping his gaze fixed outside. "It is. But it's part of the job. We'll figure it out."

Isabella moved closer, placing a comforting hand on his arm. "I know you, George. You won't rest until you find the truth. But don't let this consume you. You have to take care of yourself too."

George nodded, the weight of the situation bearing down on him. "I know. It's just hard. This case... it's personal in a way I never imagined."

The couple stood in silence, the ticking of the kitchen clock a subtle reminder of the passing time. Isabella finally broke the silence. "Whatever happens, I'm here for you. We'll get through this together." "And remember, George, you're more than just a detective. You're a person, too. And people need support."

George took a deep breath, the faintest hint of resolve returning to his posture. "Thanks, Izzy. That means everything to me."

He finished his coffee, setting the empty mug on the counter with a decisive clink. The normalcy of the morning stood in stark contrast to the chaos of his thoughts, a juxtaposition that mirrored the complexity of his life at the moment.

As George prepared to leave for the station, he paused at the door, turning back to look at Isabella. "I'll be late tonight. There's a lot to go through at the office."

Isabella nodded, understanding the unspoken weight of his words. "Just come back safe to me, George. That's all I ask."

George leaned in, kissing her forehead. "I will. Always."

With one last look at the peaceful kitchen, a stark contrast to the chaos of his professional life, George grabbed his coat and headed out the door. The normalcy of his home life stood in sharp contrast to the complexities of the case that awaited him, a case that was becoming increasingly personal and fraught with unspoken fears.

As George navigated the familiar streets of Leeds, the city was just beginning to stir under the early morning light. Behind the wheel of his Mercedes, his mind wandered, drifting away from the looming complexities of the Santa Claus murder case to the earlier days of his career.

Back then, the world of criminal investigation had seemed more straightforward, more black and white. George remembered his first days as a detective, filled with a sense of clarity and purpose. The cases, though challenging, had seemed more manageable, the lines between right and wrong more clearly defined.

He recalled one of his first major cases, a straightforward burglary that had led to an unexpected arrest. George could still hear the voice of his then-supervisor, Detective Inspector Graham, a seasoned officer with a knack for getting to the heart of the matter.

"Beaumont, remember, it's all about following the evidence. Keep it simple," Graham had said, his voice gruff but encouraging.

"Yes, sir. It seems straightforward enough," a much younger George had replied, his confidence unshaken.

But now, years later, that simplicity seemed like a distant memory. The road ahead was clouded with personal conflicts and moral ambiguities that his younger self couldn't have imagined.

George's thoughts were interrupted by the ringing of his phone. He glanced at the caller ID—it was Detective Constable Jay Scott. He answered, switching to speaker phone.

"Good morning, Jay. Everything OK?" George asked, his voice steady despite the turmoil inside.

"Boss, we've got a lead on the Santa Claus case. Something about the murder weapon that might be worth looking into," Jay reported, his tone eager.

"Good work. Keep on it and update me when you have more," George replied, his detective instincts kicking in despite his reflective mood.

"Will do, boss," Jay responded before ending the call.

The conversation brought George back to the present, to the reality of the case at hand. The simplicity of his early career was gone, replaced by a complexity that challenged him in ways he had never anticipated.

As he continued his drive to the station, George couldn't help but feel a pang of nostalgia for those earlier days. But he also recognised that it was this very complexity, this blurring of lines, that had shaped him into the detective he was today—more thoughtful, more empathetic, and more aware of the shades of grey in the world of criminal justice.

Stepping out of his car, George felt the weight of the case settle back onto his shoulders. The early days of his career might have been simpler, but they had also been a preparation for the challenges he faced now.

* * *

Detective Constable Jay Scott knocked softly on the door of George Beaumont's office before entering. The room was dim, save for the light spilling across George's desk, illuminating the various case files spread out before him.

"Boss?" Jay's voice was cautious as he approached, holding an evidence bag carefully between his fingers.

George looked up, his face etched with the weariness of long hours spent poring over case details. "What have you got, Jay?"

Jay extended the evidence bag towards George. "Something you should see, boss." Inside was a cufflink, its design ornate and the material unmistakably expensive, glinting subtly under the office light.

Taking the bag, George held it up, examining the cufflink closely. His expression changed subtly, a mix of recognition and concern. "This looks familiar," he muttered, more to himself than to Jay.

"It should," Jay replied, watching George closely. "It matches the description of the cufflinks worn by members of the Leeds Business Club. Exclusive stuff."

George's mind raced, connecting the dots. The Leeds Business Club was no ordinary gathering. It was where the city's elite, the influential and powerful, converged. Business magnates, politicians, and high-profile figures—all rubbing shoulders under the guise of networking and socialising. And among them, Edward Beaumont, his father, was a known figure.

A silence hung in the air as George contemplated the implication. "Could be a coincidence," he finally said, his voice carrying a hint of scepticism.

Jay nodded, understanding the delicacy of the situation. "Maybe," he conceded. "But it's a lead worth following. These aren't exactly common."

George looked at the cufflink again, his thoughts clouded. The possibility of his father's involvement, however remote, added a personal dimension that he couldn't ignore. "Right," he said, finally looking up at Jay. "Have Forensics run it for prints and DNA."

"Will do, boss," Jay replied, ready to follow the orders.

"Boss, is everything alright? You seem... off," Jay ventured cautiously, his eyes carefully studying George.

George sighed, setting his pen down. "It's just the pressure, Jay. This case... it's weighing on me more than usual."

Jay moved closer, leaning against the edge of the desk. "I can only imagine. The Santa Claus murders were bad enough the first time around. This copycat, or whatever it is, it's got everyone on edge."

George rubbed his forehead, feeling the weight of unspoken truths. "Yeah, it's like we're chasing a ghost. Every lead we follow just adds to the complexity."

Jay's expression softened with empathy. "You've handled tough cases before, boss. If anyone can get to the bottom of this, it's you."

George managed a weary smile. "Thanks for the vote of

confidence, Jay. It's just... there are aspects of this case that hit closer to home than I'd like."

Jay nodded, understanding. "Sometimes the cases that affect us personally are the hardest. But they also bring out the best in us." Jay grinned. "You've taught me that, boss."

George looked at Jay, appreciating the support but also feeling the burden of keeping his true concerns to himself. "I appreciate your support, Jay. It's just a matter of putting the pieces together, as always."

Jay stood upright, ready to leave, but paused at the door. "If there's anything I can do, just say the word. We're all behind you, boss."

George spoke again, his voice steadier now. "And Jay, keep this under wraps for now. We need to be certain before we draw any conclusions."

"Understood, boss."

George, looking at the evidence bag Jay was clutching containing the ornate cufflink, called out, "Jay, wait a moment."

Jay turned back, his hand resting on the doorknob. "Yes, boss?"

George's gaze was intense, focused. "The Turner murder scene—have we got any updates on the CCTV footage? Anything that might give us a lead on the killer's identity or movements?"

Jay nodded, understanding the urgency. "I checked in with the team earlier. They're still combing through hours of footage from the surrounding area. It's a slow process, but they're prioritising any cameras that had a direct line of sight to the alley where Turner was found."

"Good," George replied, his mind clearly processing this information. "Make sure they know this is top priority. We need eyes on whoever was in that area at the time of the murder."

"I'll pass that along right away, sir," Jay assured him. "And I'll personally review the footage as soon as there's anything to report."

"Thanks, Jay," George said, a hint of gratitude in his voice. "Keep me updated. This might be our best chance at catching a break in this case."

Jay nodded once more, a determined look on his face. "Will do, boss."

After Jay left, George sat alone in his office, the silence enveloping him. He knew he had to maintain a façade of control to lead his team without allowing his personal fears to cloud his judgment. But the shadow of his father's potential involvement loomed large, a hidden spectre in a case already shrouded in darkness.

Outside, the station carried on with its usual rhythm, but inside George's office, time seemed to stand still. He realised that this case was not just a professional challenge but a personal crucible, testing the very foundations of his beliefs and loyalties.

Chapter Six

Detective Inspector George Beaumont and Detective Constable Candy Nichols arrived in Burley at the residence of Emily Turner, the sister of the late Ethan Turner. The house, nestled in a row of similar terraced homes, was modest but well-maintained. Its red-brick facade was complemented by neatly trimmed hedges and a small, welcoming front garden blooming with seasonal flowers. The front door painted a cheerful shade of blue, stood out against the more muted tones of the neighbouring houses.

George rang the doorbell, and after a brief wait, the door opened to reveal Emily Turner. She appeared to be in her late thirties, her eyes betraying a weariness that went beyond normal fatigue. She wore a simple cardigan and jeans, her hair pulled back in a practical ponytail.

"Miss Turner? I'm Detective Inspector George Beaumont, and this is Detective Constable Candy Nichols. We're investigating the circumstances surrounding your brother's death," George introduced them both with a gentle, respectful tone. They held up their warrant cards.

Emily's expression was one of resigned grief. "Yes, I was expecting you. Please, call me Emily." Her voice was soft but steady.

George nodded. "Thank you, Emily. May we come in?"

She hesitated for a moment, her gaze drifting over their shoulders as if gathering strength, then stepped aside. "Of course. Please."

As they entered, George took in the interior of the house. The hallway was narrow but bright, adorned with family photographs that seemed to capture happier times. They followed Emily into the living room, a cosy space dominated by a large, comfortable-looking sofa and a well-used armchair. A small fireplace, currently unlit, added a touch of homeliness to the room. The decor was simple and unpretentious, with a few personal touches like hand-knit throws and a small bookshelf filled with an eclectic collection of books.

Emily gestured towards the sofa. "Please, have a seat." She settled into the armchair opposite, her posture slightly tense.

George sat down, his manner compassionate yet professional. "Emily, we understand this is a difficult time for you. We need to ask some questions about Ethan. It's important for our investigation."

Emily nodded, her hands clasped tightly in her lap. "I understand. I'll help however I can."

"Did Ethan mention any problems he was facing? Any threats or unusual encounters?" George inquired.

Emily shook her head. "Ethan was private about his life. But he didn't mention anything unusual. He was just... Ethan. A bit withdrawn at times, but that was his way."

Candy, who had been observing quietly, added, "Was there anyone from his past who might have held a grudge? Any old disputes?"

"There was nothing I was aware of," Emily replied, her brow furrowing. "Ethan had his share of rough patches, but he'd moved past all that. Or so I thought."

George leaned forward slightly, his voice gentle. "Did Ethan ever mention a connection to the Leeds Business Club?"

Emily's expression changed to one of confusion. "No, Ethan wasn't the type to mingle with people like that. He kept to himself mostly."

The detectives exchanged a glance, knowing for a fact that Ethan did, in fact, mingle with people like that. George continued, "Emily, did Ethan have any routines or regular places he frequented that you know of?"

Emily thought for a moment. "Well, he was quite a regular at the local pub, The Malt and Hops. He'd go there most Fridays after work. Just to unwind, you know."

Candy, following up, queried, "Was there anyone at the pub he met regularly? Any close acquaintances there?"

Emily took a moment, her eyes gazing off into the distance as if sifting through her memories. "Ethan kept to himself a lot," she started slowly, "but he did mention a friend from the gym he went to, a Neil Roscow. He didn't talk much about him, but I know they used to grab a pint together sometimes after their workouts."

Candy, who had been taking notes, looked up. "Do you know where we can find this Neil Roscow?"

Emily shook her head slightly. "I'm sorry, I don't. Ethan wasn't one to share a lot of details. But he went to the local gym here in Burley. Maybe they'd know Neil there."

George nodded appreciatively. "Thank you, Emily. That's very helpful. We'll look into it."

Candy, delving a bit deeper, inquired, "Did Ethan ever express any concerns for his safety or mention any troubling encounters?"

Emily sighed a hint of sorrow in her eyes. "No, nothing like that. He always seemed to handle things on his own. Ethan never was one to share his worries."

Candy, looking empathetically at Emily, gently asked, "And how about his work, Emily? Any issues or conflicts there that might be relevant?"

"He never mentioned any problems at work," Emily answered. "Apparently, the kids loved him."

George, preparing to conclude the interview, added, "One last thing, Emily. Did Ethan keep any personal diaries or journals? Anything that might help us understand his state of mind before his death?"

Emily pondered for a moment before responding. "Not that I'm aware of. Ethan wasn't the type to write things down. He just... lived in the moment, I suppose."

"Emily, before we go," George began, his tone thoughtful, "is there anyone close to Ethan that you think we should speak to? Anyone who might be able to shed more light on his life recently?"

Emily hesitated for a moment as if debating whether to mention something. Then, with a slight nod, she said, "There was someone new in his life... a girlfriend, I believe. He mentioned her a few times but never gave many details."

Candy leaned in slightly, her interest piqued. "Do you know her name or where she might live?"

"Yes, her name's Jasmine," Emily replied. "Jasmine Clayton. She lives in Harehills, but that's all I know. Ethan was quite private about their relationship."

George made a mental note. "Did he seem happy with her? Was their relationship serious?"

Emily shrugged, a thoughtful expression on her face. "It

seemed casual, but he smiled whenever he mentioned her. That was rare for Ethan. So, I guess she made him happy."

Candy, always thorough, added, "Did you ever meet Jasmine or hear anything about her from Ethan?"

"No, I never met her," Emily admitted. "Ethan didn't bring her around. And he didn't say much, just that they met at a local event and hit it off."

George nodded and stood up.

As they were about to leave, Emily added, "One more thing... Ethan decided to spend Christmas with Jasmine rather than with me. It was the first time he'd done something like that."

George paused, processing this new detail. "He spent Christmas with her? In Harehills?"

"Yes," Emily confirmed. "He said Jasmine had invited him over. I didn't think much of it at the time."

George's mind began piecing together the significance of this revelation. "That's interesting," he said. Ethan's body was found in Harehills, but their house-to-house enquiries didn't pick up any information about him being there with Jasmine. George made a mental note to speak with PS Greenwood.

Candy, as if knowing what George was thinking, added, "It might be worth revisiting the area. There could be something we missed or someone who didn't come forward initially."

George concluded, "Thank you, Emily. This could be helpful. We'll look into it." He handed her a business card. "And please, if anything comes to mind, or if you need anything at all, don't hesitate to call us."

Emily accepted the card, a small, grateful smile touching her lips. "Thank you, Detective Beaumont and Detective Nichols. I just hope you find out what happened to Ethan." She wiped away a stray tear. "I just want to know what happened to him. He deserved better."

As the interview wrapped up, George and Candy thanked Emily for her cooperation. The new information provided them with additional avenues to explore—the local pub, his girlfriend, Jasmine, and the potential lead with Neil Roscow.

* * *

As they left Emily Turner's house, George steered his Mercedes through the streets of Leeds, heading towards Harehills. The morning light filtered through the city, casting long shadows on the roads.

"Better call Greenwood," George muttered, activating the car's Bluetooth system. The phone rang briefly before Police Sergeant Greenwood answered.

"Sergeant Greenwood, it's DI Beaumont. We need a team of uniforms in Harehills as soon as possible. We have a lead on Jasmine Clayton, Ethan Turner's girlfriend. She might be key to this case."

"Understood, sir," Greenwood's voice crackled through the speaker. "I'll dispatch a team right away. Do you have an address?"

"Not yet," George replied. "We're heading there now to find out more. I'll update you as soon as we have something solid."

"Roger that, sir. Good luck."

As George ended the call, Candy turned towards him, her phone in hand. "I just got off the phone with Tashan. He's found an address for Jasmine Clayton in Harehills."

"Excellent," George said, a hint of relief in his voice. "Let's head straight there."

The Mercedes wove through the morning traffic, the city slowly awakening around them. Harehills, known for its vibrant community and bustling streets, was just beginning to stir as they arrived.

Candy glanced down at her phone, reading out the address. "It's not far from here. Just a couple of streets away."

The street where Jasmine lived was bustling with the energy of a close-knit community. Her house, a two-story terraced property, stood out with its freshly painted front door and neatly arranged flower pots on the windowsill. The small front garden was well-kept, with a few ornamental shrubs adding a touch of greenery.

George rang the doorbell, and after a short wait, the door opened to reveal Jasmine Clayton. She was a woman in her early thirties, with an air of composure about her. Her expression, however, shifted to one of apprehension upon seeing the detectives.

"Jasmine Clayton?" George asked, showing his badge. "I'm Detective Inspector George Beaumont, and this is Detective Constable Candy Nichols. We're investigating Ethan Turner's death."

Jasmine's eyes widened slightly. "Yes, I'm Jasmine. What's this about?"

"We just have a few questions about Ethan," George replied. "May we come in?"

Jasmine hesitated, her gaze flickering behind her into the house. "I'm not sure that's a good idea..."

George, sensing her reluctance, gently insisted, "It's important, Miss Clayton. It won't take long."

After a moment's pause, Jasmine sighed and stepped aside,

allowing them entry. "Alright, come in."

As they entered, George noted the interior of Jasmine's home. It was modest but inviting, with warm, earthy tones and comfortable furnishings. The living room, where they were led, was compact with a well-used sofa and a small coffee table that held a few magazines and a couple of mugs. Pictures on the wall suggested a fondness for travel, featuring various landscapes and cityscapes.

Jasmine sat tentatively on the edge of an armchair while George and Candy took seats on the sofa. George initiated the interview, "Jasmine, can you tell us about your relationship with Ethan?"

Jasmine took a deep breath. "We were seeing each other, but it wasn't serious. Just... casual, you know?"

Candy asked gently, "Were you with Ethan on Christmas Day?"

Jasmine shook her head. "No, I wasn't. We had an argument on Christmas Eve. He promised to dress up as Santa Claus for a local event here in Harehills, but he bailed on that to go out drinking with some lads in the city centre."

George leaned forward, "Do you know who he was with that night?"

"No," Jasmine replied, her voice tinged with frustration. "He didn't say, and I didn't ask. I was too upset about him breaking his promise."

"And when was the last time you saw Ethan?" George inquired.

"Two days before Christmas," Jasmine said. "We met for a coffee. Everything seemed fine then."

Candy took notes, then asked, "Did Ethan ever mention any trouble he was in? Any conflicts or threats?"

Jasmine pondered for a moment before answering, "Not really. Ethan was private about certain things. But I got the feeling he was keeping something from me. I just never pushed it."

"Jasmine, did Ethan ever mention someone named Neil Roscow to you? They were friends and frequented the same gym."

Jasmine's expression shifted to one of contemplation. "Neil Roscow? Yeah, Ethan mentioned him a few times. They worked out together. I think they were quite close at one point."

Candy, keen on gleaning more details, asked, "Did Ethan talk about Neil often? Were they in contact frequently?"

"Not really," Jasmine replied, tucking a strand of hair behind her ear. "I mean, Ethan mentioned grabbing a drink with him now and then, but it seemed like their friendship had cooled off recently. Ethan didn't say much about it, and I didn't pry."

George pressed further, "Do you know if they had any falling out or disagreement?"

Jasmine shrugged lightly. "Not that I know of. Ethan never said anything about a fight or argument with Neil. It just seemed like they were drifting apart, you know? People change, move on."

Candy added another question, "Was there anything specific that Ethan mentioned about Neil that stood out to you?"

Jasmine thought for a moment before answering. "Not really. Just gym stuff, mostly. Ethan did say once that Neil was getting more serious about his training, maybe even considering competing. But that's all."

George nodded, processing this information. "Thank you,

Jasmine. This is helpful." George concluded, "Thank you for your time, Jasmine. If you remember anything else, please get in touch with us." He handed her his business card and headed for the door. Jasmine's account of Ethan's activities around Christmas provided a new perspective on his last known movements and raised questions about his companions on the night of the alleged argument.

Chapter Seven

Detective Inspector George Beaumont sat in the muted light of his office, surrounded by the ghosts of the past—case files from the infamous Santa Claus murders, both old and recent, sprawled across his desk. Each file was a reminder of a time when the lines between good and evil, right and wrong, seemed clearer. Now, those lines were blurred, obscured by personal doubts and fears.

George tried to concentrate on the files, to lose himself in the details of the cases he knew so well. But his mind rebelled, refusing to focus. The words and images before him blurred into a chaotic tapestry, each thread a reminder of his father's possible involvement.

The door to his office opened, and Detective Inspector Luke Mason walked in, his eyes immediately taking in the chaotic spread of files.

"Drowning in the past, son?" Luke asked, his voice tinged with a note of concern.

George looked up, attempting a smile that didn't quite reach his eyes. "Just revisiting some old ghosts. Trying to find something we might have missed."

Luke pulled up a chair and sat down, his gaze steady. "It's important to look back sometimes, but not at the expense of the present. What's really bothering you, George?"

George sighed, leaning back in his chair. "It's complicated, Luke. There are... aspects of this case that hit too close to home."

Luke nodded, understanding the unspoken meaning in George's words. "You're thinking about Edward again, aren't you?"

George's gaze flickered away, a silent confirmation. "First, we have his connection to Dr Ross, then we have a cufflink show up at the Turner crime scene," George explained and shook his head. "It's becoming increasingly clear that Edward is involved."

Luke placed a reassuring hand on George's shoulder. "We'll get to the bottom of this, but you can't let these doubts consume you. You're a brilliant detective, George. Trust in that."

George nodded, a mixture of gratitude and apprehension in his eyes. "I know. I just need to focus."

Luke stood, ready to leave the office. "Remember, George, sometimes the answers we seek aren't always hidden in the past."

A knock at the door interrupted George.

George, still absorbed in the aftermath of the talk with Luke, looked up as Tashan approached. The young detective's expression was a mix of determination and unease, hinting at the gravity of the information he carried.

"Boss, I've got something," Tashan began, his voice measured. "I've been digging into Dr Ross' past, trying to find anything that might link him to the victims or the OCG."

George leaned forward, his interest piqued. "And? What did you find?"

Tashan pulled up a chair, his fingers interlacing nervously. "It's about Lindsey Yardley, the pathologist. A charity funded her training. That's not unusual, but the backers of this charity are."

George's eyes narrowed. "What do you mean?"

"The charity," Tashan continued, "was set up by Edward Beaumont and other influential figures in Leeds. It seems benign on the surface but given Edward's connections with the OCG..."

George sat back, the implications of Tashan's findings sinking in. "You're suggesting that Yardley's position might not be a coincidence? That there's more to her relationship with Ross and the victims?"

Tashan nodded, his tone cautious. "It's a stretch, but we can't ignore the possibility. There's a pattern of influence here. If Edward's charity funded her training, and now she's involved in cases that directly impact our investigation into the OCG..."

George rubbed his chin, deep in thought. "This could mean Edward's reach is more extensive than we imagined. He could be manipulating events from behind the scenes, using his influence to control the narrative."

Tashan added, "And if he's doing that with Yardley, sir, who else could he be using?"

The room fell silent as the gravity of the situation settled between them. George's gaze drifted to the cityscape visible from his office window, a labyrinth of streets where unseen forces played their dangerous games.

Finally, George spoke, his voice resolute. "We need to tread carefully. If we're going to look into Yardley, we can't tip our hand."

Tashan nodded in agreement. "I'll keep digging, sir, see what else I can uncover. But we have to be discreet."

Left alone, George turned his attention back to the files, his mind a battleground of emotion. The cases he had once investigated with such clarity now seemed to mock him, their details a labyrinth with no apparent exit.

He picked up a photo from one of the older cases, studying it intently. The face of the victim stared back at him, a silent accusation from the past. George's father's words echoed in his mind, a haunting refrain that offered no solace.

Outside, the police station buzzed with the rhythmic pulse of routine. But inside George's office, time seemed suspended, the air thick with the weight of unresolved questions.

George closed the file, and his decision was made. He couldn't let his personal conflict impede the investigation. Pushing aside his doubts, he resolved to approach the case with the objectivity it deserved.

Suddenly, the incessant ringing of the phone pierced the heavy silence of George's office. He glanced at the caller ID and felt a jolt of unease. It was his father, Edward Beaumont. With a deep breath to steady himself, George picked up the receiver.

"Hello, Edward," George said, his voice carefully neutral.

"George, how are you doing?" Edward's voice was light, almost casual, but there was an underlying sharpness that didn't escape George.

"I'm fine. Just busy with work," George replied, maintaining a composed facade, though his grip on the phone tightened.

"That's good to hear. I know how demanding your job can be," Edward said, a hint of something unreadable in his tone.

George leaned back in his chair, his gaze fixed on a point on the wall. "It's part of the job. Keeps things interesting."

There was a brief pause on the line. "I've been reading about the new Santa Claus case. It seems to be quite a challenge," Edward said, his words casual but laden with unspoken curiosity.

George's heart rate quickened, but he kept his voice steady. "Yes, it's a complex case. A lot of moving parts."

Edward's chuckle came through the line, but it lacked warmth. "I'm sure you'll handle it. You always had a knack for resolving complicated matters."

George felt a twinge of discomfort at his father's words. How the hell would he know? "We're doing our best. The team is solid."

There was a knowing tone in Edward's following words. "Just be careful, George. These kinds of cases can be... consuming."

"I'm always careful," George responded, his discomfort growing. The conversation felt like a veiled dance, each participant cautious of their steps.

"Well, I won't keep you. I just wanted to check in on you. You know, a father worries about his son," Edward said, his voice softening slightly.

George's response was automatic, but his mind raced with unspoken questions. "What?"

"Look, I know I've not always been there for you, but I—"

"I've got to go," George said, interrupting his father ending the call.

As the line clicked dead, George sat motionless, the phone still in his hand. The conversation had been brief, but the undercurrents were clear. His father was probing, seeking insight into the investigation's progress.

George's thoughts were a tangle of suspicion and familial loyalty. The idea of his father being involved in the case was a dark cloud hanging over him, casting a shadow on every interaction.

The office around him felt smaller, the walls closing in as he grappled with the implications of the call. The trust he had always placed in his father was now laced with doubt, the familiar terrain of their relationship suddenly unfamiliar and treacherous.

George sat motionless at his desk, his gaze unfocused, staring at the myriad of case files that lay scattered before him. The events of the day had taken their toll, and the conversation with his father, Edward, lingered in his mind like a persistent echo.

The room, usually a haven of order and control, now felt like a confinement, a space that mirrored the turmoil within him. George leaned back in his chair, the leather creaking under his weight, his thoughts a chaotic whirlpool.

He had longed for the simplicity of the past, for the days when the lines between right and wrong were clear-cut when his path as a detective was straightforward. But those days were gone, replaced by a present mired in complexity and personal conflict.

The realisation dawned on him, heavy and inescapable—he could not keep burying his head in the sand. The past, no matter how comforting, could not provide solace for the challenges of the present.

A quiet resolve settled over him, a recognition that the path ahead would be fraught with harrowing revelations and choices. He placed the photograph back on the desk, its presence a reminder of the journey he had to undertake.

George stood up, pacing the room slowly, each step a manifestation of his shifting mindset. The detective in him, the part that sought truth and justice, was now at the forefront, ready to confront whatever lay ahead, regardless of personal cost.

As he turned back to the room, his expression hardened a reflection of the determination that had taken root within him. The longing for simpler times was still there, a faint echo in the back of his mind, but a newfound sense of purpose overshadowed it.

With a deep breath, George returned to his desk, his movements deliberate. He began organising the files, his actions methodical, each one a step towards acceptance and action.

* * *

George Beaumont was summoned into an urgent briefing. The corridors, lined with the buzz of activity, seemed to echo his increasing heartbeat as he made his way to the meeting room.

Upon entering, George found the room already filled with the core members of his team, their faces etched with a seriousness that immediately set him on edge. Detective Inspector Luke Mason, standing at the head of the table with a file in hand, nodded solemnly at George's arrival.

George took his place at the table, his eyes scanning the faces of his team. "What's up?"

Luke opened the file, revealing a series of financial records. "We've uncovered something significant. A recent financial transaction links Edward Beaumont to a known associate of the Schmidt Organised Crime Group."

The room fell into a stunned silence. George felt a chill run down his spine, the implications of Luke's words hitting him like a physical blow. His father's name, entangled with one of the most notorious crime groups in the region, was a scenario he had dreaded but never truly prepared for.

Detective Constable Tashan Blackburn, his face grave, leaned forward. "We cross-referenced the financials with known OCG activities. The link is undeniable."

George's mind raced, his professional facade struggling to mask the turmoil within. "Are we certain of this? Could there be another explanation?"

Luke shook his head. "It's clear, George. The transaction is recent and directly linked to an account controlled by your father."

Detective Constable Candy Nichols chimed in, her voice hesitant. "We need to tread carefully, given the sensitivity of this information, sir."

George nodded, the weight of his duty pressing down on him. "We will. This information stays within this room for now. I want everything we have on the Schmidt group and their associates."

Jay Scott, his expression one of concern, looked at George. "Boss, how do you want to proceed with this?"

George's gaze was fixed on the financial records, the numbers and names blurring before his eyes. "We investigate this lead like any other. We follow the evidence, no matter where it leads."

The team nodded in agreement, though the atmosphere remained heavy, charged with the gravity of their discovery.

"Keep me updated on any developments," he said, his voice carrying a newfound determination.

His hands trembled ever so slightly as he held the financial report linking his father, Edward, to the Schmidt Organised Crime Group. His team gathered inside the Homicide and Major Enquiry Team's Incident Room and watched him with a mixture of concern and uncertainty. George had always been their pillar of strength, unshakeable in the face of adversity. But now, for the first time, they witnessed cracks in his composed façade.

Detective Constable Jay Scott, ever observant, leaned in, his voice low. "Boss, are you alright?"

George looked up, meeting Jay's eyes. He quickly composed himself, his training kicking in, but the mask he wore was thinner than usual. "Yes, I'm fine. Let's focus on the task at hand."

Detective Inspector Luke Mason, standing beside George, offered a subtle nod of support. "We need to explore every avenue this information opens, regardless of personal connections," Luke said, his voice firm yet laced with empathy.

George straightened his posture, his hands now steadying as he placed the report on the table. "Absolutely. We treat this lead like any other. Objectivity is key."

Detective Constable Tashan Blackburn, known for his analytical approach, interjected. "The financial link is significant. It could suggest Edward Beaumont's involvement in funding or facilitating some of the OCG's activities."

The words hung heavy in the air, each one a blow to George's composure. He nodded, the detective in him battling with the son. "We'll need to investigate the extent of this involvement. Gather more evidence, look for patterns or other connections."

Detective Constable Candy Nichols, her eyes filled with

concern, added softly, “We’re here for you, sir. This can’t be easy.”

George offered a tight smile, appreciative of her support but unwilling to expose his turmoil. “Thank you, DC Nichols. Right now, our focus is the investigation. Let’s keep it professional.”

As the meeting concluded and the team dispersed, George remained seated, his eyes lingering on the report. The room emptied, leaving him in a silence that was both a refuge and a reminder of the storm raging within.

He leaned back in his chair, his mind racing with the implications of the revelation. The possibility of his father’s involvement, which he had fought so hard to dismiss, was now a reality he could not ignore.

Chapter Eight

In the quiet of George Beaumont's office, the only sound was the rustling of papers as he and Detective Constable Tashan Blackburn pored over the financial records. Spread out before them were bank statements and transaction histories, each line a potential clue in unravelling the mystery surrounding Edward Beaumont's involvement with the Schmidt Organised Crime Group.

Tashan, his face a mask of concentration, pointed to a series of transactions. "These here, they're periodic, large sums of money moving to an offshore account. It's been happening for years."

George leaned closer, his eyes tracing the figures that marched down the page. "That account, it's not in my father's name. But the transactions originate from one of his businesses."

"There's a pattern to these transactions," Tashan observed, his tone analytical. "It's almost as if they're scheduled. Every quarter, the same amount."

George rubbed his chin, his mind racing. "It's too systematic for a coincidence. This has to be deliberate. But why? What was he funding?"

Tashan shuffled the papers, bringing another document to

the forefront. "There's more, sir. Look at these withdrawals. They coincide with known activities of the Schmidt group."

The room felt colder, the air heavier as George absorbed the implications. "Could there be another explanation? Perhaps he was being extorted?" George asked though the suggestion sounded hollow even to his ears.

Tashan shook his head slightly. "It's possible but unlikely. The consistency, the amounts... it suggests complicity more than coercion."

George exhaled slowly, his breath a fog in the chilled air of the office. "We need to trace the end point of these transactions. Find out where the money ultimately went."

Tashan nodded, his fingers tapping a staccato rhythm on the table. "I'll get onto it. We'll need to liaise with international finance units and track the flow of money across borders."

George sat back, a sense of helplessness washing over him. The evidence was mounting, each piece adding weight to the theory of his father's involvement. "Keep me updated, Tashan. Every step of the way."

As Tashan stood to leave, George's gaze lingered on the financial records. The numbers and dates blurred before his eyes, a jumble of figures that spelt out a narrative he was reluctant to read.

"Sir," Tashan said, pausing at the door. "We'll get to the bottom of this, no matter what we find."

George nodded, his response a mere whisper. "Thanks, Tashan."

* * *

The air was tense as they waited for Michael Clarkson to

answer the door. When he did, his face registered a mix of recognition, surprise and apprehension. "Detective Inspector Beaumont, Detective Constable Nichols," he greeted, his voice laced with unease. "What brings you here?"

"Mr Clarkson, we need to talk about Ethan Turner," George said, his tone sombre.

Clarkson's face paled at the mention of Turner's name. "Ethan? What about him?"

George exchanged a glance with Candy before continuing, "He's been murdered, Mr Clarkson. We found his body Christmas evening."

The news seemed to hit Clarkson like a physical blow. He staggered slightly, bracing himself against the door frame. "Murdered?" he whispered, his eyes wide with shock.

"Yes," George confirmed gently. "We're investigating all possible connections. And we thought you should be aware, considering your past association with him."

Clarkson seemed to gather himself, a hint of fear flickering in his eyes. "You think I'm in danger too, don't you? All of us from that group a decade ago... we're all targets."

George observed Clarkson closely. "Do you have reason to believe that, Mr Clarkson?"

Clarkson ran a hand through his hair, visibly shaken. "It's just... Everyone else... they're all dead. It can't be a coincidence."

George's expression was thoughtful. "What about Danny Roberts? Do you think he could be in danger as well?"

Clarkson hesitated before answering. "Danny? I dunno. I think I'm just being paranoid. But now, with Ethan..."

Candy, who had been quietly observing, spoke up. "It's better to be cautious, Mr Clarkson. We can offer protection if you feel threatened."

Clarkson shook his head. "No, no, I don't want to make a fuss. I'll be fine. I just need to process all this."

"Can we come in and chat?"

"Of course, of course," Clarkson said.

Upon entering, they were greeted by a narrow hallway, the walls adorned with framed photographs that seemed to chronicle different stages of Clarkson's life. Some showed a younger Clarkson in various exotic locations, suggesting a past filled with adventure and travel. The wooden floorboards creaked under their feet, echoing the age of the house.

As Detective Inspector George Beaumont and Detective Constable Candy Nichols stepped into Mike Clarkson's living room, they were immediately struck by an unusual feature of the decor—a testament to Clarkson's dedication to fitness. Amidst the typical furnishings of a living room, a set of weights and a weight bench occupied a significant portion of the space.

The weight bench, robust and professional-looking, was positioned near the window, basking in the natural light that streamed in. Various sizes of dumbbells were neatly arranged on a rack beside it, indicating a routine of regular use. The presence of the gym equipment in the living room suggested that Clarkson's commitment to fitness was not just a hobby but a significant part of his daily life.

The space was unexpectedly tidy, almost meticulously so, with every item appearing to have its designated place. The living room was modest in size but well-kept. A large, comfortable-looking sofa, upholstered in dark fabric, dominated the room, facing a flat-screen television that was mounted on the wall.

Bookshelves lined one side of the room, filled with an eclectic mix of literature ranging from classic novels to contemporary thrillers and a smattering of non-fiction, perhaps indicating Clarkson's varied interests. A small fireplace, currently unlit, added a touch of homeliness to the room, with a couple of framed photographs on the mantelpiece—memories captured in time.

The decor was a blend of modern and vintage—a glass coffee table sat in the centre of the room, flanked by a pair of antique-looking brass floor lamps. The walls were painted a warm, neutral colour, complemented by the soft lighting that cast a cosy glow over the room.

Near the window stood a small desk cluttered with papers, suggesting a space where Clarkson perhaps worked or managed his personal affairs. The window itself offered a view of the modest garden outside, the curtains drawn back to let in natural light.

As George and Candy took in their surroundings, it was evident that the house, though unassuming from the outside, was a well-cared-for space, reflecting a sense of order and precision that seemed at odds with the troubled man they had come to interview. And the juxtaposition of a home gym in the living area added a unique character to the room. The usual comforts—the sofa, the television, the bookshelves—were all there, but they shared space with Clarkson's evident passion for physical fitness. The living room, therefore, was not just a place of relaxation but also of discipline and exertion.

George and Candy took a moment to observe this aspect of Clarkson's life. It was an intimate insight into his personal priorities and lifestyle—a detail that, while seemingly unrelated to their investigation, added depth to their understanding of the man they were about to interview.

George initiated the interview with a calm, methodical approach. "Mr Clarkson, we need to discuss your relationship with Ethan Turner," he began, his tone even but firm.

Clarkson shifted uncomfortably in his chair. "Ethan and I were friends years ago. But we hadn't talked much recently. Why? What does this have to do with anything?"

Candy interjected, her voice steady. "We're trying to establish a timeline, Mr Clarkson. Any interactions you had with Mr Turner in the days leading up to his death could be crucial."

Clarkson's eyes flickered with a hint of apprehension. "I told you, we hadn't spoken in ages. I had nothing to do with whatever happened to him."

George leaned forward slightly, his gaze never leaving Clarkson. "Were you aware of any issues or threats Mr Turner might have been facing? Anyone who might have wanted to harm him?"

Clarkson exhaled sharply, a mix of frustration and anxiety in his expression. "Ethan had his demons, sure. But as for someone wanting to hurt him? I wouldn't know."

The detectives exchanged a glance, picking up on the subtle nuances of Clarkson's behaviour. George continued, pressing a little harder. "Your group from a decade ago—we're looking into all possibilities. Any old grudges or unresolved disputes that could have resurfaced?"

Clarkson ran a hand through his hair, his agitation growing. "That was a long time ago. We've all moved on. I don't see how any of that is relevant now."

Candy, observing his reactions closely, noted, "Sometimes the past has a way of catching up, Mr Clarkson."

George followed up, his voice a shade more intense. "Where

were you on the night of Mr Turner's murder, Mr Clarkson?"

Clarkson's response was immediate, a touch too quick. "I was at home. Alone. But I didn't kill Ethan if that's what you're getting at."

"Can anybody confirm that?"

"No."

With nothing else to ask, the interview concluded, and George stood up, his expression unreadable. "Thank you for your cooperation, Mr Clarkson. We may need to speak with you again as the investigation progresses."

Clarkson nodded, a sheen of sweat on his brow, relieved yet still on edge. "Sure, whatever helps."

George gave him a reassuring nod. "Please don't hesitate to contact us if you need anything or remember anything that could help our investigation."

As they left Clarkson's house, the unease in the air lingered. Clarkson's fear had been palpable, a clear sign that the past was catching up in ways that none of them had anticipated.

* * *

As soon as they knocked, the door swung open, revealing Danny Roberts. Unlike Clarkson, Roberts appeared less guarded, almost carefree, as he welcomed them inside. "Detectives, nice to see you again. Come in, come in," he said with a casual wave.

The interior of Danny's house was a sharp departure from the orderly and meticulous home of Michael Clarkson. The living room was cluttered and unkempt. Magazines and newspapers were strewn across a coffee table that had seen better days, and a pile of unwashed dishes teetered precariously in the kitchen sink visible from the living room. The furniture was worn and mismatched, contributing to the overall disarray.

Clothes lay haphazardly draped over a sofa that had clearly doubled as a makeshift bed on multiple occasions. The air carried a faint, musty odour, suggesting a lack of fresh air and regular cleaning. Amidst this chaos, Danny seemed almost at ease, an indication of his disorganised lifestyle.

George and Candy, accustomed to varying living conditions in their line of work, took in the scene with professional detachment. They found a relatively clear space and began their interview.

"Mr Roberts," George started, his voice carrying a formality that contrasted with the surroundings. "We're investigating the murder of Ethan Turner and need to ask you a few questions."

Danny nodded, his demeanour becoming slightly more serious but still relaxed. "Sure, sure. Ethan was a good guy. Shame what happened."

"So you've heard of his death?"

Danny nodded. "I watched that fit reporter, what's her name, Paige something, reporting on it, like."

George narrowed his eyes and then delved into the questions, "Were you in contact with Ethan before his death? Any idea who might have wanted to harm him?"

Danny shrugged, a frown creasing his forehead. "Nah, only at the Santa Claus training. We all drifted apart, you know? As for enemies, Ethan had a few run-ins but nothing serious as far as I knew."

"You're sure that was the last time you saw Ethan?" asked Candy.

"Yeah, the Santa Claus training was the last time I saw Ethan... and Ryan Baxter, too, actually. It's strange thinking about it now."

George, his interest piqued, asked, "What's strange about it?"

Danny leaned back, a distant look in his eyes. "Well, it was Edward Beaumont who paid for that training for us. Ethan, Ryan, and me. Said it was some sort of community outreach or charity thing he was sponsoring."

Candy, looking up from her notes, inquired, "Edward Beaumont sponsored you three specifically?"

"Yeah," Danny replied. "I never knew why us specifically. I mean, he's a big name around Leeds, isn't he? It felt a bit odd, but hey, free Santa training," he said with a shrug. "But after that, things just... changed. We all went our separate ways. That training was the last time I saw either of them."

George mulled over this revelation. The involvement of Edward Beaumont, his own estranged father, in funding the training for Ethan, Ryan, and Danny hinted at a deeper connection than previously thought. "Did Beaumont have any contact with you or the others after the training?"

"Not with me," Danny said, shaking his head. "As for Ethan and Ryan, I wouldn't know. We didn't exactly keep in touch."

Candy, observing Danny's body language, added, "Your group from a decade ago—did you have any issues that might have resurfaced recently?"

Danny scratched his head, looking genuinely perplexed. "No, nothing like that. We had our fun and got into a bit of trouble, but that's all in the past."

The detectives continued their line of questioning, probing for any inconsistencies in Danny's story. Throughout the interview, Danny remained cooperative, if somewhat disorganised, in his responses. He maintained his innocence and lack of knowledge regarding any potential threats to Turner or himself.

As the interview concluded, George and Candy thanked Danny for his cooperation. Stepping out of the chaotic house, they were left to ponder the validity of Danny's statements and the role he might play in the larger puzzle of the case.

Chapter Nine

The chill in the air was a stark contrast to the oppressive atmosphere of the station as George stepped outside. He needed space, a moment of solitude to grapple with the revelations that threatened to upend his world. The streets of Leeds, usually a familiar comfort, now felt alien, a backdrop to his internal turmoil.

As he walked, his thoughts were a tumultuous whirlwind. The evidence linking his father, Edward, to the Schmidt Organised Crime Group gnawed at him. But it was more than just the professional implications; it was the personal revelations that cut the deepest.

George's mind wandered back to his childhood, to the memories of Edward's harsh conduct. The coldness in his father's eyes, the sharpness of his words—it was a form of abuse that had left deep scars, scars that George had long tried to bury.

He remembered the sting of Edward's criticisms, the way they made him feel small, insignificant. And now, facing the possibility of his father's involvement in criminal activities, those old wounds throbbed anew.

George's thoughts turned to his own children, Olivia and Jack. The love he felt for them was overwhelming, pure.

He couldn't fathom not providing them with the care and affection they deserved, the complete opposite of how Edward had treated him. It made him wonder—why? Why had Edward been the way he was?

"Was it something in your past? Something that made you so cold, so distant?" George muttered to himself, his voice barely a whisper.

He thought of Olivia's laughter, Jack's wide-eyed wonder at the world, and how he would do anything to protect that innocence, to nurture it. The idea of inflicting any kind of pain on them was unthinkable. How could Edward not have felt the same?

George's role as a detective had always been clear—to seek the truth, to serve justice. But now, that pursuit was personal, tangled up in the complicated relationship with his father. The evidence was compelling, yet part of him still hoped for an innocent explanation, a way to reconcile the father he knew with the man implicated in the documents.

The area was quiet, the occasional rustle of leaves a gentle reminder of the world moving around him. George knew he couldn't stay lost in his thoughts forever. He had a duty, both to his family and his profession.

With a heavy heart, he turned around, ready to return to the station. The path ahead was uncertain, filled with potential heartache and revelations that could change everything he knew about his father, about himself.

The cold air nipped at George's face as he walked, his thoughts swirling in turmoil. His mobile phone rang, breaking the rhythm of his footsteps. Glancing at the screen, he saw his father's name. Edward. With a hesitant hand, he answered.

"Hello, Edward," George said, his voice guarded.

"George, just checking in. How are you doing?" Edward's voice came through the phone, casual, almost cheerful, seemingly oblivious to the storm he had unwittingly stirred in his son's life.

"I'm fine. Busy, as always," George replied, his words measured, his mind racing.

"That's good to hear. Your mother is always telling me you work too hard, you know," Edward chuckled lightly.

George had no idea Edward had been in regular contact with Marie Beaumont, his mother, and his grip on the phone tightened. He'd have it out with her and get the truth straight from her mouth. "Is there something you wanted, Edward? You've been calling a lot lately."

There was a brief pause on the line. "Well, I've been thinking, George. About us. I was hoping we could reconcile; maybe I could even meet Olivia and Jack," Edward said, his tone unusually soft.

The words hit George like a physical blow. Reconcile? After years of distance, of cold indifference? The timing was too coincidental, too convenient. Fury simmered beneath his calm exterior.

"Why now? After all this time?" George's voice was steady, but the undercurrent of anger was palpable.

"People change, George. I've made mistakes, but I'm trying to make amends," Edward's voice held a note of sincerity, but to George, it sounded hollow.

"You think you can just walk back into our lives? After everything?" George's voice rose slightly, his control slipping.

"I know I haven't been the best father, but I want to try, son. I want to be part of your life, your children's lives," Edward persisted. "My grandchildren's lives."

George felt a surge of fury. The timing was too suspicious, Edward's sudden interest in reconciliation too contrived. "I can't do this right now."

Before Edward could respond, George ended the call, his hand shaking with a mixture of rage and disbelief. He stood there for a moment, staring at the phone in his hand, trying to make sense of the conversation.

Edward's words echoed in his mind, a jarring dissonance with everything he knew about his father. The man who had never shown an ounce of warmth was now seeking a relationship with his grandchildren. It didn't add up.

With a deep breath, George pocketed his phone and resumed his walk. The conversation had only added to his inner conflict. The possibility of his father being involved in criminal activities was one thing, but this sudden desire for reconciliation was another layer of complexity he wasn't prepared for.

The path back to the station seemed longer than before, each step heavy with the weight of his thoughts. George knew he couldn't let his personal feelings cloud his judgment, but separating the detective from the son was becoming increasingly difficult.

As he neared the station, George's resolve hardened. He would continue the investigation and follow the evidence wherever it led. But Edward's call had ignited a fire within him, a determination to uncover the truth, no matter how painful it might be.

* * *

Back in the austere confines of the station, George Beaumont's footsteps echoed through the corridors as he made his way to the legal advisor's office. The weight of the revelations pressed heavily on him, each step a reminder of the personal and professional tightrope he was now walking.

He knocked softly on the door marked 'HMET Legal Advisor' and entered upon the muted call to come in. Inside, Sarah Jennings, the legal advisor, sat surrounded by stacks of files and legal tomes, her sharp gaze rising to meet his.

"George, what can I do for you?" Sarah asked her voice a blend of professionalism and concern.

George took a seat, his posture rigid, the turmoil within him carefully veiled. "I need advice on a delicate matter. It's about the financial evidence linking Edward Beaumont to the Schmidt Organised Crime Group."

Sarah nodded, her expression turning serious. "I've been briefed. What specific concerns do you have?"

"It's the implications of this evidence. If it's as solid as it seems, what are our options for moving forward?" George's voice was steady, but the undercurrent of personal conflict was hard to miss.

Sarah leaned forward, her fingers interlacing. "If the evidence holds up, it's a strong indication of financial complicity with a known criminal organisation. The next steps would be to gather more concrete proof, perhaps leading to a search warrant or an arrest."

George's jaw tightened at the mention of an arrest. "An arrest... of Edward Beaumont?"

"Yes, if warranted by the evidence. But we must tread carefully, given his reputation and your connection," Sarah said, her eyes holding George's.

The reality of the situation settled over George like a shroud. His father, the man he had looked up to for so long, could soon be facing an arrest. "And if it comes to that... an arrest... I'll have to recuse myself from the case."

Sarah nodded. "That would be the standard procedure. It's important to avoid any conflict of interest or perception of bias."

George sat back, his thoughts racing. The potential fallout was immense, both professionally and personally. "Thank you, Sarah. I appreciate your guidance."

As he stood to leave, Sarah added, "George, I know this can't be easy. But you're doing the right thing by following the evidence."

Leaving the office, George felt the weight of their conversation settle around him. The gravity of the situation was now irrefutably clear. He was a detective first and foremost, but the prospect of investigating his father, potentially leading to his arrest, was a reality he had never envisioned.

* * *

As the day waned into the late afternoon, the light in George Beaumont's office had taken on a sombre hue, reflecting the gravity of the decision he was about to make. The revelation about his father, Edward, had hung over him like a dark cloud, but the time had come to act. With a resolute breath, George summoned his team for a meeting.

They gathered around the table in their Incident Room, a sense of anticipation filling the room. George stood at the head, his expression sombre, the lines on his face etched with resolve.

"Thank you all for coming," George began, his voice steady despite the storm raging within him. "We have a new direction in the investigation into the Schmidt Organised Crime Group. It involves someone close to me. My father, Edward Beaumont."

A collective gasp rippled through the team, their expressions a mixture of surprise and concern. Detective Constable Jay Scott leaned forward, his brow furrowed. "Sir, are you sure about this?"

George nodded, the weight of his decision evident in his demeanour. "Yes, I am. We have evidence suggesting financial links between Edward Beaumont and the Schmidt group. It's a lead we cannot ignore."

Detective Inspector Luke Mason, who had been watching George closely, spoke up. "This won't be easy, son. But we're with you. What's the plan?"

George took a deep breath, his resolve hardening. "We're going to conduct a detailed investigation into my father's financial dealings. I want everything scrutinised—bank accounts, business transactions, the lot."

Detective Constable Tashan Blackburn, known for his meticulous nature, nodded. "We'll need to liaise with financial institutions and possibly get some warrants. It'll be thorough."

"And be discreet," George added firmly. "This stays within our team. The implications of this investigation are far-reaching, and I don't want any leaks."

The team members exchanged glances, their faces a display of determination and loyalty. Detective Constable Candy Nichols, her voice soft but persistent, added, "You can count on us, sir. We'll handle this with the utmost professionalism."

George looked around the table, meeting the eyes of each team member. "Thank you. I know this won't be easy, especially for me. But as detectives, our duty is to the truth, no matter where it leads."

As the meeting dispersed, George remained standing, his gaze lingering on the now-empty chairs. The decision to investigate his father had been one of the hardest of his career, marking a major shift in both the case and his personal life.

Chapter Ten

After a brief knock on DCI Atkinson's door and finding no response, George Beaumont decided to seek out DSU Jim Smith for counsel. Ascending the stairs to the upper floors of the Elland Road Police Station, George's mind was awash with conflicting thoughts about his next move regarding his father, Edward Beaumont.

Outside DSU Smith's office, George paused as the secretary, a middle-aged woman with a sharp eye, asked him to wait. As he stood there, the enormity of his decision to arrest his father weighed heavily on him. It was a move fraught with personal and professional ramifications, a step that, once taken, could not be undone.

After a moment that felt longer than it actually was, the secretary nodded towards the door. "Detective Superintendent Smith will see you now, Detective Inspector Beaumont."

Entering the office, George was greeted by the familiar figure of Jim Smith. The DSU, a tall, broad-shouldered man with a distinct Geordie accent, had an air of authority tempered with approachability. Despite the seriousness of the situation, George felt a brief sense of nostalgia; he had missed working under Smith's direct supervision.

Without preamble, George got straight to the point. "Sir,

I've come to a decision about my father, Edward Beaumont. I believe it's time we brought him in for questioning."

Smith, leaning back in his chair, regarded George with a measured look. "George, I understand your eagerness to act, but we need to tread carefully. Your father is a high-profile figure. We can't afford to move without solid evidence."

George, his resolve faltering, responded, "But sir, the links we've found..."

Smith interrupted, shaking his head slightly. "It's not enough, not yet. We need more, George. More concrete evidence. I suggest you follow up on the leads in your report first."

Smith's words implied the following steps: speaking with Neil Roscow and investigating the gym and pub in Burley, which Ethan Turner was known to frequent.

"OK, sir. Thank you."

As George left Smith's office, his mind was a tumult of emotions. He had been so sure that arresting his father was the right move, yet his superior had advised patience. Smith's caution was a reminder of the complexities of the case and the need for irrefutable proof.

Descending the stairs back to his own office, George felt a sense of confusion and frustration. The path ahead was not as straightforward as he had hoped. Bringing his father to justice was not just a matter of familial betrayal but a procedural challenge that required navigating the intricate web of evidence and implications.

* * *

Detective Inspector George Beaumont and Detective Constable

Candy Nichols made their way to the gym in Burley. The visit was a crucial part of their investigation, following up on leads that connected Ethan Turner's life and potentially his death to his friend Neil Roscow.

The gym was located in a bustling part of Burley, a hub of activity with people coming and going. The exterior was unassuming, blending into the row of shops and businesses that lined the street. As George parked the car, he glanced at Candy, who was reviewing her notes. "Ready?" he asked.

"Let's do it, sir," Candy replied, her tone determined.

They entered the gym, immediately struck by the contrast between the busy street outside and the focused intensity within. The sound of weights clanging, treadmills humming, and the occasional grunt of exertion filled the air. The gym was well-equipped, catering to a diverse clientele.

George approached the reception desk, showing his badge to the young man behind the counter. "Detective Inspector Beaumont and Detective Constable Nichols. We're looking for information about one of your members, Neil Roscow." Both detectives held out their warrant cards for inspection.

The receptionist nodded, his expression turning more serious. "Sure, I know Neil. He's a regular here. Is he in trouble?"

"We just need to talk to him," George said. "Is he here now?"

"No, he was in earlier today, but he's gone now. Can I help with something else?" the receptionist offered.

George exchanged a glance with Candy, then asked, "Can you tell us about Neil's routine? And was he close with another member, Ethan Turner?"

The receptionist thought for a moment. "Yeah, they used to work out together a lot. I haven't seen them together recently, though. Neil's pretty dedicated comes in most days, early mornings or late evenings."

Candy asked, "Did you notice anything unusual about Neil or Ethan recently? Any changes in behaviour or routine?"

"Not really. Neil's always been pretty focused and keeps to himself mostly. Ethan... he stopped coming a while back. Can't say much more than that."

George said, "We need Neil's address. Can you provide that?"

The receptionist hesitated. "I'm sorry, Detective, but I can't just give out personal information about our members. You'd need a warrant or something official for that."

George's expression remained impassive, but internally, he understood the setback. "I appreciate your position," he replied. "We'll take the necessary steps."

George thanked the receptionist, and they moved away, discussing their next steps. "We need to find Neil," he murmured. "He could have key information about Ethan's last days."

Candy nodded in agreement as they left the gym. "And we should check out the pub Ethan frequented. Might find someone there who knows more."

George spoke to Candy, his tone pragmatic. "We'll need to get a warrant. It'll slow us down, but we don't have much choice."

Candy nodded, her mind already on the next step. "I'll call Tashan. He can start the paperwork. Shouldn't take too long."

* * *

George and Candy entered into what appeared to be a

quintessential English pub, with dark wooden beams, walls adorned with vintage beer adverts, and a cosy fireplace that added a touch of warmth to the dimly lit space. The atmosphere was lively yet subdued, with patrons engaged in quiet conversations over pints of ale.

In a corner, away from the casual mirth, sat Neil Roscow. He was a stocky man with a rugged look, his hands wrapped around a half-empty glass. George and Candy approached him, their expressions solemn.

"Neil Roscow?" George asked as they reached the table.

Neil looked up, a hint of recognition in his eyes. "Yeah, that's me. What's this about?"

"I'm Detective Inspector Beaumont, and this is Detective Constable Nichols. We need to ask you a few questions about Ethan Turner."

Neil's expression turned wary. "Ethan? Why? What's happened?"

George took the lead. "He's been found dead, Neil. We're investigating the circumstances around his death."

Neil's face paled slightly. "Dead? That's... I had no idea."

Candy pulled out her notebook. "Were you close with Ethan, Mr Roscow?"

"We were gym buddies, that's all. Haven't seen him much lately, though," Neil replied, his voice steady but his hands tightening around the glass.

George leaned forward slightly. "Did you see Ethan on Christmas Day or the days leading up to it?"

"No, I didn't," Neil said, shaking his head. "Last I saw him was at the gym, a week before Christmas."

"Did Ethan mention anything unusual during your last meeting? Any problems he was facing?" Candy asked, her tone curious but gentle.

Neil thought for a moment. "Not really. Ethan kept to himself mostly. Said he was seeing someone new, but that's about it."

George interjected, "Do you know Jasmine Clayton?"

Neil's brow furrowed. "Jasmine? No, can't say I do. Why? Is she involved in this?"

"We're just following up on all leads," George explained. "Did Ethan ever talk to you about any troubles he might have been in? Any conflicts?"

Neil shook his head again. "Ethan was a private guy. If he had troubles, he didn't share them with me."

Candy flipped a page in her notebook. "One last question, Neil. Where were you on Christmas Day and the following days?"

"At home with my family," Neil answered promptly. "Didn't go out much."

"Can anyone verify that?" asked George.

Neil nodded, a bit more relaxed. "Sure, my wife and kids were with me the whole time. We had family over, too. They can all vouch for me."

Candy, her pen poised over her notebook, asked, "Would you mind providing their names and contact information? We might need to follow up."

"Of course," Neil replied, reaching for a napkin and a pen from the table. He scribbled down a few names and numbers. "That's my wife, Clara, and my brother, Derek. He was there with his wife."

George took the napkin, examining the information. "Thank you, Neil. We appreciate your cooperation."

As they stood up to leave, George added, "We may need to

contact them soon just to confirm your whereabouts."

"Understandable," Neil said, offering a nod of acknowledgement.

"Thank you for your time, Mr Roscow," George said as they stood up. "If you think of anything else that might help our investigation, please contact us."

As George and Candy left the pub, they reflected on Neil's responses. The interview had provided some insights but also left unanswered questions.

* * *

Back in George's Mercedes, and processing the recent interview with Neil Roscow, Tashan's voice came through the car's speakers. "The paperwork for Neil's address is in the works, sir. Should have the warrant soon, just waiting on a judge's signature."

"Thanks, Tashan," George replied, his gaze fixed on the pub's entrance. "But we might have hit a snag. We found Neil. He claims he was with his family over Christmas and gave us a list of names for an alibi."

There was a brief pause before Tashan responded, his tone indicating something was amiss. "That's odd, sir. According to our records, Neil is single. No wife, no kids. His parents died when he was young, and there's no mention of any extended family. We're checking Council Tax records now while we wait for the warrant. See if we can get lucky with his address."

George's expression hardened. "That changes things. Stand by, Tashan."

He turned to Candy, urgency in his voice. "We need to get back in there now."

George approached the bar, his warrant card in clear view. "Excuse me," he addressed the barman, a young man wiping down glasses. "We're looking for Neil Roscow. He was here a few minutes ago. Do you know him?"

The bartender nodded, a flicker of recognition in his eyes. "Yeah, Neil's a regular. He is a quiet bloke who keeps to himself mostly. Why? What's he done?"

"We just need to talk to him," George replied. "Do you know where he lives? It's important we find him as soon as possible."

The bartender shook his head. "Sorry, detective. I don't know where he lives. He never mentioned anything personal, really."

Candy, scanning the room, approached a group of patrons at a nearby table. "Evening, folks. I'm Detective Constable Nichols. We're trying to locate Neil Roscow. Do any of you know him?"

A middle-aged woman, her hair tied back in a neat bun, looked up. "Neil? Yeah, I know him. Comes in here often. But I couldn't tell you where he lives. Sorry, dear."

George joined Candy, addressing the patrons. "If anyone has any information that could help us locate Mr Roscow, it would greatly assist our investigation."

A man in his late thirties, sitting at the end of the bar, spoke up. "I've seen Neil around. He mentioned living somewhere near Kirkstall Road, but I don't know the exact address."

George thanked him and took down his statement. The information was vague but gave them a potential area to search.

As they left the pub, George made a quick call to the station. "Tashan, we need to expand the search. Neil might be living near Kirkstall Road. Can we get teams to start looking around there?"

"On it, sir," Tashan's voice crackled over the phone.

Realising the gravity of the situation, George put out a BOLO (Be On the Lookout) for Neil. The revelation about his fabricated alibi meant he could be a key figure in the investigation, possibly more involved than they initially suspected.

The drive back to Elland Road Police Station was tense, with George and Candy discussing the implications of Neil's deception.

Upon their return to the station, George and Candy joined their colleagues in the Incident Room, the mood sombre yet determined.

Chapter Eleven

The grand hall was abuzz with the chatter and clinking of glasses as George Beaumont entered the charity event hosted by the West Yorkshire Police. The evening was dedicated to raising funds for community outreach programs, and the air was thick with a mix of formality and goodwill. George, not usually one for social events, felt a bit out of place among the well-dressed attendees, his detective's instinct never fully at rest.

As he navigated through the crowd, a man caught his attention. He was well-dressed, his suit tailored to perfection, exuding a charisma that seemed to draw people to him. This was David Hardaker, a name George had heard in passing but never met in person.

David approached George with a confident stride and an easy smile. "Detective Inspector Beaumont, isn't it? I've heard a lot about you. David Hardaker," he extended his hand.

George shook it, noting the firmness of the grip and the expensive-looking cufflink on his wrist. "Yes, that's right. A pleasure to meet you, Mr Hardaker."

"Please, call me David," he replied, his tone friendly, but there was a sharpness in his eyes that belied his casual attitude. "I've been following your work. Impressive, especially the recent developments in the Schmidt case."

George's guard went up subtly at the mention of the case. "Thank you, but I'm not at liberty to discuss ongoing investigations."

"Of course, I understand completely," David said, his smile unwavering. "I just wanted to express my admiration for your dedication. It's not often we see such commitment to justice."

There was something about David's manner that intrigued George, a sense that there was more behind his words. "I appreciate that. And you, Mr Hardaker, what brings you to this event?"

"Oh, I believe in supporting our local heroes," David replied, gesturing around the room. "Plus, it's always good to keep a finger on the pulse of the community. One never knows when such connections might come in handy."

George nodded his detective's intuition tingling. David's interest in the police work, his presence at the event—it was curious. "Connections are important," George agreed, keeping his tone non-committal.

David's gaze lingered on George for a moment longer, a hint of something unreadable in his expression. "Well, I won't keep you, Detective Inspector. Enjoy your evening."

"Wait," George said, and David turned. "Have I met you before? You look familiar?"

"I don't believe so, no." David nodded. "Have a good night."

As David moved away, mingling with other guests, George watched him, a mixture of intrigue and suspicion brewing in his mind. David Hardaker was more than just a well-dressed socialite. There was a calculated air about him, a sense of being much more involved in the city's undercurrents than he let on.

The charity event was in full swing when Detective Inspector Luke Mason found George Beaumont standing alone, his gaze fixed on the crowd. Luke approached, his experienced eyes quickly assessing George's pensive mood.

"Evening, George. You look like you've seen a ghost," Luke remarked, his voice tinged with a light humour that failed to mask his perceptiveness.

George turned, offering a half-smile. "Just thinking, Luke. This isn't really my scene."

Luke nodded, following George's gaze. "I know what you mean. These events can be... enlightening in more ways than one. Anything or anyone in particular on your mind?"

"It's David Hardaker," George said, his voice low. "I just had a conversation with him. Something about him doesn't sit right with me."

Luke's expression shifted to one of interest. "Hardaker, eh? I've heard a bit about him. Charismatic chap, but he keeps his cards close to his chest. Why, what did he say?"

"He knew about the Schmidt case. Seemed a bit too interested in it for my liking," George replied, his gaze still scanning the room.

Luke's eyes narrowed thoughtfully. "David Hardaker is a man who likes to be in the know. But you're right to be wary. In our line of work, anyone taking an undue interest in a case deserves a second look."

George looked back at Luke. "You think he could be involved somehow?"

Luke shrugged slightly. "Hard to say without more to go on. But I've learned to trust my gut, and if yours is telling you something's off, then we should keep an eye on him."

George's expression hardened slightly, the detective in him

responding to Luke's counsel. "I intend to. There's something about him that's just... off."

Luke clapped a reassuring hand on George's shoulder. "Good man. But remember, son, don't let it consume you. We've got enough on our plate with the Schmidt case as it is."

George nodded the weight of the case and his encounter with Hardaker heavy on his mind. "I know. It's just one more thing to add to the list."

The two men stood in silence for a moment, watching the ebb and flow of the event around them. The room was a whirl of light and sound, but to George, it felt distant, almost inconsequential compared to the machinations of the case that occupied his thoughts.

Luke broke the silence. "We'll figure it out, George. We always do."

George gave a determined nod. "We will. And if Hardaker is involved, we'll uncover that too."

With that, Luke excused himself, blending back into the crowd. George remained a while longer, his eyes occasionally finding David Hardaker among the guests. The evening had taken on a new dimension, the veneer of social pleasantries masking a deeper game of intrigue and suspicion.

* * *

The charity event, a microcosm of Leeds' elite, buzzed with the undercurrents of influence and power. Detective Inspector George Beaumont, a silent observer in this world of affluence, watched as David Hardaker navigated the crowd with a practised ease that spoke of his familiarity with this echelon of society.

George's eyes followed David as he made his way to Richard Harrowby, a well-known financier. Their handshake was firm, the exchange of pleasantries smooth. George couldn't hear their words, but the laughter and the knowing glances they shared spoke volumes.

"Richard, always a pleasure," David's voice carried just enough for George to catch.

"David, your insights are invaluable as always," Richard replied, his voice rich with the confidence of a man used to power.

Next, David approached Margaret Vane, a philanthropist. Her warm smile was met with David's charming nod. They conversed, and her laughter, light and genuine, echoed softly.

"Your contributions to the city are unmatched, Margaret," David complimented, his tone genuine yet calculating.

Margaret beamed. "And your support makes much of it possible, David."

George noted the ease with which David shifted his demeanour, aligning perfectly with each individual's persona. His next interaction was with Anthony 'Tony' Kendall, a real estate mogul. Their handshake was more of a power grip, the exchange brimming with the undercurrents of mutual business interests.

"Tony, your latest project is the talk of the town," David remarked, his eyes sharp and assessing.

Tony, a man of robust build and commanding presence, grinned. "And your advice was instrumental, David. We make a good team."

Julian Pierce, an art dealer, was next. Their conversation was quieter, more discreet. Julian's expressive hands moved as he spoke, his enthusiasm palpable.

"Your eye for art is unparalleled, Julian. Your gallery is a testament to that," David observed, his tone laced with admiration.

Julian's response was a mix of pride and gratitude. "Thank you, David. Your appreciation means a lot."

Catherine Devereux, a fashion icon, received a kiss on the hand from David. Her laughter, light and airy, filled the space around them.

"David, your support of the arts extends to fashion too, I see," Catherine said, her eyes twinkling.

"Only the best for Leeds' fashion queen," David replied, his compliment smooth as silk.

Finally, David engaged with Simon Trenchard, a tech entrepreneur. Their conversation seemed intense, both men leaning in, their expressions serious.

"The tech world is lucky to have a mind like yours, Simon," David said, his interest seemingly genuine.

Simon, young and energetic, nodded in appreciation. "And I'm lucky to have supporters like you, David."

As George observed, he couldn't help but notice David's skill in blending with each of these influential figures. His interactions were a dance of charm and wit, yet there was something elusive about him, a sense of playing a deeper game.

George's footsteps were measured as he approached David Hardaker for the second time, who stood alone for a moment, a glass of champagne in hand. The low hum of conversation around them provided a discreet soundtrack to the confrontation that was about to unfold.

"David," George began, his voice even but firm. "You seem to have quite the rapport with some of Leeds' most influential figures."

David turned, his smile practised but his eyes sharp. "Detective Inspector Beaumont, you've been observing me. I'm flattered."

George ignored the charm. "Richard Harrowby, Margaret Vane, Anthony Kendall, Julian Pierce, Catherine Devereux, Simon Trenchard," he listed methodically. He knew their names by heart because they were on the list of influential people known to Edward Beaumont. "You're quite connected."

David's smile didn't waver. "It's a small city, George. And in my line of work, connections are everything." He paused. "Ask your father."

George leaned in slightly, his gaze unwavering. Leeds certainly was not a small city. "What exactly is your 'line of work,' David? It seems to span quite a range of interests."

David sipped his champagne, his manner unshaken. "I'm a facilitator, George. I connect people and help them achieve their goals. It's all quite above board."

"But why the interest in the Schmidt case? And my father?" George prodded, watching David's reaction closely.

David set his glass down, his expression turning more serious. "Curiosity, George. Nothing more. Your father's a respected figure. The case is... intriguing."

"And that's all?"

David's eyes hardened, but his smile remained. "For now." He added, "I've spotted a friend of mine. Have a good night."

George turned on his heel and walked away but was sure he could feel David's gaze on his back, piercing yet puzzling. The conversation had only deepened the mystery surrounding David Hardaker.

* * *

The clatter and bustle of the event faded into the background as George Beaumont headed upstairs and entered Detective Chief Inspector Alistair Atkinson's office. The room was a stark contrast to the chaos outside, a haven of order and quiet authority. DCI Atkinson, a man whose experience was etched in the lines of his face, looked up from his paperwork as George entered.

"George, what's on your mind?" Atkinson asked, his tone indicating he already sensed the gravity of the conversation ahead.

George took a seat, his posture reflecting the seriousness of the matter at hand. "Sir, it's about David Hardaker. I have concerns regarding his connections and his recent interest in the Schmidt case."

Atkinson leaned back in his chair, his fingers steepled in front of him. "David Hardaker... Yes, I've heard the name. Influential, but somewhat elusive. What specifically concerns you?"

George exhaled slowly, choosing his words carefully. "His connections span across several influential figures in Leeds. And then there's his sudden interest in my personal life, specifically the situation with my father."

Atkinson nodded, his expression contemplative. "Intriguing. And you think there's more to it than mere social networking?"

"I do," George affirmed. "There's something about his timing, his approach. It's too calculated, too coincidental."

Atkinson's eyes narrowed thoughtfully. "Your instincts have always been sharp, George. If you suspect Hardaker's involvement goes deeper, we should definitely keep a closer eye on him."

George felt a sense of validation from Atkinson's response. "I intend to, sir. But I wanted to ensure we're on the same page, given the delicacy of the situation."

"Absolutely," Atkinson replied. "We need to tread carefully, but if Hardaker is a piece of this puzzle, we can't afford to ignore him. Keep your investigation discreet, but thorough."

George nodded, his resolve strengthening. "I'll need to pull some strings, maybe some discreet surveillance, background checks."

"Do what you need to, George, but keep it quiet. We don't want to spook him, especially if he's as connected as you say," Atkinson advised his tone a mix of caution and support.

"Understood, sir. I'll keep you updated on any developments," George said as he stood up to leave.

Atkinson gave a nod of approval. "Good. And George, be careful. We're venturing into murky waters here."

With a final nod, George left Atkinson's office, feeling the weight of the task ahead. The conversation had solidified the importance of uncovering David Hardaker's role in the investigation.

* * *

The charity event had left an unsettling residue in George Beaumont's mind as he drove through the quiet streets of Leeds. The city's night lights blurred past, mirroring the tumultuous thoughts racing in his head. His mobile phone broke the silence, vibrating against the car's console. Edward Beaumont's name flashed on the screen, sending a pulse of apprehension through George. He hesitated for a moment before answering.

"Three times in one day," George said. "What do you need?"

"George," Edward's voice came through, tinged with a warmth that felt out of place. "I hope I'm not calling too late."

"No, it's fine. What do you need?" George repeated his grip on the steering wheel, tightening.

There was a pause on the line, filled with unspoken words. "I just wanted to talk, son. I heard about the charity event tonight. Mixing with the city's elite, are we?"

George's brow furrowed slightly. "It's part of the job. You, of all people, know how it is."

"Yes, indeed I do," Edward said, his tone shifting subtly. "But it's not just pleasantries and handshakes, is it, George? This investigation you're involved in... it's dangerous territory."

The warning in Edward's voice was clear, sending a chill down George's spine. "It's what I do. I'm a detective; I uncover the truth."

"Even if that truth is closer to home than you'd like?" Edward's question hung in the air, heavy with implication.

George's heart rate quickened. "What are you saying, Edward?"

There was a sharpness in Edward's following words. "Just be careful, George. Digging too deep can have... consequences. For everyone involved."

George felt a surge of defiance mixed with concern. "Are you threatening me?"

"No, no, of course not," Edward replied quickly, the facade of warmth returning. "Just a father's concern for his son's well-being."

The conversation had taken a turn, the undercurrents of warning unmistakable. George's mind raced, trying to piece together the implications of his father's words.

"I appreciate your concern. But I have a job to do," George said, his voice steady despite the turmoil inside.

"I understand, son. Just remember, some stones are better left unturned," Edward cautioned, his tone perplexing.

George's response was firm, his resolve clear despite the emotional stakes. "We'll see. Goodnight."

As he ended the call, George's thoughts were a whirlwind of confusion and apprehension. The veiled warning from his father had heightened the emotional stakes, adding a personal dimension to an already complex case.

Driving through the quiet night, George felt the weight of the investigation pressing down on him. The conversation with Edward had revealed a disturbing facet of the case, one that intertwined his professional pursuit with a personal dilemma that could have far-reaching consequences.

Chapter Twelve

The next morning, the day after Boxing Day, Detective Inspector George Beaumont convened a strategic meeting with Detective Inspector Luke Mason and their team in their Incident Room at Elland Road station. The air was thick with determination, underscored by a sense of urgency that had settled over the team.

George leaned back in his chair, his gaze shifting between the members. "We need to refocus our investigation. David Hardaker is becoming a person of interest, and I want to know why."

Luke, his expression thoughtful, nodded in agreement. "Hardaker's been moving in influential circles, and his sudden interest in the Schmidt case raises too many questions."

Candy, her notebook open in front of her, added, "His connections span across finance, real estate, art, and tech. It's an unusual mix, indicating he's more than just a social butterfly, sir."

George folded his arms, his mind racing. "We start digging into his past. There's got to be something that ties him to the case, more than just idle curiosity."

"His financial dealings would be a good place to start," Luke suggested, his tone analytical. "We need to understand how he's connected to these sectors and what he gains from them."

Candy chimed in, her pen poised over the paper. "I can start pulling records, sir, see if there are any irregularities or links to known criminal activities."

George nodded, his focus sharpening. "Good. And let's not overlook his social connections. There might be more there than meets the eye."

Luke leaned forward, his hands clasped on the table. "What about his personal life? Any family, close relationships that could be relevant?"

"We'll look into that too," George said. "Every aspect of his life needs to be under scrutiny. But remember, we need to be discreet. Hardaker is well-connected; we don't want to tip him off."

Candy made a note, her expression serious. "Understood. It'll be thorough but low-key."

George's gaze lingered on the case files spread out on his desk. "This is more than just connecting the dots. Hardaker's a puzzle, and I have a feeling he's central to everything we're dealing with."

Luke's eyes met George's, a shared understanding passing between them. "We'll get to the bottom of this, George. Whatever it takes."

As the meeting drew to a close, the team stood, a united front against the unfolding mystery. George's last words were a quiet yet firm directive. "Keep me updated on every development. We're stepping into uncharted territory here."

* * *

It was half twelve when George ducked into the Red Lion,

shaking raindrops off his coat. The familiar scents of old wood and ale enveloped him as he paused to take in the pub's amiable din.

Making his way to the bar, George caught the attention of the portly, white-bearded barman and ordered a bitter shandy before settling onto a barstool. The understated style of the wood-clad interior, the sheer variety of cask ales behind the bar, and the lively yet cosy environment relaxed George. It was his favourite pub in Leeds now that he'd begun avoiding the Drysalters like the plague.

"Been a while, mate. The usual spot then?" asked Al as he made the DI's drink.

"Please, Al. It'll be nice to unwind for a couple of hours," he replied, offering Al a tired smile.

Al nodded knowingly, and George headed to the back corner booth, which had unofficially become his spot over the past two years. The cracked leather seats had moulded perfectly to his shape by now. George sank in gratefully and took a long swig of the crisp, sweet drink.

Soon, George would be sat across from a man who was once entrenched in the very criminal world he was trying to dismantle. The pub's low hum of muted conversations and clinking glasses provided a cover for their clandestine meeting. George's informant, a former member of the Schmidt Organised Crime Group, was a wiry man with nervous eyes that constantly darted around the room.

"You sure we're safe here?" the informant, known only as Miller, asked once he arrived, his voice barely above a whisper.

George nodded, his gaze steady and reassuring. "We're fine, Miller. Just two blokes having a pint. What have you got for me?"

Miller took a sip of his drink, his hand trembling slightly. "The OCG's planning something big. They've been moving a lot of cash around, and there's talk of a new player in town."

George leaned in, his interest piqued. "A new player? Do you have a name?"

Miller shook his head. "No, but he's someone with connections. Even the higher-ups are wary of him."

"Talk to me about the hierarchy," George urged, sensing the depth of information Miller could provide.

Miller glanced around again before leaning closer. "It's all about loyalty and fear with them. But there's a rift brewing. Some aren't happy with the current leadership. They think it's time for a change."

George's mind raced. A power struggle within the OCG could provide an opportunity for the police to exploit. "What about operations? Anything on their next move?"

"They've been quiet since Ethan Turner's murder. But there's chatter about a meeting, something about solidifying their hold over the city's underground."

George absorbed the information, his detective's mind already formulating plans. "And the meeting's location?"

"Dock Street, the old warehouse," Miller replied. "But it's heavily guarded. You won't get in easily."

George nodded, processing the risks involved. "Anything else?"

Miller hesitated, then said, "Watch your back, George. These guys... they play for keeps."

George offered a grim smile. "I always do. Thanks, Miller."

As they stood up to leave, George discreetly passed an envelope to Miller. "For your trouble," he said quietly.

Miller pocketed the envelope and hurried out of the pub,

blending into the shadows of the evening. George remained seated for a moment longer, mulling over the information he'd just received.

* * *

Detective Inspector George Beaumont sat immersed in a sea of case files. The clock on the wall ticked steadily, marking the passage of time as he delved deeper into the intricate web of the Santa Claus murders.

His eyes, sharpened by years of detective work, scanned the documents with meticulous attention. As he sifted through the details, a pattern began to emerge, subtle yet unmistakable. Each victim of the Santa Claus murders, he realised, had a connection to the Schmidt Organised Crime Group.

George leaned back in his chair, a thoughtful frown creasing his forehead. "So, they were either former members or informants or had some financial dispute with the OCG," he murmured to himself, the implications of this revelation dawning on him.

The office door opened, and Detective Constable Tashan Blackburn entered, his expression curious. "Anything new, sir?" he asked.

George looked up, his gaze intense. "Yes, Tashan. It seems our victims were not random targets. They were all linked to the Schmidt OCG in some way."

Tashan approached the desk, interest piqued. "Linked how, sir?"

George handed him a file. "Take a look. Former members who knew too much, informants who might have turned, and individuals who crossed paths financially with the group. It appears the murders were a twisted way of maintaining loyalty and enforcing silence."

Tashan leafed through the file, his brow furrowing. "That's a disturbing tactic. It means the OCG is more ruthless than we thought."

George nodded solemnly. "And more dangerous. This pattern... it's a message, a warning to anyone who dares defy them."

The room fell silent as they both absorbed the gravity of their findings. George's mind was already racing with the next steps of the investigation.

"We need to dig deeper into each victim's background, find out their exact role or connection with the OCG," George said, determination lining his voice.

Tashan agreed, closing the file. "I'll start cross-referencing their profiles with our OCG database and see if we missed any links."

George stood up, stretching his legs. "And I'll talk to some of my contacts, see if they've heard anything on the street."

As Tashan left to start his work, George turned to the window, gazing out at the cityscape of Leeds. The view was familiar, yet tonight, it seemed different, shadowed by the sinister workings of the Schmidt OCG.

* * *

Detective Inspector George Beaumont prepared to present his findings to the senior detectives. The room, usually bustling with activity, was hushed, all eyes on George. Detective Chief Inspector Alistair Atkinson, Detective Superintendent Smith, and Detective Chief Superintendent Sadiq sat across from him, their expressions a mix of curiosity and scepticism.

George cleared his throat, his gaze steady. "Thank you for joining me. I believe I've uncovered a pattern in the Santa Claus murders that links them directly to the Schmidt OCG."

DCI Atkinson raised an eyebrow. "That's a bold claim, DI Beaumont. What evidence do you have to support this theory?"

George nodded, acknowledging the scepticism. "I understand your reservations, but hear me out." He clicked a button, and the projector lit up, displaying a complex web of names and connections.

"As you can see, each victim had a direct or indirect link to the OCG," George began, pointing to the chart. "Former members, informants, even individuals with financial disputes."

Detective Superintendent Smith leaned forward, his tone cautious. "Correlation doesn't imply causation, Beaumont. How can you be sure these aren't coincidental?"

George clicked to the next slide, showing detailed timelines and financial records. "It's more than correlation, sir. Each of these victims was positioned to possess sensitive information about the OCG or to potentially threaten their operations."

Detective Chief Superintendent Sadiq, who had been quietly observing, interjected. "And what about the nature of the murders themselves? Anything that ties them to the OCG's known methods?"

"Yes," George replied, displaying crime scene photos. "The method of execution this time bears the hallmarks of the OCG's intimidation tactics."

The senior detectives exchanged glances, the initial scepticism slowly giving way to consideration. George's confidence and the weight of his evidence were beginning to make an impact.

DSU Jim Smith asked, "What was Christian Ross' involvement?"

"We're not sure yet, sir," George said, "but it appears he could have been deeply involved with the Schmidt OCG." He paused. "A hitman, if you were."

DCI Atkinson, now visibly more engaged, asked, "What's your proposed course of action, DI Beaumont?"

George took a deep breath, his resolve clear. "We need to apply pressure on known OCG affiliates, increase surveillance, and dig deeper into the financial trails. I also suggest we use this pattern to predict and potentially prevent further murders."

Detective Superintendent Smith nodded thoughtfully. "It's an aggressive strategy, but if your theory holds, it could be our best shot at dismantling the OCG's hold in Leeds."

Detective Chief Superintendent Sadiq added, "We'll need to proceed carefully. The OCG is notorious for its reach and influence. We can't afford any missteps."

"I agree, sir," George said. "But we've got a solid lead now. It's time to act on it."

The meeting concluded with a sense of cautious optimism. The senior detectives, now convinced of the validity of George's theory, gave their approval to proceed with the plan.

As George left the conference room, he felt a weight lift off his shoulders. The presentation had been a success, his theory gaining the necessary backing.

* * *

In the secluded expanse of Middleton Park woods, under the guise of a casual encounter, Detective Inspector George Beaumont met with a low-ranking member of the Schmidt Organised Crime Group. The air was crisp, the sounds of the city distant, replaced by the rustling of leaves and the occasional chirp of a bird.

The OCG member, a young man named Danny, appeared nervous, his eyes darting around as if expecting to be watched. George, dressed in plain clothes, exuded a calm demeanour designed to put Danny at ease.

"Thanks for meeting me, Danny," George began, his voice low. "I understand this isn't easy for you."

Danny, his hands shoved deep into his coat pockets, nodded. "I... I don't know how much more of this I can take, Inspector. It's not what I signed up for."

George could sense the fear and disillusionment in Danny's voice. "You're doing the right thing. What can you tell me about the OCG's operations?"

Danny hesitated, then sighed. "It's... it's all gotten out of hand. The violence, the threats... I joined for the money, but this..." His voice trailed off, filled with regret.

"Focus on what you know, Danny. Any information could be crucial," George encouraged, his tone reassuring.

"The Santa Claus murders... they're a message. A warning to anyone who thinks about crossing the OCG," Danny revealed, a shiver running through his voice.

George's expression remained impassive, but inwardly, he was processing every word. "A warning? Can you elaborate?"

Danny looked around again before continuing. "The victims... they either knew too much or owed too much. The OCG doesn't forgive debts, Inspector. Not in money, not in loyalty."

George's mind was racing, piecing together the information with what he already knew. "Do you know who's behind these murders, Danny?"

"I... I don't know names. But there's talk about someone high up, someone making examples," Danny said, his voice barely a whisper.

George nodded, understanding the gravity of what Danny was sharing. "Are you telling me Dr Christian Ross didn't kill the other Santa Claus victims?"

"I don't think he murdered them himself, no, but he was involved in the decision-making."

"And the OCG's next move? Anything you've heard?"

"They're planning something big. A power move to consolidate their hold over the city," Danny divulged, his fear palpable.

George reached into his pocket and handed Danny a card. "If you think of anything else, anything at all, you contact me. It's encrypted, untraceable."

Danny took the card, his hand trembling. "I just want out, Inspector. I never wanted any of this."

George's gaze was sympathetic yet firm. "We'll do what we can to help, but your safety depends on you staying under the radar for now."

As they parted ways, George watched Danny disappear amongst the trees, his figure soon swallowed by the shadows. The meeting had confirmed his suspicions about the OCG's brutal methods of maintaining control.

Chapter Thirteen

In the police station's tech lab, Detective Inspector George Beaumont watched as Detective Constable Tashan Blackburn worked his magic on a series of encrypted communications intercepted from the Schmidt Organised Crime Group. The air was charged with a tense anticipation, the whirring of computers and the faint hum of the air conditioning the only sounds in the room.

"Any luck, Tashan?" George asked, his voice low, as he leaned over Blackburn's shoulder.

Tashan, his eyes fixed on the screen, fingers rushing over the keyboard, nodded without looking up. "I'm getting there, sir. These guys know their stuff, but they're not as clever as they think."

George's gaze was fixed on the screen, a myriad of codes and symbols cascading down. The complexity of the task was evident, but so was Tashan's skill.

After several tense minutes, Tashan's fingers stilled, and he leaned back. "Got it," he announced a triumphant tone in his voice.

George's eyes narrowed as he read the decrypted text. "This is it. It looks like they're planning a meet. Time and place are here."

Tashan pointed to the screen. "There, the old warehouse on Dock Street. Tomorrow night."

George's mind raced with the implications. "This could be our chance to catch them red-handed. We need to set up surveillance, maybe even an intervention."

Tashan turned to George, his expression serious. "We'll need backup, sir. This could get hairy."

George nodded, already formulating a plan. "I'll talk to DCI Atkinson and get the green light. We can't let this opportunity slip through our fingers."

As George stood up, ready to leave the lab, he paused, looking back at Tashan. "Good work. This could be the break we've been waiting for."

Tashan offered a small smile, the satisfaction of a job well done evident in his eyes. "Just doing my part, sir."

* * *

In the Incident Room at Elland Road Police Station, a web of financial transactions stretched across multiple screens, each one a thread in the complex tapestry of the Schmidt Organised Crime Group's operations. Detective Inspector George Beaumont and Detective Sergeant Yolanda Williams stood before the digital display, their expressions a blend of concentration and concern.

"These transactions," George pointed at the screen, his finger tracing lines that connected various accounts, "they're not just random movements of money. They're deliberate, calculated."

Yolanda, her eyes scanning the data, nodded in agreement. "It's a pattern of money laundering, and look here," she gestured towards a series of dates and amounts, "each significant transaction corresponds with the dates and locations of the Santa Claus murders, sir."

George leaned in closer, his gaze intense. "So the OCG was paying off someone at each location. It's not just about laundering money; it's bribery, keeping the locals quiet, or maybe paying off a killer."

Yolanda's eyes met George's, reflecting the gravity of their discovery. "This is big, George. It ties the OCG directly to the murders."

George stepped back, absorbing the implications. "We need to trace these transactions to their source. Find out who was on the receiving end."

Yolanda was already typing rapidly on a keyboard. "I'm cross-referencing the accounts with known OCG associates. If we're lucky, we'll get a match."

The room was filled with the soft clicking of keys and the occasional beep of incoming data. George and Yolanda worked in tandem, piecing together the puzzle.

After a few moments, Yolanda straightened up, a triumphant look on her face. "Got something, sir. One of the accounts is linked to a known OCG enforcer. He's been spotted at several of the murder locations."

George's eyes narrowed. "That's our connection. We need to bring him in for questioning."

Yolanda's fingers flew over the keyboard, pulling up more information. "He's slippery, but now that we know who we're looking for, we can track his movements."

George turned away from the screen, his mind racing with the next steps. "Good work, Yolanda. This could be the break we've been waiting for."

Yolanda nodded, a determined look in her eyes. "We're close, sir. We're finally close to cracking this."

* * *

The evening had settled over Leeds like a heavy blanket, shrouding the city in shadows. In a nondescript van parked discreetly down the street from a known Schmidt Organised Crime Group hideout, Detective Inspector George Beaumont and Detective Constable Jay Scott sat in silence, their eyes trained on the dimly lit building ahead.

The van, equipped with surveillance gear, was their temporary command post. The air inside was thick with anticipation; the only sound was the quiet hum of the surveillance equipment. George's eyes were focused, his expression a mask of concentration as he observed the comings and goings at the hideout.

"Anything yet, boss?" Jay whispered, breaking the silence, his gaze never leaving the binoculars.

George shook his head slightly. "No, it's been quiet. Too quiet, maybe."

The hideout, a rundown building with boarded-up windows, had been under their watch for hours. The stillness of the scene was in stark contrast to the flurry of activity they anticipated.

"You think they know we're onto them?" Jay asked, his voice low.

George considered the possibility. "Doubt it. But these guys are cautious. They won't make a move unless they're sure it's safe."

As they spoke, a black sedan pulled up in front of the

hideout. Two men stepped out, glancing around furtively before heading towards the building.

"There," George said, his tone sharpening. "That's our cue. Get the camera ready."

Jay quickly positioned the camera, zooming in on the figures. The lens whirred softly as it focused, capturing the men's faces in precise detail.

"Got them," Jay confirmed, recording their movements.

George watched intently, memorising their features. "They're new. Haven't seen them before in relation to the Schmidt group."

The men disappeared inside the building, the door closing behind them with a soft thud that seemed to resonate in the quiet street.

George reached for his notebook, jotting down the time and descriptions. "We'll run their faces through the database and see if they pop up."

Jay nodded, his eyes still on the building. "Think this could be related to the Turner case?"

"Possibly," George mused, his mind working through the connections. "Turner's murder doesn't fit the Schmidt's usual MO, but we can't rule anything out."

They sat in silence for a while longer, the surveillance equipment whirring softly. The street outside remained still, the occasional passer-by oblivious to the operation unfolding in the van.

After a few more minutes, the two men re-emerged from the hideout, quickly getting into the sedan and driving off. George and Jay watched them go, the tail lights disappearing into the night.

"Let's pack up," George said, closing his notebook. "We've

got what we came for."

* * *

The air in DCI Alistair Atkinson's office was laden with anticipation as Detective Inspector George Beaumont laid out the evidence linking the Santa Claus murders to the financial activities of the Schmidt Organised Crime Group.

DCI Atkinson, seated behind his imposing oak desk, listened intently, his fingers steepled under his chin. His eyes, usually a penetrating stare, softened as George presented the meticulously gathered data.

"Your findings are impressive, DI Beaumont," Atkinson finally said, leaning back in his chair. "It appears you've uncovered a significant piece of the puzzle."

George, standing confidently yet respectfully before the DCI's desk, nodded. "Thank you, sir. The pattern is clear—the OCG's financial transactions are inextricably linked to the murder locations. We're not just looking at money laundering; it's direct involvement in the crimes."

Atkinson's gaze shifted to the evidence spread across his desk. "This level of corruption and manipulation... it's more extensive than we initially thought."

George's expression was resolute. "Yes, sir. And it's crucial we act on this information swiftly. The longer we wait, the more entrenched the OCG becomes."

Atkinson stood up, a sign of his engagement and respect for the gravity of the situation. "I agree. You have the green light to pursue this lead further, George. What do you need?"

George didn't hesitate. "Additional resources would be beneficial—more officers for surveillance and analysis, and perhaps enhanced tech support to dig deeper into the financial trails."

Atkinson walked over to the window, looking out over Leeds. "You'll have it. I'll allocate additional human resources and equipment. We need to dismantle this network before more lives are lost."

George's stance relaxed slightly, a silent acknowledgement of the support. "Thank you, sir. I'll coordinate with the teams and formulate a plan of action."

Atkinson turned, his expression now one of determination mirroring George's. "This is a pivotal moment in our fight against the OCG, Beaumont. Your work could be the key to bringing them down."

George gave a curt nod, the responsibility of the task not lost on him. "I understand, sir. We'll proceed with caution but with the necessary force."

As George prepared to leave, Atkinson added, "And George, keep me updated on every development. This case has far-reaching implications. We need to stay one step ahead."

"Of course, sir. You'll be the first to know of any progress," George assured before exiting the office.

* * *

Detective Inspector George Beaumont, armed with the information gleaned from his covert meeting with the informant, Miller, and stakeout with Jay, stood before his team, a detailed map of the Schmidt Organised Crime Group warehouse on Dock Street spread out on the table.

"Listen up," George began, his voice steady yet charged with the gravity of the situation. "Based on what we've learned, we're planning a raid on this OCG warehouse." He pointed to the map, his finger tracing the layout of the building and its surroundings. "The DCI has given us the green light."

Detective Inspector Luke Mason, standing beside George, interjected, "We need to consider every angle. This isn't going to be straightforward."

Detective Constable Tashan Blackburn, known for his technical expertise, spoke up from the back of the room. "The warehouse is heavily guarded, and the layout is complex. There are multiple entry and exit points."

George nodded, acknowledging Tashan's assessment. "That's why we need to be meticulous. We'll approach from two sides. Tashan, you'll lead Team A through the rear entrance. Luke, you take Team B through the front. I'll coordinate from the mobile command unit."

Detective Constable Candy Nichols, her expression focused, asked, "What about civilian safety, sir? If things go south..."

"We minimize collateral damage at all costs," George replied firmly. "Our aim is to apprehend, not escalate. Non-lethal tactics unless absolutely necessary."

Luke, studying the map, added, "Timing is crucial. We strike at 0200 hours when their guard is likely to be lowest. We need the element of surprise."

The room fell silent as the team absorbed the details of the plan. George's eyes swept over his team, each member keenly aware of the risks involved.

"Communications will be key," George continued. "Constant updates. If anyone spots anything out of the ordinary, you report it immediately." He paused. "The AFOs are there to do the hard work, so let them do their jobs."

Tashan chimed in, "I'll set up jamming devices to disrupt

their communications. It'll give us an edge."

George gave a curt nod. "Good. And remember, the OCG is dangerous and unpredictable. Expect resistance."

Candy, her gaze resolute, said, "We're prepared, sir. We've trained for this."

George looked at each of his team members, their faces a blend of determination and resolve. "This operation could significantly disrupt the OCG's activities in Leeds. It's a big step towards dismantling their network. But don't put yourself at risk."

Luke added a note of caution. "But let's not underestimate them. We stick to the plan, watch each other's backs."

George's expression hardened with resolve. "We go in smart, we go in prepared, and we bring them down."

Chapter Fourteen

Outside the stoic façade of Elland Road Police Station, a cluster of journalists and cameras gathered, buzzing with anticipation. Detective Inspector George Beaumont, standing beside a podium adorned with the police crest, prepared to address the media. The evening sky was a sombre grey, a fitting backdrop for the gravity of the occasion.

Detective Chief Inspector Alistair Atkinson stepped up first, his voice clear and authoritative. "Thank you all for coming. Today, we acknowledge a significant breakthrough in the investigation of the Santa Claus murders, thanks to the diligent efforts of DI George Beaumont."

The reporters shifted, their cameras focusing on George, who stood stoically, a hint of unease hidden behind his professional image.

Atkinson continued, "DI Beaumont's discovery of financial links between the murders and an Organised Crime Group has been instrumental in advancing our investigation."

George, now stepping forward, faced the sea of lenses and microphones. "Thank you, DCI Atkinson. Our team has worked tirelessly on this case. It's a collaborative effort, and this breakthrough brings us closer to delivering justice for the victims and their families."

A reporter from the front row called out, "DI Beaumont, how significant is this discovery in the context of the investigation?"

George answered, "It's a pivotal moment. It gives us a clearer picture of the OCG's involvement and its methods. We're now able to target our investigation more effectively."

Another reporter asked, "Does this mean you're close to making arrests?"

George responded, his tone measured, "We're following several leads. I can't comment on specific details at this stage, but we are making progress."

The flashes of cameras punctuated each question, capturing George's composed responses. His colleagues, standing to the side, watched with a newfound respect. George's breakthrough had not only advanced the case but also elevated his standing within the force and with the media.

A journalist from a local paper chimed in, "How does this impact the OCG's operations in Leeds?"

George regarded the reporter, aware that his answer would be scrutinised. "Our goal is to dismantle their network. This development disrupts their activities and sends a clear message that we are closing in on them."

As he continued to detail the police's efforts, a hand shot up from the back. Emma Clarke, known for her community activism, her presence always commanding attention. Her gaze was direct, challenging, yet respectful.

"DI Beaumont, how does the police plan to address the concerns of residents, particularly in the areas most affected by these crimes?" she asked, her tone firm but concerned.

George met her eyes, recognising the importance of her question. "We understand the community's concerns and are increasing patrols in high-risk areas. We're also working closely with local leaders to address safety issues."

Emma nodded, jotting down notes, then followed up. "And what about the youth in these areas? They need more than just increased police presence."

George paused, choosing his words carefully. "You're right, Emma. It's about more than policing. We're engaging with youth groups and local schools to provide support and prevent them from being drawn into criminal activities."

The room buzzed with the scratching of pens on paper, reporters capturing every word. George's answers were measured, reflecting a deep understanding of the community's needs.

Emma continued, "Many in the community feel that the police are not approachable. How will you change this perception?"

George's response was immediate and sincere. "We're holding community meetings, inviting residents to speak directly with officers. It's about building trust and showing that we're here to serve and protect everyone."

As the briefing came to a close, George stepped away from the podium, the reporters dispersing to file their stories, buzzing with the new information. George, deep in thought, thought about the many challenges facing his city and how he was committed to making a difference, one step at a time.

Detective Sergeant Yolanda Williams approached George, a smile of genuine admiration on her face. "Well done, sir. You've handled that brilliantly," she said.

George gave a modest nod, his gaze lingering on the dispersing crowd. "It's not over yet, Yolanda. But today, we've shown them we're on the right track."

Yolanda's expression turned serious. "And the spotlight is on us now, more than ever."

George looked back at the police station, his resolve firm. "Then let's make sure we're ready for what comes next."

* * *

The aroma of freshly ground coffee filled the air as Detective Inspector George Beaumont sat in a corner of a quaint café near Elland Road Police Station. Outside, the city of Leeds went about its business, oblivious to the weight of the case resting on George's shoulders. He cradled a steaming cup of coffee, his mind momentarily drifting from the complexities of the investigation.

The recent breakthrough in the case had brought a sense of pride, yet with it came an overwhelming responsibility. The journey to this point had been arduous, marked by sleepless nights and relentless pursuit of justice. He sipped his coffee, the warmth a brief respite from the chill of his thoughts.

"More coffee, detective?" the friendly barista, a young woman with a bright smile, asked as she approached his table.

George looked up, offering a small, appreciative smile. "Please, just a bit more. Thank you, Lucy."

As she poured the coffee, Lucy's curiosity got the better of her. "I saw the press briefing on TV. Must feel good to make such a big breakthrough, right?"

George nodded, a thoughtful expression crossing his face. "It's a step forward, but there's still a long way to go. Each breakthrough brings its own set of challenges."

Lucy leaned against the table, her interest evident. "But you must be proud, catching the bad guys and all that."

George chuckled softly, a hint of humility in his laugh. "It's not quite like in the films, Lucy. It's a team effort, and every case has its own complexities. Pride is mixed with a sense of duty."

Lucy nodded, her gaze reflecting admiration. "Still, it's pretty impressive. We all feel a bit safer knowing you're on the case."

George sipped his coffee, considering her words. "I appreciate that, Lucy. We do what we can to keep the city safe. It's not just a job for us; it's a commitment to the people."

The conversation was interrupted by the café's door chiming as a new customer entered. Lucy excused herself, flashing George another friendly smile. "Well, we're all rooting for you, detective."

Left alone with his thoughts again, George reflected on Lucy's words. The public's perception of their work was often simplified, unaware of the intricacies and emotional toll it took. Yet, it was these small interactions, these snippets of appreciation, that reminded him of the impact of their work beyond the confines of the police station.

Finishing his coffee, George stood up. As he walked out of the café, the weight of the case settled back on him, but now mixed with a renewed sense of purpose. The journey had been long, and the road ahead was uncertain, but moments like these provided a subtle reassurance that their efforts were not in vain.

* * *

George Beaumont sat in his car outside his home, the engine idling softly as he stared into the quiet suburban street. It was late, the moon casting a pale glow over the peaceful suburb. His mind, usually a whirlwind of case details and strategies, had momentarily quieted, allowing him a rare moment of reflection.

His phone buzzed, breaking the silence. It was Isabella, his fiancée. He smiled, feeling a wave of warmth at the sight of her name on the screen.

"Hey, Izzy," George answered, his voice softening.

"Hi, George. Just saw the news. You were brilliant," Isabella's voice came through, filled with pride and affection.

George chuckled a hint of modesty in his tone. "It's just part of the job, Izzy. But thank you."

"No, really, George. What you're doing... it's important. You're making a difference," Isabella insisted, her words sincere.

George leaned back in his seat, the comfort of Isabella's words wrapping around him like a warm blanket. "It feels like a never-ending battle sometimes. But hearing that from you... it means a lot."

Isabella's voice was soft but firm. "You're too hard on yourself. You've achieved so much. The whole city is talking about your breakthrough in the case."

George sighed, a mixture of exhaustion and contentment in his breath. "I just want to see it through, Izzy. To bring some peace to those families, to make our city safer."

"I know you will. You have this incredible ability to see things through, no matter how tough they get," Isabella said, her admiration for him evident.

George's gaze drifted to the darkened windows of his home, a symbol of the personal life he often had to put on hold for his work. "I couldn't do it without your support, Izzy. You and the kids... you're my anchor."

Isabella's laughter, light and melodic, filled the car. "Well, just make sure you come inside soon. It's cold out there, and you need your rest."

George smiled, his heart lightened by the conversation. "I will. I'll be right in. Love you, Izzy."

"Love you too, gorgeous. See you in a bit," Isabella replied, ending the call.

George sat for a moment longer, the sense of purpose and determination solidifying within him. The challenges of the case and the weight of responsibility all seemed manageable with the support of his family. He turned off the engine and stepped out of the car, the crisp night air greeting him.

As he walked to his front door, George felt a renewed sense of resolve. The investigation, with all its twists and turns, was more than just a job. It was a commitment to justice, to the safety of his community, and to the ideals he had dedicated his life to upholding.

* * *

Inside, the warm, inviting aroma of tea filled the air. Isabella was in the kitchen, skilfully manoeuvring pots and pans. Olivia, their baby daughter, cooed and gurgled in her playpen, her little hands reaching out as George entered.

"Daddy's here!" he announced in a playful tone, scooping Olivia into his arms. Her giggles filled the room, a sound that always managed to ease the weight of his day. He twirled her around, her laughter a melody that soothed his weary soul.

Isabella looked over, a smile on her face. "You two are just adorable," she said, her eyes sparkling with affection.

George set Olivia down in her high chair, joining Isabella in the kitchen. "Something smells amazing," he complimented, peering over her shoulder.

"Just a simple pasta bake," Isabella replied, "But I've added a few of your favourites."

They settled at the dining table, Olivia in her high chair, babbling happily. The room was filled with the warmth of family, a haven from the outside world. George shared the highlights of his day, carefully omitting the grimmer details to preserve the sanctity of their home life.

As they ate, George's expression turned serious. "I shouldn't be telling you this, but there's going to be a raid tonight.

Isabella reached across the table, her hand finding his. "Please, be careful."

George met her gaze, the depth of his love for her evident in his eyes. "I will, Izzy. I always am." His voice was firm, reassuring.

"I know you have to do this, but Olivia and I... we need you, George. Just promise me you'll come back to us."

George squeezed her hand gently. "I promise, Izzy. You're my world. You and Olivia are why I do all this—to make sure you're safe."

The conversation shifted as they finished their meal, focusing on lighter topics, but the unspoken understanding lingered in the air. The upcoming raid was a necessary part of his duty, yet it brought an undercurrent of risk that they both acknowledged.

Later, as George stood at the sink, methodically washing up the dinner dishes, Isabella joined him to help dry the pots. The cosy domesticity of the moment was tinged with the unspoken understanding that something was weighing heavily on George's mind.

Isabella picked up a tea towel, her movements gentle and deliberate. "George," she began cautiously, "you've been a bit distant since you got home. Is everything okay?"

George paused, his hands submerged in soapy water. He glanced over his shoulder, offering her a half-smile. "I'm fine, Izzy. Just a lot on my mind with the case."

But Isabella knew him too well. She placed a hand on his arm, prompting him to face her. "It's more than just the case, isn't it? You can talk to me, George."

There was a moment's hesitation before George relented, his expression softening. "It's about Edward. DSU Smith... he wants me to focus on other suspects instead of him. It's confusing. Part of me thinks it's the right call, but..."

Isabella's eyes were full of empathy. "But you're not sure if it's because there's not enough to go on or if it's to protect him, given his status?"

"Exactly," George sighed, drying his hands on a towel. "I want to follow where the evidence leads, but there's this nagging doubt. What if we're missing something crucial by not pursuing him more aggressively?"

Isabella leaned against the counter, considering his words. "It's a tough position, George. But remember, you've always been one to trust your instincts. Maybe Smith is being cautious, but that doesn't mean you stop looking at all angles, including your father."

George nodded, the lines of conflict evident on his face. "You're right. It's just hard, Izzy. He's my dad, but the evidence... it's hard to ignore."

Isabella reached out, her touch reassuring. "I know it's difficult, but you're doing the right thing, George. Following the evidence and being thorough—that's who you are. Whatever the outcome, you'll know you did everything by the book."

George's gaze met hers, gratitude and love in his eyes. "Thanks, Izzy. I don't know what I'd do without you."

Chapter Fifteen

Under the cloak of darkness, the silent streets of Leeds bore witness to a meticulously planned operation. Detective Inspector George Beaumont, clad in tactical gear, led a team, including a squad of AFOs and his detective team, towards the Schmidt Organised Crime Group warehouse on Dock Street. The night was eerily still; the only sound was the muffled footsteps of the police unit advancing with stealth.

George signalled to his team, his hand movements precise and calculated. Every member knew their role, the hours of planning and preparation culminating in this moment. Beside him, Detective Inspector Luke Mason and Detective Constable Tashan Blackburn moved with equal caution, their eyes scanning the shadows.

As they neared the warehouse, George's voice was a whisper in the team's earpieces. "Remember, no unnecessary risks. We need them alive for questioning."

The warehouse loomed ahead, a fortress of illegal activities now vulnerable to the law. George and his team split into their designated groups, encircling the building.

Tashan, leading Team A, reported in a hushed tone, "In position at the rear entrance, sir."

Luke, at the front, whispered back, "Team B ready."

George gave the signal, and in a coordinated move, both teams breached the warehouse. The sound of doors being forced echoed through the building as they flooded in, tactical lights piercing the darkness.

"Police! Hands where I can see them!" The AFO squad leader bellowed, his team swiftly moving in to secure the area. George's detectives followed them inside. The warehouse, filled with crates and contraband, was a hive of illegal operations now exposed.

Amid the chaos of the raid, George found himself face to face with one of Jürgen Schmidt's top henchmen. Oleksander Jones, a towering figure with a scarred face and eyes that spoke of many violent encounters, sneered at George, his stance aggressive and challenging.

George, his heart pounding but his expression calm assessed his opponent. He remembered his boxing training, the countless hours spent in the ring, preparing for moments like these. The henchman lunged forward, his movements swift but predictable to George's trained eye.

With a fluid motion honed by years of training, George sidestepped the attack, his own body coiling with controlled power. The henchman's momentum carried him forward, and George seized the opportunity, landing a solid punch to his midsection.

The henchman grunted, surprise flashing in his eyes, but he quickly recovered, swinging a heavy fist towards George. George ducked, feeling the rush of air as the fist passed over his head. He countered with a swift uppercut, connecting with the henchman's jaw.

"You don't want to do this," George warned, his voice steady despite the adrenaline coursing through his veins.

The henchman, now furious, launched another attack, throwing a series of wild punches. George, drawing on his experience in the ring, deftly blocked and dodged, his movements precise and efficient.

"I'm the police! Stand down!" George commanded, but his words seemed to fuel the henchman's rage.

In a final, desperate move, the henchman pulled a knife, the blade glinting in the dim warehouse light. George's eyes narrowed, his focus intensifying. He couldn't afford a misstep now.

As the henchman lunged, George stepped inside his reach, using his own momentum against him. With a swift motion, George disarmed him, sending the knife clattering to the floor. A well-placed jab to the henchman's solar plexus winded him, and George quickly subdued him, twisting his arm behind his back.

"You're finished, Jones," George said, the authority in his voice unmistakable.

Oleksander, now gasping for breath, ceased his struggles, the fight leaving his body. George, his breathing heavy, maintained his grip, ensuring the henchman was securely restrained.

Detective Inspector Luke Mason arrived, his gun drawn. Seeing the situation under control, he holstered his weapon and moved to assist George.

"Good work, son," Luke said, helping to handcuff the henchman. "You alright?"

George nodded, releasing a breath he hadn't realised he'd been holding. "Yeah, I'm fine. Let's get him out of here."

As an AFO pair led the henchman out of the warehouse, George's mind was already moving on to the next phase of the operation. The physical altercation had been brief but intense, a testament to George's training and resolve.

Other OCG members had been caught by surprise and were quickly apprehended. Handcuffs clicked as crucial figures of the criminal network were secured. George moved through the warehouse, his trained eyes assessing the scene.

"Sir, we've found something," Candy called out from a corner of the warehouse. She held up bags filled with what looked like drugs and stacks of cash.

"Good work, DC Nichols," George responded, satisfaction in his voice. "Let's make sure we catalogue everything. This is the evidence we need."

Meanwhile, Tashan was at a computer terminal. "Sir, I've found encrypted files here. Could be crucial to their operations."

George approached, looking over Tashan's shoulder. "Can you crack it?"

Tashan nodded, already working on the encryption. "I'm on it, sir."

The operation continued with military precision, each team member methodically searching and securing evidence. Luke oversaw the arrest of the OCG members, ensuring each one was read their rights.

As the operation wound down, George stood in the centre of the warehouse, surveying the success of their raid. They had struck a significant blow to the OCG, disrupting their network and seizing crucial evidence.

"OK, regroup," George ordered. "Let's get these criminals processed and this evidence back to the station."

As they exited the warehouse, the first light of dawn was beginning to break, casting a soft glow over the scene of their victory. George's face was set in a stoic expression, but the satisfaction of a job well done was evident in his eyes.

* * *

The aftermath of the raid on the Schmidt Organised Crime Group warehouse left Detective Inspector George Beaumont with a trove of seized items to examine. In the privacy of his office at the Elland Road police station, he sat surrounded by boxes of financial records, correspondence, and various other documents that could potentially unravel the intricate web of the OCG's operations.

George's eyes were focused, his mind absorbed in the task at hand. He methodically sifted through each piece of evidence, his fingers occasionally pausing to underline or note down critical information. The room was silent except for the soft rustle of paper and the occasional scribble of his pen.

Detective Constable Tashan Blackburn entered, his expression serious. "Find anything useful, sir?"

George looked up, his gaze intense. "It's like solving a complex puzzle, Tashan. But yes, there are patterns emerging. Look at this." He pointed to a series of transactions on a financial record.

Tashan leaned over the desk, studying the document. "Large sums being transferred to off-shore accounts. And these names..." His voice trailed off as he recognised some of them.

"Exactly," George said, a hint of grim satisfaction in his voice. "High-profile individuals, some in positions of power. It seems our OCG has been busy."

The implications were clear. The OCG had entangled itself

with influential figures, making the case more complex and dangerous.

Tashan's brow furrowed. "This is going to ruffle some feathers, sir."

George nodded, a determined look in his eyes. "We knew this wouldn't be easy. But we can't shy away from the truth. We need to follow the evidence, no matter where it leads."

He turned his attention back to the documents, his focus unwavering. The task was daunting, but George was not one to back down from a challenge.

As he continued to work, the pieces of the puzzle slowly began to fit together. Each financial record and each piece of correspondence added another layer to the story of the OCG's reach and influence.

Hours passed, and the only sound in the room was the turning of pages and the occasional murmur of conversation between George and Tashan. The meticulous examination was a testament to George's dedication and expertise.

Finally, George leaned back in his chair, a weary sigh escaping his lips. "We've got enough to start building a case. These links are just the tip of the iceberg."

Tashan nodded in agreement. "It's going to be a long road ahead, sir."

George stood up, stretching his tired muscles. "Yes, but it's a road we have to take. We owe it to the city, to the victims of this OCG."

He gathered the most critical documents, his mind already planning the next steps. "I'll brief DCI Atkinson first thing in the morning. We need to strategise our approach, especially now that we're dealing with high-profile targets." He added, "Go home and rest. Be back here for nine."

Tashan collected the remaining papers, ready to assist George in whatever came next. "Thank you, sir."

Chapter Sixteen

Detective Inspector George Beaumont's stride faltered slightly as he approached Elland Road station. The weight of the night's raid hung heavily on his shoulders, exhaustion seeping into his bones. The station, a looming structure of grey and blue, stood as an unyielding testament to law and order in the heart of Leeds.

Inside, the corridor's fluorescent lights flickered, casting shadows that danced across George's path. He navigated the familiar maze of hallways, each step echoing in the silent building, towards Detective Chief Inspector Alistair Atkinson's office.

Upon reaching the office, George paused, noting the unexpected presence of Detective Constable Tashan Blackburn. Tashan, young and earnest, had a way of wearing his emotions openly. Today, his usual buoyancy was replaced by a sad gravity that mirrored George's own mood.

"Tashan didn't expect you here," George remarked, his voice betraying a hint of surprise as he entered the office.

"Sir, I thought you might need a hand with the briefing," Tashan replied, shifting uncomfortably in his chair.

DCI Atkinson's office, a room steeped in the legacy of countless solved cases, felt oppressively quiet. The walls, lined with shelves of case files and commendations, bore witness to a career's worth of dedication.

Alistair Atkinson, a man whose reputation for tenacity was as well-known as his disdain for small talk, gestured them to sit. "Beaumont, Blackburn, report."

George settled into the chair, his weary mind focusing on the task at hand. "The raid, sir. It was more complicated than we anticipated."

The air in the room seemed to grow denser as George recounted the events. Each detail, from the unexpected resistance they faced to the scant evidence they were able to recover, painted a picture of a plan unravelling.

"And the Schmidt OCG?" Atkinson's voice cut through the narrative, sharp and direct.

George exchanged a glance with Tashan, the unspoken concern evident in their eyes. "We couldn't tie them directly, sir. It's like they knew we were coming."

Atkinson leaned back; his fingers tented in contemplation. "We need something concrete, Beaumont. This case is slipping through our fingers."

George felt the frustration simmering within him. The elusive nature of this investigation was unlike anything he had encountered in his extensive career. "We're doing everything we can, sir. But it's like chasing shadows."

Tashan, usually reserved in the presence of Atkinson, spoke up. "Sir, there's something else. The CCTV footage we recovered—it's not much, but it might give us a lead."

Atkinson's gaze sharpened. "Well? Out with it, lad."

Tashan detailed the grainy footage, describing the vague outline of a figure who could be vital to resolving the mystery. George listened, admiration growing for the young detective's keen eye.

As the meeting concluded, George lingered by the door. The weight of responsibility, the pursuit of justice, felt heavier than ever. "We'll get them, sir," he said, more to himself than to Atkinson.

Atkinson's response, a simple nod, was all the assurance George needed. He stepped out of the office, the image of the shadowy figure from the CCTV footage imprinted in his mind.

* * *

Detective Sergeant Yolanda Williams sat back in her chair, her eyes scanning the timeline laid out on the screen before her. The Homicide and Major Enquiry Team detectives had worked hard on it.

The dim light of the CCTV suite mirrored the complexity of the case she was entangled in. Ethan Turner's last hours were sprawled across her monitor, a digital mosaic of movements and encounters, each piece a clue in the intricate puzzle of his murder.

"Christmas Eve... a time for joy, but not for Ethan," Yolanda murmured, her fingers tracing the timeline. She started from the top, reconstructing Ethan's day in her mind.

On Christmas Eve morning, Ethan's day seemed ordinary; captured in fragments of CCTV footage, he was carrying shopping bags and laughing with friends—typical festive preparations in Leeds city centre.

During the afternoon at a café, surrounded by friends, Ethan was the picture of holiday cheer. Yolanda could almost hear the clatter of dishes, the murmur of conversation, the carefree laughter that must have filled the air.

Early evening, she saw Turner in the pub, where his demeanour changed. Yolanda pictured Ethan there, the light dimmer, the crowd thicker, his laughter a bit forced. A place where troubles could be drowned or deepened.

At eight that night, the argument with Jasmine Clayton, his girlfriend, was a turning point. Yolanda knew how quickly words could escalate, how plans could change on a whim.

Yolanda sifted through the witness statements detailing Ethan's whereabouts between nine and eleven that night. They described Ethan, Neil Roscow, and others hopping between bars. She imagined the blur of faces, the clink of glasses, the increasing haze of alcohol.

The nightclub's CCTV showed Ethan leaving at half eleven, his steps slightly unsteady, his expression clouded.

Yolanda's gaze lingered on the gap. Two hours were lost to the night, two hours where Ethan's fate was sealed, between midnight and two Christmas morning. That's what they needed to find, and fast.

But because they knew roughly when he died, Yolanda checked the CCTV they had on Harehills, and around half two that morning, a disturbance near the ginnel caused a solitary resident to leave their house, startled by a noise but too wary to investigate. Candy had already interviewed the resident and had received nothing to go on.

And then Yolanda knew that by six that Christmas morning, Ethan's body was already staged in the ginnel, a grim Christmas display. Yolanda could almost feel the chill of that discovery, the silent scream of the scene.

The phone rang, breaking the silence. Yolanda answered, her voice steady. "DS Williams."

It was Detective Constable Tashan Blackburn. "DS Williams,

we've got something on Turner's phone records. A text, around 11.45 pm. It might fill in the gap."

Yolanda's heart quickened. "I'll check the CCTV."

She stood up, the timeline etched in her mind.

* * *

In a modest Leeds terrace, Detective Constables Candy Nichols and Jay Scott stood facing a local woman named Anna Greyson, a woman whose eyes flickered with an unease that reached beyond the ordinary. The dim light from the overhead bulb cast more shadows than illumination in the cramped living room, painting a stark contrast with the bright blue of their police vests.

"C'mon, love, anything you can tell us about that night could be crucial," Candy prodded gently, her voice a soft lilt in the tense air.

The woman, wrapped tightly in a shawl despite the stuffiness of the room, wrung her hands. "I... I did see him, the Turner lad, with someone," she began, her voice a hesitant whisper.

Jay leaned forward, his notebook ready. "Can you describe the man he was with?"

She hesitated, her eyes searching the room as if the walls might whisper the answers. "He was tall," she began slowly, her voice barely above a whisper. "Broad and... well, muscled, I suppose. And he had brown hair." Her words trailed off, lost in the air of doubt that filled the cramped room.

Jay scribbled down her description, but his mind was already racing, drawing parallels. Tall, broad, muscled, brown hair, he thought. The description was eerily similar to that of two men who had been looming large in their investigation—Neil and David. Both fit the bill, their physical similarities a nagging complication in the puzzle they were desperately trying to piece together.

Neil and David, two names that had been circulating with increasing frequency in the team's discussions. Both had connections to the case, both had reasons to be in the vicinity and crucially, both shared an almost uncanny resemblance in stature and appearance.

Too much of a coincidence? Jay wondered internally, his detective's mind wrestling with the implications. The similarity in their descriptions was either a red herring or a vital clue, and it was his job, along with the rest of the team, to figure out which.

Candy exchanged a glance with Jay, a silent communication of shared frustration and understanding. She turned back to the witness. "Was there anything distinctive about him? Anything at all?"

The woman's eyes searched the corners of the room as if hoping to find her answer hidden in the cobwebs. "He... he had this air about him like he was used to being in charge. But I didn't see his face clear enough."

Jay scribbled down her words, his expression impassive yet thoughtful. "Did you hear anything? Any part of their conversation?"

The woman shook her head, her eyes now fixed on the worn carpet. "No, they were just... walking by. But something about them didn't feel right. It was in the way they talked, all hushed, like."

Candy sensed the witness's growing discomfort, the fear that seemed to seep into her very bones. "It's alright. You've been very helpful," she reassured, her tone softening.

As they stepped out into the chilly Leeds evening, the sky a blanket of unforgiving grey, Candy let out a slow breath. "That wasn't much to go on."

Jay closed his notebook, his face etched with the day's weariness. "But it's another piece, isn't it?"

They walked in tandem down the narrow street, their footsteps echoing off the rows of terraced houses. The air was heavy with the scent of rain, the kind that threatened to wash away more than just the grime of the city.

"Back to the station, then?" Jay asked, his voice barely louder than the rustle of the wind.

Candy nodded, her mind already racing ahead to the puzzle pieces waiting for them, each one a fragment of a larger, darker picture. "Yeah. There's still work to be done."

* * *

Detective Sergeant Yolanda Williams's eyes were fixed on the grainy footage flickering across the screen.

The image on the monitor showed a figure, unmistakably Ethan Turner, his movements slightly staggered as he approached a parked car in the early hours of Christmas morning. Yolanda leaned closer, her brow furrowing as she scrutinised the vehicle's number plate. The screen's bluish glow cast a pallid light on her face, deepening the lines of concentration etched there.

As the car's doors opened and Ethan slipped inside, Yolanda's fingers danced across the keyboard, capturing the time stamp and vehicle details. She reached for her phone, dialling Detective Inspector George Beaumont's number. Her voice, when she spoke, was a blend of urgency and precision. "Sir, it's Yolanda. You need to see this."

George, having just briefed DCI Atkinson and stepped onto the HMET floor, felt his phone vibrate. The sound of Yolanda's voice instantly sharpened his focus. "What have you got, Yolanda?"

"I've found footage of Ethan, early Christmas morning during the missing hours. He gets into a car, and I've got the plate," Yolanda replied, her words slicing through the static of the line.

George's mind raced as he moved briskly through the bustling floor of the HMET, the buzz of activity around him fading into a distant hum. He ducked into a quieter corner, pulling out his notebook. "Give me the plate number."

Yolanda relayed the details, each digit punctuating the thickening plot. George's pen flew across the page, and then he paused, his instincts kicking in. "I'm running it through the DVLA now. Hold on."

The phone pressed against his ear, and George's other hand worked swiftly on his tablet. The seconds stretched out, laden with anticipation. Then, the DVLA's database yielded its secrets.

"Damn," George muttered under his breath. "The car's registered to Neil Roscow, Ethan's gym buddy."

Yolanda's intake of breath was audible. "Neil? Jesus."

George's mind was already racing ahead. "I need to get an update on the BOLO for Neil. Hang tight, Yolanda. This is big."

He ended the call and dialled Police Sergeant Greenwood's number. The line clicked, and a voice emerged, crackling with static. "PS Greenwood."

"Greenwood, it's DI Beaumont. Any news on the BOLO for

Neil Roscow?"

The response was quick, tinged with the frustration of dead ends. "Nothing yet, sir. He's disappeared."

George's jaw set firmly. "Keep pushing. We've got him tied to Ethan Turner's final hours. He's key to cracking this."

Chapter Seventeen

Detective Inspector George Beaumont stood motionless, his gaze fixed on the house at the end of a quiet Leeds street in Gipton. The evening air was crisp, the onset of night casting shadows across the pavement. Beside him, Detective Constables Jay Scott and Candy Nichols huddled in the unmarked car, their eyes equally trained on the building.

"This is it, then?" Candy's voice was low, barely more than a whisper, as she glanced at the file in her lap.

George nodded. "The last text from Ethan's phone was traced here via cell site analysis."

Jay, his youthful face etched with concentration, peered through the binoculars. "No movement yet. It's been quiet since we got here, boss."

The house, a plain two-story structure, seemed ordinary, almost painfully so. But George knew better. In his years on the force, he had learned that appearances in Leeds often deceived.

"Keep your eyes peeled," George instructed, his voice a steady command. "Whoever's inside could lead us to Ethan's final hours."

The interior of the car was suffused with a tense silence, broken only by the occasional crackle of the radio. Time seemed to slow, each second stretching out as they waited.

Candy's eyes never left the house. "You think this is OCG-related, sir?" she asked, her tone reflecting a mix of curiosity and concern.

"Possibly," George replied his thoughts on the complex web they were untangling. "But there's more to it. Ethan's involvement was deeper than we initially thought."

The house remained still, its windows dark, giving nothing away. George's eyes, however, didn't waver. He had learned patience over his long career and knew the value of waiting for the right moment.

Jay shifted in his seat, breaking the stillness. "If Ethan was meeting someone here, it could have been about the financial scheme we uncovered."

"Exactly," George said, his mind racing with possibilities. "And if Marcus 'The Hawk' Hawkinson is involved, this goes way beyond a simple OCG operation."

The mention of Marcus's name hung in the air, a reminder of the stakes they were dealing with.

The radio crackled to life, startling them. "DI Beaumont, we've got movement inside the house," came the voice of Detective Constable Tashan Blackburn, stationed at a vantage point on the opposite side.

George's hand moved instinctively to his earpiece. "Confirm visual on the individual," he ordered calmly.

"Affirmative, sir. One male, with red hair, matches the description we have for Hawkinson."

George's jaw tightened. "Understood. Maintain surveillance. No one goes in until we have confirmation of identity and backup in place."

Candy glanced at George, her expression a mix of admiration

and concern. "You think Hawkinson's the key to all this?"

George's gaze didn't leave the house. "He's a piece of the puzzle. But there's more to it. Ethan's death, the OCG, the financial schemes—it's all intertwined."

Jay nodded, his youthful eagerness tempered by the gravity of the situation. "So we wait for Hawkinson to make a move?"

"Aye, we wait," George affirmed, his voice steady. The game of cat and mouse was a familiar one, but the rules were constantly changing.

Outside, the night deepened, the streetlights casting a soft glow on the house. Inside the car, the three detectives remained vigilant, each lost in their thoughts, each aware that the night's events could change the course of their investigation.

In the distance, a dog barked, a lone sound in the quiet street. George's eyes remained fixed on the house, his mind working through scenarios, strategies, and outcomes.

* * *

Strangely, Marcus Hawkinson had come voluntarily and was now sitting opposite George in an interview room at Elland Road station. Marcus, a figure of imposing stature, sat with an eerie calmness that belied his reputation in the criminal underworld.

After turning on the tape and reeling off the usual spiel, George leaned forward, his gaze fixed on Marcus. "Mr Hawkinson, your presence at the residence linked to Ethan Turner's last movements raises some questions."

Marcus's eyes, cold and calculating, met George's. "What questions?"

George said, "Let's talk about Neil Roscow and his involvement in the OCG's operations."

A faint smile played on Marcus's lips. "Neil," Marcus began, his voice smooth and controlled, "is a pawn in a much larger game. A game he's no longer useful in."

George's eyes narrowed, sensing the undercurrents in Marcus's words. "And Ethan Turner? How does he fit into this game?"

Marcus leaned back, his gaze unwavering. "Ethan stumbled upon something he shouldn't have. His murder... it was meant to send a message to Neil. But it was not Neil who killed him."

George's pen paused over his notebook. "Are you saying the OCG planned to frame Neil for Ethan's murder?"

Marcus's nod was almost imperceptible. "Neil's unpredictability made him a liability. Framing him for murder would serve two purposes: remove the liability and close the Ethan Turner case."

George absorbed this information, the pieces of the puzzle slowly falling into place. "So, Ethan's death was a strategic move within the OCG?"

"Exactly," Marcus replied. "A power play. And I want out of it."

"Then why dress him up as Santa? Why not just kill him and dispose of his body discretely?"

"I've no idea." Marcus paused. "As I said, I want out of it. So I'm trying to stay out of everything. The less I know, the better."

George's expression hardened. "Why should we believe you, Marcus? You've been at the heart of the OCG's operations for years."

Marcus's eyes flickered, a hint of something deeper behind

them. "Even a hawk can tire of the hunt, Detective. I've seen enough bloodshed."

George studied Marcus for a long moment. "What do you want in return for your cooperation?"

"Protection," Marcus said simply. "And a way out of this life."

The room fell silent, the weight of Marcus's revelation hanging heavily between them. George finally stood up, his decision made. "We'll need everything you have on the OCG, Marcus. Names, operations, locations."

Marcus nodded, a trace of relief in his eyes. "You'll have it all, Detective."

As George left the interview room to speak with his superiors, his mind was racing. The case had taken a significant turn, and Marcus Hawkinson, once a man shrouded in fear and respect, was now their unlikely ally.

* * *

Detective Inspector George Beaumont watched as his team, usually a well-oiled machine, showed signs of strain. Detective Sergeant Yolanda Williams and Detective Constable Tashan Blackburn were locked in a heated discussion, their voices low but intense.

"We're chasing shadows, Sarge. Every lead turns to dust," Tashan said, frustration lacing his words.

Yolanda, usually the epitome of calm, shot back, "We can't afford to lose focus now. There's more at play here than we're seeing."

Across the room, Detective Constable Candy Nichols leaned against her desk, her expression troubled. "What if we're too late?" she murmured, more to herself than anyone else. "What if Neil's already been dealt with by the OCG?"

George, taking in the scene, knew they needed to regroup. "Alright, team meeting, ten minutes," he announced. "Have a drink, eat some food, but come back refreshed.

The team gathered a circle of weary but determined faces. George stood at the head of the room, his presence commanding attention.

"We've hit a wall," he began, his tone steady. "But we can't let frustration cloud our judgment. This case... it's a maze, and we're close to the centre."

Yolanda nodded, her earlier fire subdued. "We need to reassess our approach. Double-check our leads, re-examine the evidence."

Tashan, running a hand through his hair, added, "And what about Marcus Hawkinson? He's a key piece in this puzzle."

George's gaze swept over the team. "Marcus is our wildcard. But our immediate concern is finding Neil Roscow. Alive."

Candy's voice was hesitant but firm. "Sir, if the OCG has targeted Neil, we might be running out of time."

George nodded, acknowledging her point. "Time is not on our side. But we can't rush in mindlessly. We need to be methodical, precise."

The room fell silent; each member was lost in their thoughts. George continued, "Let's go back to the basics. Review everything from the beginning. We might have missed something in our initial assessments."

Yolanda's eyes met George's, a silent promise of unwavering support. "We'll turn this case inside out if we have to."

Tashan, his earlier frustration now channelled into determination, said, "I agree. We're not letting this case go cold.

Not on our watch."

Candy, though still worried, nodded in agreement. Her resolve, like that of her colleagues, was clear.

George looked around at his team, a sense of pride mingling with the weight of responsibility. "We're up against a formidable enemy. But we've got something they don't—a commitment to the truth."

As the meeting dispersed, each member returned to their tasks, a renewed sense of purpose in their steps. George watched them, knowing the road ahead was fraught with uncertainty. But he also knew that his team was the best of the best, and together, they would navigate the treacherous waters of this investigation.

* * *

Detective Inspector Luke Mason sat alone in his office, the gentle hum of the police station in the background forming a comforting yet distant soundtrack. The room was a testament to his long and storied career in the police. The walls were adorned with commendations and certificates, each a silent witness to his years of dedication and hard-won victories.

Luke's gaze wandered around the room, settling on a photograph framed in simple wood. It was an image of his younger self, fresh-faced and eager, just starting in his career. He picked it up, his fingers tracing the glass as a wave of nostalgia washed over him. The young man in the photo had no idea of the complexities and moral ambiguities he would face in the years to come.

The room was quiet, save for the ticking of a small clock on his desk—a rhythmic reminder of the passing of time. Luke's eyes moved from the photo to the other mementoes scattered around the office: a commendation for bravery here, a group photo from a successful case there. Each item held a story, a memory of a time when the lines between right and wrong seemed clearer, more defined.

As Luke sat there, lost in his thoughts, the weight of his experience hung heavy in the air. He had seen so much over the years: the best and worst of humanity, the grey areas where good and evil blurred. His career had been a constant battle between the pursuit of justice and the realities of a flawed world.

He set the photo down and leaned back in his chair, his eyes closing momentarily. In the stillness of the room, he allowed himself a rare moment of introspection. He thought of the young detectives he had mentored, especially George Beaumont. George, with his fierce determination and unyielding sense of justice, reminded Luke so much of himself at that age.

But there was a hardness in George that Luke recognised, a rigidity forged by personal demons and a relentless drive to right the wrongs of the world. Luke knew all too well the toll that this job could take on a person's soul. He had seen it in others and felt it in himself.

Chapter Eighteen

Upstairs in the IT Forensics Lab, Detective Inspector George Beaumont and Forensic IT Specialist Karen Willis huddled over a computer screen. The room was stark, illuminated by the cold glow of monitors displaying lines of data and digital reconstructions.

Karen's fingers hovered over the keyboard, her expression a mix of concentration and apprehension. "I've managed to recover a series of deleted messages from Ethan Turner's phone," she began, her voice steady despite the gravity of her findings.

George leaned in closer, his eyes scanning the screen. "What do they tell us, Karen?"

"There's a series of exchanges between Ethan and Jasmine Clayton, his girlfriend." Karen clicked, bringing up a string of messages on the screen. "They discuss an illegal financial scheme, likely money laundering, connected to the OCG."

George's brow furrowed as he read the messages. "He was in deep," he muttered, more to himself than to Karen.

"Quite deep," Karen agreed. "And it seems he was planning to get out." She pointed to a message where Ethan vaguely mentioned exposing the scheme if he couldn't leave safely.

George straightened up, his mind racing with the implications. "This could be why the OCG targeted him. He became a liability."

Karen nodded, her gaze still fixed on the screen. "Ethan's fear comes through in these messages. He knew the risks."

"It's also the reason why he was working as a shopping centre Santa," George said aloud. It linked Edward Beaumont to the OCG, too.

The room fell silent, save for the soft hum of computer fans. George paced slowly, his thoughts swirling. "We need to talk to Jasmine again. There's more to her story than she's told us."

Karen clicked through the messages, her expression sombre. "If Ethan was threatening to expose the OCG, it puts Jasmine in a dangerous position as well."

George stopped, turning to face Karen. "Keep digging into these messages, Karen. Anything else Ethan might have left behind could be key."

Karen's response was a simple nod, her focus unwavering as she delved back into the data.

Back in the Incident Room, the team was absorbed in their various tasks, the air thick with determination and focus. George cleared his throat, capturing their attention. "We've got a new lead," he announced, his voice carrying the weight of his experience and authority.

He briefed them on the recovered messages, watching as expressions of realization and concern crossed their faces. "This changes our perspective. We need to re-evaluate our suspects, our leads... everything."

Detective Sergeant Yolanda Williams nodded, her expression steely. "We'll start by revisiting Jasmine Clayton. She knows more than she's letting on."

Detective Constable Tashan Blackburn added, "And we need to keep a closer eye on the OCG's movements. If they feel cornered, they might act out."

George surveyed his team, a sense of pride mingling with the gravity of the situation. "We're up against a formidable enemy, but we've got the truth on our side. Let's get to work."

* * *

Later, George stood in the Incident Room, his eyes fixed on the map spread out before him. The location pinpointed was an abandoned warehouse on the outskirts of the city, its image grainy on the satellite photo. Beside him, Forensic IT Specialist Karen Willis adjusted her glasses, her voice steady as she presented her findings.

"The geolocation data from Ethan's phone places him at this warehouse on Christmas Eve, the night he disappeared," Karen said, her finger tracing the route on the map.

George's brow furrowed, the pieces of the puzzle slowly fitting together in his mind. "A warehouse we thought was insignificant," he mused, his voice a deep rumble. "It's been used by the OCG for their discreet meetings. We've never linked it to them before. It's always appeared abandoned."

Karen nodded, her expression solemn.

A heavy silence filled the room as the implication of this revelation sank in. George broke the silence, his decision clear. "We need to talk to Marcus again. He might shed more light on this."

Detective Sergeant Yolanda Williams, who had been quietly observing, spoke up. "But why would Ethan be there? And with Marcus?"

George leaned back against the table, his gaze distant. "The messages we recovered suggest Ethan was planning to leave the OCG. And we know that Marcus was, too. This meeting could have been about their exit strategy."

"Then why didn't Marcus tell us this when we interviewed him?" asked Jay.

"I don't know, Jay, but it might be because we didn't ask him that specific question," said George.

The team exchanged glances, the gravity of the situation evident in their expressions. Detective Constable Tashan Blackburn, his youthful face marked with concern, added, "If they were both planning to leave the OCG, that puts them both in danger."

George nodded, his thoughts aligning with Tashan's. "Exactly. We need to understand what happened at that warehouse. It could be the key to unravelling this entire case."

The team stood in contemplative silence, each member processing the information and its potential implications. Luckily, they still had Marcus at the station, his deal being checked by lawyers and higher-ups in the police.

George's voice cut through the quiet. "Let's interview Marcus. We need answers, and we need them now."

The interview room door opened to reveal Marcus 'The Hawk' Hawkinson sitting calmly, his presence dominating the small room.

"Marcus," George began, his voice measured, "we know about the warehouse. We know you were there with Ethan."

Marcus met George's gaze, his expression unreadable. "OK, Detective, but be aware you're delving into dangerous waters."

George leaned forward, his eyes locked on Marcus's. "Why

were you there, Marcus? What was the meeting about?"

Marcus's gaze shifted, a flicker of something crossing his face. "It was about freedom, George. Freedom from the life we've been trapped in."

The room grew still, the weight of Marcus's words hanging in the air. George knew they were on the brink of uncovering something monumental. "We need to know everything, Marcus. Every detail could lead us to the truth."

Marcus sighed, a look of resignation on his face. "Very well. But understand, the truth is a double-edged sword."

* * *

Luke Mason leaned against the Incident Room's wall, his arms folded, observing the scene before him. His eyes, seasoned with years of experience, lingered on the younger detectives, Tashan Blackburn and Candy Nichols, who were animatedly discussing the latest developments in the case. Their energy was palpable, their gestures emphatic, their voices intermingling in a chorus of theories and conjectures.

There was a bittersweet expression on Luke's face, a mixture of pride and a faint, unspoken melancholy. He watched as Tashan, with a hunger in his eyes, laid out his analysis on the map, his finger tracing the routes and locations with precision. Candy, equally engaged, countered with her insights, her voice strong and confident.

The room was alive with the buzz of activity, phones ringing, keyboards clattering, and the occasional raised voice as frustration or excitement took hold. It was a scene Luke had been part of for decades, one that had defined his life. But now, standing on the periphery, he felt an unfamiliar sense of detachment, a quiet realisation that his time in this world was drawing to a close.

He remembered his early days on the force, the rush of adrenaline, the relentless pursuit of justice, the camaraderie. He had been like Tashan and Candy once, full of ambition and determination, but time had a way of changing things, of mellowing out the fiery passion into a steady, glowing ember.

A faint smile touched Luke's lips as he saw Tashan's animated hand gestures, mirroring his own from years gone by. He could see his younger self in these detectives, in their unwavering commitment to the job, their belief that they could make a difference. It was heartening yet poignant, a reminder of the relentless march of time.

His gaze shifted around the room, taking in the faces of the team. Each one was focused, driven by a shared purpose, a collective desire to bring closure to a case that had gripped the city with fear. Luke felt a surge of pride, knowing he had played a role in shaping some of these detectives, in guiding them through the complex and often treacherous path of criminal investigation.

But along with pride, there was a tinge of sadness. Mason knew that soon, these halls, these faces, would continue without him. The thought was sobering, a stark reminder of his impending retirement. His role had been his identity, his life. Stepping away from it felt like leaving behind a part of himself.

Lost in thought, Luke was startled when Jay approached him, his expression one of concern. "You alright, Sarge... I mean, sir?" Jay asked, his voice tinged with genuine care.

Luke nodded, pulling himself back to the present. "Just reminiscing, lad. You never really prepare for this moment, you know, stepping away from all this," he gestured around the room.

* * *

"Let's cut to the chase, Marcus," George began, his voice steady. "What is this freedom and truth you speak of?"

Marcus, a figure who commanded respect even in handcuffs, leaned back. "It was about getting out, George. We both wanted out of the OCG. It's not the life I want any more."

George's eyes narrowed, analysing every word. "And Ethan? Why did he want out?"

"He got in too deep with the money laundering scheme," Marcus replied, a hint of remorse flickering in his eyes. "The risk got too high, even for him."

George leaned forward, his gaze unflinching. "Was he planning to expose the OCG?"

Marcus nodded slowly. "Ethan had evidence against the group. He thought it was his ticket out, a way to keep them off his back."

Detective Sergeant Yolanda Williams, sitting beside George, interjected, "So, he became a liability to the OCG."

"Exactly," Marcus confirmed. "In our world, liabilities don't last long."

George scribbled notes before looking up again. "Tell us about the power struggle within the OCG."

Marcus sighed, the weight of his secrets apparent. "There's a faction within the group that wants to change the status quo. Ethan's death was a move in this internal chess game. They're cleaning house, getting rid of anyone who's not fully in their pocket."

Detective Constable Tashan Blackburn, who had been listening intently, asked, "Who's leading this faction?"

Marcus hesitated, his loyalty to the underworld code battling with his desire for a new life. Finally, he said, "I can't give you names, not yet. But they're high up, and they're ruthless."

George sat back, processing the information. "Your plan to leave the OCG, how does that fit into all this?"

"I've seen enough blood, George," Marcus said, his voice tinged with a rare vulnerability. "I want out, but it's not easy to just walk away from the OCG."

Yolanda leaned in. "So, you and Ethan were planning to leave together?"

"In a way," Marcus replied. "Our paths aligned. He had the evidence; I had the means to disappear."

George's thoughts were racing. "And now Ethan's dead because of it."

Marcus nodded solemnly. "Ethan underestimated how far they would go to keep him silent."

The room fell silent, the gravity of Marcus's revelations sinking in. George finally broke the silence. "We need to protect you, Marcus. If what you're saying is true, you're in as much danger as Ethan was."

Marcus's gaze met George's. "I know the risks, Detective. But I'm tired of looking over my shoulder."

George stood up, signalling the end of the interrogation. "We'll arrange for your protection. But in return, we need everything you know about the OCG's operations."

Marcus nodded in agreement, a man resigned to his fate.

As George and his team left the interrogation room, he called for a meeting. The team gathered around the incident room table, each member aware that the case had taken a significant turn.

"We've got a new angle," George announced, filling them in on Marcus's testimony. "Ethan's murder was more than just a hit. It was part of an internal struggle within the OCG."

Yolanda looked up from her notes. "So, Neil Roscow might be a red herring."

"Perhaps," George said. "But we can't rule him out yet. We need to dig deeper into this power struggle Marcus mentioned."

Tashan added, "If we can identify the faction leaders, we might be able to anticipate their next move."

George nodded. "Exactly. We need to stay one step ahead."

Candy, who had been quiet, spoke up. "What about Jasmine Clayton? She must know more than she's told us."

George agreed. "We'll need to bring her in again. But carefully. We don't want to spook whoever's watching her."

The team dispersed each member with a renewed sense of purpose.

Chapter Nineteen

Detective Inspector George Beaumont stood at the head of the Incident Room in Elland Road Police Station, his team gathered around the table, their faces a blend of determination and concern. The air was thick with the anticipation of the next phase in their intricate investigation.

"Right," George began, his voice carrying a sense of urgency. "We need to bring Jasmine Clayton in for another interview, but we have to be cautious. If our suspicions are correct, she's being watched."

Detective Sergeant Yolanda Williams, always the voice of reason, spoke up. "How do you propose we do this, sir? A direct approach might tip off whoever's keeping tabs on her."

George nodded, acknowledging her point. "We'll have to be discreet. Candy, I want you and Jay to bring her in. Make it look like a routine follow-up, nothing that would raise any alarms."

Detective Constable Candy Nichols, her expression serious, replied, "Understood, sir. We'll handle it."

With their instructions clear, Candy and Detective Constable Jay Scott left the station and headed towards Jasmine Clayton's residence. The city of Leeds bustled around them, a stark contrast to the gravity of their task.

Arriving at Jasmine's apartment, they maintained a casual behaviour. Candy knocked on the door, her heart racing with the uncertainty of what they might uncover.

Jasmine opened the door, her face a picture of surprise. "Detectives? Is everything OK?"

Candy offered a reassuring smile. "We just need to ask you a few more questions, Jasmine. Routine follow-up."

Jasmine hesitated for a moment before nodding. "Sure, let me grab my coat."

As they escorted Jasmine to their unmarked car, Candy and Jay exchanged subtle glances, aware of the importance of their actions. The ride back to the station was quiet, Jasmine sitting in the backseat, lost in her thoughts.

Back at the station, George was waiting. He greeted Jasmine with professional warmth. "Thank you for coming in, Jasmine. We just need to clarify a few details."

In the interview room, Jasmine sat across from George and Yolanda, her hands clasped tightly in her lap. George, after turning on the recorder and reeling off the typical spiel, began the interview with routine questions, easing into the more critical aspects of the case.

"Jasmine, we need to understand your relationship with Ethan Turner," George said, his tone gentle yet probing. "Was there anything he might have shared with you about his activities outside of work?"

Jasmine's eyes flickered with a mix of fear and uncertainty. "Ethan was a private person. He... he didn't share much about what he did outside of our relationship."

George noted her hesitation. "We believe Ethan was involved in something dangerous. Anything you can tell us could be crucial."

Jasmine took a deep breath, her resolve wavering. "He mentioned meetings late at night, but he never said with whom. I didn't ask. I was scared to know."

Yolanda leaned forward, her voice soft yet insistent. "Cut the crap, Jasmine."

Jasmine's gaze drifted away, lost in thought, as a memory from Christmas Eve surfaced unbidden. The room around her faded into the background as she relived the moment with vivid clarity.

It was a cold, festive evening, and Jasmine and Ethan were in his apartment, the sound of distant carolers seeping through the walls. The room was warmly lit and adorned with Christmas decorations.

"Ethan, there's something I need to tell you," Jasmine began, her voice trembling with a mix of fear and regret.

Ethan, sensing the seriousness in her tone, turned to face her. "What is it, Jasmine?"

She took a deep breath, gathering her courage. "I'm not who you think I am. The OCG sent me... to keep an eye on you."

Ethan's face hardened, his anger palpable. "You've been spying on me? All this time?"

Jasmine's eyes filled with tears. "I was, at first. But Ethan, I swear, what I feel for you now... it's real. I never meant to fall for you, but I did. I'm so, so sorry."

Ethan paced the room, his hands clenched into fists. "How can I trust anything you say? How do I know this isn't another lie?"

Jasmine reached out to him, a plea in her eyes. "I understand why you're angry. But my feelings for you... they're the one true thing in all this mess."

Ethan stopped, his expression torn between hurt and confusion. "This changes everything, Jasmine. I don't know what to believe any more."

Jasmine's voice was barely a whisper. "I understand if you can't forgive me. But please, believe that I love you."

Back in the present, Jasmine's eyes refocused on George and Yolanda, the memory fading but leaving a trail of pain and regret. She wiped away a tear that had escaped down her cheek.

"I need to tell you the truth about Christmas Eve."

George, observing her emotional turmoil, spoke softly. "What happened that night, Jasmine?"

"I told him the truth about why I initially became his girlfriend." Jasmine swallowed hard, her voice breaking. "He was angry, understandably. But I told him the truth about how I felt. I hoped he would understand."

Yolanda leaned in, her tone gentle. "And did he?"

Jasmine shook her head, a sense of loss in her eyes. "We never got the chance to resolve it. After that night, everything changed."

George and Yolanda exchanged a glance, the significance of her statement not lost on them. "So you were sent by someone to keep an eye on him?"

Jasmine nodded.

"Is there anything else you haven't been honest with us about?"

"No, nothing else." She paused. "That was earlier Christmas Eve. Later, I called him, and we argued again at eight. It had nothing to do with him playing Santa Claus. That was a lie."

"You're sure there's nothing else?" asked George.

"I'm sure."

"Jasmine," George continued, "we found your DNA at one of the crime scenes. If there's nothing else, how can you explain that?"

Jasmine's face paled. "I... I have no idea how that could be. I've never been to any crime scenes."

Putting that answer to one side for now, George, with a attitude that was both firm and empathetic, leaned forward. "Jasmine, you mentioned Ethan had meetings late at night. Did he ever mention anyone else involved? Any names that kept coming up?"

Jasmine hesitated, her eyes flickering with recollection. "He was always vague about it. But he mentioned a 'benefactor' once or twice. Someone who was backing him, I think. He never said a name, though."

Yolanda, who had been taking meticulous notes, looked up. "And these meetings, did he ever say where they took place?"

"No, he was very secretive about that," Jasmine replied, a tinge of frustration in her voice. "I always got the feeling he was protecting me from something despite me keeping that terrible secret from him."

George's thoughts were racing. A benefactor. Could this be linked to Dr Ross or even Edward Beaumont? The pieces were starting to form a disturbing picture.

Yolanda, picking up on George's train of thought, asked, "Did Ethan ever display any unusual behaviour after these meetings? Anything that seemed out of the ordinary for him?"

Jasmine nodded slowly. "He would be anxious, on edge. More than once, he came back looking... frightened, almost."

The detectives exchanged a glance, the significance of her statement not lost on them. George's voice was thoughtful when he spoke again. "It sounds like Ethan was involved in something much bigger than he anticipated. Something dangerous."

Jasmine's hands were trembling slightly now. "I just thought he was stressed from work. I never imagined..."

Her voice trailed off, the burden of her realisation evident in her eyes. George and Yolanda could see the pieces falling into place for her, the horrific understanding of her involvement, however unwitting, in a much larger game. And in Ethan's murder.

"We need you to tell us who in the OCG gave you the job of keeping an eye on Ethan, Jasmine," said George.

Jasmine's hands twisted in her lap, her eyes flitting between George and Yolanda. "It wasn't like that... not exactly," she began, her voice faltering. "The OCG didn't directly hire me. It was more like... they found me."

George leaned forward slightly, his interest piqued. "Found you? How? Who?"

Jasmine took a deep breath, steadying her nerves. "I was in a difficult place financially, and I got involved in some minor illegal activities. That's when they approached me. A man, he never gave his name, but he knew everything about me. My debts, my activities..."

"Describe the man for me, Jasmine," George prompted, his voice calm yet commanding.

Jasmine hesitated, her eyes searching the space in front of her as if the details were written in the air. "He was... ordinary in appearance. Not someone you'd notice in a crowd," she started, her voice tinged with the effort of recollection.

"Can you be more specific? Height, build, age?" George prodded gently, encouraging her to delve deeper into her memory.

"He was tall, I suppose. Not giant. His build was muscled, but not in a way that stood out," Jasmine continued, her gaze now distant, lost in the memory.

"And his age?" Yolanda Williams, sitting beside George, asked softly.

Jasmine paused, considering. "He was middle-aged, maybe in his mid-forties. His hair was brown, but I remember seeing flecks of grey at the temples."

George nodded, absorbing every detail. "What about his face? Any distinguishing features?"

Jasmine closed her eyes for a moment, concentrating. "His face was... unremarkable. But his eyes were a deep blue, cold, and calculating. It's the one thing that really stood out to me. He always wore a suit, always immaculate, like he took great care in his appearance."

"Did he have an accent? Anything that might indicate where he's from?" George asked, aware that every little detail could be a vital clue.

"Not really, no distinct accent. His voice was normal, Yorkshire. He was careful with his words, always measured and precise," Jasmine described, her brows furrowed in concentration.

Yolanda, her pen poised over her notebook, asked, "Did you ever meet with this man again? Any more instructions or payments?"

"A few times," Jasmine admitted. "In public places, always different. I never knew when he would contact me. He paid me in cash and said it was best I didn't know too much for my own safety. He said it was safer that way. As for contact, he always said he would reach out to me when needed," Jasmine answered, a hint of fear creeping into her voice as she recalled the encounters.

George's expression hardened slightly. "Did this man give you any specific instructions? Anything about what to look for or report back?"

"He was vague," Jasmine replied. "Just to keep them informed if Ethan did anything unusual, met with anyone new. I didn't know it would lead to this... to murder."

George leaned back, his mind racing with the implications of her statements. "Did Ethan ever suspect you were reporting on him?"

Jasmine's eyes welled up with tears. "I don't think so. I tried to keep it as normal as possible. But when I told him the truth that night, he was devastated. I think he felt betrayed, not just by me but by everything he thought he knew."

The room fell silent for a moment, the weight of her confession hanging heavily. George finally spoke, his voice a mix of sympathy and professionalism. "Jasmine, this information is crucial. It helps us understand the network we're dealing with. Your cooperation is invaluable."

Jasmine wiped a tear from her cheek, her voice barely a whisper. "I just want to make things right, somehow."

The interview wrapped up with George assuring Jasmine that they would do everything in their power to get to the bottom of this. As she was escorted out of the room, George turned to Yolanda, his expression grave.

"We're dealing with something much bigger than a series of isolated incidents," he said. "This benefactor Jasmine mentioned and the fear Ethan exhibited... It's all pointing to a larger conspiracy."

Yolanda, ever the pragmatic one, replied, "We need to tread

carefully, sir. If there's someone pulling the strings from the shadows, they won't take kindly to us messing up their plans."

George nodded, a sense of determination setting in. "We'll unravel this, Yolanda. No matter how deep we have to dig."

* * *

The day's events had taken a toll on George as he sat alone in the quiet of his home. The clock on the mantle ticked steadily, marking the passage of time. His gaze was fixed on the dancing flames in the fireplace, but his mind was far away, entrenched in the complexities of the case he was unwinding.

Isabella, his partner, entered the room, her presence a comforting one. "You coming to bed?" she asked, her voice soft with concern.

George looked up, managing a weary smile. "Soon."

Isabella sat beside him, her hand finding his. "You need to sleep."

"I know." He nodded, the weight of responsibility evident in his eyes. "It's just... it's bigger than we thought, Izzy. The OCG has its claws in deep. We're not just up against criminals; we're up against a system."

Isabella squeezed his hand, understanding the gravity of his words. "But if anyone can get to the bottom of this, it's you, George."

George's gaze returned to the fire, the flickering flames reflecting in his eyes. "I keep thinking about the victims, the lives ruined by these criminals. We owe it to them to bring the OCG down."

Isabella leaned her head on his shoulder. "And you will. You have the determination and the skill. Just remember, you're not alone in this."

George let out a slow breath. "I know. It's just... the deeper we go, the more dangerous it becomes."

The silence that followed was a comfortable one, filled with mutual understanding and shared commitment to justice. Isabella's presence was a reminder of the life outside his work, a life that provided balance and perspective.

"This case... It's going to test the team and me, Izzy. But I'm ready for it," George said, a renewed determination in his voice.

Isabella looked up at him, her eyes full of admiration. "I know you are. And I'll be here every step of the way."

Chapter Twenty

In the bustling HMET floor of Elland Road Police Station, the arrival of Dr Samuel Hughes, a forensic toxicologist, cut through the usual hum of activity. Detective Inspector George Beaumont, sensing the gravity of the moment, quickly convened an emergency meeting in the cramped conference room. The team gathered around the table, their expressions a mix of anticipation and concern.

Dr Hughes, a man whose presence commanded respect, adjusted his glasses as he faced the team. "Thank you for seeing me on such short notice," he began, his voice calm yet carrying an undercurrent of urgency.

George nodded, his gaze intense. "What have you found, Dr Hughes?"

"The toxicology reports on the Santa Claus victims," Dr Hughes started, pausing to ensure he had everyone's attention. "They've all been poisoned with Digitalis."

A murmur rippled through the room. George leaned forward, his brow furrowed. "All of them? What do you mean?"

Dr Hughes shook his head. "It appears all four Santa Claus victims, plus Oliver Hughes from a decade ago, were poisoned with Digitalis."

The revelation hung heavily in the air, and George's mind

raced. "But why? Why use poison?"

Dr Hughes adjusted his spectacles, a gesture that bespoke his meticulous nature. "Digitalis is not just any poison. It's subtle and hard to detect unless you're specifically looking for it. It seems the killer, or killers, wanted the deaths to appear natural or caused by other means."

Detective Inspector Luke Mason interjected, "So, the previous assumptions about the cause of death were incorrect?"

"Exactly," Dr Hughes confirmed. "The symptoms of Digitalis poisoning can easily be misinterpreted. For example, skin discolouration could be explained as bruising." He paused. "It's a clever choice for a murderer aiming to mislead."

George's hands clenched into fists under the table. The implications were significant—they weren't just dealing with a series of killings; they were dealing with a methodical, calculating murderer.

Detective Constable Tashan Blackburn leaned in, his youthful face etched with confusion. "But why now? Why have we only found out about this after a decade?"

Dr Hughes pondered the question, his eyes reflecting years of experience. "I think that's obvious, is it not?"

George stood up, pacing the length of the room. It meant that Dr Ross was definitely involved in the previous four murders. He said this to the room, and Dr Hughes nodded. "It also most likely means Christian Ross was an OCG member."

The team watched as George processed this new information, his usually composed demeanour giving way to a rare display of agitation.

Luke, ever the voice of reason, added, "We'll need to liaise with the coroner's office and review the post-mortem reports of all the victims."

"And the Digitalis," George mused aloud. "Where did it come from? How did the killer obtain it?"

Dr Hughes interjected, "That, Detective, is another puzzle. Digitalis isn't commonly found. It requires specific knowledge to use it effectively."

"So, Digitalis," George said, his voice tinged with contemplation. "Tell me about it."

Dr Hughes adjusted his glasses, nodding in agreement. "It's derived from the foxglove plant. It's a potent cardiac glycoside used medically for heart conditions. But in high doses, it's lethal."

George leaned forward, his interest piqued. "Lethal, how?"

"It increases the force of heart contractions," Dr Hughes explained. "An overdose can lead to cardiac arrest. The symptoms — nausea, vomiting, diarrhoea, confusion, blurred vision, and changes in colour perception — are often mistaken for other ailments."

George rubbed his chin, deep in thought. "So, detecting it in toxicology tests..."

"It requires specific screening," Dr Hughes interjected. "Because of its therapeutic use, it's not typically screened for in standard autopsies."

George's gaze was steely, his mind racing with the implications. "Who could get their hands on such a substance?"

Dr Hughes listed the possibilities. "Home cultivation is one, though it requires botanical knowledge. Theft from a medical facility is another. It could also be purchased online through unregulated marketplaces. But the most plausible scenario is pharmaceutical theft."

George's thoughts immediately turned to Dr Christian Ross, the pathologist involved in the previous Santa Claus murders.

"Could Ross have had access to Digitalis?"

"Absolutely," Dr Hughes affirmed. "Pathologists are involved in patient care and research. They have access to a range of pharmaceuticals, including Digitalis, for testing and analysis."

George sat back, his mind a whirlwind of scenarios. "So, Ross could've used Digitalis without raising suspicion. He knew not to screen for it and could explain away the symptoms."

"Exactly," Dr Hughes agreed. "It's a poisoner's dream substance, in a way."

The room was silent for a moment, the weight of the discovery settling over them. George finally stood up, pacing slowly. "This changes our perspective on the entire case. If Ross was using Digitalis, and now our current victims are poisoned with the same substance..."

"It suggests a pattern, a connection," Dr Hughes said, finishing George's thought.

George stopped pacing, turning to face the toxicologist. "We need to re-examine all the evidence, all the autopsy reports. We might have overlooked something crucial."

Dr Hughes nodded. "I'll coordinate with the coroner's office. We need to scrutinise every detail."

As Dr Hughes left the room, George remained, lost in thought. The revelation about Digitalis opened up new avenues in the investigation, avenues that were dark and treacherous. He knew they were up against a cunning adversary, one who understood the art of deception and murder. But also someone who had intricate knowledge of medicine.

* * *

Later, in the Incident Room, Detective Inspector George Beaumont and his team gathered around the cluttered table, the air heavy with the gravity of their latest revelation. The walls, lined with photographs and string-connected evidence, seemed to close in on them, a stark reminder of the case's complexity.

George, standing at the head of the table, looked at each member of his team. "If Ross was using Digitalis, he must've had an accomplice. It's not a substance you use casually."

Detective Inspector Luke Mason, his brows knitted in thought, leaned forward. "You're thinking Dr Lindsey Yardley?"

George nodded slowly. "She had access to Digitalis through Ross before and now in her role as a pathologist. It's a starting point."

Detective Constable Tashan Blackburn, his youthful face etched with concentration, chimed in, "But Dr Yardley's reputation is spotless. Approaching her could be tricky."

"That's true," George acknowledged, his gaze thoughtful. "We need to tread carefully. We can't afford to tip her off or cause undue alarm."

Detective Constable Candy Nichols, leaning against the wall, added, "If we're wrong about her, it could compromise the entire investigation."

Luke tapped his pen against his notepad. "We could start by discreetly reviewing her professional and personal connections. See if there's any link to Ross or the OCG."

Tashan nodded in agreement. "And cross-reference her movements with the timeline of the murders. If there's a pattern, it might give us something concrete."

George absorbed their suggestions, his mind a chessboard of

strategies. "Right. Let's divide the tasks. Candy and Tashan, you two take the lead on cross-referencing Dr Yardley's movements. DI Mason, work with the IT team on digging deeper into her connections."

The team nodded, a silent agreement of their roles in the intricate dance of investigation.

George's voice held a note of caution as he concluded the meeting. "Remember, we're working with suppositions. Until we have solid evidence, Dr Yardley remains a person of interest, nothing more."

As the team dispersed to their respective tasks in the outer shared office, George remained at the table, his thoughts lingering on the potential implications of their findings. The revelation about Digitalis not only pointed to a methodical killer but also to a broader network of deceit and betrayal.

Once George had left, Detective Sergeant Yolanda Williams sat alone, surrounded by stacks of files and flickering computer screens. Her eyes, sharp and focused, scanned through the reams of evidence, searching for any overlooked thread that might connect Dr Lindsey Yardley to their sprawling investigation.

The room was silent except for the soft hum of computers and the occasional rustle of paper as Yolanda methodically worked her way through the files. She paused occasionally, her mind weaving together the fragments of information, looking for a pattern, a clue, anything that might hint at Dr Yardley's involvement.

Meanwhile, in his office, Detective Inspector George Beaumont sat behind his desk, a furrow of concern etched into his brow. The revelation about Digitalis and its potential link to Dr Yardley weighed heavily on him. His gaze drifted to the window, where the cityscape of Leeds stretched out, a maze of streets and secrets.

George's thoughts were interrupted by a knock on the door. "Come in," he called, his voice steady despite the turmoil in his mind.

Detective Constable Tashan Blackburn entered a sheaf of papers in his hand. "Sir, I've been looking into Dr Yardley's background. There's nothing so far that directly ties her to the OCG or Ross."

George nodded, his expression thoughtful. "Thank you, Tashan. Keep digging. We can't afford to overlook anything."

Tashan hesitated before speaking again. "Sir, if Yardley is innocent, this could damage her reputation and career."

George leaned back in his chair, aware of the delicate balance they needed to maintain. "I know, Tashan. We have to tread carefully. But we can't ignore a potential lead, no matter how sensitive."

"But there are other pathologists, sir, why Lindsey?"

"Christian was her mentor, and she often deputised for him," George said. "If nothing comes of it, we'll look elsewhere."

Tashan nodded and left George's office without a word. The news was troubling everyone.

Back in the Incident Room, Yolanda continued her meticulous examination of the evidence. Her eyes landed on a series of emails between Dr Yardley and an unknown contact. The correspondence was cryptic, but something about it niggled at the back of her mind.

She leaned closer to the screen, her fingers tapping on the keyboard as she cross-referenced dates and times with the timeline of the murders. A slow realisation began to dawn on her, the pieces of the puzzle starting to fit together in a new and unexpected way.

In his office, George's phone rang, jolting him from his thoughts. It was Yolanda. "Sir, I think I've found something. There's a pattern in Yardley's emails that correlates with the timeline of the murders. It's tenuous, but it's there."

George's pulse quickened. "Good work, Yolanda. Bring everything you have. We'll meet in the Incident Room."

As Yolanda and George convened in the Incident Room, the evidence laid out before them, the gravity of their discovery hung in the air. They were on the brink of a breakthrough, but the path forward was fraught with uncertainty.

"We need to approach this cautiously," George said, his voice low. "If we're wrong about Yardley, the consequences could be severe."

Yolanda nodded in agreement, her expression resolute. "But if we're right, we could be one step closer to solving this case."

The room fell silent as they both contemplated their next move. Outside, the city of Leeds continued its ceaseless rhythm, unaware of the drama unfolding within the walls of the police station.

Inside, George Beaumont and Yolanda Williams stood at the heart of the investigation, their determination unwavering as they navigated the complex web of crime and deception, a testament to their commitment to uncovering the truth, no matter how hidden it might be.

Chapter Twenty-one

Detective Inspector George Beaumont and Detective Sergeant Yolanda Williams sat in the Incident Room, pouring over Neil Roscow's phone records. The room was hushed, save for the occasional hum of machines and the soft tapping of keys. Stacks of files and papers lay scattered across the table, each one a piece of the intricate puzzle they were trying to solve.

"Anything yet, Yolanda?" George asked, his voice low and steady.

Yolanda, her eyes scanning line after line of data, shook her head slightly. "It's like looking for a needle in a haystack, but... wait." Her finger paused over a series of texts. "Here, sir, look at this."

George leaned in, his gaze focused on the screen. The text messages were between Neil and an unknown contact, their content cryptic yet suggestive of something more than a casual conversation.

"Can you pull up the full thread?" George asked, his mind already racing with possibilities.

Yolanda clicked through the records, bringing up the entire conversation. "It's like they're speaking in code. But it's clear they were planning something."

George rubbed his chin thoughtfully. "We need to find out

who this unknown contact is. It could lead us to Neil... or to something bigger."

At that moment, Karen Willis, the Forensic IT Specialist, entered the room, her expression serious. "You called me about tracing a number?"

"Yes," George replied, gesturing to the screen. "We need to find the origin of these messages."

Karen settled in front of the computer, her fingers flying over the keyboard. "Let me see what I can do."

The room fell into a focused silence as Karen worked, the only sound the occasional click of her mouse.

After several minutes, Karen leaned back, her expression one of triumph. "Got it. The number belongs to a burner phone, but I traced it back to a location in Harehills."

Yolanda's eyes widened. "Harehills? That's where Ethan's body was found."

George stood up, his mind working through the implications. "This could be the break we've been looking for."

Karen printed out the information and handed it to George. "I'll keep digging, see if I can find any more connections and figure out who the burner belongs to."

"Good work, Karen," George said, his voice appreciative. "Yolanda, let's get a team together. We need to check out this location."

As they left the computer lab, the pieces of the case slowly began to fall into place in George's mind. Each clue, each piece of evidence, was bringing them closer to the truth.

The building in Harehills stood like a forgotten relic from a bygone era. It was an old textile mill, a remnant of Leeds' industrial past, now abandoned and desolate. The structure was imposing, with its tall, red-brick walls weathered by years of neglect and windows either boarded up or shattered, leaving gaping holes that stared out like hollow eyes.

As they approached, the crunch of gravel underfoot broke the eerie silence that enveloped the area. The mill loomed over them, its towering chimney no longer billowing smoke but standing as a silent sentinel. Ivy crept up its sides, nature slowly reclaiming the man-made monolith.

"Be on your guard," George cautioned Yolanda as they prepared to enter the building. "We don't know what we might find in there."

Yolanda nodded, her expression determined. "Let's find out what Neil was hiding."

The main entrance, a large double door, was ajar, hanging off its rusted hinges. The faint smell of dampness and decay wafted from within. Graffiti adorned the outer walls, cryptic tags that were the only signs of human presence in recent times.

Inside, the vast open space of the mill was a testament to its once bustling activity. Now, it was a cavernous void, with remnants of machinery and textile equipment scattered about, rusted and forgotten. Shafts of moonlight pierced through the broken roof, casting ghostly beams across the dust-laden floor.

George and Yolanda tread carefully, their torches cutting through the darkness. The air was stale and heavy with the scent of mould and old fabric. The echoes of their footsteps filled the space, a stark reminder of the building's desolation.

In a secluded corner of the mill, they found what Neil had been hiding. Covered with a tarpaulin sheet, they discovered a cache of items that were immediately recognisable—more Santa Claus memorabilia, similar to those found at the murder scenes, and a collection of documents and photographs. Among these were maps of the city with specific locations marked and photos that seemed to surveil various individuals, including some of the victims.

Yolanda lifted one of the photographs with gloved fingers, her expression turning grave. "Sir, these are surveillance photos. Neil was tracking someone."

George examined the maps, his mind piecing together the implications. "He was onto something... or someone. This wasn't just obsession; it was methodical planning."

As they left the mill, the weight of their discovery hung between them. The building, once a beacon of industry, now stood as a silent witness to a modern mystery, a piece in the complex puzzle of crime and deceit that George and Yolanda were determined to solve.

* * *

Back in the bustling Incident Room, Detective Constables Tashan Blackburn and Candy Nichols were hunched over a bank of monitors, their faces illuminated by the glow of the screens. Around them, the room hummed with the quiet intensity of focused investigation.

"Look at this," Tashan said, pointing to a timestamp on Neil's phone records. "This message, it's sent right before he disappears from the CCTV."

Candy leaned in, her eyes tracing the line of text on the screen. "It mentions a meeting. Can we match the location to any of the CCTV footage?"

Tashan scrolled through the video feeds, his fingers deftly navigating the controls. "Here, this is Neil's last known location. If we can track where he went from here..."

The two detectives worked in tandem, cross-referencing data with a meticulous precision borne of hours of training and experience. The room around them faded into a blur as they focused solely on the task at hand.

Meanwhile, in his office, Detective Inspector George Beaumont and Detective Sergeant Yolanda Williams were deep in discussion. The air was thick with the gravity of their findings.

Moments earlier, Karen Willis, the Forensic IT Specialist, her workstation aglow with the data they had painstakingly been unravelling, paused over the keyboard, her expression one of disbelief. She picked up the phone, and when it was answered, she said, "DI Beaumont, you need to see this," her tone laced with a mix of surprise and gravity.

George immediately headed upstairs, and when he focused on the screen where Karen pointed, he asked, "What is it?"

"This burner phone we've been tracking, the one connected to Neil's messages," Karen began, her voice steady despite the bombshell she was about to drop. "It's not a burner. It's registered. Registered to Dr Lindsey Yardley."

The revelation hit George like a physical blow, his mind reeling from the implications. "Yardley? Are you certain?"

"Absolutely," Karen replied, turning the screen to show him the digital trail she had uncovered. "I triple-checked. The number traces back to her. She's the unknown contact in Neil's texts."

George stood back, absorbing the news. Dr Lindsey Yardley, a respected pathologist, was now a central figure in their investigation. It was a twist he hadn't seen coming.

"Could she have been involved in all this?" George pondered aloud, more to himself than to Karen. "And if so, to what extent?"

Karen shrugged, a gesture of uncertainty. "It's hard to say, but this connection... it changes everything."

George rubbed his chin, his mind working through the new scenario. "We need to approach this carefully. Yardley's professional standing makes her a sensitive target. So we keep this close to the chest for now." He paused. "The team will start digging into Yardley's financials, her communications, anything that might give us more context to these messages."

Karen turned back to her computer, her fingers flying over the keys. "On it, DI Beaumont."

Back in the present, George said, "Yolanda, this message Neil sent could be key," his voice low and thoughtful. "It hints at a meeting at a private residence. Could be Yardley's."

Yolanda, her expression serious, nodded. "If it is Yardley's, we need to approach this carefully. She's a respected pathologist. We can't afford to spook her."

George leaned back in his chair, his mind working through the implications. "We'll need to set up surveillance, see who comes and goes. If Neil was meeting with Yardley, it could tie her directly to the case."

Yolanda considered this, her brows furrowed. "But we need to be discreet. If Yardley is involved, she'll be on high alert for any police activity."

George stood up, his decision made. "I'll arrange for an unmarked car, keep it low-key. We can't tip our hand, not yet."

Back in the Incident Room, Tashan and Candy had made a breakthrough. "Got it," Tashan exclaimed, a triumphant note in his voice. "Neil's path from the last CCTV sighting leads towards a residential area. It could be where he was heading for the meeting."

Candy peered at the screen, her detective instincts kicking in. "We need to pass this on to DI Beaumont and Yolanda. It could be the piece of the puzzle we've been missing."

The two detectives quickly gathered their findings, the evidence a tangible thread in the complex web of the investigation.

In George's office, the information from Tashan and Candy only deepened the intrigue. George pondered the next move, aware of the delicate balance they needed to maintain.

"We're close, Yolanda," George said, a determined edge to his voice. "We just need to fit these last pieces together."

Yolanda nodded, her resolve mirrored in her steady gaze. "We'll get there, sir. One step at a time."

* * *

The evening air was tense as Detective Inspector George Beaumont and his team, shrouded in the dim light of dusk, approached a nondescript residence in Seacroft, Leeds. The operation, green-lit by DCI Atkinson, was a calculated move, a silent dance of strategy and anticipation.

Beside George, Detective Sergeant Yolanda Williams adjusted her earpiece, her eyes fixed on the house. "Warrant's secured, sir. PS Greenwood's team is in position."

George nodded his expression a mask of concentration. "Remember, we go in quietly. No alarm, no tipping our hand."

The team, a blend of seasoned detectives and uniformed officers led by Police Sergeant Greenwood, moved with practised precision. The street was quiet, the house seemingly innocuous, but George knew appearances in their line of work were often deceiving.

As they breached the door, the sound of splintering wood shattered the silence. Inside, the house was cloaked in shadows, the air stale and heavy with the scent of disuse.

"Clear!" PS Greenwood's voice echoed through the empty corridors.

The team methodically swept through the house, but it was as George feared—the property was empty. However, in the living room, amidst a clutter of mundane items, lay a chilling discovery.

"Sir, look at this," Yolanda called out, her voice taut.

George approached, his eyes widening at the sight. Spread across the room was an array of Santa Claus memorabilia—figurines, costumes, and decorations—eerily similar to the items found at the murder scenes.

His mind raced, the implications clear and unnerving. "This is it. This is our link to the murders."

The team gathered around, the gravity of the discovery dawning on them. George reached for his phone, dialling DCI Atkinson with a sense of urgency.

"Sir, it's DI Beaumont. We're at the Seacroft residence. It's empty, but we've found something—Santa Claus memorabilia, like the ones at the crime scenes."

The voice of DCI Atkinson, calm yet authoritative, came through. "Understood, George. I'll get Kent and the SOC team there immediately. Secure the scene."

As the call ended, George turned to his team, his voice firm. "We hold the fort until SOC arrives. No one touches anything. This is a goldmine of evidence."

The team nodded their expressions, a mixture of determination and solemnity. As they waited, the house seemed to whisper secrets, the memorabilia a silent testament to the twisted mind they were chasing.

Yolanda, standing beside George, spoke softly. "Whoever lived here, they're deeply connected to the murders."

George's gaze was steely. "And we're going to find out who."

The wait for the Scene of Crime Team felt like an eternity. The house, once a place of presumed innocence, now loomed as a cornerstone of their investigation.

When Kent and his team arrived, the atmosphere shifted. The SOC officers, clad in protective gear, moved in with clinical efficiency, their equipment whirring and flashing as they began to process the scene.

George watched, his thoughts a whirlwind. Each piece of evidence collected was another step closer to the truth, another fragment of the dark puzzle they were assembling.

As the night deepened, the lights from the SOC team's work flickered in the darkened rooms, casting shadows that danced across the walls. Outside, the quiet street of Seacroft stood in stark contrast to the flurry of activity within the house.

Chapter Twenty-two

The morning sun barely penetrated the dense clouds over Leeds as Detective Inspector George Beaumont strode into the station, his mind already churning with the complexities of the case.

Detective Sergeant Yolanda Williams approached him, a file in her hand, her expression grave. "Sir, we've got the results from the lab. Lindsey Yardley's prints and DNA were on the Christmas decorations from the Seacroft residence."

George's stride paused, the implications of this discovery settling over him like a heavy cloak. "Yardley's?" he echoed, the pieces of the puzzle clicking into place yet raising more questions.

Yolanda nodded, her brows furrowed. "Yes, we cross-referenced it specifically against the Contamination Elimination Database. It's a definitive match."

George rubbed his chin, deep in thought. "But why weren't her prints or DNA found at the previous four murder scenes?"

Yolanda shrugged slightly, her usual composure tinged with uncertainty. "That's the million-pound question, isn't it, sir? It suggests she was more careful, or perhaps not directly involved in those."

George motioned for Yolanda to follow him to his office, his mind racing. Once inside, he sat down, leaning back in his chair, his gaze distant.

"We need to scrutinise every aspect of Yardley's life—her activities, associations, everything," George said, his voice carrying a note of urgency.

Yolanda, standing by the desk, replied, "We're already on it. But if she's involved, she's been extraordinarily cautious until now."

Detective Constable Tashan Blackburn entered the office, a folder under his arm. "Sir, I've been reviewing Yardley's financials and communications. There's nothing overtly suspicious, but there are gaps, periods where her activities are unaccounted for."

George's eyes narrowed. "Gaps? Around the time of the murders?"

"Possibly, sir," Tashan replied, his youthful face marked with concentration. "It's like she's living a double life."

The room fell silent as the gravity of the situation settled over them. George stood up, pacing the small space. "We're missing something, a key piece of this puzzle. Yardley's involvement doesn't fit the pattern cleanly."

Yolanda chimed in, "Could she be a red herring, planted to throw us off the scent?"

George stopped pacing, turning to face his team. "It's possible. But we can't ignore the evidence. For now, we treat her as a primary suspect."

The team nodded in agreement, a silent acknowledgement of the path they were about to tread.

George looked out the window, his gaze settling on the city skyline. "This case is more than just a series of murders. It's a web of deceit and hidden truths. And we're going to unravel it."

As Yolanda and Tashan left the office, George remained with his thoughts a complex tapestry of theories and possibilities. The case had taken a turn, and with it, the stakes had risen.

* * *

Early morning light filtered through the clouds as Detective Sergeant Yolanda Williams and the team, including Detective Constable Jay Scott, arrived at Dr Lindsey Yardley's residence, the search warrant firmly in Yolanda's grasp. The air was crisp, carrying a sense of solemn duty as they prepared to delve deeper into the life of the respected pathologist.

"Remember, we need to be thorough but respectful," Yolanda instructed, her voice firm yet measured. "Yardley's reputation is on the line."

Jay nodded, his expression serious. "Understood, Sarge. Let's get to it."

The team dispersed, entering the residence with practised efficiency. The house was a portrait of professional elegance—clean lines, minimalistic décor, and an air of sterile precision.

As Jay moved through the living room, his eyes were drawn to a bookshelf. Among the medical textbooks and journals, he noticed a series of older, more peculiar books on toxicology. His fingers traced the spines, a sense of foreboding growing within him.

"Look at this," he called out, holding up one of the books.

Yolanda joined him, her gaze falling on the book's title—a treatise on the use of natural poisons throughout history. "Interesting reading material for a pathologist," she noted, her tone laced with suspicion.

Meanwhile, in Dr Yardley's office, other team members sifted through paperwork and files. One detective held up a calendar, his finger on a series of dates. "These dates coincide with the murders," he said, a hint of disbelief in his voice.

Yolanda, joining him, examined the calendar. "We need to cross-reference these with her phone and email records. See if there's any communication on these days."

As the search continued, Jay discovered a drawer. After a moment's hesitation, he carefully opened it, revealing its contents. Inside, among various personal items, were several vials and a notebook filled with meticulous notes. The notes referenced multiple poisons and their effects, detailed in a clinical, almost cold manner.

Yolanda, peering over Jay's shoulder, felt a chill run down her spine. "This could be the connection we're looking for."

The team's attention turned to the vials. "We need the forensic experts to examine these," Yolanda stated. "See if there's any trace of Digitalis."

As they carefully packaged the items for transport, the gravity of their discovery weighed heavily on them. The search had revealed a side of Dr Yardley that was in stark contrast to her public persona.

Back at the station, George Beaumont awaited their return, his office a haven of quiet amidst the station's usual hustle. Yolanda briefed him on their findings, her voice steady but tinged with unease.

"Books and detailed notes on poisons, vials... it's compelling, George," she said, laying out the evidence on his desk.

George leaned back, his gaze fixed on the items. "It's circumstantial, but it's a start. We need those forensic results. If Digitalis is present..."

Yolanda nodded, her thoughts mirroring his. "It would place Yardley at the heart of the murders."

The room fell silent, the evidence laid out before them a silent testament to the complexity of the case. George finally spoke, his voice resolute. "Keep me updated on the forensic results. This case just took a significant turn."

* * *

Detective Inspector George Beaumont sat in the sparse interview room of Elland Road Police Station, his eyes fixed on the door. The room was stark, with only the essential furnishings—a table, a few chairs, and a one-way mirror. The air was heavy with anticipation. George knew the delicacy of the situation at hand. Arresting Dr Lindsey Yardley wasn't a decision taken lightly, given her esteemed professional status. He planned each question in his mind, a diplomatic approach to unravel the truth without prematurely casting aspersions.

The door opened, and Dr Yardley was escorted in by two of Police Sergeant Greenwood's uniformed officers. Her posture was erect, her expression a mask of composed professionalism, but her eyes betrayed a flicker of apprehension.

"Dr Yardley, thank you for coming in," George began, his tone measured, betraying neither accusation nor empathy.

She sat down, her hands folded neatly on the table. "Detective Inspector Beaumont, I presume this is about the recent... unpleasantness?"

George nodded. "Yes, Dr Yardley. I'm sure you understand the seriousness of the situation."

"I do, but I assure you, my involvement is purely professional," she replied, her voice steady.

George leaned forward slightly, his gaze unwavering. "We found your fingerprints and DNA on items closely linked to the murders. How do you explain that?"

Dr Yardley's composure faltered slightly. "I can't. I've never been near those...items. It must be a contamination error."

"Contamination?" George echoed, scepticism lacing his tone. "That seems unlikely, given the extent of your presence on them."

Her eyes flickered, a silent battle of thoughts playing out behind them. "I don't know what to say, Detective. I'm as baffled as you are."

George shifted gears, his approach cautious yet probing. "Let's talk about your relationship with Ethan Turner. Were you aware of his activities outside of work?"

She hesitated, then sighed. "No."

"But your prints, your DNA," George pressed on, watching her reaction closely. "They place you at the heart of this case."

Dr Yardley's facade of calm began to crack, a hint of agitation seeping through. "I am a pathologist, Detective. My work brings me into contact with all sorts of...material. But that doesn't make me a murderer."

George sat back, his mind working through her responses, weighing her words against the evidence. "What about Neil Roscow? Were you in contact with him?"

Her response was immediate, a touch too quick. "No, never. I don't even know him."

George's eyes narrowed slightly. "Yet, we have evidence suggesting otherwise. Phone records, meetings..."

Dr Yardley shook her head, a trace of desperation creeping into her voice. "It's not what you think. I can explain."

George's voice was firm, yet not unkind. "Then please, Dr

Yardley, explain. Help us understand your side of the story."

As she began to speak, her words spilling out in a mix of justification and fear, George listened intently. Each sentence, each pause, was a piece of the puzzle he was determined to solve.

* * *

George sat in the small break room near the interview suites, a cup of untouched coffee growing cold in front of him. His mind was a swirl of thoughts, churning around the latest turn in the investigation. The interview with Dr Lindsey Yardley had left more questions than answers, a frustrating puzzle that seemed to deepen with every piece they uncovered.

Detective Sergeant Yolanda Williams entered the room, her footsteps a soft echo on the linoleum floor. She pulled up a chair opposite George, her expression mirroring his concern.

"Sir, I've been going over Dr Yardley's statements," Yolanda began, her voice measured. "There's something off. It's like she's telling us what we expect to hear, not what actually happened."

George rubbed his temples, feeling the weight of the case pressing down on him. "I know, Yolanda. Every answer she gives, it's too... convenient. Like she's been coached."

Yolanda nodded in agreement. "Exactly. And the evidence linking her to the crime scenes, it's almost too perfect. It's as if someone wants us to focus on her."

George leaned back, his gaze distant. "A red herring," he mused, the words tasting bitter in his mouth.

Yolanda leaned forward, her eyes intent. "If Yardley is a diversion, then we're missing the real player in this game.

Someone's orchestrating this, and they're always one step ahead."

The realization was a cold splash of reality. George stood up, pacing the small room, his frustration palpable. "This case... it's like a web, and we're stuck in the middle of it."

Yolanda watched him, her own frustration a silent echo. "So, what's our next move?"

George stopped pacing, his determination resurfacing. "We go back to the beginning. Re-examine everything. There's a piece we're missing, a connection we've overlooked."

Yolanda stood up, her resolve firming. "I'll get the team on it, sir. We'll comb through every piece of evidence, every statement, every lead."

George nodded, a plan forming in his mind. "And I'll take another run at Yardley. There's something she's not telling us. I can feel it."

As they left the break room, the station around them buzzed with the usual activity, a stark contrast to the complex puzzle they were trying to solve. George knew they were up against a cunning adversary, one who was manipulating the investigation with skill and precision.

He returned to the interrogation room, his mind clear, his focus sharp. Dr Yardley sat there, her composure still intact, but George could see the cracks beginning to show.

"Dr Yardley," he began, his voice calm but firm. "Let's go over this one more time. And this time, I want the truth, not a story designed to mislead us."

Dr Yardley met his gaze, a flicker of uncertainty in her eyes. George knew he was on the right track. The truth was there, hidden beneath layers of deception, and he was determined to uncover it.

Chapter Twenty-three

In the interview room, Detective Inspector George Beaumont and DI Luke Mason sat across from Oleksander Jones, his solicitor beside him.

"Mr Jones, we need to discuss your ties to the Organised Crime Group (OCG) involved in the recent murders," George said, his tone measured.

Jones remained stoic, his response a simple, "No comment."

Luke tried a different angle. "Your connections to the OCG aren't just casual. We've evidence linking you directly to them."

Again, Jones replied, "No comment."

The detectives persisted, detailing the connections and evidence they had gathered. Despite their efforts, Jones's response was always the same: a resolute "No comment."

In a final attempt, George leaned forward. "We have enough to arrest you as a member of the OCG, Jones. Your solicitor knows it too," he said, glancing at the solicitor, who gave a subtle nod.

"There's a chance for a reduced sentence if you agree to become an informant," George offered, watching Jones's reaction closely.

Jones shook his head, his lips parting only to say, "No comment."

As George and Luke stood to leave, Jones called out, "OK. I'll give you something. But not everything." He paused. "I want protection before I give you more."

George's grin was immediate as he sat back down. Jones looked between the two detectives, his demeanour shifting. "Dr Christian Ross," he began, his voice steady, "was a powerful member of the Schmidt OCG. Had been for over a decade."

George and Luke exchanged a quick glance, recognising the significance of this revelation. But it was something they already knew.

"Tell us something we didn't already know, Jones."

The solicitor said, "You're not being fair, detectives."

Frustrated but not surprised, George and Luke left the room. Approaching the desk sergeant, George said firmly, "Charge Oleksander Jones. His silence speaks volumes."

George headed straight for his office with Christian Ross in his mind and once there, he sat, a stack of old case files spread out before him. The room was quiet, save for the soft ticking of the clock on the wall. He sifted through the files, looking for anything they might have missed in the case involving Dr Lindsey Yardley, who had like Jones, also resorted to giving a 'no comment' interview.

His fingers paused on a faded photograph tucked between the pages. It was an old, grainy image, but the faces were unmistakable. There, smiling at the camera, was a young Dr Christian Ross, standing next to a man who bore a striking resemblance to David Hardaker.

George leaned back in his chair, his eyes fixed on the

photograph. The connection between Ross and Hardaker was a revelation, a piece of the puzzle he hadn't anticipated.

At that moment, Detective Sergeant Yolanda Williams entered his office, her expression curious. "Sir, you called?"

George handed her the photograph. "Look at this, Yolanda. Who do you think it is?"

"Looks like David Hardaker to me, sir."

"Exactly. Ross and Hardaker, together. We need to dig into this."

Yolanda examined the photo, her brow furrowing. "That's a significant find. I'll start looking into their history right away."

As Yolanda left the office, George's mind raced with the possibilities. The link between Ross and Hardaker could be a critical lead in solving the complex web of the case.

* * *

Later, Yolanda returned with a file in her hand. "Sir, I've got something," she said, her tone indicative of a breakthrough.

George looked up, anticipation building. "What did you find?"

Yolanda opened the file, revealing her research. "Dr Ross and David Hardaker had a past collaboration in medical research. Ross was in need of funding, and Hardaker provided it through his contacts."

George leaned forward, absorbing the information. "Funding for what exactly?"

"It's unclear, but it seems to be related to pharmaceutical research, possibly experimental," Yolanda replied, her voice laced with suspicion.

George's thoughts turned to the current case. "And now Ross is dead, and Hardaker is a key figure in our investigation. This connection could be more than coincidental."

Yolanda nodded in agreement. "It suggests a deeper involvement. Hardaker's funding could have been for something illicit, something Ross was a part of."

George stood up, a sense of urgency in his movement. "We need to follow this lead. See where it takes us. Hardaker's role in this could be pivotal."

Yolanda gathered the files, her determination evident. "I'll get the team on it. We'll pull everything we have on Hardaker and Ross and see if there are any more connections."

As Yolanda left to coordinate with the team, George stood by the window, gazing out at the cityscape of Leeds. The case was evolving, each discovery leading them deeper into a maze of secrets and lies.

The revelation of Ross and Hardaker's past collaboration added a new layer, a thread in the tapestry of crime that George was determined to unravel.

Meanwhile, Detective Constables Jay Scott and Candy Nichols sat in a small, unremarkable interview room at the Elland Road Police Station, facing a former colleague of Dr Christian Ross. The colleague, a middle-aged man named Jerry Northfield with a weary expression, seemed hesitant, his fingers fidgeting nervously on the table.

"Can you tell us about Dr Ross's meetings with David Hardaker, Mr Northfield?" Jay asked, his voice calm yet insistent.

Jerry sighed, a look of reluctance in his eyes. "Christian and David, they met often. Always in private, always seemed... secretive."

"Secretive how?" Candy probed, her gaze sharp and focused.

"Unusual times, odd places. It wasn't regular professional meetings. More like... covert discussions," the man replied, his voice trailing off.

Jay exchanged a glance with Candy, both sensing the significance of this revelation. "Did you ever hear what these meetings were about?"

The man shook his head. "No, but Christian changed after those meetings started. Became more distant, guarded."

Upstairs in his office, Detective Inspector George Beaumont mulled over this new information. The connection between David Hardaker and Dr Ross was becoming clearer, and the potential involvement of Digitalis was a lead he couldn't ignore.

George's thoughts were interrupted by a knock on the door. Detective Sergeant Yolanda Williams entered, her expression serious.

"Sir, I've arranged for you to meet with some of Hardaker's known associates," she reported.

George stood up, his resolve firming. "Thank you, Yolanda. It's time we got some answers."

* * *

In the Red Lion pub, George sat across from a man known to be an associate of David Hardaker. Harold Jenkinson, rugged and unshaven, eyed George warily.

"I don't know what you want from me, Detective," the man said, his tone defensive.

George leaned forward, his gaze unwavering. "I need to

know about David Hardaker's relationship with Dr Christian Ross, Mr Jenkinson. Were they working on something together?"

The man hesitated, glancing around the pub before leaning in closer. "David always had big plans, big ideas. Ross was part of that. Something about new medical breakthroughs, experimental stuff."

George's mind raced, piecing together the puzzle. "Did this involve Digitalis?"

The man's eyes narrowed slightly. "Maybe. David was always talking about using what's natural, finding new ways to treat diseases."

George sat back, a mix of frustration and determination settling over him. The pieces were falling into place, but the whole picture was still elusive.

"Thank you," George said, standing up. "You've been helpful."

As he left the pub, the evening air felt crisp against his skin, a stark contrast to the stuffy atmosphere inside. The city of Leeds, with its hidden stories and unseen truths, was a landscape of complexity and mystery.

Back at the station, George convened with his team, sharing the new information, before heading upstairs to the IT lab.

Karen Willis, the Forensic IT Specialist, sat intently in front of her computer. Her fingers moved rapidly over the keyboard, decrypting a series of emails that had just come to light. George and Detective Constable Candy Nichols stood behind her, watching the screen with bated breath.

"There," Karen announced, a triumphant note in her voice as lines of decrypted text appeared on the screen. "Emails between David Hardaker and the late Dr Christian Ross."

George leaned in, his eyes scanning the content. The emails were cryptic, but the undertone was clear—there was a deeper conspiracy at play, one that tied David and Dr Ross together in ways they hadn't anticipated.

"This is big," George muttered, his mind racing with the implications. "They were planning something... something more than we thought."

Candy, her expression a mix of concern and frustration, interjected, "But what does this mean for the rest of the case, sir? Are we missing other leads while focusing on this?"

George turned to her, his gaze thoughtful. He knew she was talking about Edward despite not saying his name. "It's a valid concern, Candy. We can't afford tunnel vision. We need to ensure we're covering all angles."

Karen turned in her chair, addressing them both. "This conspiracy... it could be the key to understanding the entire case. But it's complex, layered."

George nodded, a sense of resolve washing over him. "We need to untangle this web. Piece by piece."

The room fell silent, the weight of their discovery hanging heavily in the air. George knew they were delving into dangerous territory, a realm where the lines between victim and perpetrator were blurred.

* * *

Detective Chief Inspector Alistair Atkinson sat stiffly. Across from him, Detective Superintendent Smith and Detective Chief Superintendent Sadiq, their expressions stern and expectant, awaited updates on the Santa Claus murders.

Atkinson cleared his throat, his voice steady but betraying

an undercurrent of urgency. "The investigation is progressing, but we're grappling with complex layers and unexpected revelations," he began, his gaze fixed on the two senior officers.

DSU Smith leaned forward, her hands clasped tightly. "Complexity is not what the public wants to hear, Alistair," she said sharply. "They want answers, resolutions. The media is breathing down our necks, and our credibility is at stake."

DCS Sadiq nodded in agreement, his face etched with concern. "We need a breakthrough, and we need it fast. The city is on edge, and every day without an arrest only fuels the fear and speculation."

Atkinson, feeling the pressure mounting, responded with a controlled calmness. "I understand the stakes. We've identified a new lead with pathologist Lindsey Yardley, a previously unknown connection in the case. This could be the key to unlocking the entire case."

The revelation was not new to them, but the reality of their situation quickly overshadowed it. "Time is not a luxury we have," DSU Smith stated. "We need tangible progress, Alistair. The department can't afford another misstep."

As the meeting concluded, the senior officers' words echoed in Atkinson's mind—a constant reminder of the thin ice on which they all tread. Stepping out of the conference room, he pulled out his phone, dialling with a sense of purpose.

The call connected, and Atkinson's tone was a blend of frustration and determination. "We're facing significant challenges here," he spoke into the phone, his voice low. "The higher-ups are demanding quick results, but this case is anything but straightforward."

He listened intently, his expression turning grim as he

received news of further bureaucratic constraints being placed on the investigation. "Understood," Atkinson replied tersely, ending the call with a sense of foreboding.

He stood for a moment, gazing out the window at the cityscape. The burden of leadership weighed heavily on him, the balancing act between solving a complex case and managing the expectations of superiors and the public.

* * *

Later, in his office, George sat alone, reflecting on the twisted path the investigation had taken. The walls, adorned with maps and photos of the case, seemed to close in on him. The case had started as a straightforward murder investigation, but now it had spiralled into a complex web of deceit and hidden agendas.

His thoughts were interrupted by a knock on the door. Detective Sergeant Yolanda Williams entered, a file in her hand.

"Sir, we've cross-referenced the email dates with other case events," she said, laying the file on his desk.

George opened the file, his eyes scanning the contents—the dates aligned with key events in the case, painting a picture of a meticulously planned conspiracy.

Yolanda watched him, her expression serious. "Marcus Hawkinson has given us a location."

George looked up, meeting her gaze. "Let's get out there, then."

Yolanda nodded, a silent acknowledgement of the task ahead. "We'll follow your lead, sir."

Chapter Twenty-four

In an unmarked police car, Detective Inspector George Beaumont and Detective Constable Jay Scott sat in weighted silence, their eyes piercing through the darkness towards a desolate warehouse in an industrial quarter of Leeds. The area, steeped in the city's industrial past, echoed with the faint hum of machinery long silenced. The night was deep, wrapped in the city's historical gloom, punctuated only by a flickering street lamp nearby, its stuttering light casting elongated shadows. This was a notorious haunt of Jürgen Schmidt's henchmen, a place where Leeds' rougher edges met the underbelly of crime. The air was tinged with the bitter scent of the nearby factories, a constant reminder of the city's hard-working roots.

The car was equipped with the latest surveillance gear, but the stakeout was a test of patience and endurance. George's eyes, sharp and focused, scanned the area, taking in every detail. Jay, equally alert, monitored the feed from their hidden cameras.

"Anything yet, boss?" Jay whispered, his voice barely audible over the hum of the surveillance equipment.

George shook his head, his gaze not leaving the warehouse. "Nothing. It's quiet, too quiet."

Hours had passed with little activity, but both men knew

that the situation could change in an instant.

Jay adjusted his position, trying to ease the discomfort of sitting for so long. "You think they got wind of us?"

George considered this. "Doubtful. We've been careful. It's more likely they're being cautious. The OCG doesn't take chances."

The silence settled over them again, broken only by the occasional crackle of their radios. George's mind, constantly analysing, ran through possible scenarios and contingencies for every action.

A flicker of movement caught his eye. "Hold on," he murmured, pointing to a shadow moving near the warehouse.

Jay leaned forward, his attention fixed on the figure. "One of Schmidt's guys?"

"Possibly. Let's not jump to conclusions," George cautioned, his hand moving to the car's ignition in case they needed to move quickly.

They watched as the figure approached the warehouse, looked around furtively, and then slipped inside. George's hand tightened around the steering wheel.

"Time to move in, boss?" Jay asked the eagerness in his voice tempered with discipline.

George weighed the options. "Not yet. Let's see if anyone else shows up. We need more than one man to make a case."

The minutes stretched into an hour. Then, another figure appeared, followed by two more. Each entered the warehouse in the same cautious manner.

"That's our cue," George said, his voice low but decisive. "Let's go."

Quietly, they exited the car, moving towards the warehouse with practised stealth. Their footsteps were soundless, their movements calculated. Every step was taken with the utmost care, their training evident in their precision.

As they neared the warehouse, George signalled to Jay, indicating they should split up to cover both entrances. Jay nodded, understanding the plan without words.

The stillness of the industrial area was abruptly shattered as several of Jürgen Schmidt's men emerged from the shadows, their intentions clear in their swift, menacing approach towards Detective Inspector George Beaumont and Detective Constable Jay Scott.

"Boss, we've got company!" Jay hissed, alerting George to the sudden danger.

George's eyes narrowed as he assessed the situation. They were outnumbered, and the element of surprise lost. "Stay sharp, Jay. Back to the car, now!"

One of Schmidt's men, larger than the others, lunged at George, a crude weapon in hand. George sidestepped, his years of experience in the field evident in his swift response. He delivered a sharp blow to the man's midsection, temporarily winding him.

Jay, meanwhile, grappled with another assailant, managing to disarm him before pushing him away with a well-placed kick. "We need to get out of here, boss!"

Detective Inspector George Beaumont and Detective Constable Jay Scott found themselves in a perilous foot chase as they tried to escape. Their pursuit of key Schmidt OCG members had led them into a maze of dark alleys and abandoned buildings, the danger palpable in the air.

"Left here, boss!" Jay shouted, his voice echoing off the grimy walls as they turned sharply into another narrow passageway.

George, his senses heightened, followed closely, his years of experience evident in his swift, calculated movements. The sound of their footsteps was a rapid staccato against the cobblestones, the only noise in the otherwise silent night.

With Jürgen Schmidt's men in close pursuit, every shadow seemed to loom threateningly, every sound a potential give-away of their location.

George, his breaths measured despite the adrenaline surging through his veins, managed to fumble for his radio while keeping an eye on the dimly lit path behind them. "Control, this is DI Beaumont. We need urgent backup. Suspects from Schmidt OCG in pursuit," he whispered into the radio, his voice a low murmur.

Jay, standing watch, his body tensed for any sign of their pursuers, nodded at George. "Where do you reckon they'll come from, boss?"

George glanced around the desolate surroundings, his mind racing. "Could be any direction. We need to stay out of sight until backup arrives."

They moved deeper into the labyrinth of alleys, their footsteps silent on the damp cobblestone. The night was oppressively quiet, the distant hum of the city a stark contrast to their immediate peril.

Finding a recessed doorway, George signalled to Jay to take cover. They crouched in the shadows, the cold seeping through their clothes. George's eyes never stopped moving, scanning the darkness for any sign of movement.

"How long do you think before backup gets here?" Jay asked, his voice barely audible.

"Hard to say," George replied, his tone calm despite the uncertainty. "But we have to stay put. It's too risky to move now."

The minutes stretched on, each one feeling longer than the last.

Suddenly, a distant sound caught George's attention—the faint echo of footsteps. He gestured to Jay to be silent, his own body tensing.

The footsteps grew louder, then stopped. George could feel his heart pounding in his chest, his senses heightened to their limit.

A figure appeared at the end of the alley, silhouetted against the faint light. George's hand instinctively went to his sidearm, but he held off from revealing their position.

The figure moved on, the sound of footsteps fading into the night. George let out a quiet breath, the danger momentarily averted.

"We can't let our guard down," he murmured to Jay. "They're still close."

Jay nodded, his expression one of focused determination. "We'll be ready, boss."

Time seemed to slow as they waited in the darkness, the weight of their situation pressing down on them.

The sound of sirens cutting through the tense night air was the first sign of backup arriving for George and Jay.

Parked in the industrial district's shadowy expanse, George's team and several police cars converged on the scene, creating a tight perimeter around a cluster of Schmidt's henchmen, who stood stock-still.

George, calm but authoritative, stepped forward to lead the confrontation. The henchmen, now cornered, looked defiant yet wary, aware that their position was compromised.

"Evening, gentlemen," George began, his voice firm but not

provocative. "You're a long way from home. Care to explain what brings you to this part of Leeds at this hour?"

The leader of the group, a burly man with a scar across his cheek, sneered. "We're just enjoying the night air. Is there a law against that now, Detective?"

George met his gaze evenly. "When it involves members of the Schmidt OCG, it certainly raises questions. Especially given recent events."

Jay, standing a few steps behind George, watched the henchmen closely, ready to act at a moment's notice.

The stand-off was palpable, each side measuring the other. George knew he had to tread carefully; any wrong move could escalate the situation.

"I'm more interested in what you know about the Santa Claus murders," George continued, watching for any reaction that might give him an advantage.

The henchmen exchanged glances, a flicker of unease in their eyes. The leader maintained his defiant stance, but George could sense the uncertainty beneath it.

"You think we had something to do with that?" the leader challenged, trying to mask his hesitation.

"Let's just say your boss has a reputation for making problems disappear," George replied, his tone suggesting more than he let on.

The stand-off continued, the henchmen seemingly weighing their options. George could see the wheels turning in their minds, the realization that they were in a precarious position.

"You don't want to go down for Schmidt's dirty work," George pressed, his voice low and persuasive. "Help us out, and we can offer protection."

The leader scoffed, but there was less conviction in his voice this time. "And why should we trust you?"

"Because right now, I'm your best chance at getting out of this without a lengthy prison sentence," George stated, his confidence clear. "We know the OCG's involved. What we don't know is how deep this goes. Give us something to work with."

There was a tense silence as the leader seemed to consider George's offer. The other henchmen shifted uncomfortably, the reality of their situation sinking in.

Finally, the leader nodded, albeit reluctantly. "Alright. I don't know much about the murders, but I heard talk about a big payoff. Someone high up was getting nervous about loose ends."

George's expression remained unchanged, but inwardly, he knew this was a significant lead. "Do you have a name?"

The leader shook his head. "No names. But I can give you a location where I heard some of the higher-ups meet."

Satisfied, George signalled to his team to move in and detain the henchmen. "We'll take it from here. And we'll be in touch about that protection."

As the henchmen were led away, George turned to Jay, a look of quiet triumph in his eyes. "We've got a new lead, Jay. Let's see where this takes us."

* * *

In the wake of the confrontation with Schmidt's henchmen, the industrial district's cold, eerie silence returned. Detective Inspector George Beaumont surveyed the scene, his mind still processing the tense encounter. As the last police car departed, his keen eye caught a glimmer on the ground near where the henchmen had stood.

"Jay, over here," George called out softly.

Detective Constable Jay Scott, who was ensuring the area was secure, joined George. "What is it, boss?"

George pointed to a smartphone lying near a discarded pile of crates. "Looks like one of our friends dropped something."

Putting on a glove and pulling out an Exhibit bag he kept inside his trench coat, George carefully picked up the phone, holding it up for examination. The device was modern; its screen cracked but was still functional. George's experienced instincts told him this was no ordinary loss.

"This could be significant, Jay. Could have messages, contacts, anything," George said, his voice laced with anticipation.

Jay leaned in, his curiosity piqued. "Think it's password protected?"

George turned the phone over in his hand. "Only one way to find out." He pressed the power button, and the screen flickered to life, surprisingly unlocked.

"Looks like luck is on our side for once," Jay remarked, a slight smile on his face.

George navigated through the phone, his eyes scanning the content. Text messages, recent calls, and a slew of apps filled the screen. But it was the messaging app that caught his attention.

"Here, look at this," George said, opening a conversation thread filled with cryptic messages.

Jay read over his shoulder. "Seems like code. Arrangements for meetings, maybe pickups or drop-offs?"

"Could be," George mused, his mind already racing with possibilities. "We need to get this to Karen in IT. They can extract more information, maybe even track locations."

The two men stood in the dim light, the implications of their find slowly dawning on them. This phone was a direct line into the operations of the OCG, a breakthrough in their investigation.

George said, "Let's get back to the station. We need to act on this quickly."

As they walked back to their car, parked a discreet distance away, the quiet of the night enveloped them. Jay broke the silence, his voice contemplative. "You ever think about what it'd be like, boss? A normal job, no stakeouts or confrontations?"

George glanced at him, a wry smile on his lips. "Sometimes, Jay. But this is what we do. It's not just a job; it's who we are."

Chapter Twenty-five

Back at Elland Road Police Station, the atmosphere in the incident room was charged with a palpable intensity. Detective Inspector George Beaumont, surrounded by his team, held the recently acquired smartphone—a crucial piece of evidence that could potentially unravel the nefarious web woven by the Schmidt Organised Crime Group.

George looked over to Detective Constable Jay Scott and Detective Sergeant Yolanda Williams, who were waiting expectantly. "We may have just found our golden ticket," he said, his voice a mix of hope and caution.

Yolanda leaned in, her eyes sharp. "What's on it, sir?"

George handed the phone to the tech specialist, who was already set up with his equipment. "Let's find out," he said, watching intently as Karen began to extract data.

The room fell into a tense silence, broken only by the occasional click of the keyboard. Screens around them displayed streams of data being pulled from the phone, a digital unveiling of secrets.

After a few moments, Karen looked up. "Got something here. There are messages that directly link this phone to Schmidt. Looks like he's been coordinating activities personally."

George's focus intensified. "Can you bring up these messages?"

Karen nodded, pulling up a string of communications on the main screen. The messages were coded, but the implication was clear: instructions for meet-ups, transactions, and, chillingly, veiled references to the Santa Claus murders.

Yolanda's eyes narrowed as she read the screen. "This is it, sir. This is our direct link to Schmidt."

George nodded, a sense of vindication in his gaze. "We knew he was involved, but this is hard evidence. He's been orchestrating the murders, using them as a tool for his criminal enterprise."

Jay, who had been quietly observing, spoke up. "It's like he's been playing chess with people's lives."

George turned to the team. "This information changes everything. We need to move fast now. Schmidt will realize we have this phone, and he'll go to ground."

Yolanda stepped forward, her expression one of determination. "What's our next move, sir?"

George looked at each member of his team, his resolve clear. "We build our case. This phone is the key. We'll need to work through the night, cross-reference every piece of information with our existing data."

The team nodded in unison, ready for the task at hand. The room buzzed with renewed energy as they set to work, each member playing a crucial role in the intricate puzzle.

George stood back for a moment, watching his team. The weight of the case was heavy, but the sense of purpose was heavier. They were on the brink of a breakthrough that could bring down one of the city's most notorious criminals.

* * *

The room was stark and functional, the walls devoid of decoration, creating an atmosphere of solemnity. Detective Inspector George Beaumont sat across from the broad sniper, Martin Shaw, a tall and seasoned marksman with brown hair and blue eyes. The man had years of experience. The Professional Standards investigator, Detective Chief Inspector Helen Barnes, presided over the meeting, her presence a reminder of the gravity of the situation.

Martin Shaw, his uniform immaculate, his posture rigid, appeared stoic, yet there was a hint of tension in his eyes. He was well aware of the scrutiny he was under following the incident at Edward Beaumont's residence.

DCI Barnes initiated the interrogation with a professional yet stern tone. "Officer Shaw, let's go over the events that led to you discharging your weapon at Dr Christian Ross."

Martin nodded, his voice steady but betraying a hint of the weight he felt. "I was positioned with a clear line of sight to the study window. My primary objective was to ensure the safety of all involved, including Mr Edward Beaumont."

George observed silently, his expression neutral, yet his mind was awash with the implications of the sniper's actions.

"Walk us through the moment you decided to take the shot," DCI Barnes continued, her pen poised above her notepad.

Martin took a deep breath, recalling the tense moments. "I observed Dr Ross through the scope. He appeared agitated, moving erratically. When he raised the gun and pointed it at Mr Beaumont, I had to make a split-second decision."

DI Barnes pressed on, "Did you consider any non-lethal alternatives before firing?"

"The situation escalated rapidly," Martin explained. "Given the distance and the immediate threat to Mr Beaumont's life, there was no viable non-lethal option."

Barnes interjected, her voice calm but firm. "Officer Shaw, were you aware of any prior relationship between Dr Ross and Mr Beaumont that might have influenced the situation?"

Martin shook his head. "No, ma'am. My focus was solely on the potential threat. I acted to neutralise the immediate danger."

DI Barnes noted his response, her expression unreadable. "Officer Shaw, your record indicates exemplary service and judgment. This incident, however, has significant ramifications. It's vital we understand every detail."

Martin's response was measured, his training evident in his composure. "I understand the gravity of the situation, ma'am. My actions were in line with the protocol for an imminent threat to life."

George knew the complexities of such split-second decisions. The line between heroism and scrutiny was perilously thin.

DI Barnes concluded the session with a final question. "Is there anything else you wish to add, Officer Shaw, that might shed further light on your decision-making process?"

Martin paused, his gaze steady. "Only that I acted with the intent to save a life. The outcome was tragic, but given the same circumstances, my duty to protect life and prevent harm remains paramount."

The meeting adjourned, leaving a heavy silence in its wake. Martin Shaw stood up, his expression still composed, yet the burden of his actions was palpable.

George approached him, placing a hand on his shoulder.

"Martin, you had a tough call to make. We all know that."

Martin nodded, a flicker of gratitude in his eyes. "Thank you, sir. I just hope the investigation brings some clarity."

As Martin Shaw left the room, George remained, deep in thought. The shooting, while justified in the moment, opened a Pandora's box of ethical and procedural questions. The line of duty was often a tightrope walk over moral and legal complexities.

In the quiet of the room, George Beaumont pondered the weight of responsibility that every officer carried, the decisions made in the blink of an eye that could alter lives forever. The pursuit of justice was a journey fraught with challenges and choices, each with its own shadow and light.

* * *

In the quiet solitude of his office at Elland Road Police Station, Detective Inspector George Beaumont sat at his desk, the events of the night replaying in his mind. The dim light from his desk lamp cast long shadows across the room, mirroring the darkness that seemed to envelop his thoughts.

He leaned back in his chair, his eyes drifting to the framed photo on his desk. It was a snapshot of happier times—George, smiling, with his arm around Isabella, Jack in front of him and Olivia in her mother's arms. The picture was a stark contrast to the world he was currently entrenched in, a world of danger and moral ambiguity.

George picked up the photo, his fingers tracing the edges of the frame. "What I wouldn't give for a simple day," he murmured to himself.

The phone's discovery and the subsequent linking of

Schmidt to the Santa Claus murders had been a significant breakthrough. Yet, with each step closer to the truth, the danger seemed to grow, an ever-present shadow looming over him and his team.

George set the photo back down, his gaze now fixed on the file in front of him—a file that contained the key to dismantling Schmidt's OCG. The responsibility weighed heavily on him, but it was a weight he had chosen to bear.

The room was silent, save for the occasional rustle of paper as George reviewed the evidence once more. Every detail mattered; there was no room for error. The lives of innocent people and the safety of his city depended on their next moves.

His thoughts were interrupted by a soft knock on the door. Detective Constable Jay Scott peeked in, a look of concern on his face.

"Everything alright, boss?" Jay asked, stepping into the room.

George managed a tired smile. "Just going over everything again. We can't afford to miss anything."

Jay nodded, understanding. "We're all behind you, boss. We'll get Schmidt and his lot."

George's smile widened slightly. "I know, Jay. Thanks. That's enough for tonight, though. Go home to your family."

Jay hesitated, then nodded. "Alright, boss. See you in the morning."

As Jay left, George turned his attention back to the file, his mind once again consumed by the case. The stakes were higher than they had ever been.

He stood up, stretching his tired muscles, and walked over to the window. The city was quiet at this hour, a stark contrast to the turmoil that lay just beneath its surface.

George's reflection stared back at him in the glass—a man who had dedicated his life to fighting crime, to protecting those who couldn't defend themselves. The job had its costs, but he had never wavered in his commitment.

George remained by the window, the cityscape a tapestry of light and shadow under the night sky. The silence of the office was a stark contrast to the clamour of his thoughts, each one a thread in the intricate web of the investigation.

He glanced at the clock, noting the late hour, and realised he needed a brief respite from the all-consuming nature of the case. Reaching for his phone, he dialled a number he knew by heart. After a couple of rings, the familiar, warm voice of Isabella answered.

"George, it's late. Everything OK?" Isabella's voice was tinged with concern, a testament to the countless nights his work had intruded upon their lives.

"Just wrapping up here," George replied, his tone softening. "How was your day?"

Isabella chuckled softly, a sound that always brought him a sense of peace. "She's finally asleep. Had a bit of a fussy day, but she's calm now. Spent the afternoon trying out the new baby mobile you got her. She seems to love it."

George smiled, imagining the scene. "Glad to hear she likes it. I just wish I could be there more, to see these moments."

"I know, love. We both do. Olivia might not understand it now, but she will. Just don't work yourself too hard."

He sighed, feeling the weight of balancing his demanding job and family life. "I promise to make it up to both of you. Maybe this weekend, we can spend some quality time together, just the three of us."

"That would be lovely, George. We miss you around here."

Their conversation drifted to lighter topics, providing a much-needed break from the mental toll of his work. Isabella's voice was a soothing presence, grounding him to a life outside of crime and investigation.

Eventually, George glanced at the files on his desk, a reminder of the unfinished business that awaited him. "I should let you go. It's late, and I've still got a bit to do here."

"OK, George. Just remember, we're here for you. Olivia and I. We love you."

"I love you both, too," George replied, feeling a sense of warmth enveloping him despite the chill of the night.

As the call ended, George stood in the quiet of his office, Isabella's words echoing in his mind. He knew the job demanded much of him, often more than was fair to his family. Yet their support was his anchor, a reminder of why he pursued justice with such relentless determination.

Chapter Twenty-six

George's eyes, once weary with doubt, now held a resolute determination that Sunday morning. He adjusted his tie, the gesture slow and deliberate. He was no longer just a detective on a case; he had become a crusader against a tide of corruption that had hit too close to home.

As he buttoned his jacket, the door to the locker room opened, and Detective Sergeant Yolanda Williams walked in. "Morning, George. You're in early."

George glanced at her reflection in the mirror. "Couldn't sleep. Too much on my mind."

Yolanda leaned against the lockers, her expression one of understanding. "Big day today. We're getting closer to the OCG."

George turned to face her, his stance firm. "We are. But it's more than just bringing down the OCG now. It's about setting things right, about justice."

Yolanda nodded. "And your father?"

George paused, his jaw setting. "He's a part of this, whether I like it or not. My feelings towards him won't change what needs to be done." He paused. "And I've been told to leave it to the NCA, so that's exactly what I'm doing."

The conversation was interrupted as Detective Constable

Jay Scott entered the room, his usual energetic demeanour slightly subdued. "There's been another Santa Claus murder, boss."

George's resolute gaze shifted towards Jay Scott, the gravity of another murder adding a new layer of urgency to their mission. "Another murder?" he asked, his voice steady despite the rising tide of concern within him.

Jay nodded, a grim expression on his face. "Yes, boss. Early this morning. It's got the same MO as the others. The victim was found in a back alley in Chapeltown, dressed in a Santa outfit."

George exhaled slowly, the weight of their responsibility settling heavily on his shoulders. "The OCG is still at it, then. They're making a statement."

Yolanda straightened up, her features hardening with resolve. "We need to get to the scene, see what we can find. Maybe this time, they've left us something more."

George grabbed his coat, his movements precise and determined. "Let's hope so. We're running out of time and options. The OCG isn't slowing down, and neither can we."

As they left the Incident Room, the station was already buzzing with activity, a hive of officers and detectives preparing for the day ahead. George, Yolanda, and Jay made their way through the corridors, their steps echoing with purpose.

Arriving at the crime scene, they were greeted by the all-too-familiar sight of police tape and flashing lights. The early morning air was crisp, the dawn light casting long shadows across the alley where the latest victim lay.

Stuart Kent's Crime Scene Investigators were already at work, meticulously collecting evidence. George watched them for a moment before kneeling beside the victim. His gaze was intense, searching for the minutest details that might have previously been overlooked.

An older PC signed George, Tashan and Jay into the scene and handed them their protective gear.

After suiting up, George crossed through the tape and crouched beside the body, his eyes scanning for any clue, any sign that might lead them to the killer. The victim, another unfortunate soul caught in the OCG's web of terror, was a grim reminder of the stakes.

The pathologist from Bradford, Dr Helen Simmons, arrived. She was greeted by Detective Inspector George Beaumont and his team, who stood by the cordoned area, waiting for her assessment.

Dr Simmons, a seasoned professional with a pragmatic approach to her work, knelt beside the victim, her tools in hand. The alleyway, now a site of meticulous investigation, was quiet except for the distant hum of the city waking up.

After a thorough examination, Dr Simmons stood up to address George and his team. Her expression was sombre, reflecting the gravity of her findings.

"Detective," Dr Simmons began, addressing George directly, "the brutality of this murder is... unsettling. The victim's head was beaten to a pulp. It's one of the worst I've seen."

George's brow furrowed deeply, his thoughts clouded with the horrific nature of the crime. "Was this level of violence necessary to kill the victim, or does it suggest something more?"

Dr Simmons shook her head slightly, her eyes reflecting a professional yet empathetic concern. "The overkill here is indicative of extreme rage or a desire to send a message. The force used was far beyond what was needed to kill."

Yolanda interjected, her voice steady despite the gruesome details, "This is normally how the OCGs leave a message."

"Yes," Dr Simmons replied. "However, the nature of the injuries could suggest a personal vendetta. However, without knowing the victim's identity, it's hard to determine the motive definitively."

George looked back at the scene, his mind working through the implications. "Thank you, Dr Simmons. Please let us know as soon as you have more information from the autopsy."

As Dr Simmons nodded and returned to her work, George and Yolanda stepped away from the scene to discuss their next steps.

"The level of violence here... it fits the usual pattern of the OCG," George mused, his gaze distant. "But if this is personal, it could mean a shift in the dynamics of what we're dealing with."

Yolanda agreed, "We need to find out who this victim is. Their identity could be the key to understanding the motive behind this brutality."

"Time of death, Dr Simmons?" asked George.

"Based on the body's condition and the temperature here, I'd say the time of death was in the early hours. But given the cold weather, it's difficult to ascertain more precisely."

George nodded, understanding the challenges posed by the weather. "Anything unusual about this one?"

Dr Simmons hesitated, her expression turning more serious. "I don't want to speculate without a full autopsy, but there might be signs of poisoning. We should get the body to the lab for a detailed examination."

George's mind raced with the implications. Another potential poisoning added another layer of complexity to the already intricate case. "Thank you, Dr Simmons. Please keep us updated on your findings."

As Dr Simmons and her team prepared to transport the body, George turned to Detective Sergeant Yolanda Williams, his thoughts evident in his furrowed brow. "If this victim was also poisoned, we're looking at a pattern, a signature method. It could link back to the same source."

"Bastard hasn't left a trace again," said Jay.

George didn't respond immediately, his attention fixed on a small, almost imperceptible mark on the ground near the outline. "Maybe," he finally said. "But every killer makes mistakes. It's our job to find them."

Jay crouched beside him. "What are you thinking, boss?"

George pointed to the mark. "See this? It's slight, but it's a scuff mark. It could indicate a struggle, maybe something the victim did in their final moments."

Jay followed his gaze, nodding slowly. "I'll make sure the CSIs get a cast of it."

George stood up, his eyes still scanning the area. He moved slowly along the alley, pausing occasionally to examine something that caught his eye. Every piece of trash, every stain on the wall, every uneven cobblestone was a potential clue.

Detective Sergeant Yolanda Williams approached, holding a small evidence bag. "Found this near the entrance, sir. It's a piece of torn fabric; it could be from the victim or the killer."

George took the bag, examining its contents closely. "Good find, Yolanda. Get it to the lab, see if they can match it to anything."

Stuart Kent, the Scene of Crime Manager, approached

George, his expression grave.

"Good morning, Stuart. Have we been able to ID the victim yet?" George asked, his voice tinged with a mix of urgency and frustration.

Stuart, methodical and thorough in his approach, nodded grimly. "We're working on it, George. The condition of the face has made visual identification impossible. We're going to have to rely on dental records or fingerprints."

George ran a hand through his hair, his mind racing with the implications. "Let's get on it quickly. Knowing who the victim is could be crucial in understanding why they were targeted."

Stuart turned to his team, issuing instructions with a calm efficiency. "Get a Lantern device over here ASAP."

As the SOC team set to work with practised precision, George watched the scene playing out before him like a well-rehearsed but grim ballet. The meticulous search for evidence, the careful handling of the body, every step was a reminder of the brutal reality of their work.

Yolanda, who had been coordinating with the uniformed officers securing the perimeter, joined George. "Any luck with the ID?"

George shook his head. "Not yet. Stuart's team is on it. We're going to need to wait for fingerprint confirmation."

"Makes our job harder," Yolanda remarked, her gaze surveying the scene. "Not knowing who the victim is stalls a lot of our avenues of investigation."

George's eyes remained fixed on the SOC team. "Every victim is a piece of the puzzle. This brutality, the overkill... it's sending a message. We just need to figure out what it is."

Yolanda nodded in agreement, her mind equally troubled by the savage nature of the crime. "We'll get to the bottom of this, sir. We have to."

Jay, who had been examining the perimeter, called out, "Boss, you might want to see this." He was pointing to a piece of evidence partially hidden in the shadows.

George and Yolanda joined him, their attention focused on what Jay had found—a small, crumpled piece of paper. George carefully picked it up, unfolding it to reveal a hastily scribbled message.

"It's a location and a time," George said, reading the note. "This could be where they're meeting next."

Yolanda's eyes met George's, a spark of hope amidst the despair. "This could be our chance to catch them in the act."

George nodded, his determination renewed. "We set up surveillance on this location. If we're right, we could finally get the break we need."

Stuart Kent, the Scene of Crime Officer, briskly approached Detective Inspector George Beaumont, a sense of urgency in his stride. The crime scene, still buzzing with forensic activity, had yielded a crucial piece of information.

"DI Beaumont, we've got an ID on the victim," Kent announced, his expression grave. "We used the Lantern device for rapid fingerprint analysis. It's Michael Clarkson."

George's expression tensed at the mention of the name, a stark realisation hitting him. "Mike Clarkson? He's one of the two surviving members of that group involved with the OCG a decade ago."

Kent nodded, his eyes reflecting the significance of this discovery. "Yes, it's him. This changes the complexion of the case, doesn't it?"

"It does," George agreed, his mind racing with the implications. "Clarkson's past with the OCG, his survival from the previous ordeal... This isn't random. It's a targeted killing."

Detective Sergeant Yolanda Williams, who had joined them, added, "This could mean a shift in the OCG's focus, or it could be settling old scores. We need to dig deeper into Clarkson's recent activities and associations."

George turned to Kent. "Stuart, I want a full forensic sweep of Clarkson's residence, his workplace, everywhere he frequented. We need to find any connection to the current OCG activities or any potential threats he might have received."

"Already on it," Kent replied, his professionalism evident. "We'll comb through everything."

Turning to Yolanda, George said, "Let's get back to the station. We need to piece together Clarkson's last few days. There has to be a trail that led to this."

As they left the scene, George's thoughts were with Mike Clarkson, a man whose past had seemingly caught up with him in the most brutal way. The streets of Leeds carried on with their usual bustle, the morning progressing as if nothing had happened. But for George and his team, the day had taken a significant turn.

In the Incident Room, George stared at the whiteboard filled with names, dates, and connections. Mike Clarkson's name was now at the centre, a new focal point in the intricate web of their investigation.

Chapter Twenty-seven

The overcast sky loomed above as Detective Inspector George Beaumont and Detective Constable Jay Scott pulled up outside the grimy garage where Mike Clarkson had been employed before becoming a personal trainer. The air was heavy with the scent of oil and rubber, the sounds of the city a distant hum. George's expression was one of determined focus, his mind already framing the questions he needed answers to.

Stepping into the garage, they were greeted by the clatter of tools and the rhythmic thumping of a car being worked on. The manager, a burly man with grease-stained overalls, approached them warily.

"Can I help you, officers?" he asked, eyeing their badges.

George nodded. "We're investigating Michael Clarkson's death. We'd like to ask a few questions about him."

The manager's face tightened, a mixture of surprise and discomfort evident in his eyes. "Mike? Sure, but I don't see what I can tell you. He was just a regular guy. A hard worker."

George observed the surroundings, the array of tools neatly lined up, the cars in various states of repair. "Did you notice any changes in his behaviour recently? Anything unusual?"

The manager scratched his head, thinking. "Well, as you know, he hasn't worked here for six months or so, but I see him a lot." The man scratched his arse. "Now that you mention it, he did seem a bit on edge these past few weeks. Jumpy, like he was expecting trouble."

Jay, taking notes, interjected, "Did he mention anything about his personal life? Any problems he was facing?"

"No, he kept to himself mostly. But he was spending a lot of time at The Rusty Anchor after being at the gym all day. Maybe people there know more."

Thanking the manager, George and Jay left the garage, their next destination clear. The Rusty Anchor, a local pub known for its colourful clientele, could hold the key to understanding Clarkson's state of mind in his final days.

The pub, nestled in Burmantofts, had a weathered sign swaying gently in the breeze. As they entered, the smell of stale beer and the sound of a lone darts game in progress greeted them.

The bartender, a middle-aged woman with a no-nonsense appearance, looked up as they approached. "What can I get for you, gentlemen?"

"We're not here for a drink," George said, showing his warrant card. "We're looking into Mike Clarkson. He was a regular here, we hear."

The bartender's eyes softened slightly. "Mike? Yeah, he was in here most evenings. He kept to himself mostly, but he seemed troubled lately."

"Troubled how?" Jay asked, his pen poised over his notepad.

"Stressed, like he was carrying the world on his shoulders. He'd sit in that corner," she pointed to a secluded booth, "and stare into his pint. Sometimes talked to a few of the regulars, but I couldn't tell you about what."

George scanned the pub, noting the few patrons who seemed

engrossed in their own worlds. "Do you remember seeing him with anyone in particular? Any new faces?"

She thought for a moment. "There was this one guy who came in a couple of times with Mike. Didn't fit in here—too polished, too... watchful. They'd talk in hushed tones."

"Can you describe him?" George pressed, sensing a lead.

"Tall, dark hair with streaks of grey. Had a look about him, like he was used to being in charge," she described.

As they left The Rusty Anchor, George felt the pieces of the puzzle slowly starting to align. Clarkson's behaviour and the mysterious associate—were all threads in a larger tapestry that was slowly coming into focus.

In the car, George turned to Jay. "We need to find out who this man is. He could be the link we've been looking for."

The drive back to the station was silent; both men lost in thought.

* * *

Detective Inspector Luke Mason and Detective Constable Tashan Blackburn hunched over a grainy monitor. The footage, timestamped and unsteady, showed a scene outside a notorious OCG hotspot in Leeds. The area, known for its shadowy dealings, now offered a crucial piece of evidence.

"There," Luke pointed to the screen where Dr Lindsey Yardley, her face animated in anger, was caught in a heated exchange with Neil Roscow. The intensity of their argument, even without sound, was palpable.

Tashan leaned in closer, observing every gesture. "She's not just arguing; she's furious. Look at her body language."

Luke nodded, his mind racing with implications. "And Neil...

he seems defensive, almost scared."

The detectives watched as the argument reached its peak, with Lindsey jabbing a finger at Neil before storming off, leaving Neil visibly shaken. The footage then faded to the routine activity of the night.

"We need to dig deeper into this," Luke said, his voice firm. He started typing on his computer, pulling up financial records.

Minutes later, he whistled softly. "Look at this. Bank transfers from Neil to Lindsey. And not just small amounts."

Tashan's eyes widened. "You think she's involved in his criminal activities, sir? Could be why she was so angry?"

"It's starting to look that way," Luke replied. "Could be blackmail, or maybe she's more involved than we thought."

The detectives knew they had to tread carefully. Dr Lindsey Yardley, a respected pathologist, now appeared to be a suspect in a complex web of crime.

"Let's bring her in for questioning, sir," Tashan suggested. "We need to confront her with this."

A while later, in an interview room, Dr Yardley sat, her poise betraying nothing of the storm that might be raging within. Luke and Tashan entered, their expressions neutral yet determined.

"Dr Yardley," Luke began, "we have evidence suggesting your involvement in financial transactions with Neil Roscow. Can you explain these?"

Lindsey's face remained impassive. "Neil and I had a... professional arrangement."

"Professional? We have footage of you two outside a known OCG spot, arguing heatedly. Doesn't seem very professional," Tashan countered, his gaze unwavering.

Lindsey sighed, a flicker of annoyance crossing her features. "That was a personal matter. Neil owed me money for... a consultancy I provided."

The detectives exchanged a glance. Luke pressed on. "What kind of consultancy requires meeting at a known OCG hotspot, Dr Yardley?"

She hesitated, then replied, "It was confidential. I can't divulge patient information."

"But the money," Tashan interjected, "why the substantial amounts? And why the heated argument?"

Lindsey's composure cracked slightly. "I was advising him on a matter. The argument was about his delay in payment. I assure you, it has nothing to do with his... other activities."

Luke leaned forward. "We find that hard to believe, given the circumstances."

After the questioning, Luke and Tashan stepped out of the room, their minds abuzz with theories. "She's hiding something," Luke said. "But we need more to pin her down."

"Agreed, sir," Tashan replied. "Let's go over everything again. We're missing something."

* * *

The morning light filtered weakly through the blinds of Detective Inspector George Beaumont's office, casting long, slender shadows across the room. He sat, a figure of concentration, his eyes poring over Michael Clarkson's financial statements, which lay scattered across his desk.

Detective Sergeant Yolanda Williams entered, her footsteps a soft echo on the wooden floor. "Got the warrants, sir. We can legally dig deeper into Clarkson's finances now."

George looked up, his gaze intense. "Good. These unexplained cash deposits and withdrawals in Clarkson's account are our best lead yet."

Yolanda pulled up a chair, her eyes scanning the bank statements. "These deposits are substantial. Far more than you'd expect from a personal trainer." She shrugged. "Unless he was training a celebrity or actor, I guess."

"And the withdrawals," George added, tapping a finger on a particularly large figure on the statement. "Always in cash, always just under the amount that would trigger a report. He was trying to stay under the radar."

The room was steeped in silence, broken only by the occasional rustle of paper as they sifted through the documents. George's mind was a whir of theories and conjectures, each more complex than the last.

Yolanda picked up another statement, her brow furrowing. "Look at this pattern. The deposits started small, then gradually increased over time. Like he was being slowly drawn deeper into something."

George leaned back in his chair, his thoughts turning over. "It's as if he was being paid for services or information. Maybe the OCG was using him for something more than we initially thought."

There was a knock at the door, and Detective Constable Jay Scott entered, a file in hand. "I've cross-referenced Clarkson's withdrawal dates with known OCG activities, boss. There's a correlation. Every time there's a spike in their activity, Clarkson withdraws a large sum of cash."

George's eyes narrowed. "He was being paid to facilitate their operations. It's becoming clearer."

Yolanda nodded in agreement. "We need to track where this

money was going. Any regular payments or purchases that stand out."

Jay flipped open his notebook. "I've got a team working on tracing the serial numbers of the notes. And I'm checking for any high-value items he might have bought."

George stood up, his figure casting a long shadow against the wall. "We also need to consider who else might be involved. Clarkson couldn't have managed this alone. There's a bigger network here."

The room was filled with a palpable sense of determination. Each of them knew the importance of the task at hand, the need to untangle the web of financial transactions that Clarkson was entangled in.

Yolanda's voice was resolute. "We'll get to the bottom of this, sir. Follow the money, as they say."

George nodded, a steely glint in his eyes. "Exactly. And when we do, we'll uncover more than just Clarkson's role in all this. We're going to expose the entire operation."

As they left the office, the station buzzed around them, the usual hum of activity. Outside, Leeds carried on, oblivious to the dark undercurrents flowing beneath its surface. But within the walls of the police station, George Beaumont and his team were steadily peeling back the layers of deception and crime, inching ever closer to the truth.

* * *

The bitter winter chill hung in the air as Emma Clarke stood outside the small community centre, a haven for those shattered by the recent wave of crimes that had plagued Leeds. She adjusted her scarf and took a deep breath, steeling herself for the heart-wrenching task ahead.

Inside, the room buzzed with subdued conversations. Faces etched with grief and anger huddled together, seeking solace and understanding. Emma knew that behind every pair of haunted eyes was a story of loss, of lives torn apart by the ruthless hand of crime.

Emma looked at the group, her heart heavy. She had seen too many lives shattered by senseless violence, too many families torn apart. "We'll get through this together. Leeds is strong, and we won't let these criminals destroy our community."

As Emma moved through the room, she listened to the stories of loss and pain. Each tale was a thread in the tapestry of suffering that crime had woven through Leeds.

In a corner of the room, a group of children huddled together, their faces painted with a mixture of fear and curiosity. Emma approached them, crouching down to their eye level. "Hey there," she said with a warm smile. "I know this is a tough time, but we're all here to support each other. If you ever want to talk or if you're scared, find one of us grown-ups, okay?"

A young boy named James, no more than seven years old, nodded solemnly. "Will the bad people go away, Miss Emma?"

Emma's heart ached for the innocence that had been stolen from these children. "The police are working on it, James. They're doing everything they can to make sure Leeds is safe again."

She continued to speak with the children, assuring them that the community was a shield against the darkness that had descended upon their town. The children's laughter, though fragile, was a glimmer of hope in the midst of despair.

Chapter Twenty-eight

The day was overcast, the heavy clouds mirroring the mood that hung over Detective Inspector George Beaumont as he made his way to Daniel Roberts' residence. The air was thick with the impending rain, the streets of Leeds echoing with the muted sounds of a city carrying on unknowingly above the undercurrents of its darker side.

Danny Roberts' house was a modest semi-detached in a quiet suburb, the garden unkempt. He knocked on the door, the sound sharp in the stillness of the afternoon.

The door opened to reveal Danny, his appearance markedly aged somehow since they last spoke. His eyes, once bright and full of life, now held a wariness born of hard years.

"Mr Roberts, I'm Detective Inspector Beaumont. May I have a word?" George asked, his tone professional yet not without empathy.

"I remember who you are." Danny's gaze was cautious but resigned. "I was wondering when you'd show up. Come in."

Inside, the house was sparse, the furnishings minimal. They sat in the small living room, where Danny faced George with a resigned expression.

"I suppose this is about Mike Clarkson," Danny began, his voice tinged with a mixture of sadness and fatigue.

"Yes," George confirmed. "I need to understand your relationship with him, especially any recent interactions."

Danny sighed, a deep, weary sound. "Mike and I... we go way back. But things changed. He got involved with some dangerous people. I tried to warn him."

"Can you tell me about these people?" George pressed, observing Danny's reactions closely.

Danny hesitated, then spoke in a low voice. "It's the OCG, OK. I admit it. And I'm next, right?"

"We have no reason to believe that," said George. George leaned forward, his eyes locking onto Danny's. The air in the room felt heavy, charged with unspoken fears and secrets. "Danny, we need to understand the nature of your involvement with the OCG. It's crucial for us to protect you and others who might be in danger."

Danny's gaze dropped to his hands, which were clenched tightly together. He seemed to wrestle with his thoughts, the internal struggle evident on his weathered face. "I... I was never 'in' with them, not like Mike. But I knew things, overheard things. That's enough for them, isn't it?"

Yolanda, who had been quietly observing, added gently, "Anything you can tell us could help. Not just in solving Mike's case, but in keeping you safe."

Danny looked up, his eyes meeting George's. "They're everywhere, aren't they? In the shadows, behind the deals... I've seen them around, making plans, talking in hushed voices. Mike got in over his head. Said he was just doing them favours, but I could see it was more than that." He paused. "I only did the Santa stuff, I swear."

George leaned in slightly. "Did Mike ever discuss his dealings with them? Anything specific?"

Danny shook his head. "He kept it close. But I could tell it was eating at him. He was scared, paranoid even." With a note of regret in his voice, he said, "But I could see the change in him. He got deeper and started taking risks... I warned him, told him to get out."

George nodded, understanding the gravity of the situation. "And these risks, did he ever mention specifics?"

Danny shook his head slowly. "Just that he was moving stuff for them, big stuff. He said it was getting too hot and that he wanted out. But you don't just walk away from the OCG, do you?"

George's expression remained impassive, but his mind was racing. "We're doing everything we can to dismantle their operations. But we need as much information as possible. Anything else you can remember could be vital."

Danny sighed, a deep exhalation that seemed to carry the weight of his worries. "There was talk of a big deal, something that was going to set them up for a long time. Mike didn't give details, just said it was big and dangerous."

Yolanda interjected, "Do you know when this deal was supposed to happen or who was involved?"

"It's already in motion," Danny said, his voice barely above a whisper. "But names, no. Mike never mentioned names. He was scared and said this was bigger than anything they'd done before."

George took notes, his mind piecing together the information. "Was there anyone else who might have been involved with Mike and the OCG?"

Danny paused, a shadow crossing his face. "There was a guy, new in town—a real estate developer. Mike met with him a few times. Didn't seem like the regular business type, if you know what I mean."

George's interest was piqued. "Do you have a name?"

"Richard Hallworth," Danny said. "Drove a fancy car, wore expensive suits. Didn't fit in around here."

Thanking Danny, George left, his next course of action straightforward. He needed to delve into Richard Hallworth's background.

The visit to The Rusty Anchor pub later that evening yielded more insights. The bartender, a middle-aged man with a keen eye, remembered Hallworth.

"Yeah, I saw him with Mike a couple of times. They kept to themselves, always talking hushed like. Looked serious."

George stood up, his decision made. "We're going to increase surveillance around your place, Danny. And we'll look into this deal. You've been a great help."

As they left Danny's house, the evening sky was turning a darker shade of blue, and the streetlights were beginning to flicker on. George and Yolanda walked back to their car in silence, each lost in their thoughts.

In the car, George broke the silence. "This 'big deal' could be our chance to hit the OCG where it hurts. We need to move fast, gather as much intel as we can."

Yolanda nodded, her expression set in determination. "I'll coordinate with the team and see if we can pick up any chatter about this deal."

The car pulled away, leaving Danny's house and its secrets behind.

George's visit to Hallworth's last known address led to a dead-end, the luxury apartment vacated recently. The neighbours knew little, but one comment stood out.

"He was always on the phone and looked stressed. I saw

him arguing with someone a few nights ago. Couldn't catch who, though."

Back at his office, George sat in the dim light, the pieces of the puzzle slowly forming a clearer picture. Clarkson's deepening involvement with the OCG, Hallworth's mysterious presence, and the increasing danger that seemed to surround their activities.

Each revelation added a layer to the intricate web of crime and deceit that George was determined to unravel.

* * *

In a separate interview room at Elland Road Police Station, Detective Constables Candy Nichols and Jay Scott sat across from a nervous-looking witness, the room feeling even more constricted than usual. The man, a local shopkeeper, fidgeted in his chair, his eyes darting around the room.

"So, Mr Davies, you mentioned seeing Dr Lindsey Yardley and Neil Roscow together?" Candy began, her voice calm and measured, aiming to put the witness at ease.

Mr Davies nodded, swallowing hard. "Yes, Detective. Several times, late at night. They met in the alley behind my shop. It always seemed... secretive."

Jay leaned forward, his attention sharpened. "Can you describe these meetings? Anything you noticed about their behaviour or what they exchanged?"

The shopkeeper wrung his hands, the memory clearly unsettling. "Well, it was odd, you know? They always looked around as if making sure no one was watching. And Lindsey... she always had this briefcase with her."

"A briefcase?" Candy prompted, her interest piqued.

"Yes," Mr Davies continued, "They'd exchange what looked like documents. Neil seemed anxious, always checking over his shoulder."

Jay scribbled notes, his mind racing with the implications. "Did you ever hear anything they said?"

Mr Davies shook his head. "No, Detective. They kept their voices low, but it was clear they didn't want to be seen or heard."

Candy exchanged a glance with Jay, both detectives sensing the gravity of the witness's account. "And how often did these meetings occur?"

"Several times over the past month. Always late at night. It was strange... I never thought Lindsey, a respected doctor, would be involved in something like this."

The detectives thanked Mr Davies, assuring him his information was invaluable. After he left, they sat in silence, contemplating their next move.

"This changes things," Candy said, her voice tinged with concern. "If Lindsey was passing documents to Neil, she could be more than just a casual acquaintance."

Jay nodded in agreement, his expression grave. "We need to speak with Lindsey again. This time, we press her on these meetings."

In George Beaumont's office, where the DI was working with DS Williams, Candy and Jay briefed him on their interview with Mr Davies. George listened intently, his eyes narrowing as the pieces of the puzzle began to fit together in a disturbing picture.

"Alright," George said, his decision firm. "Speak with Lindsey Yardley. We need to confront her with this new information."

* * *

The relentless rain pattered against the windows of the small, cluttered office where Detective Inspector George Beaumont and Detective Sergeant Yolanda Williams sat, their gazes fixed on the array of Clarkson's phone and email records spread before them. The dim light from the desk lamp cast long shadows across the papers, mirroring the dark undercurrents of the case they were unravelling.

George's eyes were narrowed in concentration as he sifted through the call logs, each number a potential key to unlocking the secrets Clarkson had taken to his grave. "We need to find the source of these encrypted calls. They could lead us straight to the heart of the OCG's operations."

Yolanda, her fingers tapping rhythmically on the keyboard, replied, "I'm on it. I've got the telecoms team tracing the numbers. It's a deep dive, but we'll get there."

The room was filled with a palpable sense of urgency, the sound of the rain a constant reminder of the storm they were navigating. George picked up a series of emails, his eyes scanning the cryptic language used.

"Look at this," he said, pointing to a specific email. "The language here is guarded, almost coded. But there's an undercurrent of threat."

Yolanda leaned over, her keen eyes quickly assessing the content. "You're right. It's subtle, but it's there. Like they're reminding Clarkson of his place."

The phone on George's desk rang, breaking the intense focus in the room. He answered, his voice brisk. "DI Beaumont."

After a few moments of listening, a quick nod, and then he hung up, a look of triumph in his eyes. "That was the telecoms team. They've traced the unknown number. It belongs to a burner phone, but they've managed to pinpoint its last known location."

Yolanda's eyebrows raised in anticipation. "Where?"

"A rundown industrial estate in Holbeck on the outskirts of the city. It's been a hotspot for dubious activities in the past."

George stood up, a new energy in his movements. "We need to check it out. If we're lucky, we might catch a break."

The drive to the industrial estate was tense, the rain creating a blurred curtain against the car windows, distorting the familiar cityscape into something more ominous. As they navigated the narrow, winding roads, the sense of stepping into unknown territory grew stronger.

The industrial estate was desolate, a collection of abandoned warehouses and derelict buildings. They parked the car and stepped out, the rain a relentless companion. George's senses were heightened, every sound and movement amplified in the vast emptiness.

Yolanda pointed to one of the warehouses. "That's where the signal was last detected. Let's check it out."

They approached cautiously, their steps echoing in the vast open space. The warehouse loomed ahead, its large, rusted doors slightly ajar.

Inside, the air was musty, the only light coming from the cracks in the boarded-up windows. They moved slowly, their eyes scanning the shadows.

George's foot hit something with a soft thud. He looked down to find a discarded burner phone; its screen cracked.

"This is it," he murmured, picking it up carefully. "This could be our direct line to the OCG."

Yolanda examined the phone. "We need to get this to

forensics and see if they can retrieve anything from it, sir."

As they made their way back to the car, the weight of their discovery hung heavily between them. The burner phone was a tangible link, a whisper in the dark that promised to lead them closer to the truth.

Back at the station, George and Yolanda sat in George's office, the burner phone now in the hands of the forensics team. The rain had eased, but the sense of a storm still brewing was palpable.

"We're getting closer, Yolanda," George said, a determined edge to his voice. "Every step takes us deeper into their world, but we're not backing down."

Yolanda nodded, her expression one of resolve. "We're in this together, sir. We'll see it through to the end."

Chapter Twenty-nine

The evening draped its shadow over Leeds as Detective Inspector George Beaumont and Detective Sergeant Yolanda Williams made their way to the flat where the individual involved in the heated argument with Mike Clarkson lived. The building, nestled in a less affluent part of the city, wore its age like a badge, its walls echoing stories untold.

It had been DC Candy Nichols who had notified them of Alan Turner's argument with Clarkson during her research into Clarkson's recent interactions and acquaintances. So they'd immediately headed to interview him.

They ascended the creaky stairs, the sound of their footsteps muffled by the faded carpet. At the door of the flat, George knocked firmly, his posture tensely anticipative.

The door swung open to reveal a man in his mid-thirties, his face marked by a life that hadn't been kind. His eyes flickered with a mix of suspicion and curiosity. "Yes?"

"Mr Alan Turner?" George asked, his warrant card in clear view. "We're investigating the death of Mike Clarkson. We understand you had an altercation with him recently."

Alan's expression shifted, a flicker of recognition passing through his eyes. "Yeah, that's me. But it was nothing, just a disagreement."

Yolanda stepped forward, her tone gentle yet probing. "We need to understand the nature of this disagreement, Mr Turner."

Alan sighed, running a hand through his hair. "Alright, come in."

The flat was sparse, the furniture worn but clean. They sat in the small living room, Alan perched nervously on the edge of an armchair.

"It was about money," Alan began, his gaze fixed on the floor. "Mike owed me. He was acting all strange, said he was in trouble but wouldn't say why."

George leaned in, his voice steady. "What kind of trouble? Did he mention anyone he was afraid of?"

Alan hesitated, then spoke in a hushed tone. "He mentioned being followed and said he was in deep with some bad people. I thought he was just making excuses for the money."

Yolanda's voice was soft but insistent. "Did he mention any names, Mr Turner?"

"No, no names. Just that he was scared. Said it was bigger than he thought, something about getting out."

The detectives exchanged a glance, the pieces slowly falling into place. George stood up, his decision made. "Thank you, Mr Turner. If you remember anything else, please get in touch with us."

Their next stop was the home of Clarkson's close friend, Peter Walsh, who lived in a quiet suburban area. The street was lined with neatly kept houses, their windows glowing warmly against the twilight.

Peter, a man in his late forties, greeted them at the door, his face lined with worry. "Detectives, please come in. I've been expecting you since I heard about Mike."

In the comfort of Peter's living room, amidst family photos and soft furnishings, the conversation took a more sombre turn.

"Mike confided in me a few weeks back," Peter said, his voice heavy with concern. "He was terrified, kept saying he'd got involved with something he couldn't control."

George, sitting across from Peter, asked, "Did Mike specify what he was involved in? Any details that could help us?"

Peter shook his head sadly. "He was vague and said it was too dangerous to talk about. But he mentioned something about a deal gone wrong, something that put him in the cross hairs."

Yolanda, her pen poised over her notebook, queried further. "Did he ever express fear for his life, Mr Walsh?"

"Yes," Peter replied, a tremor in his voice. "He said he feared he wouldn't make it out alive. I never imagined it would come to this." He paused. "He didn't give me a name when I asked but did give me a hint. The guy shares a surname with a Rugby League player from Yorkshire."

As they left Peter's house, the night had fully descended upon Leeds, casting a cloak of darkness over the city. George and Yolanda walked back to their car, their minds heavy with the revelations of the evening.

"It's clear Clarkson was deeply entangled in something dangerous," George mused, his thoughts troubled. "Fear was a constant companion in his final days."

Yolanda nodded in agreement, her expression resolute in the glow of the streetlights. "We need to uncover what that 'something' was. Clarkson's fear might just lead us to his killer."

The drive back to the station was quiet; both detectives lost in thought.

* * *

Detectives Luke Mason and Tashan Blackburn were hunched over a desk littered with papers and photos. The dim light from the lamp cast a subdued glow, adding to the room's intense atmosphere.

"We've been looking at this all wrong," Luke said, his voice low and thoughtful as he sifted through the evidence. "That argument between Lindsey and Neil—it's not what we thought."

Tashan, leaning back in his chair, rubbed his chin thoughtfully. "You mean the shopkeeper's account that Jay and Candy took, sir? About the heated exchange?"

Luke nodded, pointing to a transcript of a recent interview. "Exactly. According to new statements, Lindsey was confronting Neil about his illegal activities. She didn't know about the nature of his business when she loaned him the money."

Tashan's eyes widened slightly. "So, the bank transfers we found... they were repayments for a loan she gave him unknowingly?"

"Seems like it," Luke confirmed, his expression turning pensive. "Lindsey's involvement in this might be far less sinister than we suspected. She might just be an unwitting participant."

The detectives sat in silence for a moment, absorbing the implications of this revelation. It painted a completely different picture of Dr Lindsey Yardley, one that moved away from the narrative of her being a willing accomplice.

"We need to speak with her again then, sir," Tashan said

decisively. "Clear up this misunderstanding, get her side of the story." He smiled. He had always thought Lindsey was innocent.

Luke nodded in agreement, a sense of urgency in his movement as he stood up. "Let's do it. We can't keep chasing shadows."

Ten minutes later, in an interview room, Lindsey Yardley sat across from Luke and Tashan. The room, stark and uninviting, echoed with the weight of their discussion.

"Lindsey, we've come across some new information," Luke began, his tone deliberately neutral. "It appears that the money you lent to Neil Roscow was used for purposes you weren't aware of."

Lindsey's face softened slightly. "I had no idea to begin with," she said, her voice tinged with frustration. "When I found out what Neil was using the money for, I was furious. That's what the argument was about."

Tashan leaned in, his expression one of professional curiosity. "So, you're saying you were an unwitting participant in his activities?"

Lindsey nodded, her posture conveying a mix of relief and exasperation. "Absolutely. I'm a doctor, not a criminal. I loaned him money thinking it was for a legitimate business."

Luke and Tashan exchanged glances, the new information reshaping their understanding of the case. "We appreciate your honesty, Lindsey. This certainly changes things," Tashan said, his tone implying a shift in their investigation.

Tashan was about to stand up when Luke stopped him. "It was a lot of money, Lindsey."

"It's not a crime, is it?"

"Not if you weren't aware and Neil lied to you," Luke

explained. "I guess I'm just curious as to why you'd lend him so much money."

Lindsey's cheeks coloured at the question.

"Well?" asked Luke.

Lindsey hesitated, her cheeks still flushed with colour. "Neil and I... we have history," she began cautiously. "Our families were close when we were younger. When he came to me with his business proposal, it seemed legitimate, and I wanted to help."

Luke nodded, understanding the nuances of such a personal connection. "So, it was more than just a financial transaction. There was a trust, a bond from the past."

"Exactly," Lindsey affirmed, a hint of sadness in her voice. "I believed in him, in his vision. It's only later I realised the true nature of his activities."

Tashan leaned back, processing her words. "That must've been quite a shock for you, realising you'd been deceived."

"It was," Lindsey admitted, her expression a blend of regret and resolve. "But now, I just want to help set things right."

"I still don't think you're being entirely honest with us," Luke said.

Lindsey, reflecting on her relationship with Neil, shared with a certain wistfulness, "We were together when I was fifteen, and he was seven years older. He always had this respectful, caring side to him, which made me trust him deeply." This revelation painted a picture of a bond formed in the bloom of early adulthood, a connection that evidently had a profound impact on Lindsey's decisions and her trust in Neil.

The detectives exchanged a look, a silent agreement on the complexity of human relationships and the pain of betrayal.

"We'll do our best to untangle this, Lindsey," Luke assured her, his tone sincere. "Your cooperation is invaluable." Again, Tashan got up to leave, but Luke stopped him. With a hint of frustration, he asked Lindsey, "Why didn't you mention your past with Neil before? During the initial investigation?"

Lindsey sighed, a conflicted look crossing her face. "I knew how it would look—a personal connection, the money... I thought it would cast unnecessary suspicion on me and complicate the investigation. I wanted to help, not become a distraction." Her words reflected the dilemma she faced, torn between honesty and the fear of being wrongly implicated due to her past with Neil.

"And the DNA and prints on the Christmas ornaments?"

She shrugged. "I've known Neil for a long time, so I could have handled them at one point."

As Lindsey left the room, escorted by a police constable back to her cell, the detectives remained, pondering the complexity of the case. "We were so focused on finding a connection," Luke mused, "we almost missed the truth."

"Yeah, sir," Tashan agreed, standing up. "It's a reminder that things aren't always as they seem. We need to keep digging but with a clearer perspective."

* * *

Their CCTV suite at Elland Road Police Station, usually bustling with activity, was unusually quiet as Detective Inspector George Beaumont and Detective Sergeant Yolanda Williams sat hunched over a bank of monitors. The glow from the screens cast an eerie light on their faces, illuminating their expressions of intense concentration.

On the screens flickered various CCTV footage from around Leeds, the images grainy and often jumpy but potentially crucial to their investigation. George's eyes were fixed on one particular screen showing a feed from a camera near a known OCG hangout.

"There," he pointed to a shadowy figure entering the frame. "That could be one of Clarkson's unknown contacts. See the way he's looking around? Like he's trying to avoid being noticed."

Yolanda leaned closer, her eyes narrowing as she studied the figure. "He's cautious, that's for sure. Can we enhance the image? Get a better look at his face?"

George nodded, reaching for the keyboard. With a few keystrokes, he zoomed in on the figure, the image pixelating slightly before sharpening again. A hat partially obscured the man's face, but there was enough to suggest he wasn't just an ordinary passer-by.

"He looks familiar," Yolanda murmured, her brain rifling through the mental catalogue of known associates of the OCG. "Can't place him, though. We'll need to run this through facial recognition."

George sat back, his gaze still on the screen. "Keep an eye on the hangout spots. If he's a regular, he'll show up again."

They switched their attention to another screen showing footage from a camera outside a pub where Clarkson was known to meet his contacts. The time stamp on the footage indicated it was from a few nights before Clarkson's murder.

"There," Yolanda said suddenly, pointing to a figure lurking in the background. "That man there, talking to Clarkson. He's been in and out of the frame for the past few minutes."

George studied the footage, noting the man's body language.

"He's careful, keeping his distance, but definitely interested in Clarkson. Could be another link."

The detectives continued their vigil, the room filled with the hum of the machines and the occasional soft click of a mouse. Each frame of footage was scrutinised, and each individual was assessed for potential connections to their case.

After several hours, George leaned back in his chair, rubbing his tired eyes. "We've got some leads. Let's get these images out to the team and see if we can put names to these faces."

Yolanda stretched, her muscles aching from hours of sitting. "I'll coordinate with the tech team and get them working on enhancing the images. We're close, sir. I can feel it."

As they left the room, the weight of their findings hung heavily between them. The CCTV footage had provided them with tantalising glimpses into Clarkson's last days, each frame a potential clue in the intricate puzzle they were piecing together.

The corridors of the police station were quiet as they made their way back to their office, the rest of the building seemingly asleep. But for George Beaumont and Yolanda Williams, the night was far from over. The city of Leeds, with its dark corners and hidden secrets, was a tapestry of stories waiting to be uncovered.

In his office, George sat down heavily, his mind still on the footage. "We're solving it, Yolanda. Bit by bit, we're getting to the truth."

Yolanda nodded, a determined glint in her eye. "And we won't stop until we've brought whoever's responsible to justice."

* * *

Chapter Thirty

The rhythmic tapping of keys filled the air in the digital forensics lab of Elland Road Police Station, where Detective Inspector George Beaumont and Detective Sergeant Yolanda Williams stood over the shoulder of Forensic IT Specialist Karen Willis. The glow from multiple computer screens illuminated the trio, casting an almost spectral light in the otherwise dim room.

Karen's fingers danced across the keyboard with practised ease as she navigated through the labyrinth of Mike Clarkson's digital life. George watched intently, his keen mind piecing together the fragments of information that flickered across the screen.

"We've managed to break into Clarkson's laptop and phone," Karen began, her voice a monotone of concentration. "He was meticulous about his digital footprint. Lots of encrypted files, secure communications."

Yolanda leaned in, her eyes scanning the screen. "Any idea what he was trying to protect?"

Karen nodded, clicking on a folder. "He did extensive research on data encryption and secure messaging apps. It's like he was paranoid about being monitored."

George's expression was pensive, his brain turning over the

implications. "He knew he was in dangerous waters. Was trying to keep his tracks covered."

Karen opened a series of browser history tabs, the list extensive and varied. "Look at this," she said, pointing to a series of searches. "He was looking into ways to disappear, new identities, even offshore banking."

The room fell into a thoughtful silence, each member of the team contemplating the significance of Clarkson's actions. It painted a picture of a man desperate to escape, to shed the skin of his current life for something new, something safer.

Yolanda broke the silence, her tone laced with curiosity. "Was he planning to run? Start over?"

"It seems likely," George replied, his gaze still fixed on the screen. "He knew too much, got too involved. He was looking for a way out."

Karen continued to sift through Clarkson's online activity, her fingers a blur of motion. "There's a series of deleted emails here. I'm trying to recover them, but it looks like they were sent to an unknown recipient. Could be key."

George's mind was already racing ahead, the pieces of the puzzle slotting together in his head. "Keep at it, Karen. Those emails could be our best lead yet."

Back in his office, George sat staring out of the window, the cityscape a mosaic of light and shadow. Yolanda sat opposite him, her mind equally absorbed in thought.

"He was scared, Yolanda," George said, his voice a murmur. "Scared enough to want to disappear."

Yolanda nodded, her eyes reflecting a mix of empathy and determination. "And that fear led him to his death, sir. We need to find out who he was talking to, who he was afraid of."

The room was steeped in a sombre atmosphere, the reality

of Clarkson's plight a stark reminder of the dangers lurking beneath the surface of their city. The rain began to fall outside, a gentle patter against the window, a rhythmic reminder of the passing of time.

"We'll find the truth," George said, his voice now firm with resolve. "For Clarkson and all those caught in this web."

The rain continued to fall, a soft accompaniment to their thoughts.

* * *

Detective Constables Candy Nichols and Jay Scott pored over a tangle of family trees and bank statements, their focus unwavering. The room, steeped in the muted bustle of the police station, felt like a world apart, a sanctuary for unravelling the complexities of their case.

Candy, her eyes tracing a lineage chart, broke the silence. "Jay, look at this," Candy said, her mind racing with the implications. "Lindsey wasn't funding criminal activities. She was trying to stop them."

The revelation cast a new light on the investigation. The secretive meetings and the document exchanges were all part of Lindsey's efforts to gather evidence against Neil, intending to report him to the police.

"Her behaviour makes sense now," Jay mused, a note of admiration in his voice. "She was working undercover in her own way, gathering intel on Neil's activities."

Candy nodded, the pieces of the puzzle finally fitting together. "We need to inform the team. This changes everything."

The detectives made their way to George Beaumont's office,

where the hum of diligent work filled the air. But George wasn't there; he was still out, working on Mike Clarkson's background and last hours.

Jay pulled out his mobile, placed it on his desk in the shared office, and called DI Beaumont.

As they briefed George on their findings, his tone shifted from scepticism to understanding.

"So Lindsey was operating solo, trying to bring Neil down?" George asked, leaning back in his chair.

"Exactly," Candy confirmed. "She used her connection to get close, collect evidence."

George let out a long breath, the weight of the revelation evident in his posture. "We need to protect her. If Neil finds out..."

"We're on it, sir," Jay assured him. "We'll ensure Lindsey's safety."

"Before you go, I need help figuring out a timeline for Michael Clarkson's last hours before his murder," George said.

"We'll get right on it," Jay said.

After the call had finished, the reality of the situation settled in. Their investigation, once a labyrinth of suspicion and doubt, had found a semblance of clarity.

* * *

The sky was a palette of greys as Detective Inspector George Beaumont and Detective Sergeant Yolanda Williams drove through the quiet streets of Leeds to the modest house where Mike Clarkson's ex-wife, Sarah, lived. The garden was well-tended, a stark contrast to the turmoil that lay within the walls of the house.

Sarah Clarkson opened the door, her features etched with the lines of worry and loss. She ushered them into a neat living room, where faded photographs of happier times adorned the walls.

"Thank you for seeing us, Mrs Clarkson," George began, his tone respectful. "We need to understand more about Mike in the weeks before his death."

Sarah sat down, her hands clasped tightly in her lap. "I wish I could help, but Mike and I... we weren't close after the divorce. He changed, became distant, secretive."

Yolanda leaned forward, her voice soft. "Did he ever mention feeling threatened or scared?"

Sarah's eyes flickered with a remembered fear. "He did once. He said he was in over his head with something. But he wouldn't give me details. I thought it was just talk." She wiped away a stray tear. "I didn't bloody believe him, did I?"

George's gaze was sympathetic but probing. "Did he have any unusual visitors or make any strange phone calls that you know of?"

"No, but he was always cautious. Used to look over his shoulder like he was being followed," Sarah replied, a shiver running through her. "It's what ended us, to be honest, his paranoia." She shrugged. "Well, that and the jealousy."

After leaving Sarah's house, George and Yolanda drove to the suburb where Mike Clarkson had lived. The houses were close together, and the community was tight-knit. They stopped at a neighbour's house, an elderly lady named Mrs Thompson, known for her keen observation skills.

Mrs Thompson welcomed them in, her eyes sharp beneath her grey curls. "Detectives, about Mike? It's a terrible thing, his death."

George nodded. "We're trying to piece together his last few days. Did you notice anything unusual?"

Mrs Thompson thought for a moment. "Well, there was a car, a black sedan, parked outside his house a few times. Didn't recognise it. And there was a man, always wore a hat and coat, visited Mike a couple of times."

Yolanda took notes, her interest piqued. "Can you describe the man, Mrs Thompson?"

"Tall, dark coat, always kept his head down. Had a sense of... urgency about him," Mrs Thompson described, her gaze distant as she recalled the details.

George exchanged a look with Yolanda, and the significance of Mrs Thompson's observations was not lost on them. "Thank you, Mrs Thompson. You've been very helpful."

As they left, the evening was drawing in, casting long shadows across the streets of Leeds. The car ride back to the station was quiet, both detectives lost in thought, piecing together the fragments of Mike Clarkson's last days.

In George's office, the lights were dim, the cityscape outside a mosaic of light and dark. "Clarkson was scared, running from something... or someone," George mused, staring out the window.

Yolanda, sitting across from him, added, "The black sedan, the mysterious visitor. It's clear he was involved in something dangerous. We need to find out who this visitor was and what their connection to Mike was."

George turned from the window, his expression one of resolve. "We're getting closer, Yolanda. Closer to understanding the web Clarkson was entangled in."

The room was silent, save for the faint sounds of the

city outside. George sat down at his desk, the files and photographs spread out before him like pieces of a puzzle waiting to be solved.

"We need to keep digging," he said, picking up a photograph of Clarkson. "Every detail, no matter how small, could lead us to the truth."

Yolanda nodded in agreement, her eyes scanning the files. "I'll go through his phone records again, see if we missed anything. Maybe there's a pattern we overlooked."

* * *

Later, Detective Constables Candy Nichols, Jay Scott, and Tashan Blackburn, along with Detective Inspector Luke Mason, huddled around a cluttered desk, piecing together the final hours of Michael Clarkson's life.

"Let's start with the pub visit," Candy suggested, pointing to a series of time-stamped CCTV images. "He was a regular here, right?"

"Yeah," Jay replied, zooming in on a frame where Clarkson was seen laughing with a group of acquaintances. "Looks like a normal evening for him. But notice the change in his demeanour over time."

The timeline shifted to late evening, marked by a pivotal phone call. Luke pointed to a CCTV image showing Clarkson stepping outside, phone to his ear. "Here. He looks agitated after this call. Something must have rattled him."

Tashan, reviewing Clarkson's phone records, added, "The number he called is unregistered, but the location ping puts it near an industrial area. I've already checked, and it's a dead end, but it suggests something covert."

The detectives pondered the significance of this call, each aware of its potential link to Clarkson's fate.

"We need to focus on this meeting," Luke said, pointing to another CCTV clip. It showed Clarkson meeting an unidentified figure in a secluded area. "This has to be crucial."

The footage was grainy, the figures barely discernible in the shadows. "Can we enhance this?" Candy asked, squinting at the screen.

"I'll get the tech team on it," Jay offered, reaching for his phone. "Maybe they can clear it up, get us an ID."

As the evening progressed, so did their investigation. The detectives looked at the last known image of Clarkson, time-stamped just before the timeline went blank.

"This is it, the last sighting before he's found dead," Tashan said, his voice low. The image showed Clarkson walking alone, his figure swallowed by the night.

The room fell silent; each detective lost in thought. The gap in the timeline represented the unknown, the critical hours of Clarkson's life that led to his untimely death.

Candy broke the silence. "We have a pub full of potential witnesses, an agitated phone call, a secretive meeting, and a time gap we can't account for. This is more than just a murder; it's a puzzle we need to solve."

Luke nodded in agreement. "Let's split up. Jay, you and I will go back to the pub and see if the regulars remember anything about that night. Tashan, Candy, you two dig deeper into that phone call and track down who he was meeting."

The detectives stood up, each acutely aware of the importance of their next steps. As they filed out of the office, the determination to uncover the truth about Michael Clarkson's final hours was etched on their faces.

Chapter Thirty-one

The day was wearing into a drizzly evening as Detective Inspector George Beaumont and Detective Sergeant Yolanda Williams found themselves in the plush office of a high-end real estate agent in Leeds. The walls were adorned with images of luxurious properties, and the air was tinged with a scent of affluence. They were there to unravel the enigma surrounding the recent property transaction by Mike Clarkson.

"Mr Clarkson's property sale," George began, his voice deliberate, "it was handled through this agency, correct?"

The agent, a well-dressed man with a carefully manicured beard, nodded, his attitude a mix of professionalism and caution. "Yes, Detective. It was a rather swift transaction, quite unusual."

Yolanda, her eyes scanning the opulent office, asked, "Unusual in what way?"

The agent hesitated, then responded, "Well, the buyer was eager to close the deal. Paid in cash, a substantial sum. It's not every day we see transactions like that."

George's gaze was unwavering. "And the buyer, can you tell us anything about them?"

"Privacy policies, I'm afraid. But I can say they weren't local. Seemed more... international. You'll need a warrant."

As they left the estate agent's office, the pieces of Clarkson's puzzle were slowly assembling in George's mind. The luxury car, the property sale, the cash—it all pointed towards something more significant than mere financial gain.

Their next stop was a high-end car dealership on the outskirts of Leeds, where Clarkson had recently purchased a luxury car. The showroom gleamed with polished cars and the promise of speed and luxury.

The salesman, upon recognising the detectives, approached with a practised smile, which faltered under George's direct gaze.

"We're interested in a transaction involving Mike Clarkson," George stated. "He bought a car here recently?"

The salesman's smile had now fully retreated. "Yes, a top-of-the-range model. Paid in cash. It was an unusual sale but not unheard of in this business."

Yolanda, her eyes skimming over the cars, queried, "Any idea where Mr Clarkson got that kind of cash?"

The salesman shrugged. "We don't pry into our clients' personal affairs as long as their money is good."

Back in the car, George and Yolanda sat in contemplative silence, the puzzle pieces clicking together in their minds.

"The cash for the car," Yolanda mused, "it suggests Clarkson had access to a significant amount of money. Money that wasn't from his job at the gym."

George nodded, his thoughts mirroring Yolanda's. "It points to an undisclosed income source. Possibly from his dealings with the OCG."

The car wove through the streets of Leeds, the cityscape a blur of grey and muted colours. George's mind was abuzz with theories and possibilities, the case unfolding like a complex tapestry.

In his office, George sat behind his desk, the files of Clarkson's financial records spread before him. Each document, each transaction, was a clue in the intricate labyrinth of corruption and deceit they were navigating.

"We need to trace the flow of this money," George said, his voice a determined rumble. "Find out where it's coming from and where it's going. That's the key to unlocking Clarkson's involvement with the OCG."

Yolanda, her eyes sharp and focused, added, "And if we can prove the money is tied to criminal activities, we might just be able to pull the whole operation apart."

* * *

In the shadowed streets of Shadwell, the surveillance team watched Neil Roscow with bated breath. Hidden within the confines of their unmarked car, they observed him pacing near the designated location, a nervous energy about him.

"He's definitely waiting for someone," whispered Sergeant Phillips, her eyes not leaving the binoculars.

Neil Roscow was loitering near an old, graffiti-laden phone box.

Detective Constable Harris, seated beside her, nodded. "Could he be the killer? This changes everything."

Phillips reached for the radio. "We need to call DI Beaumont. He'll want to know about this development."

In his office, George Beaumont's phone rang, pulling him from his thoughts. "Beaumont here," he answered.

"Sir, it's Phillips. We're observing Roscow at the location. He's acting suspiciously. Could be our man."

George's mind raced. When Jay had found the small, crumpled piece of paper at the Clarkson murder scene, he didn't expect it to be Roscow.

"Sir, should we bring him in?" Sergeant Phillips's voice crackled through the speaker.

George pondered the implications. Arresting Roscow could prematurely reveal their hand, but letting him roam could risk losing a vital lead. The decision weighed heavily on him.

"No, keep on him," George instructed. "I want every move he makes monitored. I'll get my team to get me his phone records, bank statements, everything. We need to understand his role in this before we make a move."

Phillips acknowledged the order.

George hung up, his gaze lost in the maze of possibilities this new development presented. Roscow's involvement was a significant twist, potentially a breakthrough in the case. But the decision on how to proceed was critical. He could only hope he'd made the right decision.

He reached for his phone again, dialling Luke Mason. "Hiya Luke, I want a deep dive into Neil Roscow's life," he said, explaining what Sergeant Phillips had told him.

After hanging up, George turned to his computer, pulling up Roscow's file. His eyes scanned the information, searching for connections, patterns, anything that might provide insight into Roscow's motives.

As George set his team in motion, the surveillance team, eyes glued to Roscow, reported every move, every fleeting glance.

Roscow, unaware of the watchful eyes of the surveillance team, his gaze kept shifting to his wristwatch, a look of growing impatience etched on his face. Each glance seemed to stretch longer, his frown deepening. The cold air of the evening did little to dampen his evident anxiety. It was clear that the person he was waiting for was significantly late, or perhaps, had decided not to show at all. Roscow's frequent, restless glances around, punctuated by the occasional running of his fingers through his hair, painted a picture of a man grappling with uncertainty and, possibly, the dawning realisation of a plan falling apart.

* * *

The steady hum of the police station served as a backdrop to Detective Inspector George Beaumont and the team as they delved into the labyrinthine task of connecting Mike Clarkson's movements to the Organised Crime Group's operations. Maps, timelines, and photographs were strewn across the large table in the incident room, creating a tapestry of information.

George, his brow furrowed in concentration, traced a line on the map with his finger. "Look at this, Yolanda. Clarkson's frequent visits to the warehouse district coincide with the spikes in OCG's known drug shipments."

Yolanda leaned over the table, her eyes following the timeline. "And these cash withdrawals from his account, sir. They match up with the dates of these shipments. He was more than just an errand boy; he was involved in the logistics."

The room was charged with a palpable intensity as they pieced together Clarkson's hidden life. George tapped on a photograph pinned to the board, showing Clarkson speaking with a known OCG member. "He was in deep, right in the thick of their operations."

Yolanda, her hands on her hips, looked thoughtfully at the board. "But what motive could the OCG have for killing him? He was an asset to them."

George, turning to face her, said, "Unless he became a liability. What if he was planning to leave, or worse, to turn informant?"

The theory hung in the air between them, a chilling possibility in the murky world they were navigating. Yolanda picked up a series of bank statements, her finger tracing the figures. "These large deposits into his account stopped abruptly two weeks before his death. Something changed."

George nodded, his mind racing with the implications. "He knew too much, maybe saw something he wasn't supposed to. We need to dig deeper into the OCG's recent activities to see what was different."

As night fell, the incident room became a beacon of light in the darkened station. George and Yolanda, along with a team of dedicated officers, continued to work tirelessly, cross-referencing data and chasing down leads.

The clock ticked on, marking the passage of time in their relentless pursuit. George stood back from the table, his eyes scanning the web of information. "There's a pattern here, an underlying current that we're not seeing yet."

Yolanda, rubbing her tired eyes, replied, "We're close, sir. It's like a puzzle, and Clarkson is a crucial piece."

George picked up a series of photos, each showing Clarkson in different locations around Leeds. "He was always on the move, but these weren't random movements. He was orchestrated, controlled."

Yolanda pointed to a series of dates on the timeline. "These dates, they're key. Something significant happened within the OCG. We need to find out what it was."

* * *

Detective Inspector Luke Mason, along with detectives Jay Scott and Tashan Blackburn, sat huddled in a cramped, cluttered office, the glow of the computer screens casting a pale light on their focused faces. The directive from Detective Inspector Beaumont was clear: delve into Neil Roscow's life, uncover every hidden crevice, every shadowed connection.

"Right, let's start with his financials," Luke suggested, his fingers flying over the keyboard. "See if there's any unusual activity or large transactions."

Jay leaned over, pointing at the screen. "There, look at that spike in his account two weeks ago. That's unusual for a man of his means."

Tashan chimed in, her voice steady and analytical. "Cross-reference that with known payments to criminal organisations. It could be a payoff or blackmail."

The team's investigation dug deeper, combing through Roscow's phone records, emails, and social media accounts. Each piece of information was scrutinised, debated, and logged.

"Who are these people he's been in contact with recently?" Tashan asked, zooming in on a series of names and numbers.

"Some are known associates of the OCG," Luke answered, his expression growing grimmer. They had hit gold with the mobile phone left behind at the raid. "But others... they're not on any of our radars. We need to find out who they are."

The room was tense, the air thick with concentration. The detectives were piecing together a complex jigsaw, each revelation adding to the emerging picture of Neil Roscow.

Jay pulled up a map on the screen, marking out locations Roscow had visited in the past month. "He's been all over Leeds, but there's a pattern here. These areas align with recent criminal activities."

Luke nodded, his mind racing. "We need to put a tail on him and see if he leads us to anyone else in the network."

The scene shifted as the team set up surveillance operations, coordinating with other units and setting up discreet watch points across the city.

Chapter Thirty-two

The lab was unusually quiet when Detective Inspector George Beaumont entered, the hum of equipment creating a backdrop to his heavy thoughts. Forensic Analyst Karen Willis looked up from her microscope, her expression sombre.

"We've got the results from the cufflink analysis, DI Beaumont," she began, her voice tinged with caution.

The DI had forgotten all about the cufflink until he'd received an impromptu call from Karen.

George's gaze was intense, his anticipation palpable. "And?"

Karen hesitated, then spoke, "It's a familial match to you, George. About 25% DNA shared. It could be a grandad, an uncle, a nephew... or a half-sibling."

The revelation hit George like a physical blow. He leaned against the cold metal table, his mind racing. "That's... impossible. I don't have any... any half-siblings." He paused. "I don't think I've even got any uncles, and I'm sure my grandfathers are both dead.

Karen offered a sympathetic look. "I can only tell you what the science shows, DI Beaumont. Maybe there's something in your family history you're not aware of."

George's thoughts turned turbulent. His family history was

a closed book, one he hadn't dared to open in years. The idea that it held secrets that were now surfacing was unsettling.

Leaving the lab, George walked through the corridors of the station, each step heavy with the weight of the discovery. He needed answers, and there was only one place to start.

* * *

The evening draped its shadow over Leeds as Detective Inspector George Beaumont drove through the winding roads to Cookridge. His mind was a tumult of emotions, each turn bringing him closer to a confrontation he never imagined. The Beaumont family home, a symbol of old wealth and hidden stories, stood imposingly as he pulled into the driveway.

George's heart pounded as he rang the bell, the chime echoing through the grand hall. Edward Beaumont, his father, answered with an expression of surprise and wariness.

"George, to what do I owe this unexpected visit?" Edward's voice held a note of unease.

"I need answers," George said, stepping into the familiar yet now estranged environment of his childhood home. "About our family. Do I have an uncle, a nephew, or a half-sibling?"

Edward's face registered shock, then a resigned understanding. He motioned for George to follow him into the study, a room filled with memories and unspoken truths.

"Sit down, George," Edward began, his tone heavy with a lifetime of secrets. "You were never supposed to be burdened with this."

George's patience was thinning. "Just tell me, Dad. Is there someone else in our family?"

Edward sighed, a look of regret crossing his features. "You

and I, George, we were both only children. And your grandfather, my father, he passed away over twenty years ago."

George processed his father's words. The familial DNA connection to the case was making less sense.

"So, you're saying there's no one else? No other family member who could be involved in this case?" George pressed, his voice tinged with frustration and disbelief.

Edward shook his head slowly. "I'm sorry, George. I wish I had the answers you're looking for, but our family tree doesn't branch out like that."

George stood up, the weight of unanswered questions bearing down on him. "Then how do you explain the DNA evidence? It links to our family."

Edward's eyes met George's, a mixture of sorrow and helplessness within them. "I can't explain it, George. But I swear to you, there's no one else."

The conversation reached a stalemate, with more questions than answers. George realised that the path to uncovering the truth would be more complex than he had anticipated.

As he left the house, the night air felt colder, the darkness deeper. The drive back to the city was a blur, George's thoughts lost in a maze of confusion and doubt.

* * *

George, frustration etched across his face, drove through the quiet streets of Morley. His destination was his mother's house.

Arriving at the modest home, George was greeted by his mother, Marie Beaumont, her face reflecting surprise and concern. "George, I was just about to set off to yours. Is everything OK, love?"

Inside, sitting at the kitchen table, George didn't waste time. "Mum, I need to know—do I have any half-brothers?"

Marie looked taken aback, a frown creasing her forehead. "Half-brothers? No, George, you're my only child. What's this about?"

George exhaled, the weight of the case and his family's tangled history pressing down on him. "It's part of the investigation. We found a familial DNA match. I thought... I don't know what I thought."

Marie reached across the table, her hand gently touching his. "I've only given birth to you, my dear. There's no one else."

His next question felt heavier. "Do you have any brothers? An uncle I might not know about?"

Marie nodded slowly. "Yes, I have a brother, your Uncle Jack. But he's been living in Spain for over thirty years. We barely speak—just Christmas cards once a year. Why?"

The revelation made George's mind race. Uncle Jack, an almost mythical figure in his family lore, now a person of interest in his case. "I never met him, right?"

"No, he moved away before you were born," Marie confirmed, a hint of sadness in her voice. "Your maternal grandfather passed away too, long before you came into this world."

George stood up, his mind a storm of thoughts and theories. "Thanks, Mum. I just had to be sure."

Marie looked up at her son, her eyes filled with worry. "George, whatever you're tangled up in, please be careful."

"I will, Mum," George reassured her, though his own certainty wavered. "Do you want a lift?"

"No love, I need to do some stuff before I come over."

George's drive back home was shrouded in contemplation. The cold Leeds night did little to ease the turmoil of his thoughts. As he pulled up to his house, adorned with Christmas lights, a semblance of normality in his tumultuous world, George felt a wave of disconnect. The festive facade seemed at odds with the darkness he was delving into.

Stepping inside, the warmth of the house enveloped him, a stark contrast to the chill in his bones. Olivia, his infant daughter, lay peacefully in her crib, her gentle breathing a reminder of the purity and innocence that still existed in the world. George lingered by her side, a tender smile crossing his face as he watched her sleep. In that moment, he found a fleeting sense of peace, a respite from the relentless demands of his investigation.

Leaving Olivia's room, George slumped onto the sofa, the weight of the case pressing down on him. Isabella, sensing her husband's distress, joined him, her presence a comforting anchor. She sat beside him, her hand finding his in the dim light of the living room.

"Everything alright?" Isabella asked, her voice tinged with concern.

George let out a heavy sigh. "It's complicated. The DNA results from the cufflink... they've led me to a dead end. I spoke to both Mum and... Edward. Edward insists there's no one else in our family, but Mum mentioned an uncle in Spain. It doesn't add up."

Isabella listened intently, her eyes reflecting the depth of her understanding. "Maybe there's something they're not telling you. Families have their secrets, George."

He nodded, his mind racing with possibilities and unanswered questions. "One of them is lying, Isabella. I can feel it. But why? What are they hiding?"

Isabella squeezed his hand, offering silent support. "You'll figure it out, George. You always do. Just don't let it consume you."

George looked at her, the complexity of his emotions mirrored in his eyes. "I won't. But this case... it's personal now. It's not just about finding the truth; it's about understanding my own past."

The room fell into a comfortable silence, the soft glow of the Christmas lights casting gentle shadows. Isabella leaned her head on George's shoulder, a gesture of solidarity in the face of uncertainty.

"You're not alone in this, George," she whispered. "We're here for you, Olivia and I. Whatever this journey uncovers, we'll face it together."

George felt a surge of gratitude for Isabella's unwavering support. In the labyrinth of his investigation, she was his constant, his guiding light.

He leaned back, closing his eyes for a moment, allowing himself to be anchored by the warmth of his family.

Chapter Thirty-three

In the quaint Italian restaurant nestled in the heart of Morley, a suburb steeped in the history of Leeds, Detective Inspector George Beaumont and Isabella, his fiancée, shared a rare, tranquil evening. The restaurant's walls, adorned with black and white photos of old Leeds, whispered stories of a bygone era. As New Year's Eve unfurled outside, the soft clatter of dishes and the low murmur of other diners blended with the aroma of authentic Italian cuisine, creating a cocoon away from George's chaotic work life. It was a night where the world seemed to pause and reflect and, for them, a moment to cherish amidst the echoes of Leeds' vibrant yet historical tapestry.

The restaurant buzzed with the soft murmur of conversations and the clinking of glasses, but in their secluded corner, it felt like they were in a world of their own. The warm glow of the candle on their table flickered across their faces, casting a romantic ambience.

George, usually so consumed by his cases, appeared more relaxed. Isabella, elegant and radiant, her eyes sparkling in the candlelight, held his gaze with an affectionate smile.

"You know, this feels like a dream," Isabella said, her hand reaching across the table to clasp his. "It's not often we get to escape like this."

George's response was a tender smile, a rare sight that spoke volumes. "I know. I'm sorry my work often takes me away. But tonight, it's just us."

Isabella started with a light-hearted topic, and George listened intently, always fascinated by the shine in her eyes as she spoke. "Remember when we first met at Sarah's birthday party? You were so engrossed in that crime novel, oblivious to the party around you."

George chuckled, "Ah yes, my love for mystery novels." He was with Mia at the time, who had plans with her own friends, but Sarah had pleaded with him to attend, so he'd gone, and, to be frank, he'd been instantly enamoured by Isabella Wood. "But then, you came over, and suddenly, the party became much more interesting."

"I did notice you put that book down a bit too quickly," she said with a wink.

As the conversation continued, they discussed their shared love for travel. "I've been thinking about our honeymoon," Isabella said dreamily. "Maybe a trip to Italy? To see Venice, Florence..."

George nodded in agreement. "That sounds perfect. A trip where we can just relax, explore, and enjoy each other's company." He raised his brows. "Though, is there any point in going somewhere nice if we're not going to leave the hotel?"

Isabella giggled. "I guess we'll have to have two honeymoons then."

Finally, they touched upon their family life, especially concerning Olivia and their upcoming wedding. "I can't believe how fast Olivia is growing. She'll be walking down the aisle with us at this rate," George said with a soft smile.

Isabella laughed, "She's our little star. And speaking of the wedding, I've been looking at some floral arrangements. Something classic and elegant, what do you think?"

George's eyes lit up as Isabella described her ideas for the ceremony.

"I've been thinking about the venue," Isabella said, her eyes alight with excitement. "The old chapel on the outskirts of Leeds. It's nestled among rolling hills, with a view of the cityscape in the distance. It's quaint, intimate... perfect for us."

George imagined the chapel, a relic of Victorian architecture, its ancient stones whispering stories from a bygone era. The way the morning light would filter through its stained-glass windows, casting a kaleidoscope of colours across the wooden pews. He pictured them there amidst the scent of old wood and echoes of history, exchanging vows in a place that felt timeless.

"The chapel, it's not just beautiful; it represents something," Isabella continued, her voice tinged with reverence. "It's like Leeds itself—a blend of history and modernity, resilience and charm. Imagine saying 'I do' surrounded by such history."

George nodded, deeply moved. He could almost hear the faint rustle of the trees surrounding the chapel, the distant hum of the city, a testament to the vibrant life outside its serene walls. "It sounds magical, Isabella. A perfect blend of our love and the spirit of Leeds."

George nodded, his expression one of contentment. "It sounds wonderful. I can't wait to be your husband, Isabella."

The waiter arrived with their meals, a symphony of Italian aromas enveloping the table. As they savoured the flavours, their conversation continued, brimming with hope and anticipation for their future together.

"You know, I never imagined I'd find someone who'd understand my life, the demands of my job," George admitted, a hint of vulnerability in his voice. "You've been my rock, Isabella."

Isabella reached over, her touch gentle. "And you've been mine, George. We've faced a lot, but it's only made us stronger."

The clatter of dishes and the distant sound of a violin added to the restaurant's charm, but for George and Isabella, it was as if they were in their own secluded world. They laughed, reminisced about how they met, and shared their aspirations for the years ahead.

As the clock neared midnight, the restaurant's atmosphere became festive, with patrons ready to welcome the New Year. George and Isabella joined in the countdown, their voices mingling with others in a chorus of anticipation.

"Happy New Year, Isabella," George said as the clock struck twelve, his voice filled with emotion.

"Happy New Year, George," Isabella replied, her eyes glistening with happiness.

They toasted to the New Year, their glasses clinking in a promise of love and companionship. The world outside continued its relentless pace, but in that moment, time stood still for George and Isabella.

After their meal, they strolled through the quiet streets of Morley, hand in hand, the crisp night air filled with the promise of new beginnings. Their conversation turned to Olivia and their puppy, Rex, waiting for them at home with Marie, George's mother.

"I can't wait to see Olivia's face when she sees the little teddy I got her," Isabella said, her voice warm with maternal love.

"And Rex," George added with a laugh. "He's probably turned the house upside down by now."

They reached their car, reluctant to end the evening but filled with a sense of peace and happiness. As they drove home, the streets lit by the soft glow of streetlights, George and Isabella knew that no matter what challenges the future held, they would face them together, strengthened by their love and the family they were building.

In the quiet of their home, with their daughter and puppy, the troubles of George's work felt distant. For tonight, they were just a family, basking in the joy of each other's company, ready to face the New Year with hope and love.

* * *

The early hours of the New Year enveloped Leeds in its silent embrace as George tossed restlessly in his bed. His mind, unable to escape the clutches of the case, conjured images that flickered like shadows on the wall. In his uneasy slumber, a recurring vision emerged—the cufflink, its intricate design glinting in the dim light.

George's subconscious mind sifted through memories, searching for a connection. A fragment surfaced—the Boxing Day charity event at Elland Road station, a gathering clouded with official handshakes and polite conversations. In his dream, he saw himself extending a hand to somebody, noticing the glint of a cufflink at their wrist. The very same cufflink now haunting his investigation.

George tossed and turned, his subconscious constantly revisiting the charity event and the shaking of hands. It was like that until dawn when suddenly he awoke with a start, the remnants of the dream lingering like a whisper. The room was still; the only sound was his own heavy breathing. George lay there in the dark, the realisation dawning upon him. He had seen that cufflink before, on David Hardaker's wrist.

The following morning hours found him in his study, surrounded by case files and notes. The light of the desk lamp cast a focused glow on the papers in front of him. George's mind raced, piecing together the fragments of his dream with the reality of the investigation.

He remembered the firm handshake with Hardaker, the brief eye contact, and now, the crucial detail of the cufflink. It was more than a mere accessory; it was a tangible link to the mystery enveloping the case.

But what did that mean?

Was Hardaker a relative?

And who was he related to?

As the first light of dawn crept through the window, George felt a renewed sense of purpose. He needed to revisit the details of the charity event and scrutinise every interaction and every piece of footage available. The cufflink was a clue that he couldn't ignore, a breadcrumb on the trail leading to the truth.

He picked up his phone, dialling his team to arrange an urgent meeting. "We need to review everything from the Boxing Day event. Look for Hardaker; focus on the details," he instructed, his voice steady and determined.

The team responded with their usual efficiency, understanding the urgency in their boss's voice. They knew George

Beaumont, a detective with a knack for finding connections in the most intricate of cases.

As George prepared to leave, he paused for a moment, looking at the photo of his family on the desk. The case was personal in a way he never anticipated. But amidst the complexities of his investigation, his family remained his anchor, a reminder of the world beyond the shadows of crime and deceit.

With a deep breath, George stepped out into the morning light, ready to face the day's challenges. The streets of Leeds were slowly awakening to a new year, the city a mosaic of stories and secrets. And Detective Inspector George Beaumont was determined to unravel the mystery that now intertwined his professional duty with his personal history.

Chapter Thirty-four

The cold bite of New Year's Day hung in the air as Jay and Luke stepped into The Crown and Anchor, a quaint pub nestled in the heart of Chapeltown. It was a place where whispers of secrets often mingled with the scent of ale and where locals gathered to escape the bitter winter winds.

Their mission was clear: to gather any slivers of information about the night Clarkson had vanished into the shadows. The pub's dimly lit interior greeted them with the soft murmur of conversation and the clinking of glasses. A scattering of regulars sat huddled in corners, their faces etched with the lines of years spent in this establishment.

Approaching the worn wooden bar, Jay and Luke took a moment to scan the room. The bartender, a stout man with a gruff expression, acknowledged them with a nod.

Their target was a group of regulars huddled around a corner table. The trio consisted of Fred, an elderly man with a shock of white hair; Mary, a middle-aged woman with a penchant for gossip; and Tommy, a burly fellow whose silence often spoke volumes.

Luke, the more personable of the two, ventured towards them. "Good afternoon, folks. Mind if we join you for a moment?"

Fred, the elder of the group, peered at them through a pair of wire-framed spectacles. "Depends on what you're after, detectives."

Jay and Luke exchanged a glance before Luke spoke with a charming smile. "Just a bit of information, if you don't mind. We're looking into something that happened around here not too long ago."

Mary leaned forward, her eyes sharp with curiosity. "Oh? What's this all about, then?"

Jay, choosing his words carefully, said, "You see, there was a man who goes by the name of Clarkson. He was last seen around these parts on a night not unlike this. We're just trying to piece together what happened that evening."

Tommy, who had remained silent until now, grunted in acknowledgement. His expression was guarded, but there was a flicker of something in his eyes, a hint of recognition.

Fred adjusted his spectacles and leaned in closer. "Clarkson, you say? Can't say I remember anything out of the ordinary that night. Just the usual crowd, you know."

Mary chimed in, her voice tinged with curiosity. "But now that you mention it, there was something a bit odd. Old Pete, he was sitting right over there," she gestured to a corner, "kept glancing towards the door like he was expecting someone."

Luke's interest was piqued. "Old Pete, you say? Do you know where we can find him?"

Fred scratched his head, deep in thought. "Well, he's not a regular regular, if you catch my drift. But he does come in from time to time. Haven't seen him lately, though."

Jay leaned in, his tone casual. "Any idea where he might be now?"

Tommy finally spoke, his voice gruff. "Last I heard, Pete hangs around that abandoned warehouse down by the river. Bit of a recluse, he is."

Their conversation was interrupted by the sound of a darts game in progress. It was a raucous affair, with the patrons cheering on the players. But amidst the noise, Jay caught a snippet of conversation from the neighbouring table.

"...heard they found something strange down by the river in Holbeck..."

The words hung in the air, a tantalising hint of something amiss. Luke's eyes met Jay's, and they exchanged a knowing glance.

Before they could delve further into the cryptic remark, Fred spoke up again. "You two, be careful poking around down there. It's not the safest place, especially after dark."

Jay nodded, his mind already racing with possibilities. "Thanks for the tip. We'll keep that in mind."

As they left The Crown and Anchor, the bitter cold had intensified, but the glimmer of a lead warmed Jay and Luke. Old Pete and the abandoned warehouse down by the river held secrets, and they were determined to uncover them.

* * *

The fluorescent lights of the police station buzzed overhead, casting a barren glow in the corridor leading to the interview suites. George, weary from a long week of chasing leads and battling shadows, trudged down the hallway, the weight of unsolved mysteries heavy on his shoulders.

As he approached the interview suite, he noticed a figure standing by the door. Harold Jenkinson, a wiry man with sharp features and a penchant for digging into the darkest corners of criminal enterprises, turned to face George as he approached. There was an urgency in Harold's eyes, a flicker of determination that caught George's attention.

"Harold," George greeted him, his tone a mixture of surprise and curiosity. "What brings you here?"

Harold's response was terse as he gestured towards the interview room. "I've got something you need to hear, Detective Inspector Beaumont. It can't wait."

Without waiting for George's consent, Harold pushed open the door and entered the room. George followed, closing the door behind them. The room was stark, with a table in the centre and two chairs on opposite sides. It was a place where truths were extracted and secrets laid bare.

Harold wasted no time. He reached into his coat pocket and produced an envelope, placing it on the table before George. "I've been doing more research into Hardaker and Ross," he began, his voice low and urgent. "They were definitely researching Digitalis."

George's eyes widened as he studied the envelope, his mind racing to comprehend the significance of the information within. Digitalis, a deadly poison that had recently made an appearance in their investigation, was a troubling piece of the puzzle.

"Why are you sharing this with me, Harold?" George asked, his voice steady but laced with curiosity. "What's your angle in all of this?"

Harold leaned forward, his gaze unwavering. "Look, George, I might be a pain in the arse most of the time, but this case... it's different. There's something rotten here, something that goes deeper than we can imagine. I can't ignore it any longer."

George studied Harold's face, searching for any sign of deceit. He had clashed with the relentless researcher on numerous occasions, but now, in this stark interview room, their roles were reversed. Harold seemed sincere, driven by a sense of purpose that transcended their usual disagreements.

"Alright," George conceded, opening the envelope and pulling out a stack of documents. He began to scan through them, his mind working to connect the dots. "This information could be crucial. We need to find out where they were sourcing the Digitalis from."

Harold nodded, his expression grim. "That's what I thought. I've been digging into their contacts, trying to trace the supply chain. But George, you need to be careful. Whoever's behind this won't hesitate to eliminate anyone who gets too close."

George's jaw tightened as the gravity of their situation settled in. The stakes were higher than he had ever imagined, and the shadows that loomed over this case seemed to grow darker with each revelation.

"Thanks for this, Harold," George said, genuine gratitude in his voice.

A rare hint of a smile accompanied Harold's nod of agreement.

With that, they both knew that their uneasy alliance was born out of necessity, a shared determination to uncover the truth, no matter how dangerous the journey.

As George left the interview suite, he felt a renewed sense of purpose. He headed back upstairs to the HMET floor, where his team awaited. Tashan, the tech wizard of the group, was deep in thought, his fingers dancing across the keyboard as he accessed databases and followed the Digitalis trail.

George approached him, his voice firm. "Tashan, we need

to find out where Hardaker and Ross were getting their supply of Digitalis. It's our best lead right now."

Tashan nodded, his eyes fixed on the screen. "I'll start by tracing any known suppliers and connections in the criminal underworld, sir. If there's a source, we'll find it."

As George watched his team work tirelessly, he knew that Harold's unexpected revelation had set them on a path fraught with danger. But they were detectives, driven by an insatiable thirst for the truth, and they would stop at nothing to unravel the mysteries that lay before them.

* * *

The Homicide and Major Enquiry Team floor of the police station buzzed with a sense of urgency. Tashan, the tech whiz of George's team, sat hunched over his computer, fingers flying across the keyboard with practised ease. Beside him, Candy, the meticulous and detail-oriented detective, poured over transcripts and phone records. Their mission was to unravel the mystery behind the agitated phone call to Clarkson, a call that held the key to their investigation.

Tashan's brow furrowed as he navigated through layers of encrypted data. "This call was made from a burner phone," he muttered to himself, frustration evident in his voice. "But we've got a partial signal ping from a nearby cell tower."

Candy leaned closer, her eyes scanning the transcript of the call. "Let's run that ping through the database. We might get lucky and find a match."

With a few keystrokes, Tashan initiated the search, and the computer screen flickered to life with a map of the area marked with signal strength indicators. They watched as the search algorithm worked its magic, narrowing down the possibilities.

Minutes passed in tense silence, broken only by the soft hum of electronics. Then, a ping on the map caught their attention. It was faint, but it was there—a signal that matched the location of Clarkson's last known whereabouts.

Candy's eyes widened. "That's it! We've got a match."

Tashan nodded, satisfaction evident in his expression. "Now, we just need to cross-reference it with CCTV footage and see who was in the vicinity at that time."

As they continued to work, piecing together the puzzle, the significance of this call became increasingly clear. It was the thread they had been searching for, the link between Clarkson and his mysterious contact. If they could identify the person on the other end of that call, it could lead them one step closer to the truth.

Candy pulled up the CCTV footage for the designated area, her fingers dancing across the keyboard. The screen split into multiple windows, each displaying a different angle of the street where the call had been made.

Tashan leaned in, studying the footage intently. "There," he pointed at one of the screens. "A man in a dark coat, standing near the phone booth. That's our guy."

Candy quickly captured a screenshot and enhanced the image. They now had a clear picture of the man's face, albeit partially obscured by a low cap.

"We need to run facial recognition on this," Tashan said, determination in his voice. "It's our best shot at identifying him."

Candy nodded and uploaded the image to the facial recognition software. They watched as the program scanned its vast database, searching for a match. The seconds ticked by agonisingly slow.

Then, a notification popped up on the screen. "Match found," it read.

Tashan and Candy exchanged triumphant glances as the software displayed the man's identity. His name was Stephen Foster, a name that meant nothing to them at first.

But as they dug deeper into Foster's background, they uncovered a web of connections that sent shivers down their spines. Foster had a history of involvement in organised crime, with ties to a notorious drug cartel operating in the city. He was known for his cruelty and ability to stay one step ahead of the law.

"This just got a whole lot more complicated," Candy remarked, her voice tinged with unease.

Tashan agreed, his eyes fixed on Foster's image on the screen. "Foster's no small fry. If he's involved, this case goes deeper than we thought."

The agitated phone call to Clarkson had taken on a new significance. It was a direct link to a dangerous criminal with a reputation for leaving no loose ends. The investigation had just escalated, and the stakes were higher than ever.

As they continued to delve into Foster's background, Tashan and Candy couldn't help but feel a sense of foreboding. They were treading on dangerous ground, and the path ahead was shrouded in darkness. But they were detectives, driven by a relentless pursuit of the truth, and they would stop at nothing to bring those responsible to justice.

Chapter Thirty-five

The air in the briefing room at Elland Road Police Station was thick with anticipation as Detective Inspector George Beaumont settled into a seat among his colleagues. The room, usually a hive of activity, was hushed, the mood sombre. They were there for a classified briefing, one that promised to unveil the depth of the Schmidt Organised Crime Group's infiltration into the city's fabric.

A senior intelligence officer, a man with sharp features and an air of authority, stood at the front. He cleared his throat, his eyes sweeping across the room. "Thank you for coming at short notice. What you're about to see is classified. The extent of Schmidt's OCG's influence is more pervasive than we imagined."

George leaned forward, his expression one of focused attention. Around him, his colleagues mirrored his seriousness. This was no ordinary briefing; the stakes were higher than ever.

The officer clicked a remote, and the screen lit up with a web of connections—names, places, transactions. It was a daunting sight, each thread a vein feeding into the OCG's heart.

"As you can see," the officer continued, "Schmidt's reach

extends into various sectors. We're not just dealing with the underworld here. There are indications of influence in politics, even within our own ranks."

A murmur rippled through the room. George felt a knot tighten in his stomach. The idea of corruption within the police was a bitter pill to swallow.

"Politics?" a detective two seats down from George asked, his voice tinged with disbelief.

The officer nodded grimly. "Yes. We have evidence suggesting that certain politicians are under Schmidt's thumb, either through blackmail or bribery."

George interjected, "And within the police?"

The officer met George's gaze, his expression grave. "We suspect there are officers who might be compromised. It's a small number, but it's significant enough to be a concern."

The room fell silent, the weight of the information pressing down on them. George's mind raced, his thoughts a whirl of implications and strategies.

"So what's our play?" George finally asked, his voice steady despite the turmoil in his mind.

"We tighten our inner circle," the officer replied. "Trust is paramount now. We proceed with caution, focus on gathering more intelligence."

George nodded, his resolve firming. "We need to root out this corruption, expose Schmidt's reach. It's the only way to dismantle his network."

The briefing continued, the officer outlining their next steps, the need for discretion, and vigilance. George absorbed every detail, already formulating plans in his mind.

Each slide presented by the senior intelligence officer peeled back layers of a painful truth that George had been reluctant to confront—his father, Edward Beaumont's, deep involvement with the Schmidt Organised Crime Group.

"This," the officer said, pointing to a grainy photograph of a man in a clandestine meeting, "is your father, Edward Beaumont. We captured this two months ago."

George's jaw tightened as he stared at the image. It was undeniably Edward, engaged in what appeared to be an intense conversation with known OCG members. The backdrop was a secluded warehouse, a frequent haunt of the group.

A bitter taste filled George's mouth. He had harboured suspicions, but seeing the tangible proof was a different ordeal. "What was the nature of the meeting?" he asked, his voice steady despite the turmoil inside.

The officer clicked to the next slide—financial records. "Your father's been making regular transactions to accounts linked to the OCG. Large sums. It appears he's been funding them, possibly laundering money through his business."

George's colleagues cast sympathetic glances his way, aware of the personal blow this revelation represented.

"George," Detective Sergeant Yolanda Williams began, her voice filled with concern, "are you okay to..."

George raised a hand, cutting her off. "I'm fine, Yolanda. Continue, please," he said, directing his words to the officer.

The officer nodded, proceeding with the briefing. He outlined the extent of Edward's involvement—it was substantial and long-standing. George absorbed every word, every image, his mind racing.

As the briefing concluded, the room slowly emptied, leaving George sitting there, lost in thought. The evidence was irrefutable, yet he struggled to reconcile the man in the photographs with the father he knew.

Detective Constable Jay Scott approached hesitantly. “Boss, if there’s anything I can do...”

George looked up, his expression a mask of professionalism. “Thank you, Jay. We just need to focus on the case. This... this is just another piece of the puzzle.”

Jay nodded, understanding the unspoken pain behind George’s words, and left him to his thoughts.

Alone, George replayed the briefing in his mind. The image of his father mingling with criminals was a stark contradiction to the man who had raised him. It raised questions about their past, about the truth behind the facade of a respected businessman.

He stood up, his resolve hardening. This personal revelation would not deter him. If anything, it strengthened his determination to bring down the OCG and uncover the full extent of their corruption.

* * *

Detective Inspector George Beaumont, his mind a turbulent sea of emotions, made his way to the office of Detective Superintendent Jim Smith. The revelations about his father, Edward Beaumont, had left him grappling with a blend of personal anguish and professional duty. The hallways of the police station, usually a familiar comfort, now felt oppressively narrow as he approached Smith’s office.

Knocking firmly, George entered the office to find Superintendent Smith seated behind his desk, a figure of authority and experience. “Sir, I need to discuss an urgent matter,” George began, his voice betraying his inner turmoil.

Smith looked up, his expression one of concern. “What is it,

George?"

"It's about my father, Edward Beaumont. We have evidence linking him to the Schmidt OCG. I believe we have enough to bring him in," George stated, the words tasting like ash in his mouth.

Smith's expression shifted to one of caution. "George, I understand this is personal for you, but you need to tread carefully. Your father is a prominent figure in Leeds."

George's frustration simmered just below the surface. "That shouldn't matter. The evidence is clear. He's involved in funding and laundering for the OCG."

Smith leaned back in his chair, his gaze steady. "The NCA, who you've just been in a meeting with, I believe, has advised that we leave this in their hands."

George felt a surge of disbelief. "Leave it with the NCA? Sir, we have the opportunity to act now. We can't just sit back."

Smith's tone was firm. "George, your involvement in this case is becoming too personal. I need you to focus on other angles of the investigation. Let the NCA handle your father."

George's hands clenched into fists at his sides. "With all due respect, sir, we can't ignore this. He's a key player in this entire operation."

Smith's voice was unwavering. "I understand your position, George, but my decision stands. We can't afford to jeopardise this investigation or your career over a personal vendetta."

George's sense of justice warred with the command from his superior. "I will follow orders, sir. But I'm afraid I have to disagree with this decision."

Without waiting for a response, George turned and left Smith's office, the door slamming shut behind him with a resonant thud that echoed down the corridor. His stride was brisk as he descended the stairs to the car park, his mind a whirlwind of conflicted thoughts.

Why is Smith stopping me from arresting Edward when he's clearly involved? We have evidence, undeniable proof of his crimes, George thought, his frustration boiling over. Is it because of my father's status, his influence in Leeds? Or is there more to this than I'm seeing?

He reached his car, pausing for a moment to collect his thoughts. This isn't just about my father any more. It's about the integrity of the law, the principles I've sworn to uphold. If the system is protecting him, then what does that say about our fight for justice?

George slid behind the wheel of his car, his resolve hardening. I may have to follow orders, but this isn't over. I'll find a way to bring him to justice, one way or another. The truth can't stay buried forever.

As he drove away from the station, the city of Leeds sprawled before him, a complex tapestry of light and shadow. George Beaumont, a man torn between duty and a painful personal truth, knew that the road ahead would be fraught with challenges. But he was resolute, determined to confront the bitter reality of his family legacy.

* * *

In the affluent suburb of Cookridge, the Beaumont residence stood imposingly, its opulence a stark contrast to the inner turmoil Detective Inspector George Beaumont felt as he approached. The revelations about his father, Edward Beaumont, had left him with a heavy heart, a mix of disbelief and a sense of duty compelling him to seek the truth.

George rang the bell, the familiar chime echoing through the grand hallway. The door opened, revealing Edward, his appearance as impeccable as ever, but his eyes betraying a flicker of surprise.

"George, this is unexpected," Edward said, his tone carefully neutral. "To what do I owe this visit?"

George stepped inside, his gaze unwavering. "We need to talk. About your involvement with the Schmidt OCG."

Edward's expression hardened momentarily before he regained his composure. "Please, come in. Let's discuss this like civilised people."

They moved to the study, a room lined with shelves of antique books, the air heavy with the scent of aged leather. George declined his father's offer to sit, preferring to stand.

"I've seen the evidence: the meetings, the transactions. You can't deny it," George said, his voice firm.

Edward poured himself a drink, his back to George. "You always were headstrong. Like your mother." He turned, offering a dismissive smile. "You've misunderstood, George. Business dealings can often be misconstrued."

"It's more than just business dealings. You're funding them, laundering their money. You're complicit in their activities," George countered, his frustration mounting.

Edward sipped his drink, his demeanour unnervingly calm. "You've made quite the name for yourself, George. A respected detective. But this is out of your depth. These are dangerous accusations."

George's jaw clenched. "I'm not here to play games. What you're involved in... it's serious. People are getting hurt."

Edward set his glass down, his eyes meeting George's. "You think you understand the world, but you only see a fraction of it. I do what I must to protect our interests."

"Our interests? What about the law? What about what's right?" George's voice rose, his emotions close to the surface.

Edward's expression was one of cold pragmatism. "The world isn't black and white, George. You, of all people, should know that."

George shook his head, disappointment etched on his features. "I can't ignore this. I won't. I'm giving you a chance to come clean, to make this right."

Edward walked to the window, looking out over the manicured gardens. "You always were idealistic. It's a dangerous trait. I suggest you leave this alone for your own sake."

George's resolve hardened. "I can't do that. I won't." He paused. "You can't seriously expect me to believe these... these justifications," George said, his voice a controlled blend of incredulity and anger.

Edward, seated comfortably in his leather armchair, regarded his son with a disconcerting calmness. "George, you've always been naïve about the ways of the world, about what it takes to maintain a legacy."

"A legacy built on criminal activities? On blood money?" George's tone rose, his fists clenched at his sides.

Edward sighed, a hint of exasperation in his gesture. "You see it as black and white. But life, George, is about the shades in between. Our family's status, our legacy, it requires... accommodations."

"Accommodations?" George echoed, incredulous. "Is that what you call funding criminal enterprises? Being complicit in murders?"

Edward's expression hardened. "I did what was necessary for our family, for our name. You've benefited from it, whether you acknowledge it or not."

George's expression was one of disbelief, his father's justifications striking him as both absurd and appalling. "Benefited? I've spent my career upholding the law, trying to do what's right. And you... you undermine everything I stand for."

Edward leaned forward, his eyes locking onto George's. "I've made sacrifices, difficult choices for the greater good of our family. You might not understand or appreciate it now, but one day, you will see the wisdom in my actions."

"The wisdom in breaking the law? In betraying everything our family should stand for?" George's voice was laced with bitterness.

Edward rose from his chair, his conduct still eerily composed. "This world is a chessboard, George. You either play the game, or you're a pawn. I chose to play."

George shook his head, a mix of sadness and disgust in his eyes. "And in doing so, you've become just as corrupt as those you associate with. You've lost sight of what's truly important."

Edward walked to the window, looking out into the night. "One day, you'll understand that some rules need to be bent for the greater good."

George watched his father, a man he once respected, now a stranger shrouded in moral ambiguity. "No, Edward. You're wrong. And I can't... I won't be a part of this."

Edward turned, his gaze cold and distant. "Then you do what you must, George. But be warned, the path you're choosing is fraught with consequences you may not be ready to face."

Chapter Thirty-six

The flickering fluorescent lights cast an eerie glow in the cramped office where Karen Willis sat hunched over her computer. It had taken her hours of painstaking work, but she had finally managed to unearth the deleted emails that Clarkson had sent to an unknown recipient. The contents of those emails were a missing piece of the puzzle, and Karen was determined to solve it.

As she read through the messages, her brow furrowed in concentration. The words hinted at a deeper conspiracy, one that had remained hidden until now. Clarkson had been in communication with someone named 'Richard Hallworth,' and the nature of their correspondence was cryptic, filled with coded language and veiled references.

Karen's fingers danced across the keyboard as she cross-referenced the email address associated with Hallworth. She dug deeper into the digital trail, tracing IP addresses and following every lead. It was a tedious process, but Karen was relentless.

Meanwhile, George, having returned from Cookridge fired up, had taken a keen interest in Hallworth as well. He had a nagging feeling that this name held the key to resolving the mystery that had consumed their investigation. The more he delved into Hallworth's supposed background, the more suspicious it became.

"Karen, have you found anything on this Hallworth character?" George's voice crackled down the phone.

Karen glanced at the screen filled with data, her eyes narrowing. "I've traced the emails to an encrypted server, but I'm getting close. It won't be long now."

George hung up and headed upstairs. As he waited for Karen's findings, he couldn't shake the feeling that something was amiss. Hallworth's identity seemed elusive, his background shrouded in secrecy. There was no trace of him in any official records, no digital footprint that suggested he existed.

And that's when it hit George—a chilling realisation that sent a shiver down his spine. Hallworth couldn't be a real person. It was an identity, a carefully constructed facade meant to conceal the true identity of the recipient.

"Karen, keep digging," George urged, his voice edged with urgency. "But don't focus on Hallworth as a person. Focus on who might be behind that name."

Karen nodded, her fingers flying across the keyboard as she redirected her search. She began to delve into the connections, the subtle hints and clues that Clarkson's emails had left behind. The pieces of the puzzle started to fall into place.

George's mind raced as he considered the possibilities. If Hallworth was a cover, then who was the puppet master pulling the strings? The answer seemed to hover just out of reach, tantalisingly close yet frustratingly elusive.

As he sifted through the information, one thought gnawed at George's conscience. Neil and Edward. The two names that had haunted him since the beginning of the investigation.

Could one of them be Hallworth? It made sense, given their proximity to the case and their potential motives.

George shared his suspicions with Karen. "I think Hallworth is connected to Neil or Edward. It's the only explanation that makes sense."

Karen's eyes widened as the pieces of the puzzle fell into place. "You're right, DI Beaumont. It all fits. But we need concrete evidence."

George nodded, his jaw set with determination. "I'll dig deeper into Neil and Edward's backgrounds. We need to find a link, something that ties them to Hallworth."

The room felt charged with anticipation as George and Karen continued their investigation. The weight of the unknown hung heavily in the air, but they were the police, driven by an unrelenting pursuit of the truth.

* * *

The afternoon sun cast long shadows across the city as George strode purposefully toward the estate agency. It had taken a day or two of persistence and a mountain of paperwork. Still, he finally had the warrant he needed to delve into the mysterious property sale involving Mr Clarkson. The estate agent's cooperation was crucial, and George was determined to get the answers he sought.

Inside the office, a middle-aged woman with a professional demeanour greeted him. Her nameplate read "Sarah Reynolds, Senior Agent."

"Good morning, Detective Inspector George," she said with a polite smile, her fingers deftly typing on the keyboard. "How can I assist you today?"

George returned the smile, though the weight of the investigation pressed on his shoulders. "I appreciate your help, Miss Reynolds. I'm here to inquire about a property sale that took place recently. The property belonged to a Mr Clarkson."

Sarah nodded, her gaze attentive. "Ah, yes, the Clarkson property. That was a rather unique transaction, I must say."

George leaned forward, his interest piqued. "Unique in what way?"

Sarah hesitated for a moment as if choosing her words carefully. "Well, the buyer insisted on a certain level of anonymity. They used a pseudonym during the entire process."

George's eyebrows furrowed. Anonymity in a property sale was unusual, to say the least. "Do you have the pseudonym they used?"

Sarah nodded and retrieved a file from her desk, placing it in front of George. "The buyer went by the name 'Richard Hallworth.' Very discreet, I must say."

George scanned the documents, noting the details of the property sale. It was clear that 'Mr Hallworth' had gone to great lengths to keep their identity hidden.

"I need to know more about Mr Hallworth," George said, his tone firm but not accusatory. "Can you provide any information about this buyer?"

Sarah nodded again, her fingers dancing across the keyboard as she accessed her database. "Of course, Detective Inspector. Mr Hallworth presented himself as an international buyer, and the transaction was conducted in cash. It was a substantial amount, which raised some eyebrows here at the agency."

George's heart quickened. Cash transactions of that magnitude were rarely seen in legitimate property sales. "Can you tell me about the source of the funds? Where did Mr Hallworth obtain such a significant amount of cash?"

Sarah hesitated once more, her gaze fixed on George. "I'm afraid I've no idea, and we didn't ask too many questions, given the international nature of the transaction."

As long as you're getting paid, you don't care, George thought. It was frustrating, but George understood the delicate position Sarah was in. He leaned in closer. "Miss Reynolds, I can assure you that this matter is of utmost importance to an ongoing investigation. Any information you can provide may help us prevent further criminal activities."

Sarah sighed, her professional facade giving way to a touch of sympathy. "All I know is the funds were transferred through several offshore accounts before the cash transaction took place." She paused. "Make your own mind up about that."

George's mind raced. Offshore accounts, cash transactions, and anonymity—it was a recipe for money laundering and illegal financial activities commonly associated with organised crime groups. The connection between Mr Hallworth and the OCG was becoming clearer.

"Thank you, Miss Reynolds," George said, his gratitude evident. "You've been incredibly helpful. Is there anything else you can share about Mr Hallworth or the property sale?"

Sarah shook her head, her expression apologetic. "I'm afraid that's all I know, Detective Inspector. Mr Hallworth was quite guarded about his personal information, even wearing a facemask and hat when inside the estate agency."

George nodded, his mind already racing with the new leads and connections. "You've given me valuable information, Miss Reynolds. I appreciate your cooperation."

As George left the estate agency, the weight of the revelation settled on his shoulders. Mr Richard Hallworth had provided a crucial link between the property sale, money laundering, and the organised crime group they were investigating. The pieces of the puzzle were falling into place, and the path to uncovering the truth was becoming clearer.

* * *

George and his team converged on the location that had once been Mr Clarkson's property. It had taken painstaking investigation and the cooperation of the estate agent to uncover the truth—but George was convinced they were standing before a safe house and operational base for the OCG they had been pursuing relentlessly.

This was the moment they had been building toward, the climax of their investigation. George felt the weight of responsibility pressing upon him; they were about to confront the heart of the organised crime group that had plagued their town.

Hawkinson, the informant who had led them to this pivotal moment, stood by, his face etched with anticipation and a hint of anxiety. He had provided valuable information that had brought them here, but he also had his own agenda—a deal with the authorities that hinged on the success of this operation.

George exchanged a meaningful glance with his team, their expressions a mix of determination and apprehension. This was a make-or-break moment, and they knew it.

With a quick nod, George took out his phone and dialled Detective Superintendent Smith, who had been instrumental in orchestrating the delicate deal with Hawkinson. The call was answered promptly, and George wasted no time.

"Sir, it's DI Beaumont. We're at the location, and it's confirmed—a safe house and operational base. Hawkinson's here, and he's anxious about the deal."

On the other end of the line, Smith's voice was calm but businesslike. "George, you know the terms. If Hawkinson provides all the necessary information and this operation is successful, the deal is done. We'll protect him as agreed."

George nodded, though he knew that protecting Hawkinson would be a complex and challenging endeavour. "Understood, Smith. We'll do our part."

As George ended the call, he turned to Hawkinson and relayed the news. The informant's eyes widened with a mix of relief and apprehension. The deal was in motion, and he had played his hand.

The armed officers (AFOs) approached the entrance, their movements precise and calculated. George and his team of detectives remained in the van, watching the unfolding operation through the body cameras worn by the AFO team.

The door to the safe house creaked open, revealing a dimly lit interior shrouded in shadows. The AFO team moved with caution, their firearms held firmly, their senses heightened to the slightest sound or movement.

And then, in the heart of the safe house, their target emerged from the darkness. It was David Hardaker, the elusive mastermind behind the criminal operations that had plagued their city. George uttered his name with a mix of anger and frustration, the weight of their long pursuit settling heavily on his shoulders.

Hardaker's face displayed a complex blend of defiance and

resignation. He knew that his carefully constructed facade had finally crumbled, and he was now facing the consequences of his actions.

Meanwhile, Karen Willis, the team's dedicated tech expert, had been working tirelessly to unlock the smartphone they had found during the raid. Her fingers raced across the screen as she delved into its contents, her eyes widening with a sudden realization. The information she had uncovered was a treasure trove of evidence linking Hardaker directly to the heart of the OCG.

Unable to contain her excitement and dread, Karen immediately called George, her voice trembling with anticipation. "DI Beaumont, you need to see this," she urged urgently.

George, still fixated on the video footage, replied with a sense of urgency in his tone. "I'm a bit busy right now, Karen. What have you found?"

Karen wasted no time in briefing George about the incriminating evidence against Hardaker. "I'm looking at it right now," she said. "We've got him, George. This is the evidence we've been searching for."

The implications of their discovery raced through George's mind. They finally had the damning evidence needed to bring down Hardaker and dismantle the entire criminal organization that had plagued their town for so long. It was a breakthrough they had all been waiting for.

But just as it seemed like victory was within their grasp, chaos erupted. A sudden explosion rocked the safe house, and a thick plume of smoke billowed into the air. Panic set in as armed members of the Organised Crime Group emerged from the shadows, their guns blazing.

The AFOs found themselves under heavy fire, their training

and instincts kicking in as they sought cover and returned fire. Hardaker, seizing the chaos as an opportunity, made his escape amidst the confusion, disappearing into the smoke and darkness.

George's heart sank as he watched the scene unfold through the body cameras. Their meticulously planned operation had cracked in an instant, and their elusive target had slipped through their fingers once again.

The sound of gunfire and shouting filled the air as the AFOs engaged in a desperate firefight with the OCG members. George knew that they were in a race against time to apprehend Hardaker before he could disappear completely.

As the chaos continued to escalate, George made a quick decision. He called for backup and prepared to join the fray, determined to bring Hardaker to justice, no matter the cost. The hunt for the elusive criminal had reached its most critical moment, and the stakes had never been higher.

Chapter Thirty-seven

Karen Willis had been working tirelessly, her fingers playing an arpeggio across the keyboard as she attempted to decrypt the information on Clarkson's laptop. It was a race against time, a battle of wits against the criminal sophistication of the organised crime group they were up against.

George stood nearby, his expression a mix of anticipation and impatience.

The laptop held the key to resolving the mystery they had been chasing for so long. It was a puzzle that had led them through the dark underbelly of their town, and they were on the brink of uncovering the truth.

But George's mind was still on the raid.

The smoke billowed around the safe house, obscuring vision and adding to the chaos. George's heart pounded in his chest as he watched David Hardaker slip away. He knew they had to act quickly to prevent the OCG members from making a clean escape.

"Fall back!" George shouted into his radio, his voice cutting through the commotion. "We can't let them get away!"

The AFOs retreated, their training kicking in as they moved to more advantageous positions. Shots rang out from both sides, a deadly exchange of gunfire that echoed through the building. Bullets ricocheted off walls, and the smell of gunpowder hung in the air.

There was no time to wait. George knew they had to keep the pressure on the OCG members and prevent them from regrouping.

So George, with his team of detectives close behind, sprinted through the smoke-filled corridor, guided only by the flashing red dots on their body cams. They reached the main entrance just as a smoke bomb went off, further reducing visibility.

As they burst out of the safe house, George could see figures moving through the haze. The OCG members were making a run for it, disappearing into the cover of the surrounding darkness.

"Engage!" George ordered, and his AFOs opened fire, their shots carefully aimed to suppress the escaping criminals. The sound of gunfire filled the night, punctuated by shouts and the occasional scream.

But David Hardaker was nowhere in sight. He had slipped away in the confusion, leaving George seething with frustration. The one chance they had to capture him had slipped through their fingers.

"We need to regroup!" George called out, his voice hoarse. They couldn't afford to let Hardaker disappear into the shadows. "Secure the area!"

But as the AFOs secured the area and searched for any remaining OCG members, George couldn't shake the feeling that this was far from over.

Finally, Karen's face lit up with triumph. She turned to George, her eyes sparkling with excitement. "I've got it. There's more on this laptop than we could have ever imagined."

George leaned closer, back in the present, his heart racing. "What is it, Karen? What have you found?"

With a sense of gravitas, Karen began to explain. "It's

information on a significant event that happened within the organised crime group, marked by the dates Yolanda pointed out earlier."

The weight of her words hung in the air as George processed the implications. Yolanda's cryptic clues had pointed them in the right direction, and now they were on the verge of a breakthrough.

"Tell me more," George urged.

Karen continued, her voice filled with urgency. "This event was the orchestration of a major criminal enterprise—a launch of a new, highly profitable, illegal, sophisticated scheme. It involved high-stakes cybercrime, an international smuggling operation, and the establishment of a new, powerful drug trafficking route."

The magnitude of what she was describing sent shock waves through George. It was a criminal empire of unprecedented scale and complexity. Schmidt's organised crime group had transcended mere local operations; they were now a formidable international force.

"Clarkson's movements around Leeds," Karen added, "they were precise and controlled, suggesting his crucial role in this operation. It seems he might have been a key coordinator or a liaison between different factions of the OCG."

George's mind raced as he absorbed the revelation. Clarkson, the man he had visited countless times during the last three weeks, had been a linchpin in the organization's grand design. His death was not a mere coincidence; it was a calculated move by those who wanted to protect the secrets of this criminal empire.

George's determination hardened as he realised the gravity of their mission. "Karen, we need to dig deeper into this event, into every detail. We need to know who was involved, how it operated, and how we can dismantle it."

Karen nodded, her eyes reflecting the same resolve. "We have the resources of the NCA at our disposal. We can trace the connections, follow the money, and expose every facet of this criminal enterprise."

As they stood, surrounded by the evidence of their discovery, a sense of purpose filled the air. The pursuit of justice had taken on a new dimension, and they were determined to bring down those responsible for this vast criminal empire.

* * *

George and his team huddled around a large wooden table strewn with documents and photographs. The weight of the case bore down on their shoulders as they delved deeper into David Hardaker.

"Hardaker's connections are like a spider's web," George remarked, his voice heavy with contemplation. "He's tied to influential people across various sectors—business, politics, even the arts. It's as if he's been strategically positioning himself for years."

Luke, ever the analytical mind of the team, chimed in, "If we want to understand his motivations and unravel this web, we should start with his financial records. Money often reveals a person's true intentions."

George nodded in agreement. "That's a good point, Luke. Scrutinize his bank statements, investment portfolios, and any unusual transactions. Look for ties to suspect organizations or any financial anomalies."

Tashan interjected, "We should also dig into his communication trails—emails, phone records, and social media, sir. There might be hidden messages or connections that can lead us to the heart of this operation."

Karen added, "Don't forget his past employment and business ventures. We need to examine his career history, partnerships, and any business dealings that might have links to our case."

As the discussion continued, they delved deeper into Hardaker's personal life. Candy voiced her thoughts. "His personal relationships could hold the key. We should investigate his close associates, family, and social circles. There might be someone with a motive or valuable information." She also suggested, "Property holdings could provide insights as well. Let's look into his real estate transactions, property ownership, and any related disputes or anomalies."

Sergeant Greenwood, who had been relatively quiet until now, spoke up. "Travel history might reveal something. Check his records for any unexplained trips or visits to relevant locations."

The room fell into contemplative silence as they considered the multitude of avenues they needed to explore. The complexity of the case weighed heavily on their minds.

George, ever the determined leader, broke the silence. "This investigation won't be easy. We're dealing with a man who has left no stone unturned in concealing his tracks. But we can't afford to be passive observers. We need to act swiftly and decisively."

As they began to divvy up the tasks, an undercurrent of doubt and scepticism lingered in the room. Jay couldn't help but voice his concerns. "Boss, this case is like chasing shadows. Are we even capable of cracking it?"

George met her gaze with unwavering resolve. "Jay, I won't pretend this won't be a challenge. But we have something they don't—dedication, a commitment to justice, and a belief that we can make a difference. We owe it to our community to bring down this criminal empire."

The room echoed with a renewed sense of purpose. They were a team bound by a common goal—to expose the truth, no matter how elusive it might be.

* * *

George and his team had been painstakingly decrypting the information they had obtained from both the mobile phone and Clarkson's laptop. The revelations they sought were about to come to light.

Karen had been the linchpin in this operation. Lines of code scrolled across her computer screen, and she muttered to herself as she worked.

And then it happened.

A moment of silence fell over the room as Karen's eyes widened, and her fingers froze on the keyboard. The decrypted information was finally revealing its secrets, and the implications were staggering.

George leaned over her shoulder, his eyes fixed on the screen and his heart pounding in his chest. The words on the monitor confirmed their worst fears.

"Edward Beaumont," Karen said, her voice barely above a whisper, "Schmidt's second in command."

The room seemed to close in on them as the weight of that revelation settled in. Edward Beaumont, the man they had been chasing, had been right under their noses all along, operating in the shadows as Schmidt's trusted lieutenant.

But the revelations didn't stop there.

Karen continued to decrypt the data, and the room grew even quieter.

And then, the final piece of the puzzle fell into place.

"David Hardaker," Karen said, her voice trembling with disbelief, "He's their third."

George felt a rush of emotions sweep over him—shock, anger, frustration.

The team exchanged glances, each one processing the magnitude of what they had just discovered. Edward Beaumont and David Hardaker, two names that would forever be etched in their memories as the architects of a criminal empire.

George knew he had to act quickly. He couldn't let this information go to waste. It was time to pay a visit to Detective Superintendent Smith, the man who had ordered George to ignore any involvement pertaining to Edward. They needed to arrest both Edward and David before they could slip away again.

He stood up abruptly, his chair scraping against the floor, and addressed his team with a sense of urgency. "We've got them," he said, his voice resolute. "Edward Beaumont and David Hardaker. We know who they are, and whilst I don't know where David Hardaker is, I know where to find Edward Beaumont."

Jim said, "Get your team in here, George. You all need to hear what I've got to say."

Chapter Thirty-eight

The atmosphere in Detective Superintendent Smith's office was tense as George and his team sat around a polished wooden table. The truth they were about to uncover was about to reshape their understanding of the case.

Jim Smith, a stern and experienced senior Geordie detective, leaned forward, his hands clasped on the table, his gaze steady. He had been waiting for this moment, and now it was time to reveal the secrets he had been guarding.

"Edward Beaumont," Smith began, his voice steady, "is working undercover for the NCA."

The words hung in the air, heavy and unexpected. George couldn't hide his disbelief. "Undercover? You expect us to believe that?"

Smith nodded, unfazed by George's scepticism. "It's true. Edward had been embedded within the OCG for years. Over a decade. We needed his intel to dismantle the entire operation, and that's why I insisted on the NCA handling this case."

George couldn't hide his anger. He had been kept in the dark about Edward's true role, and it felt like a betrayal. "You lied to us, sir. You kept us in the dark."

Luke Mason intervened, his voice calm but authoritative. "Son, hear him out. There's more to this than we know."

Smith continued, explaining how they had been coordinating with the NCA, protecting Edward's cover for the sake of the larger operation against the OCG. He revealed the depth of Edward's sacrifice, the risks he had taken, and the information he had gathered over the years. He looked George in the eye when he talked about the sacrifice he made by not seeing his family.

But George was still sceptical. "And what about David Hardaker? Did you know about him too?"

Smith hesitated for a moment, and then he nodded. "We knew he was involved because of what Edward told us, but naturally, we couldn't risk exposing Edward. We needed to maintain the illusion that he was still loyal to the OCG."

The room was filled with a heavy silence. George felt a whirlwind of emotions—anger, frustration, and a sense of betrayal. He had been kept in the dark, and it was hard to accept.

Jim spoke up again, his voice measured. "George, we're all on the same side here. Edward's sacrifice has been immense, and we need to trust the plan. We've been working towards dismantling the OCG, and we can't jeopardise that now."

George leaned back in his chair, running a hand through his blond hair. He was torn between his loyalty to his team and his duty to the larger operation. The situation was complex, and there were no easy answers.

After a moment of tense silence, George finally spoke, his voice softer but still filled with frustration. "I don't like being kept in the dark, sir, but I understand the bigger picture now. We need to work together to bring down the OCG."

Smith nodded, a sense of relief washing over him. "I'm glad you see it that way, George."

The confrontation had cleared up misunderstandings and suspicions, leading to a newfound understanding between them. They were all working towards the same goal, and it was clear they needed to trust each other to achieve it.

George couldn't help but feel a grudging respect for Jim Smith. He had made difficult decisions to protect Edward's cover and the larger operation. It was a reminder of the complex and morally ambiguous nature of their work in the world of crime and justice.

* * *

Sitting in his office, George's heart pounded in his chest as he processed the implications. He had been suspecting his own flesh and blood for too long now. Instead, it was Neil and David who were the ones deeply involved in criminal activities.

They still had a BOLO on Neil, which had been about as helpful as a chocolate fireguard, but George needed to follow protocol and initiate one on Hardaker.

Greenwood picked up after a few rings, and George wasted no time. "Sergeant, it's DI Beaumont. We need to put out a BOLO on David Hardaker. He's a prime suspect in the case."

There was a brief pause on the other end of the line before Greenwood responded. "Understood, sir. I'll get the team on it right away. Do you have any specific details we should include in the BOLO?"

George quickly described David Hardaker—height, build, any known associates, and the fact that he was connected to the OCG. He emphasised the need to apprehend him as soon as possible, as the case had taken a personal turn. George also ensured the borders knew about him, too.

After ending the call, George leaned back in his chair, his mind still reeling from the shock of the revelation.

* * *

The small community of Harehills had always regarded Emma Clarke with a sense of trust and respect. Her role as a pillar of the neighbourhood went beyond her official duties as a local council member. She was the one people turned to when they needed assistance, guidance, or simply a friendly face. It was a responsibility she took to heart, and as she sat in her cosy living room, she couldn't help but feel the weight of it.

Meanwhile, Neil Roscow, a man with a chequered past and a desire for redemption, had found himself unexpectedly entangled in the web of events that had unfolded in Leeds. His own involvement in questionable activities had led him down a path of uncertainty, but now he had a chance to make amends to prove that he could be on the right side of the law.

The room was dimly lit, the soft glow of a table lamp casting gentle shadows across the worn wooden floor. Emma sat in her favourite armchair, a cup of tea in hand, her thoughts drifting to the countless times she had been a source of solace for her fellow residents. It was a role she had embraced willingly, but it also came with its share of challenges.

As she pondered the trust that her community placed in her, a knock on the door interrupted her reverie. Emma's heart skipped a beat, and she set her tea aside before rising from her chair to answer it.

On the other side stood a middle-aged woman, her face etched with worry and fear. She was a familiar face in the neighbourhood, someone Emma had known for years.

"Jane," Emma said with a warm smile, though concern lurked in her eyes. "What brings you here at this hour?"

Jane hesitated for a moment before speaking, her voice trembling slightly. "Emma, it's... I've just witnessed a kidnapping."

Emma's brow furrowed as she ushered Jane inside and offered her a seat. "Take a deep breath, Jane. Tell me what happened."

Tears welled up in Jane's eyes as she recounted the disturbing scene she had witnessed. David Hardaker, a name that had become synonymous with danger in Leeds of late, had been violently assaulting Daniel Roberts before forcing him into a car. The brutality of the encounter had shaken Jane to her core.

Emma's heart sank as she listened to the harrowing tale. She knew that David Hardaker was a man to be feared, and his involvement in such a violent act was deeply troubling.

But Neil, who had been silently observing the conversation, saw an opportunity. He knew Roberts and Hardaker, too, and he was desperate to clear his name from the cloud of suspicion that hung over him.

"Jane," Neil spoke up, his voice steady, "we need to do the right thing here. We should call Detective Inspector Beaumont and let them know where Roberts has been taken."

Emma nodded in agreement, her sense of duty resolute. "You're right, Neil. We can't let this go unchecked. It's our responsibility to ensure justice is served."

As Emma reached for her phone to make the call, she couldn't help but feel the gravity of the situation. The trust that the community had placed in her was not to be taken lightly. She was their advocate, their protector, and, in this moment, their beacon of hope.

Meanwhile, George sat in his office, a storm of thoughts swirling in his mind. The revelation about Edward had sent shock waves through his world. Family ties tangled in a web of criminality—it was a nightmare he couldn't escape.

His mobile phone buzzed on the desk, the screen displaying an unknown number. He hesitated for a moment, his mind still entrenched in the troubling discoveries. But curiosity got the better of him, and he answered the call.

"Detective Beaumont," a voice on the other end spoke urgently, "it's Neil and Emma."

"Who?"

"Neil Roscow."

George's heart raced as he recognised the man's voice; his urgency was palpable.

Emma's voice trembled as she spoke, "Detective Inspector Beaumont, I don't know if you remember me, but my name is Emma Clarke; we spoke at a press conference. And at Ethan Turner's murder scene."

George remembered the woman. How could he not? She'd left a lasting impression on him, one that commanded respect. "Where are you, Emma? I need you to keep Neil occupied so I can arrest him."

"There's no time, detective," Emma said. "And Neil is innocent, anyway. Well, innocent of murder, at least." She paused, panting. "I'm calling about Danny Roberts. A friend of mine saw David Hardaker kidnap him. The man was ruthless, George."

Neil chimed in, his voice equally filled with distress, "I know where David's taken Danny, George. It's an old factory on the outskirts of town. We need to act fast."

"Whereabouts on the outskirts?" George asked, and David explained about the factory in Holbeck beside the river."

The weight of the situation pressed down on George, and he knew that every moment counted. Danny Roberts was in grave danger, and David Hardaker was a man capable of unspeakable violence.

"Stay where you are," George ordered, his tone firm. "I'm mobilising a raid group, and we're heading to that location immediately."

The urgency in George's voice was matched by his actions. He hung up the call and swiftly contacted his team, relaying the critical information. The clock was ticking, and they couldn't afford to waste any time.

Within minutes, the raid group assembled, each member armed and ready for the confrontation ahead.

* * *

The old factory loomed in the distance, its decrepit walls bearing witness to decades of secrets and shadows. George led his team, their hearts pounding with a mix of anticipation and trepidation. The rescue of Danny Roberts was their paramount mission, and they knew the dangers that lay ahead.

Danny's life hung in the balance, and George's determination burned brighter than ever.

The team moved cautiously, their every step calculated. The old factory was a maze of corridors and chambers, a labyrinth that concealed danger at every turn.

And then, in the interior of the factory, they found him. Danny Roberts, bound and battered, but his eyes still held a glimmer of resilience.

George's heart sank as he saw Danny's condition, the realisation of the horrors he had endured at the hands of David Hardaker. But there was no time for sentimentality. They had to move fast.

The moment of truth arrived with a suddenness that left everyone breathless. David Hardaker emerged from the shadows, a sinister grin on his face. In his hand, he held a handgun, its cold metal glinting in the feeble light.

George's instincts kicked in, and he shouted for his team to take cover. But before he could react, before the darkness of the factory could swallow them whole, something unexpected happened.

Danny Roberts, battered and bruised, but with a fire in his eyes, acted with a bravery that none could have foreseen. With a swift and selfless movement, he threw himself in front of George just as David squeezed the trigger.

The deafening sound of gunshots echoed through the factory, a jarring cacophony that seemed to freeze time itself. For a brief moment, all was still, as if the world held its breath.

And then, as the acrid smell of gunpowder hung in the air, reality crashed back with a vengeance. Danny lay on the cold factory floor, a pained expression etched on his face, a crimson stain spreading on his chest. David, too, was on the floor, spasming from a gunshot to the knee.

George, still reeling from the shock, knelt beside Danny, his hands trembling as he tried to apply pressure to the wound. The team watched in stunned silence, their faces a mix of horror and admiration.

"Danny, why?" George's voice was filled with a mixture of gratitude and anguish.

Danny managed a weak smile, his breaths shallow and

laboured. "You're more important than me, Detective."

The depth of Danny's sacrifice hung heavy in the air, a stark reminder of the unexpected heroism that could arise in the darkest of moments. He had taken a bullet to protect George, a man who had once been a suspect but had become a symbol of justice.

As the ambulance sirens wailed in the distance, the team sprang into action, ensuring that Danny received the medical attention he so desperately needed. George's gratitude was immeasurable.

Chapter Forty

"It's not over, Detective Inspector," Hardaker sneered, his voice dripping with venom. "You might have me now, but you and your family are not safe."

George's heart skipped a beat at the ominous words. He knew that Hardaker was a man of his word, and the threat was not to be taken lightly. Panic seized him as he considered the possible targets of Hardaker's twisted vendetta.

Isabella, his fiancée, and Olivia, their baby daughter, immediately came to mind. They were the centre of his world, and the mere thought of them in danger sent a chill down his spine. Without wasting a moment, he pulled out his phone and dialled Isabella's number.

As the phone rang, George's mind raced with a thousand terrible scenarios. He imagined Hardaker's associates lurking in the shadows, waiting for the perfect moment to strike. He feared for Isabella and Olivia's safety with every passing second.

Finally, Isabella's voice came through the line, and George's heart soared with relief. "Izzy, where are you?" he asked urgently.

Isabella's voice was calm and composed, a stark contrast to George's frantic state. "I'm in Middleton with my grandma and grandad, George," she replied. "We decided to visit them; why?"

A wave of gratitude washed over George as he realised that Isabella and Olivia were safe, far from the clutches of danger. He breathed a sigh of relief, but his mind was still racing with concern for his family.

"Stay there, Isabella," he instructed. "Don't come back until I give you the all-clear. I'll explain later."

With a promise from Isabella to stay put, George ended the call. His next call was to Mia, his ex, who should be with their son, Jack.

Mia answered on the second ring, her voice hushed. "George."

George wasted no time. "Mia, where are you?"

"I'm with Jack at Ryan's place," she replied. "Is something wrong?"

George's heart sank as he thought about the innocent little boy who was his world. "Mia, stay where you are," he said urgently. "Don't go anywhere. I need to make sure you and Jack are safe."

Mia's voice trembled with concern. "George, what's going on? Why are you so worried?"

George's mind was racing, his thoughts consumed by the danger that lurked in the shadows. "Someone dangerous has made threats, Mia. I can't take any chances. Just stay put, and I'll be there as soon as I can."

With the promise to keep Jack safe, George ended the call. He knew he had to act quickly, his father's life hanging in the balance.

As he rushed to his car, the weight of his responsibilities bore down on him. The need to protect his family, his fiancée, his daughter, and his son was a burden he carried with unwavering determination.

The road to Cookridge seemed endless, every second ticking by like an eternity. Thoughts of his father, Edward, flooded his mind. Was he in danger, too? Had Hardaker's threats extended to him?

The ominous words of David Hardaker echoed in his mind, a constant reminder that the storm was far from over. With each passing mile, George's determination grew stronger. He would protect his family at all costs, even if it meant facing the darkest corners of his past.

The mansion in Cookridge stood in eerie silence as George's car pulled up to the imposing oak door. He felt a growing unease gnawing at his gut. The mansion, as always, exuded an unsettling stillness.

With a sense of foreboding, George pulled out his phone and tried to call his father, Edward. His fingers tapped impatiently on the screen as he waited for a response. But there was nothing—only the cold indifference of a switched-off phone.

Panic welled up inside him as he realised the gravity of the situation. His father's car was parked in the driveway, a silent witness to the ominous quiet that enveloped the mansion. The oak door, a symbol of security and sanctuary, stood resolute, refusing to yield to George's urgent push.

His eyes scanned the surroundings, searching for any sign, any clue that could explain the eerie calm. And then he saw it—a glint of light, distant and deadly, in the foliage that concealed the mansion.

Instinctively, he dropped to the ground, his heart pounding in his chest. There was no doubt about it—a sniper rifle was trained on the mansion, and George was dangerously exposed.

Fear and adrenaline surged through him as he realised the gravity of the situation. The OCG had infiltrated everywhere, and they were ready to strike with deadly precision. He couldn't risk calling for backup; the sniper would take him out before help could arrive.

With a surge of determination, George knew he had to act. He pulled out his phone once more, desperation driving his actions. Pretending to speak to his father, he raised the phone to his ear, his voice shaking with feigned concern.

"Edward, it's George," he said in a hushed tone. "I'm just outside. Can you please unlock the door?"

There was no response, but George knew he couldn't afford to wait any longer. He had to take a risk. With the phone still pressed to his ear, he retreated to his car and started the engine.

The tires crunched on the gravel driveway as he slowly began to pull away from the mansion. But then, halfway down the driveway, he made a daring decision. He cut the engine and switched off the lights, leaving the car in darkness.

His heart raced, and every nerve in his body screamed at him to turn back and escape the looming danger. But George couldn't abandon his duty, not when the threat was so close.

Carefully, he stepped out of the car and closed the door with utmost caution. He moved like a shadow, creeping back towards the mansion. The fading daylight cast long shadows, adding to the treacherous atmosphere.

His senses were heightened, every rustle of leaves, every creak of a branch, magnified in the stillness. He knew he was tangling with a sniper without a weapon of his own, and the odds were stacked against him.

As he approached the mansion, George's eyes scanned the

surrounding foliage, searching for the source of the glint he had seen. The sniper was out there, hidden, waiting for the perfect shot.

Time seemed to stretch as George inched closer to the mansion's entrance. The oak door stood as an impenetrable barrier, a silent sentinel guarding the secrets within. But beyond it, the danger lurked, hidden by shadows and malice.

George knew that one wrong move could seal his fate, but he couldn't let fear paralyse him. He had to find his father and confront the threat that had invaded their sanctuary.

The sun dipped below the horizon, casting the mansion and its surroundings into darkness. George's heart pounded in his chest as he took a deep breath, preparing to breach the mansion's defences.

And then, as if conjured from the shadows themselves, a figure materialised before him. Martin Shaw, the man he had once considered a trusted colleague, stood there, cold and calculating, his sniper rifle pointed straight at George's heart.

Time seemed to slow to a crawl as the reality of the situation settled over George like a suffocating shroud. He was trapped, vulnerable, and at the mercy of a man who had become his enemy.

"Why, Martin?" George's voice trembled with a mix of fear and confusion. "Why are you doing this?"

Martin's lips curled into a sinister smile, his eyes devoid of remorse. He relished in the moment, basking in the power he held over George.

"Why, indeed," Martin replied, his voice dripping with a cocky arrogance that sent shivers down George's spine. "You see, George, I was groomed for this from the very beginning."

The revelation hit George like a physical blow. Groomed?

From the beginning? The pieces of the puzzle began to fall into place, and he couldn't help but ask, "Groomed by who?"

Martin's expression remained tauntingly smug as he continued, "The Schmidt OCG, George. They got to me when I was just a young boy. I was a member of the Horsforth Rifle & Revolver Club, and they saw my talent. Being a police sniper was the perfect cover for someone with my skills."

George's mind raced, trying to process the shocking information. Martin, a double agent within the police force, had been planted there by the OCG. It was a chilling revelation that shook the very foundation of George's understanding of the world.

"Why?" George pressed, desperation seeping into his voice. "Why become a hitman for the OCG?"

Martin's disposition shifted, his confidence unshaken as he revealed his true motives. "It's what I was ordered to do!" He shook his head. "You wouldn't understand."

"Help me understand, Martin."

"Piss off," Martin said. "Get on the ground with your hands behind your head."

"Why did you kill Christian Ross if you were an OCG member, Martin?" George asked, getting onto his knees."

"I needed to ensure my cover was intact, George." He shrugged. "Plus, I had orders."

George's mind raced, connecting the dots. Martin had killed Christian Ross to maintain his cover, and he had nearly killed Edward too. The pieces of the puzzle clicked into place, revealing a complex web of intrigue and betrayal. "From Schmidt?"

"That's not really a concern for a dead man, is it?"

"If I'm a dead man, then you may as well tell me," George

said, his voice trembling with a mixture of fear and anger.

Martin's smirk widened as he replied, "From your father, George."

"What."

"Your father instructed me to kill Christian if he ever put him in danger," Martin explained. "But that's not all, George. I also had orders to kill Edward, too."

"What? Why?"

"Because Schmidt knows everything. Even that your father is a mole."

"So why didn't you kill Edward when you had the chance, Martin?"

"Because you were there, George. You noticed I'd shot Christian immediately. It was important not to blow my cover. So, I had to put down my weapon as you asked."

The revelation sent a chill down George's spine. He had unwittingly prevented Martin from carrying out a deadly mission. But the danger was far from over. Martin's sniper rifle was still pointed at him, and the threat was very real.

George knew he had to tread carefully. He couldn't afford to make a wrong move.

"Why tell me all of this now, Martin?" George asked, his voice steady despite the fear that coursed through him. "As you said, I'm a dead man."

Martin's eyes narrowed, and for a moment, doubt flickered across his face. "I suppose I wanted you to know the truth before I kill you."

George's heart raced, but he couldn't let fear consume him. He continued with the Control questions. "Tell me, Martin, who else in the force is involved with the OCG?"

Martin hesitated for a fraction of a second, and in that

moment, George saw a flicker of uncertainty. It was a crack in the facade, a vulnerability he could exploit.

"I won't give you that information," Martin replied, his voice firm but lacking the earlier arrogance.

George pressed on, "How many operations have you compromised, Martin? How many lives have been lost because of you?"

The questions hung in the air, a weight that bore down on both men. Martin's face contorted with a mix of anger and frustration.

"You don't understand, George," he said, his voice strained. "I had no choice. They had leverage over me. My family."

George's mind raced as he pieced together the puzzle. Martin had been trapped in a web of coercion and fear, forced to betray everything he had once held dear. It was a tragic revelation, and for a fleeting moment, he felt sorry for the sniper.

"Where is he, George? Tell me where Edward is so I can finish my mission. I heard you on the phone with him."

George's jaw tightened as he stood his ground. "I wasn't talking to Edward, Martin," he replied, his voice steady despite the threat that loomed over them. "I saw the scope glint. I knew you were here."

Martin's eyes narrowed, his scepticism clear. "You're bluffing, George."

George's gaze remained unwavering. "I'm not lying. There's someone else here with us."

Martin's frustration boiled over as he pulled a hunting knife from its sheath, its gleaming blade a menacing promise.

"No, there isn't, George; you always were a terrible liar."

"I'm not lying."

Martin stepped closer, and George watched only the blade of the knife.

"Tell me. Otherwise, I'll kill you, too."

"I'm a dead man anyway, right?" George grinned. "That's what you said, right?"

"But oh, what an honour it would be for me to kill you, George," Martin hissed, the knife glinting in the dim light. "An honour to eliminate someone on Schmidt's list."

"What?" George's mind raced, and he seized the opportunity to pry for information. "Schmidt's list? Tell me more about it, Martin."

But Martin was determined to take control, his voice laced with threats. "Where is Edward? Tell me, or I'll make sure Mia and Jack and Isabella and Olivia pay the price."

George's lips remained sealed, his resolve unshaken. He knew he couldn't give in to Martin's demands. The stakes were too high, and the lives of his loved ones hung in the balance.

Suddenly, a movement in the corner of George's eye caught his attention. It was a shadow, a figure lurking in the darkness.

Chapter Forty-one

As George's heart raced, he realised that Edward had arrived, unseen and unheard, poised to intervene.

Meanwhile, Martin took a step closer, the hunting knife glinting ominously. He was about to make his move, to eliminate the only obstacle standing between him and his mission.

But just as Martin lunged forward, ready to strike, Edward emerged from the darkness, a fire poker clutched tightly in his hand. With a swift and powerful swing, he brought it crashing down on the side of Martin's head.

The blow landed with a sickening thud, and Martin crumpled to the ground, the hunting knife slipping from his grasp. He lay there, stunned and defeated, blood trickling from the wound on his temple.

George and Edward stood side by side, their eyes locked on the fallen figure of Martin Shaw.

Edward's face was a mix of anger, determination, and relief as he looked at George. He had arrived just in time to save his dad from a deadly threat.

The darkness that had hung over them was slowly receding, replaced by the flickering light of resolve. They had faced a formidable enemy, but they had emerged victorious.

As George and Edward stood together in the aftermath, they knew that crucial revelations had been unveiled. The truth about Martin Shaw's allegiance and the mysterious Schmidt's list had come to light, adding layers of complexity to the already intricate web of deceit.

The surroundings seemed to come alive with new meaning. The darkness that had once concealed danger now held the promise of justice and redemption.

"I'm assuming you know my secret, son?" Edward asked.

George's eyes locked onto Edward's, searching for any sign that this was some sick joke, a twisted attempt to throw him off balance. But all he found in Edward's gaze was raw honesty and a hint of desperation.

"You're with the NCA?" George asked, his voice barely more than a whisper.

Edward nodded, his expression grave. "Yes, George. I've been deep undercover, working to bring down the Schmidt OCG from the inside."

The darkness of the night seemed to press in on George, the weight of the truth bearing down heavily. George's heart pounded in his chest, his mind racing to process the enormity of the truth Edward had finally admitted.

"Why?" George finally managed to utter, his voice hoarse with disbelief. "Why didn't you tell me?"

Edward's shoulders slumped, the weight of his double life finally taking its toll. "I couldn't, George. It was a matter of life and death, not just for me but for everyone involved. If they had even suspected that I was a mole, they would have killed me, and the entire operation would have crumbled."

George's fists clenched involuntarily. The anger was building within him, a simmering rage at the betrayal, at the knowledge that he had been kept in the dark for so long. But he also understood the gravity of the situation. Taking down the Schmidt OCG had been their top priority, and Edward had sacrificed everything to see it through.

"And David Hardaker?" George pressed, his mind still struggling to piece together the puzzle. "Was he part of your mission, too?"

Edward nodded, his face grim. "Yes, George. David Hardaker is a high-ranking member of the Schmidt OCG. I had no idea until recently. I was this close to taking him down myself when you stumbled upon the safe house. I had to protect my cover."

George felt a chill run down his spine. The pieces were falling into place, but the picture they painted was far more complex than he could have ever imagined.

"What now?" George asked, his mind racing to find a way forward. "What's the plan?"

Edward's expression turned grave. "You need to interview David and learn the truth for yourself."

George recoiled, his thoughts racing. "What truth?"

"It needs to come from him, not me, son," said Edward, reaching out for his boy.

Wary and conflicted, George took a step back from Edward. The lines between personal and professional had blurred beyond recognition. He couldn't fathom the complexity of the situation, the layers of deception that had woven their lives together.

With a shrug, Edward turned around and headed for the mansion.

He stood guard over Martin, the fire poker clutched tightly in one hand, ready to defend himself.

Shaking his head and watching as his father abandoned him yet again,

George reached for his phone. He dialled a familiar number, a number that would bring in the reinforcements they needed. As the call went through, George couldn't help but wonder how many more secrets were buried beneath the surface, waiting to be unearthed. In the world of crime and deception, nothing was ever as it seemed, and trust was a fragile commodity.

Chapter Forty-two

The hospital ward was cold and sterile, a stark contrast to the heat of the pursuit that had led to David Hardaker's capture. Handcuffed and defeated, he sat in a wheelchair a day later, across from George, a malevolent glint in his eyes that sent shivers down George's spine.

Yesterday's events played back in George's mind like a film on a loop. David, after being disarmed by a shot to the knee, had received immediate medical attention. Medics had worked swiftly to stabilise him, their hands moving with practised precision to control the bleeding and ensure his vital signs remained stable before transport to the hospital.

Upon arrival at the hospital, the flurry of activity continued. David underwent a thorough assessment by medical professionals, with X-rays and other imaging revealing the extent of the damage. The bullet had shattered part of his knee, a cruel irony for a man who once prided himself on his physical prowess. Surgeons had worked meticulously to remove the bullet, repair the damaged tissues, and stabilise the knee joint. David would face a long road to recovery, one that would start in prison.

Now, in the quiet of the hospital ward, the gravity of the situation settled heavily on George. He watched David, who sat motionless except for the occasional flicker of pain across his face.

"Talk to me, David," George said, his voice low and steady. "Tell me your story."

David's eyes, which had been fixed on a distant point on the wall, slowly turned to meet George's. There was a hint of resignation in his gaze, a subtle acknowledgement of his defeat.

"It all began with our father," David began, his voice a mere whisper. "You were the golden child, the one he had in Scotland after he'd left me and mum to fend for ourselves in Leeds."

"Our father?" asked George.

"Yes, brother, our father," said David. "Surely you've realised this by now?"

The revelation hung in the air, heavy and undeniable. George's mind reeled, piecing together fragments of past conversations, fleeting glances, and unspoken truths. The narrative he had known his entire life was unravelling, thread by thread.

David continued, his voice gaining strength. "He never told you, did he? About me, about us. You lived with the privileges of his name while we were left in the shadows."

The words struck George like physical blows. He had always known his father to be a man of secrets, but this... this was a chasm that yawned wide open, threatening to swallow the very foundation of his identity.

"But why now, David? Why reveal this after all these years?" George's voice was strained, struggling to maintain composure in the face of this seismic shift in his reality.

David's laugh was hollow, devoid of any real humour. "Because it's time you knew the truth, George. The full truth of who you are, of who we are."

The room seemed to close in around them, the sterile walls of the hospital ward echoing back their conversation in hushed, ghostly whispers. The revelation was not just about lineage; it was a testament to a lifetime of choices, paths taken and not taken, and the inexorable pull of blood ties.

George looked at David, really looked at him, seeing not just the man who had become his nemesis, but the brother he never knew he had. The resemblance was there, in the set of their jaws, the intensity of their gazes—a mirror reflecting a shared lineage, yet fractured by a lifetime of different experiences.

"And what now, David?" George's question was laden with a myriad of emotions - confusion, anger, but also an undeniable undercurrent of empathy.

David's expression softened, the hardness in his eyes giving way to something more vulnerable, more human. "Now? Now you understand why I did what I did. It wasn't just about revenge or jealousy. It was about claiming what was rightfully mine – recognition, a place in this world."

George listened, his expression unreadable. Deep down, he already knew; he knew from the moment he'd heard 'familial match', and the tale was extremely familiar, yet hearing it from David's lips lent it a raw, visceral quality.

David's voice was a low murmur, heavy with the weight of unspoken years. "Mum tried, she really did. But there was always this... emptiness, you know? A place where he should've been." His gaze drifted away, lost in the shadows of the past. "I remember sitting at the window, waiting for a dad who'd never come. The other kids, they had their fathers. I just had this void, this aching void."

He shifted uncomfortably, the handcuffs clinking softly. "It wasn't just the absence; it was the silence. The unspoken truth was that he had another life, another son. You." David's eyes, now glistening with a sheen of unshed tears, met George's. "And me? I was just the forgotten one, left behind."

A sigh escaped his lips, laden with the weight of a lifetime's resentment. "I just wanted to be seen, George. To be acknowledged. To have my place in the family. But it was like I didn't exist." He paused, his voice barely above a whisper. "And for a long time, I wished I didn't."

The air in the room felt heavy, thick with the tangible sorrow of a life defined by absence and neglect. David's story was a tapestry of pain and longing, each word a thread weaving a portrait of a boy, and then a man, consumed by the need for recognition from a father who was never there.

"But why the revenge, David? Why go to such lengths?" George's question hung in the air, heavy with the weight of years of bitterness and misunderstanding.

David's laugh was bitter, devoid of humour. "Revenge? It was never just about revenge. It was about proving I was just as good, if not better than you. About making him see he chose the wrong son."

The silence that followed was palpable. George could feel the layers of hurt and rivalry that had driven David to his current predicament. It was a twisted path, one paved with misguided intentions and a desperate need for validation.

"I understand the need to prove yourself, David. But the cost... Look where it's brought you," George said, his voice tinged with regret.

David's eyes darkened, the glint of malice reappearing for a fleeting moment. "Yes, look where it has brought me. And you, brother, always the hero."

The conversation was interrupted by the arrival of a nurse, her presence a stark reminder of the reality they faced. As she checked David's vitals, George took a step back, his mind racing with the implications of David's words.

When the nurse left, David spoke again, his voice softer. "You always had the life I wanted, George. A career, a family, respect."

George's reply was measured, his gaze steady. "But at what cost, David?"

"Everything, you idiot!" said David. "Anyway, in the end, I didn't need to prove myself, did I?"

"What do you mean?" asked George.

The room seemed to grow colder as David leaned forward, a conspiratorial glint in his eyes. "Well, I had my own father, didn't I? Somebody far superior to Edward Beaumont."

"Schmidt?" George ventured, recalling the name from past cases.

David shook his head, a smirk playing on his lips. "Christian Ross."

The name hung in the air, heavy with implication. George felt a chill run down his spine. Christian Ross—the late pathologist, a figure who loomed large in the shadows of their past, now cast in a new, ominous light.

George leaned in, his voice low. "Ross? But he was..."

"A mentor, a father figure," David interrupted, his voice tinged with a mixture of reverence and bitterness. "He saw my potential and gave me the guidance and recognition our father never did."

George's mind raced, piecing together the fragments of this new revelation. The implications were profound, reshaping his understanding of David's motivations, his actions, and the intricate web of their shared past. He thought about what Martin Shaw had told him. "Why Ross, of all people?" George pressed, his detective instincts kicking in. "What was it about him that drew you to him?"

David's eyes darkened, reflecting a depth of emotion rarely seen. "Ross understood me, understood what it was to be cast aside, to yearn for something more." His voice was almost a whisper now, laden with a lifetime of unfulfilled desires and ambitions. "He showed me that I could be more than just Edward Beaumont's forgotten son. That I could carve my own path. That together, we could be the head of the snake rather than just the belly!"

The revelation cast a new light on David's actions and on the man he had become. George could see now the pain, the longing for acceptance that had driven his half-brother to the edge of darkness. "Is it why you tried to frame Edward?"

"It was my idea to frame him for the three murders before Christmas, and Christian was up for it, especially after Edward disapproved of Christian's lover and got rid of him a decade ago."

George shook his head. "But Edward was undercover for the NCA. He was innocent."

"Edward is not innocent, he killed Oliver Hughes a decade ago," said David.

"No."

"Yes."

"But he was undercover..."

"We know about the NCA now but didn't know that then. Not until Christian figured it out did he challenge him the night of his death." David paused. "I don't know what happened with the sniper but Christian was supposed to come out alive, and Edward was supposed to be dead that night, a murderer of four people, one real and three framed." David grinned. "Your father has killed a lot more than just Hughes, though." His grin widened. "Just ask him."

George leaned forward, his eyes fixed on David, searching for any flicker of evasion.

"David, the Digitalis found to be the cause of death of all the victims—where did you get it from?" George's voice was steady, but his gaze was unrelenting.

David replied confidently, "Initially, Christian provided it. After his... death, I relied on a contact in the pharmaceutical industry."

"And you thought it would be untraceable?" George probed further.

David leaned back, a hint of arrogance in his posture. "Exactly. Digitalis has to be specifically screened for during toxicology. With Christian's help, it was easy to cover up."

George's expression hardened. David's casual admission and his lack of remorse painted a chilling picture of his involvement in the crimes.

George said, "Hughes was also killed with Digitalis, David." He paused. "You've accused Edward of murdering him, yet that's your MO." The DI shrugged. "It's not really making any sense to me."

David remained unfazed, meeting George's gaze with a cool detachment. "Hughes' death was unfortunate, but it wasn't my doing. You're trying to connect dots that don't line up, George. I had no issue with Hughes, and neither did Christian." David shrugged. "Why would Christian kill his lover?"

George, undeterred, leaned in. "But the method, David.

Digitalis was your choice of weapon. And back in the day, it was used on Hughes. It's more than a coincidence."

David shrugged, a sly smile playing on his lips. "Coincidences do happen, Detective. But if you're looking for confessions, you won't find them here."

The DI's eyes narrowed, aware that the truth was within reach, yet obscured by David's calculated responses. George said, "I understand why you tried to frame Edward for the trio of murders before Christmas, but why continue? Why kill Ethan and Mike?"

David's gaze, previously fixed on a random point on the hospital wall, slowly shifted towards George, wincing at the pain. The soft light cast a pallid glow on his face, accentuating the lines of fatigue and the remnants of resolve. "It wasn't just about framing Edward," he began, his voice a threadbare whisper, betraying a depth of emotion rarely seen. "It was about disrupting the status quo, about sending a message."

The silence that followed was heavy, laden with the weight of unsaid words and untold stories. George leaned in, his own expression a mask of professional detachment, yet his eyes betrayed a flicker of personal pain. "A message? At the cost of lives?"

David's lips twisted into a semblance of a smile, but it held no warmth. "Ethan and Mike, they were part of the system, a system that glorified people like your father while leaving others in the shadows. They needed to be removed to make a point."

George's hand clenched involuntarily, the mention of their father igniting a flash of anger. "So, this was all some twisted form of justice? For being abandoned, for living in the shadows?"

David's laughter was hollow, echoing off the walls of the room. "Justice? No, George. It was retribution. A way to balance the scales, to show that even those in the shadows can reach out and cause chaos in the light."

The conversation was interrupted by a nurse entering the room, her presence a stark reminder of the reality outside their familial drama. She checked David's vitals. Once she left, the conversation resumed, albeit with a more subdued tone.

"You didn't just reach out, David. You destroyed lives," George said, the edge in his voice sharper than before.

David's response was slow and contemplative. "Yes, and in doing so, I stepped out of the shadows. I made sure that your father, the world, saw me."

George's gaze was unyielding. "And was it worth it? Stepping out into a spotlight stained with blood?"

The question hung in the air, unanswered. David's expression shifted, the facade of resolve crumbling, revealing a glimpse of the vulnerability beneath. "I don't know, George. At times, it felt like the only way to claim my existence."

"And now?" George asked, the question hanging between them, charged with unspoken implications.

David leaned back, the ghost of a smile on his lips. "Now, I've made my mark, haven't I? In a way that neither our father nor Christian could ever ignore."

George sat back, his mind a whirlwind of thoughts and emotions. The room felt smaller, the walls closing in as he grappled with the weight of David's words. He looked at his half-brother, seeing him not just as the antagonist in their shared story, but as a man shaped by a complex tapestry of neglect, ambition, and a desperate need for validation.

Chapter Forty-three

Detective Inspector George Beaumont sat in the sparsely furnished break room of the police station, a steaming cup of coffee forgotten in his hands. His thoughts were tumultuous, swirling with the aftermath of the case and the revelations about his family. The room was quiet, save for the distant hum of the station beginning to stir with activity.

The door creaked open, and Detective Superintendent Jim Smith entered. Smith was a towering figure in the force, not just in stature but in experience. His presence commanded respect, and his advice was often sought after in times of crisis.

"George," Smith greeted, his voice a deep rumble, "mind if I join you?"

George looked up, a semblance of a smile flickering on his face. "Of course, sir."

Smith took the seat across from him, his eyes assessing George with a mix of concern and understanding. "You've been through the wringer, son. The David case, your father's revelations... it's a lot for anyone to handle."

George sighed, his gaze drifting to the window where the first light of dawn was beginning to seep through. "It's been...overwhelming, sir. The case was complex enough, but learning about my father's life as an undercover agent has thrown everything I thought I knew into question."

Smith nodded, his expression thoughtful. "It's never easy, reconciling the man we thought we knew with the reality. But it's part of growing, part of understanding the world isn't always black and white."

George's fingers tightened around his mug, the warmth seeping into his palms. "I always saw things in a clear light, sir. Right and wrong, justice and injustice. But now..."

"Now you see the shades of grey," Smith finished for him. "It's a sign of growth, George. A good detective needs to understand the complexities of human nature. It's not just about solving cases; it's about understanding the people behind them."

The room fell into a comfortable silence, the two men lost in their thoughts. George finally spoke, his voice hesitant. "Do you think I'm cut out for this, sir? After everything that's happened, I wonder if I'm really meant for this job."

Smith leaned forward, his eyes locking onto George's. "You're one of the best detectives I've seen in my years of service. Your dedication and your ability to see beyond the obvious is what makes you stand out. This case, your father's story, it's tested you, yes, but it's also given you a depth of understanding that few possess."

George pondered Smith's words, the doubt within him beginning to ebb. He had always respected Smith, not just as a superior but as a mentor, and his affirmation meant more than he could express.

Smith continued, "Life throws us curveballs, George. It's how we handle them that defines us. You've shown resilience, empathy, and a willingness to confront difficult truths. Those are qualities that make a great detective."

A faint smile touched George's lips, a sense of clarity beginning to dawn within him. "Thank you, sir. I...I needed to hear that."

Smith stood up, his chair scraping softly against the floor. "I'll leave you to your thoughts. Just remember, George, this job, it's not just about solving crimes. It's about understanding the human condition, and you have a knack for that."

As Smith stood up, George felt a renewed sense of purpose. The conversation had not only reassured him but had also provided a glimpse into his future in the force. He understood now that his experiences, both personal and professional, had shaped him into the detective he was today.

"As a father myself who hasn't always made the best decisions, I'd be forever grateful if either of my children decided to hear my side of the story."

Smith left, and George stood up, placing his empty mug on the counter.

He stepped out of the break room, his steps firm and confident. The challenges ahead were many, but he knew he had the strength and the insight to meet them head-on. As he walked towards his office, he realised that this was more than just a job for him. It was a calling, one that he was now more prepared to answer than ever before.

Upstairs in his office, George leaned back in his chair, a pensive frown creasing his forehead. The case had closed, a resolution reached, yet satisfaction eluded him. His thoughts lingered not on the capture of David but on the revelations about his own family, revelations that had rattled the very foundations of his world.

The rain pattered persistently against the window, mirroring the drumming of his thoughts. He mulled over his father,

Edward, a puzzle wrapped in the guise of an everyday man. The news of Edward's life as an undercover agent with the National Crime Agency had struck George like a bolt from the blue, upending everything he thought he knew about his father.

His father's absence during his teenage years, previously a source of resentment, now took on a new, complex hue. The motivations behind Edward's choices, once obscured by a veil of misunderstanding, beckoned George with the promise of enlightenment and, perhaps, reconciliation.

The air was crisp and cold as George stepped out of his car in front of his father's modest house. He hesitated, his hand hovering over the doorbell, grappling with a torrent of emotions. Anger, curiosity, a desperate yearning for understanding. He pressed the bell.

Edward opened the door, his weathered face registering surprise that quickly morphed into a cautious welcome. "Son," he greeted, his voice a rough timbre of restrained emotion.

"Father." The word felt foreign on George's lips. He stepped inside, his eyes taking in the familiar yet distant setting of his childhood home.

"Oh, how I've longed to hear that word, son," said Edward.

They settled into the living room. The room was as George remembered: Spartan, with a hint of someone always ready to leave at a moment's notice.

Edward broke the silence, his voice steady. "I suppose you have questions."

George's gaze was steady, his voice firm. "Did you kill Oliver Hughes?"

"No, son, that was Schmidt."

"Why?"

"Simply because he was homophobic, son," Edward explained. "And Christian Ross was important to Schmidt, an important cog in his syndicate. He could see that Hughes was trying his best to get Christian to leave the life of crime behind, so he took him out." Edward let out a sigh of relief. "I won't lie, son, I expected a different question."

"It's coming, Father, believe me."

Edward nodded.

"Why live a lie?"

Edward's expression softened, a rare glimpse of vulnerability. "Why live a lie?" Edward sighed, a weary sound that seemed to carry the weight of years. "It was never my intention," he began, his eyes distant, "but the truth was more dangerous, George. To reveal my true self would have put everything at risk—my position, my influence, even my life. In the crime world, perception is everything. Weakness is not tolerated."

He paused, a sigh escaping him. "I had to play the part, maintain the facade. It was the only way to survive, to protect what I had built. But it came at a cost, a cost I didn't fully understand until it was too late." Edward attempted a smile. "When I joined the NCA, I thought I could balance both lives. But the deeper I got, the more dangerous it became."

He paused, collecting his thoughts. "I was tasked with infiltrating some of the most dangerous criminal organizations. My identity, my safety, your safety... everything was at risk."

George listened, a tumult of emotions churning within him. He watched his father, a man caught in the crossfire of duty and family love.

"I had to make a choice," Edward continued, his voice laced with regret. "I chose to protect you, even if it meant sacrificing our relationship. In fact, because I wanted to protect you, I tried to destroy our relationship. Which I regret." Edward paused. "Every moment away from you, every missed birthday, every unattended school play... it was a stab to my heart."

The room was thick with unshed tears and unspoken words. George felt the walls he had built around his heart cracking, the foundations of his long-held resentment shifting.

"I understand the duty," George said slowly, "but the silence, the abuse... did it have to be that way?"

Edward met his son's gaze. "I thought I was doing the right thing, thought I could toughen you up. But looking back, I see the scars it left on you, on our family. I can't undo the past, George, but I am truly sorry."

Silence settled between them, a bridge over years of misunderstandings.

George's thoughts turned to his own children, to the delicate balance of duty and love he navigated daily. He saw in his father's eyes a reflection of his own struggles, a parallel that softened the edges of his resentment.

"I wish things could have been different," George said, his voice a quiet admission.

"As do I, son," Edward replied, a note of sadness in his voice.

They talked for hours, unearthing memories and beginning to slowly mend bridges long thought irreparable. Edward shared stories of his missions, the dangers he faced, and the sacrifices he made. With each word, George gained a deeper understanding of the man he had only known as a distant figure.

Eventually, George stood, ready to leave. Edward stood as well, a small smile touching his lips. "Thank you, son, for listening, for understanding."

They shared a long look, a silent acknowledgement of the journey they had both undertaken. Then, with a nod, George turned and left, stepping out into the night, his heart lighter, his mind clearer.

As he drove away, the rain ceased, and the clouds parted, allowing a sliver of moonlight to illuminate the dark streets. George felt the events of the evening settle within him, not as a burden, but as a piece of a puzzle that had finally found its rightful place.

He thought about his own children, about Jack and Olivia, and the kind of father he wanted to be for them. The resolve to be present, to be a constant in their lives, grew stronger within him. He realised now, more than ever, the delicate balance between duty and family, a balance his father had struggled with and ultimately lost.

As George's car hummed along the quiet roads, he reflected on the complexities of life and the choices one makes. The understanding of his father's actions didn't erase the years of pain and absence, but it offered a perspective he had never considered. It was a realisation that, despite their best intentions, parents are fallible, human.

The city lights blurred past, each one a reminder of the cases he had solved, the lives he had touched. He thought about his team, the camaraderie and respect they shared, and the collective pursuit of justice in a world often shaded in grey.

George's mind drifted to Isabella, her unwavering support and love a constant in his tumultuous life. He recognised the sacrifices she made, the quiet strength she exhibited. He made a mental note to show her more appreciation, to make sure she knew how deeply he valued her.

As he pulled into the driveway of his home, the house was dark, save for a single light in the living room. In the stillness, George acknowledged the journey he had embarked upon that evening—a journey of understanding and forgiveness. He realised the importance of confronting the past, not to dwell in it, but to learn from it and move forward.

He entered quietly, not wanting to disturb the peace of his family.

Inside the sanctuary of his home, the chaos of his professional life was momentarily held at bay by the walls that surrounded him. He sat in the living room, the soft glow of the lamp casting a warm light over them. On one side, Isabella, his fiancée, cradled their baby daughter, Olivia, her eyes reflecting a tranquillity that soothed George's frayed nerves. On the other, Jack, his nearly two-year-old son, was constructing a haphazard tower of blocks, his concentration intense and adorable in equal measure.

George watched them, a contented sigh escaping his lips. The case that had consumed him, that had brought him face to face with his half-brother's darkest demons, was behind him now. In its wake, it had left a trail of revelations—about justice, about family, and about himself.

Isabella looked up, her hazel eyes meeting his. "You seem miles away, gorgeous," she said, her voice a gentle melody in the quiet room.

George smiled, his gaze shifting to Olivia, asleep in her mother's arms. "Just thinking about the case. It's over, but it feels like it's still with me, in a way."

Isabella nodded, understanding in her eyes. "It changed you, didn't it?"

"It did," George admitted, his voice soft. "It made me

realise how fragile life is; how our choices ripple out, touching lives we never intended to."

Jack's sudden cheer as his block tower stood tall, if only for a moment, punctuated George's thoughts. He turned to his son, pride swelling in his heart. "Good job, Jack!"

Jack beamed, his joy infectious. "Ta, Daddy!"

George rose and joined him on the floor, helping to rebuild the fallen tower. As they played, George felt a profound sense of peace. Here, at this moment, with his family, he found a balance he had long sought.

Isabella's voice, tender yet insightful, brought him back. "You've always been a man of justice, George. But I think this case... it's shown you that there's more to life than just the black and white of right and wrong."

"You're right," George said, his attention still on Jack, who was now attempting to add a toy car to the precarious structure. "There are shades of grey I hadn't considered before. It's not just about solving cases. It's about understanding the people behind them."

The tower of blocks collapsed again, eliciting another giggle from Jack. George laughed, the sound mingling with the soft cooing of Olivia and the comforting presence of Isabella. In this room, with his family, he felt a wholeness that eluded him in the outside world.

As bedtime approached, George helped Isabella put the children to bed. Jack's sleepy hug and Olivia's peaceful slumber filled him with a profound sense of purpose. He was not just a detective; he was a father, a partner, and a man with a rich tapestry of roles.

Back in the living room, Isabella and George shared a quiet moment, the silence a comfortable blanket around them.

"What's next for Detective Inspector Beaumont?" Isabella asked, a playful glint in her eye.

George smiled, a thoughtful glimmer in his green eyes. "Whatever it is, I know I'm ready for it. This case... it's taught me about the complexities of justice, about empathy. But most of all, it's shown me the importance of this," he gestured around the room, "family."

Also by Lee Brook

Book 1: THE MISS MURDERER

Book 2: THE BONE SAW RIPPER

Book 3: THE BLONDE DELILAH

Book 4: THE CROSS FLATTS SNATCHER

Book 5: THE MIDDLETON WOODS STALKER

Book 6: THE CHRISTMAS HIT LIST - a completely new version of The Naughty List, entirely re-written

Book 7: THE FOOTBALLER AND THE WIFE

Book 8: THE NEW FOREST VILLAGE BOOK CLUB

Novella 1: MISSING: MICHELLE CROMACK

Book 9: THE KILLER IN THE FAMILY

Book 10: THE STOURTON STONE CIRCLE

Novella 2: A HALLOWEEN TO REMEMBER: THE LEEDS VAMPIRE

Novella 3: ECHOES OF THE RIPPER: THE LONG SHADOW

Book 11: THE WEST YORKSHIRE RIPPER

Book 12: THE SHADOWS OF YULETIDE

Book 13: THE SHADOWS OF THE PAST

Book 14: THE ECHOES OF SILENCE

Book 15: BENEATH THE SURFACE

More coming in 2024 - see https://www.leebrookauthor.com/ for more information

Printed in Great Britain
by Amazon

42612283R00208